Matthew Tree

SNUG

AK Digital

First digital edition: March, 2013

©Matthew Tree, 2013
©AKDigital (From Antonia Kerrigan Literary Agency)
Travessera de Gràcia 22, 1º, 2ª
08021 Barcelona, Spain
www.antoniakerrigan.com

Cover design: ©Bernet Ragetli, 2013

ISBN: 978-84-616-3114-8

'Fancy, sometimes called Imagination, is not inimical to Fiction. On the contrary, they are bosom friends. But they also observe careful protocol around each other's property and around the homestead of their droll and difficult neighbour, Fact.'
Chinua Achebe, The Education of a British Protected Child (2009)

'Will you always be twelve years old?'
Harry Mulisch, The Discovery of Heaven (1992)

PART ONE: COLDWATER BAY

I WAS TWELVE

(Friday, April 12ᵗʰ)

This was back in the nineteen-seventies, when they didn't have global communications systems of any kind—we civilians didn't at any rate—no mobiles, no sat-navs, no internet, no bloody, bloody glib e-mail abbreviations like ASAP, no bloody, bloody snappy e-mail sign-offs such as 'Best'. All we had then were telephones, some of them in our homes and some of them outdoors, in red steel-and-glass cabins that frequently whiffed of piss.

I was twelve, and torn between grubbing down in the dirt and playing with Action Men (getting their stiff plastic fingers round their Armalites, twisting their torsos so they fit snugly into their snipers' lairs); and higher things, like Lucy, who was fourteen, and whose pale face with its thin eyebrows and its swishing frame of long black hair was like a door leading to a great outdoors whose unknown scenery, enticing and alarming, was hinted at on those rare occasions when she smiled.

When Lucy was around I felt silly as silly could be when handling my dolls and simulating machine-gun fire with Roger, who was also twelve but who didn't seem to understand that when Lucy appeared, our job was to leave our childish things behind and jump up like two sharp little soldiers and be charming and gallant, and offer to show her and her friend Eileen a bit of judo. That they found quite interesting, though

7

they drew the line at the ground holds, which I dearly wanted to do with Lucy as it involved us boys getting down on the grass and slipping our arms under the armpits and thighs of the girls, but no, they were having none of it.

Eileen was a red-haired freckled girl of thirteen who was Lucy's best friend, despite them being as different as chalk and cheese. I suspect Roger had a crush on her though I couldn't see what he saw in her; I mean, she was such a child. Roger, by the way, wasn't my best friend, nor me his, but we got on well together even though I found him a bit of a bore sometimes because he used to get fixed ideas into his head such as the one that a penny was a very important thing, just as important as a pound in its way, something which seemed to fascinate him, to go by the amount of times he would repeat himself on this question as if struck by a revelation. 'Struck' here is only an approximation to what really happened to Roger, who was a pondering type (with cheeks that wobbled a touch when he spoke), the type who liked to mull things over in his spare time, the type who never really got struck by anything, in fact, in whom ideas emerged slowly, like vegetables from the soil, and then wedged themselves in his brainpan, apparently for good, which meant that I had to have a certain amount of patience with Roger. Though I dare say he also had to have a certain amount of patience with me; about what I have no idea: I was as blissfully unaware of my faults as he of his.

Roger and I knew each other from school: a preparatory school in London, one of those miniature snob factories that plagued and still plague the English educational system and that was already well on the way to turning the two of us into insufferable little prigs. Not that we were conscious of that at the time, no, we were snug as bugs in a rug in the world such as we had been given to understand it, and never snugger than during that Easter holiday in 1974 when Lucy's mum and dad, together with her brother, who was in the paratroopers—something which thrilled Roger and me—made a deal with my, Eileen's and Roger's parents (who they knew) to look after all us children for a fortnight on the Isle of Wight.

Lucy's dad, Dr Whitebone, had chosen a small seaside resort on the Isle's south-west coast, Coldwater Bay, which he described to us, chuckling, upon our arrival: *No silly theme parks in good old Coldwater Bay, no glass-blowing festivals, no half-baked miniature funfairs, no old biddies stirring natural dairy fudge in unhygienic vats; none of the usual touristy nonsense one normally finds laid on in every nook and cranny of the Isle of Wight for those Below Our Class; here in Coldwater Bay there's just the essentials: one tea shop, one fish and chip restaurant, one sweet shop for you children and one pub for us grown-ups*—a quick wink startled us from the top right-hand corner of his face: *It's almost virgin territory; wonderful place.* He paused, then leaned forward over the table where we were all munching away, and stage-whispered: *What's more, it's*

British to a fault. He rubbed his hands together and barked out a laugh dry as a dog biscuit. Mrs Whitebone was busying herself with unpacking Roger's shirts: *Now, John, don't start.*

The Whitebones had rented one entire house not far off the high street of Coldwater Bay; the place was pastel-coloured inside and out; I can't remember what the colours were. The wallpaper in our bedrooms—of which Roger and I shared one, Eileen and Lucy another, Dr and Mrs Whitebone another, whereas Simon the paratrooper had the smallest bedroom all to himself (he didn't mind, he assured his mother, that it was barely a cupboard: *This is luxury compared to what you get in the army*)—the wallpaper in our bedrooms, I say, was of a bland colour, the Formica on the large kitchen table where we ate our meals was bland, indeed the floors, the walls and ceiling of every room in that building couldn't possibly have been blander.

Once we'd wolfed down our cheese and biscuits, Mrs Whitebone said she was going to go shopping for essentials and would anyone like to come. Lucy and Eileen both shot up their hands. I turned to Roger, my voice betraying eagerness: *What d'you reckon, Rodge? Give them a hand with the carrier bags?*

Well I'm not going to have much fun here on my own, am I?

The five of us walked into Coldwater Bay's Easter air. The blood in our cheeks heightened by the breeze, we walked along our street, which contained houses similar in size, shape and style to the one we had rented, all with equally similar seaside names: —Sandy Cove, Ocean Vista, Beachhead House (ours was called Seaview Heights).

Mrs Whitebone stopped a passer-by: *Excuse me, is there a grocer's near here?*

It was in the next street up, on a corner.

Roger and I had been talking about the relative merits of the Spitfire and the Hurricane, and the girls had also been chatting about something or other amongst themselves, but as soon as Mrs Whitebone pushed the door, tinkling its bell, and we trooped into the shop—crammed grotto-full with a huge array of foods, household goods and beverages—we shut up, impressed by the silence and the lack of elbow room. A full minute went by before the shopkeeper appeared.

He had a powder-puff pale face, and would have been coot-bald but for a few wisps of hair that dangled off his occiput. He wore a beige surcoat with several biros lined up in its chest pocket. On seeing us, he broke into a smile that sent creases running off to the edges of his face as if under orders: *Good morning.* Mrs Whitebone nodded, her voice cheery as wedding bells: *Good morning!* She proceeded to order, and the shopkeeper sought out the items. She glanced at the space reserved for newspapers, to the left of the till: *Is that the only one you've got?* The man nodded: *Have to go to Brook or Freshwater for the London dailies; we only stock the local paper.* He held one up high. It was called the Coldwater Bay Parish Press.

No, thank you.

Once we kids were out of there, with a carrier bag each, Lucy whispered loudly to Eileen: *What a creepola!* Eileen giggled. Lucy went on: *Did you see his eyes? I think he's on something.*

Eileen shrugged: *Maybe he's a homeopath.*

Roger turned to her: *What's a homeopath?*

Eileen glared at his interrupting mouth: *Pa says they're mad people who take little white pills that all look the same.*

Mrs Whitebone turned to Eileen with a frown: *Now, now, Eileen, there is something to be said for homeopathy.* Her tongue slid briefly over her lower lip. *That is one of the things my husband and I are in agreement upon.*

Noting our silence, she blurted: *Come on, I'll treat you to an ice cream!* She led the way into the high street, which swooped all the way down to the esplanade.

At the bottom, a coloured man in yellow PVC overalls was sweeping the pavement.

No sooner had we stepped onto the esplanade and looked over its balustrade at the thin stretch of sandy beach that lay between us and the water (its shifting bulk redoubtable, the air coursing off its surface into our faces) than I, for one, felt suddenly happy, happy as could be that there were places like this, places where there was nothing else to do but be beside the seaside at the edge of a seaside town, where we could but sip pop and suck rock and sup on battered fish when we weren't looking at the ocean, when we weren't breathing in this breeze. Mrs Whitebone spotted an ice cream machine: *Come on, everyone!*

It stood by the entrance to a sweet and souvenir shop, out of which an old lady emerged to serve us. The ice creams were of the Mr Whippy type that wasted no time in melting, so I gobbled mine down quick, the ice cream forming a satisfying lump of cold in my stomach. I stared at the shop window, which was framed by two iron arches painted blue, with its display of marzipan bacon and eggs, pink sticks of rock, of postcards showing four different views squeezed together and all but hidden by the words 'Coldwater Bay'. There were also novelty items: black kiss-me-quick hats, and severed fingers and false fangs that hung together in plastic sachets sealed by cardboard labels showing cartoon drawings of alarmed prank victims who even I knew—from their clothes and haircuts— were stuck back in the 1950s.

What with the ice cream in my belly and the esplanade and with the beach below it and the white cliffs stretching away off to its right, westward, I found it an enticing place, Coldwater Bay, and I felt it was going to be a great time we would all have there. With the added perk, for me, of Lucy's presence.

We knew nothing, nothing at all. We took for granted that our lives were ours and ours alone and would run their natural course.

Cheers.

I was twelve. And as I have already said, I was happy, thrilled, sound as a bell and rock steady on my feet. My mind back then was as bone-clean as the breeze. The world reveals itself gradually to most, the sweet things apparent first and its bitterest ingredients making their taste known later on. I had the misfortune to have the lot shoved down my gullet in one go. I was twelve.

LOG OF PROGRESS

(Friday 12th)

My bedsit, rented from the owner of the shop below, is cosy, with two electric hobs and a baby fridge and few chances of arousing suspicion given that in this land shopkeepers are discerning pillars of the community who surely wouldn't play host to anyone unsavoury.

I just laughed to myself. I've got to watch that laugh: it's the only part of me that doesn't pass. Got to slap my hand over that mouth of mine, before someone catches on.

No sooner had I darkened his doorstep than my tripe-complexioned landlord offered to help me with my case, but I insisted my way out of it. I'd already lugged it to the top of the stairs, when, for politeness' sake, he added:
Are you quite sure, sir?

Oh these people, *mungu,* these people.

The room's small and smells of dust. A sash window gives onto a view of a sash window opposite. Once in, I dumped the case on the bed and popped down to pay a month in advance, cash. He asked, voice quiet as ants, where I was from, and I spun my yarn: my father was Welsh—in the military—and my mother Italian, and as for me, I was born in Kenya, where my father happened to be stationed at the time.

He counted the wad.
Ah, I thought I couldn't place your accent.

No, it's a bit of a mishmash.

All in order.

He stuffed the notes into his sepia jacket.

Well, going to have a bit of a lie-down now.

Good idea, sir.

'Mishmash'. 'Lie-down'. I hope I'm getting my language right.

*

The day before I left for England, Mzee patted my tense and nervous shoulder:

Listen Jonas, if that fat *mkundu* Jay Edgar Hoover managed to pass for half a century, then you're certainly going to make it for a fortnight: you're credible as hell.

So far I have indeed passed, as it were, with flying colours: the pert complicity of the pink-faced passport officers at the airport; the way people sat down next to me on the Tube without a moment's hesitation; my not feeling a draft from a white soul, in fact, since arrival.

*

After my lie-down I went out, double-locking the door.

I glanced at my picture of respectability in the hall mirror.

Memories blew in. The usual.

Being made to have dawn intercourse with a hole dug out of dry earth, stark naked; being told to thump children with tree branches; walking into hospital wards, machete in hand.

I purchased sweaters, shirts and a duffle coat from the menswear shop on the high street. People treat me exactly—exactly!—as if I were one of them. Feeling peckish—'peckish'—I went into the tea shop two doors down, ordered scones and tea, took a table by the window and watched the passers-by.

Flattish-faced young women; a few families, the fathers taciturn, the mothers berating their children for behaving like children; sullen youths in bomber jackets. A stout, slow-walking policeman.

I felt what aliens must feel when they fall to Earth and see these beings who also have arms and hands and legs and feet and heads and necks, but are in fact quite, quite unalike.

Freckled people who have spent centuries spinning a cocoon in which there is only room for them.

I watched them swim past, exhaling bubbles abrupt as hiccups, hair flowing in the liquid air.

For now, I am alone.

I paid and left. Maybe I should've added 'goodbye' or 'take care' or 'cheers'. (What is *done*?)

I popped into the sweet shop and then into the fish and chip shop, further up the esplanade.

They had received plentiful goods deliveries just before the Easter break, to cope with the extra trickle of holidaymakers:

hardly any, in fact, Coldwater Bay not having the amenities of the main Wight resorts. This year, according to the chip shop woman, there are barely any due to the poor weather; what's more, the long-threatened postal and transport workers' strike—which we had been counting on—has finally been declared, so: for a month there'll be no more mail or goods delivery vans.

Back in the bedsit, I open my case and assemble the coil, buzzer, key and batteries. It's unhandy, this device, a right royal pain in the bottom, in fact. Our very own design. Slowly, as I do not wish to and indeed *must not* make any mistakes, I Morse in the first daily report—the layout of the village and my impressions, as culled from these selfsame notes—signing off with a tag plucked out of several fluttering in my head.

Anger, source of all things.

I'M NOT A

(Friday 12ᵗʰ)

Some people might think I'm obsessed with the issue. But once one has latched onto a truth, knowing it to be whole and nothing but, and when hardly anyone else seems to give a tinker's cuss about it, then it is surely only natural that it becomes the biggest bee in one's bonnet.

The problem is that the right-thinking Left have made it impossible to open up a healthy debate on the issue. As soon as they detect so much as a smidgen of anything that goes against their bloody dogmas, they start their jeering and sneering. Such ostracism, coming from the great unwashed, is quite intolerable.

*

I spotted a Negroid gentleman when driving in: the first and only one, indeed, that I have set eyes upon since our arrival in Coldwater Bay; he was working his broom hither and thither, brushing a pile of leaves off the street into the gutter.

How can people remain oblivious to the obvious? Is the fecklessness of him and his type not glaringly plain? Is it not clear from a glance at their eyes, opaque as baubles? From those sudden smiles that break out from their sullen faces for no apparent reason? Is it not clear to all but the blind from birth, I ask myself, that the womenfolk are of service to them only as peripatetic incubators and that the menfolk carry their medulla oblongata between their *legs* rather than their *ears*?

I confess I have never addressed more than a few brief words with one. Attempting a full-blown conversation must be a trial I have no intention of putting myself through: I imagine one would have to painstakingly measure one's syllables; rather as I had to do with the mentally incapacitated unfortunates I treated in my student days, during the obligatory psychiatric stint.

I WAS TWELVE

(Friday 12th)

Our ice creams finished, we trooped back to the rented house, to Seaview Heights, where Dr Whitebone and Simon the paratrooper were sitting at ease at the kitchen table, the former puffing at his pipe, the latter dragging on a fag.

Mrs Whitebone spearheaded our entrance, plonking down the shopping bags and hand-fanning her face: *You might open the window from time to time—there's the most tremendous fug in here!* Dr Whitebone leered at her, head cocked to one side: *A tremendous WHAT, dear?* Mrs Whitebone frowned: *You heard me, a tremendous* then grimaced at her husband: *Oh, John, REALLY!* Simon let off an in-the-know laugh that sounded like me and Roger's machine-gun imitations: *Hur-hur-hur-hur.*

Puzzled, I looked at Roger, but he was dead to the world, probably thinking—as was then our wont—about war. I turned to the girls. Lucy was staring into space, cheeks flushing.

Mrs Whitebone looked at her watch: *Goodness gracious, almost time for supper.* Simon stubbed out his ciggy in an ashtray that was already chock-full of butts: *Dad and I were thinking of going for a pint.* Mrs Whitebone put her hands on her hips: *Oh, very nice, and leave me here to prepare the supper for the children and then a separate one for you two when you eventually come home!* Dr Whitebone did a palms-down calming gesture: *I noticed the local pub serves food and has an outside terrace for the kiddies; we could all have supper there and give our resident chef a bit of a break; it's our first day here, after all.*

Mrs Whitebone turned to us: *Would you like that? Lucy?* Lucy smiled and nodded, and we followed her cue.

As for herself, Mrs Whitebone declined: *I'm not much of a pub person.* The rest of us—that is, me, Roger, Lucy, Eileen, Lucy's father and her brother Simon—set off, wrapped up in our padded anoraks; Lucy's, a fetching electric blue.

The houses had taken on a grey hue in the retiring light. We headed for the high street, then turned left.

The pub was a phony castle of a type I knew—from having read '101 Dalmatians'—was called a folly. Dr Whitebone waved at the half dozen empty wooden tables on its front lawn: *Sorry, kiddikins, but we can't go indoors; the law's the law.*

Roger ordered a Coke, and Eileen, an orange juice. I waited to hear what Lucy wanted: *Ginger beer, please, Dad.* Dr Whitebone turned to me. As nonchalantly as I could, I said: *Make that two.*

Simon and Dr Whitebone, going in, unleashed a flurry of chuckles and orangey light.

They reappeared within minutes, clutching drinks. I reached out for my ginger beer, meaning to help Simon because he was carrying four glasses at once, but, not seeing my proffered help, he went ahead with landing the lot on his own, which meant my hand went clunk into my drink, tipping it over and spilling its contents onto the table. Mortified, I had to make an effort not to glance Lucy's way. Dr Whitebone said: *Not to worry,* and Simon stood up: *I'll get a cloth.*

When Simon put down a fresh ginger beer on the table, Eileen was whispering: *Wow, look at those people.* Past the garden walked a most exotic-looking family, the father wearing a long white garment, with what I later learnt was called a *gutra* held down firmly on his crown. Next to him was his wife, presumably, her face surrounded by a sort of wimple. Walking behind them were two children, a girl and a boy who were five or six, both dressed pretty much the way we had been at their age.

A woman came out of the pub and set to cleaning the table surface with a grey cloth: *Well, that lot won't be coming in here, that's for sure.*

Why's that, Dad?

Dr Whitebone laughed: *Arabs don't drink alcohol, Lucy; it's against the Muslim code.* The woman finished her wiping: *Making money certainly bleeding isn't: they're rich as Croesus, that lot, got the big house on the Rise.*

Do you mean that squarish building one passes on the way into Coldwater Bay?

She nodded: *Proper manse it is; used to belong to the Stocksides before the last lord and heir made some dodgy investments; so now it's the sheik's got it.* She gave a last token rub of the table: *There you go.*

Dr Whitebone and Simon set to their pints. Each time they went into get another round—which struck me as being pretty often—they asked us if we wanted anything else ourselves, but we declined, trained as we had all been to make our drinks last as long as possible. After a few attempts at our own conversations (me with Roger, Lucy with Eileen) we kids fell silent, inhibited by the ever louder chit-chat of the men.

Then Lucy stood up: *I think I'll go for a walk.* The chatting stopped. Dr Whitebone pointed at her: *I'd feel happier if you all kept each other company, just for safety's sake.* Lucy looked at the rest of us: *Well then, are you coming or not?*

Roger got slowly to his feet: *Where are we off to?* Lucy shrugged: *To the beach, I suppose.*

As long as it's somewhere we can keep an eye on you.

Lucy narrowed hers: *At the rate you're going, pretty soon you won't be able to keep an eye on anything, Dad.* Dr Whitebone raised a mock-threatening fist: *Get along with you!*

We headed out of the pub garden. The streetlamps flickered on as we waited for a couple of cars to pass; we crossed over to the esplanade. The sky was a light shade of purple.

We leaned on the railing, and stared at the thread dividing sea and sky. Some stars had cropped up, along with half the moon. Back then, my moods would shift wholesale, like speeded-up tides: at that moment, for example, I was beset by a feeling of full-blown self-confidence, sure that I could do anything, anything at all—be a decision-maker in a dark suit in a light-filled, plush-carpeted, phone-filled office on the Continent; or a Caribbean scuba-diver, thoughts drifting amongst the highlighted fish; or just be me, myself and I, the immediate but discreet centre of attention on the part of curious girls and envious boys; or reaching out in the here and now and kissing Lucy on the lobe of her ear that now was less than a foot's distance from my lips. And then came another shift, as it hit me that nothing I could do would make an iota of difference to the quiet, patient, indifferent ink-and-blotter of sea and sky, and that I should move not one muscle so as to concentrate on that stretch of water overviewed by that expanse of air.

What are we doing here? I thought the idea was to go down to the beach.

We followed a mildly irritated Roger down the nearest steps, and padded towards the sea. A streetlamp shone yellow light over the sand.

We skirted an empty skiff, reached the edge, and contemplated this particular section of the English Channel as it dozed beast-like in the dark, our hair tinted fair from the electric light behind, our faces pale from the moonlight ahead. Here and there I could make out a sloping wave.

Roger visored his eyes: *I think there's something in the water.*

Eileen peered, face squeezed up: *And I think you're seeing things, Rodge.* I was about to second her when Lucy said, her voice pitched rather high: *He's right, there IS something.*

Where?

Wait, it's gone; no, there! I ran my line of sight off the tip of her finger: there was indeed some kind of object (not reflected light, not surfaced seaweed) in the water.

Lucy peered hard: *I've no idea what that is; maybe I should tell Dad and Simon.*

She made a beeline for the steps, skipped up to the esplanade, and waved at the pub terrace from there.

*

Dr Whitebone stared at the sea, his jury still out: *There's always plenty of debris floating about in the Channel, you know, nothing that—* Lucy pointed again: *Over there, there!* Dr Whitebone and Simon put their hands on their hips and looked in the indicated direction. The object had got closer.

Dr Whitebone opened his mouth to say something, then closed it again.

What do you reckon, Simon?

Reminds me of something I once saw in Ulster, Dad, if you get my meaning.

Really?

I'm pretty certain, but let's just wait a bit: the tide's bringing it in.

I'm not sure how much silent time passed before I heard barked, male shouts, loud as loud could be, me not realising at first that they were directed at us.

GET BACK TO THE HOUSE NOW! RIGHT NOW!

Lucy wanted to negotiate: *Daaad...* but Dr Whitebone wouldn't stop roaring: *DO AS I SAY! RIGHT THIS INSTANT! OK, Dad, OK...*

We strode pretty calmly back to the esplanade (the grown-ups' fluster notwithstanding). Just before setting foot on the steps that led up from the sand, I peeked behind me. The object was a few yards from the beach—a poorly lit lump I simply could not identify—drifting in.

*

When we went down for breakfast the next morning, Lucy's Dad and Simon and Mrs Whitebone had formed a compact group at the far side of the table; Lucy's mum was reading the spread-out newspaper over the two men's pressed shoulders. Her husband pointed at the print: *What do you think this armband business is about?* Simon shrugged: *Search me.*

The previous night, we had told Mrs Whitebone about the odd thing we'd seen in the water, but she'd made light of it: *I hope those bad little boys of mine* (an odd way, I thought, of referring to her husband, who was ancient by my standards of the time, and her son, who bore arms) *haven't been plying you with spirits.* Then she'd whipped us up some Horlicks before shooing us off to bed, it being late for us.

Sealed off in our shared bedroom, me and Roger had speculated in whispers for an hour or so. Roger's theory was that the object was an Atlantic jellyfish of the umbrella type, the biggest of its species known to man. My own, tamer, theory was that it was a capsized boat returning finally to shore. We mulled over other, increasingly improbable, possibilities, until our ideas petered out.

The morning after, no sooner had he and I bumbled into the kitchen and overheard Dr Whitebone and Simon saying something about armbands, than Mrs Whitebone cried out: *Time for brekkie!* The concentrated frown on her face transformed on the instant into a beam as Dr Whitebone folded up the paper quickly: *Hello, boys!* We were sitting down before our bowls of Weetabix when the girls came in. Mrs Whitebone plonked two more bowls and a pyramid of Long Life milk on the table, its tip snipped off.

Lucy looked over at her father and brother: *Anything in the paper about that thing we spotted in the sea?* Dr Whitebone stared at her: *What thing?* Now that was a bit thick, even for us. *Dad! Last night! That object that was in the water and you told us all to run back to the house. Remember?*

Her father nodded: *Oh, that.*

Well, what was it?

Simon and I couldn't identify it before it floated off; probably just a piece of driftwood.

I marvelled at his ease of fibbing. Simon stood up: *Right, I'm off for a shit.* Mrs Whitebone ticked him off: *Really Simon, we're not in the barracks now, you know,* but he was already out of sight, off to his 'shit'.

Dr Whitebone stood up in his turn, took the folded paper from the table, left the kitchen, and clonked upstairs. Mrs Whitebone said, in that bright way that was starting to grate on my nerves: *I need a volunteer to go out and get some bread, please!* I put my hand up.

Good for you!

She took out her purse and counted out some coins and said: *The exact amount for a loaf; we Whitebones are firm believers in thriftiness, you know,* upon which Roger dug into his back pocket and whipped out a booklet with a picture of a green box stuffed with glittering electrical appliances on its cover: *Do they give Green Shield stamps?* He held up the last page: *I've almost got a full book.* Mrs Whitebone was taken aback for a second: *We're only buying a loaf, Roger; anyway, I don't think they have Green Shield down here.*

A penny is just as important as a pound, if you think about it.

He stuffed his saver book away. Then, to my surprise, Lucy stuck her own hand up: *Is it OK if I go along? I feel like a bit of a walk.*

If you wish.

We stepped out into the brisk air, Lucy and I, this being the first time the two of us had found ourselves on our tod. I, of course, was all a-quiver. A block from the shop, Lucy tapped my arm: *You're not going to spend that money on bread, I hope?* I stopped and looked at her look of complicity, with not a clue as to what she was being complicit about. I kept my eyes wide and bright to give the impression I had hopped up onto her wavelength: *You mean...?* She nodded: *The local paper!* So she too had smelt a parental rat. We resumed our walking pace. *Of course,* I said, *but what about the loaf? Your mum gave me the exact amount, and if I don't come back with it she'll start asking questions.*

Don't worry, everything's under control.

She dug a hand into her pocket and jingled some change. I tried to keep the surprise out of my voice: *Where did you get all that from?*

She stage-whispered: *Don't tell anybody.*

OK.

She weighed me up for a second, wondering, perhaps, if I could handle the next bit of news: *I borrowed it from Mum's purse.* Confiding, she was CONFIDING in me! I did my best charming eyebrow raise: *Oh.* In fact, if one had to call a spade a spade, this was stealing she was talking about. Her confiding, her wonderful confiding, continued: *I mean, what can I do? Even though I'm fourteen now, Mum's still tighter than a gnat's bottom, moneywise; after all, I have expenses, just like anyone else.*

The shop door opened with its tinkle and out came a customer in a duffle coat that looked way too big for him.

The shopkeeper had a book open on the counter, his eyes locked onto the text, his lips twitching as he read. Lucy nudged me and nodded at the counter space where the local paper lay. I picked a copy from the top. The man glanced up from his book: *Paper?* Lucy said: *Yes, and where can I find the bread?* The man pointed: *Right behind you, my dear.*

I noticed from its layout that the man's book was a Bible. The man noticed me noticing: *A Christian, are we?*

His voice was the spoken equivalent of Vaseline.

I suppose so.

Lucy placed a loaf of sliced on the counter. The shopkeeper went on, as if repeating something learnt by rote: *You could as easily be a Muslim, as far as I'm concerned; or a Hindu; or a Jew; the Bible ain't the only holy book, you know.* Seeing that he expected me to respond, I said: *Ah.* A smile thin as wire drew itself across his face: *Sometimes I read the Koran; sometimes I try and struggle through a bit of the Talmud or the Ramayana; they all say the same thing, deep down, you know.* Lucy broke in: *How much is that altogether, please?*

Forty-seven pee.

She turned to me: *How much have you got?* I opened my palm. Lucy scooped the coins from my hand, added one of her own and handed them over: *All right?* The man nodded: *That's fine, thank you.* Lucy took the newspaper and the loaf and gave me a let's-go look.

A few yards up the road, we found a low stone wall belonging to a front yard and sat down, a mere six inches between our bums.

What an odd man, didn't you think?

She placed the Coldwater Bay Parish Press on joined knees and pointed at an item: 'What a wash-up! Boy found. Centre pages'. She flicked through the paper: *Here it is.* I reduced the six inches between us to one, close enough to catch the soap-bar smell of her skin.

MYSTERY BOY WASHED UP ON MATCOMBE

By John Craddock

Shortly after 10pm last night, in our normally sedentary village of Coldwater Bay, two London-based holidaymakers...

Lucy jabbed at the line: *That must be Dad and Simon.*

...spotted a human body drifting towards Matcombe Beach. They made an emergency call to the local constabulary from the nearby King and Country public house.

WPC Lorraine Woodstock was the first officer to arrive on the scene. She immediately called for an ambulance.

Then WPC Woodstock, now joined by fellow Coldwater Bay PC Andrew Walker, their officer in charge, Sergeant Jeffrey Hyman, and several volunteers, waded into the shallows and hauled the body in.

The deceased was coloured and in his late teens. He was wearing an unlabelled navy blue T-shirt, a pair of jeans, also unlabelled, a navy blue jersey which appeared to have been hand-knitted, and a pair of sneakers of the Czechoslovak make Bata. A white armband was tied around his left forearm.

The cadaver was transferred to St Mary's Hospital, Newport, where it was examined on arrival by pathologist Gavin Little, BM (Hons.). The *Coldwater Bay Parish Press* called the hospital for details and was informed by the duty nurse that the death had occurred within the last twenty-four hours and had been caused by drowning.

Although some two to four bodies per year are washed up on Wight's southern coastline, most of them victims of accidents at sea, Sergeant Hyman privately admitted to the CBPP that this was an unusual case: "There are just a handful of coloureds on the Isle, and the police have the names of each and every one of them, offspring included. This boy is not amongst them. We have absolutely no idea who he is."

"He just came in out of the blue," quipped WPC Woodstock.

The article was accompanied—the clipping is still in my possession—by a black-and-white photo captioned 'Local police examine mystery beach lad'. The camera's flash highlights three imposing figures dressed in black, who are, no doubt, PCs Walker and Woodstock and sergeant Hyman. They are staring downward, at a shapeless bundle.

Lucy and I leaned into the paper at the same time to get a better look. What at first looked like a mess of ink at the front turned out to be the boy's head, skewed to one side. Another, smaller, ink spot was a beshoed foot. On either side of the picture were hints of the local onlookers: a bit of anonymous arm or equally anonymous leg. Then, slowly, Lucy and I, as if by mutual accord, turned to face each other, me thrilled by the fact that we now knew something our respective friends, Roger and Eileen, didn't. Our little secret.

I think this is something important, I think that from now on we should keep our eyes peeled and our ears pricked up.

I hastened to agree, though at the time I saw this washed-up boy as being odder than he was important, convinced that he would turn out to have a reasonable explanation. Sooner or later the papers always came up with one, no matter how apparently untoward the event. I saw no reason to doubt that things would be different this time.

I was wrong of course. Time for a top-up.

LOG OF PROGRESS

(Saturday 13th)

I found the café I'd stopped by yesterday for tea and ordered breakfast, more out of curiosity than hunger; I regretted it as soon as it was placed on the table. I tried not to wince at the sight of those solid, semi-solid and liquid portions jostling about on the porcelain. I ate what I could, while catching the noises of the natives: chewing and slurping and smatterings of natter.

This log is, at least, good for honing my English. Should it fall into the wrong hands, the correctness of the language might surprise. 'Why', they may say, 'this isn't the way people like him are supposed to write: there's no overuse of the present continuous ('mother is loving me when I am borning'), there are no native-boy repetitions ('I am running quick quick'), and no cute Creole misspellings ('porson dey no fit enter here').

No, because I have taught myself this language well, given that I must not make a slip (of which, I know, there are many between cup and lip). I've familiarised myself with different social registers, so as not to use a word suitable for one class when talking in a mode habitually used by another (unless satirical intent is in order). If I were to make any gaffes, I might raise a jot of suspicion; and at this delicate stage that would be a jot too much.

Before me I have the latest issue of the Parish Press. Its gossip pages are dedicated not to local tittle-tattle but to syndicated stories about people who are famous in Britain. Models who sing. Singers who model. Presenters who both model and sing. Stars, space-fillers, faces caught pale in the flashlights, smiles askew, hair sprayed to a shine, their thoughts paraded in flimsy ink at the photos' feet.

As for us, we have had no stars for quite a while now. Even if we had, our eyes would no longer look their way.

The paper's centre pages are dedicated to our man overboard.

*

Nine pm. I went to the spot on the beach where they found him, and dawdled there. The first person down. His spirit brushed past me, leaping up from the damp sand on its way to wherever. The first person down. A raindrop made me look up. Its fellows were milling in the clouds, ready to leap.

Time to gather information. I headed for the pub.

When I said:

Evening,

the barman grinned and—nodding at the cats and dogs which had just started raining—riposted:

What's good about it?

I sat at the bar and here I still am, ears pricked up and eyes peeled.

There are hardly any holiday visitors at all—if any—as far as I can make out—and just a few villagers (older men in caps, middle-aged women, a couple of those sullen bomber-jacketed teenagers I spotted yesterday in the high street).

I overhear a wealth of grumbling about wonky carburettors, cracked patio paving, a half hour wait for the doctor. No talk at all of last night's beach corpse. Perhaps its having been packed off to the island's capital has made them lose interest. Out of sight, out of mind.

The talk gets more heavily peppered with expletives as more beer and the double-whatevers are swallowed down.

The rain has intensified and is shushing vehemently. I order a second pint.

Strange, alcohol. Given time, it will creep up the back of your neck and ruffle your head, uncle-like.

After an hour, I feel like my elbow's been welded to the bar. I might be anywhere, anywhere at all.

Nothing overheard so far has given me cause for alarm, making me feel (and with every sip more so) that for today I am on a sort of busman's holiday.

I'M NOT A

(Saturday 13th)

One is never quite sure how one might enlighten the inhabitants of a tight-knit community. Quite another thing, of course, is to sit in London and write the odd letter here and there to a national daily, each one carefully pruned so as to be in tune with the tone of the newspaper in question. I am certain I am not deluding myself when I say that over the years, my discreetly planted seeds have had their effect: whispers in many ears, behind which lurk thoughts that dare not speak their names.

When it comes to the regional periodicals, the stakes are, oddly enough, higher: one can sometimes achieve more of an impact in a rag with perhaps just a few thousand or even a few hundred readers, if one chooses one's written vein correctly. Rural people have not been so contaminated by the skewed dogmas which have been allowed to permeate most of our national organs.

I have long put behind me the aspirations of early youth, when I spent much time composing poetry and prose which, I was so very convinced, would make people's brains tingle with alertness. I imagined that one blessed day my own name might form part of that select string of authors and versifiers whose monikers are forever tripping off the tongues of the intelligent classes.

I have honed down such precipitate ambitions. While still aware that I could be rather more than a respected GP in a once elegant London neighbourhood, I have learnt to take the measure of my talent. I now care to squeeze it out in concentrated droplets, and then only when a suitable occasion presents itself.

Such as the curious event of last night. Having read the Coldwater Bay Parish Press's report the following morning, I composed a letter straight off and delivered it to the paper's editor personally (in the sticks, if one has sufficient social clout—and being a London-based doctor, I most certainly do—one can easily get the local stalwarts to do one's bidding). I explained that I would very much appreciate the immediate publication of this letter, mildly controversial though its contents might be construed by some.

The editor—Johnny, as he insisted I call him—turned out to be a prematurely aged hack who knew that life wasn't holding anything in store for him beyond the confines of Coldwater Bay; one of those men who resign themselves to their fate with the help of daily drinks and, I imagine, a patient wife; and perhaps a kiddy-wink or two to cuddle in moments of desperation.

Apropos of my letter, he said, 'That's just what we need down here, a bit of controversy,' his cheeks ruddied by chuckles. A friendly pat on my back as I left made it clear to me that my letter would be appearing the following morning, as indeed it did:

Dear Sir,

I imagine many of your readers were as shocked as I was to read of the events at Matcombe Beach on the night of the 12th last. May I venture to offer a hypothetical explanation for the appearance of this unfortunate foreign youth on our coastline?

I have it on good authority that unscrupulous individuals in some of the poorer African countries are pocketing not insignificant sums of money by promising gullible farmhand types that they will whisk them and their nearest and dearest off to the Promised Land, which is none other than the Green and Pleasant one so dear to us all. Such unscrupulous trafficking degrades both those who profit by it and those who are ensnared by them.

Without wishing in any way to condone the accidental passing away of a fellow human being, the question is undoubtedly begged: what if the boy had survived? What would we have done with him then? What, indeed, are we supposed to do with all those who, like him,

arrive unsolicited, unprepared and uneducated
in this country, year after year?

Yours,

Yours, *what?* I had used so many names over the years. Something different this time, I thought. Ah yes, whatshisname Peters. *Carl* Peters. Most appropriate.

*

Even as I was sliding the letter into the envelope, I was niggled by the tiniest of doubts and reread the final sentence: '... unsolicited, unprepared and uneducated...'. Was that, I wondered, going a bit too far? Would that raise hackles more than it would win sympathisers? No, I concluded, it was accurate. No abusive language.

I remembered an Englishwoman I met a few years ago, who had just been on holiday to some African country. She had had a splendid time but—and I was surprised that she said this, her being a Liberal voter—she had been most disappointed by the Africans themselves: *They don't do a damn thing for themselves, they're all so listless, so absolutely useless; they watch you with these dumb eyes as you go by.* She paused for a while, then wrinkled her nose (a nose which at that time I found quite delightful) and added, with unmistakable repugnance: *They're not very good at personal hygiene, either, to put it mildly.*

I would not fall into the easy trap of thinking of them as not human. They are that, of course. But if we place the qualifier 'fully' between the words 'not' and 'human', does the sentence then ring true? I rather think it does. In this sense then, we may concede, and I for one most emphatically do, that they are human, but not, indeed, *fully* so.

LOG OF PROGRESS

(Sunday 14th, Easter Day)

I'm writing this stretched out on my bed in the faint light of the small hours, above the shop of this madman, for that is what I now know him to be.

Last night, a time came when I tired of my eavesdropping and, bolstered by the beer, cosied up to the barman and asked him if I could ask him something. He started cackling:

Want the wife's phone number do you? Take her, please! Ha ha ha!

I managed to smile, said:

I hear there was a bit of an incident here last night?

I nodded in the direction of the beach. A man standing at the bar turned to us:

Too right there was.

The barman jammed a dirty jug into the rotating washer:

One of our coloured brethren came in with the tide.

The man at the bar shook his head:

Just a kid; sad.

Taking care not to rise to the bait hanging off the words 'coloured brethren', I ordered pint number three. The barman was saying to the man:

Of course it's sad; it's a death. But what was that kid doing over here in the first place? That's what I want to know.

The man at the bar shook his head again:

Could've fallen off a cliff over by Brook Bay and floated up the coast.

Another man had just installed himself at the bar:

Could be, but there aren't that many of them here on Wight, are there, though? Coloureds, I mean?

A plummy voice, so: almost certainly a holidaymaker. He was joined by a lad at the tail end of his teens. The barman shook his head:

No, not many, no.

I was halfway through my pint. My mind, swimming in silk, felt it might say anything it wanted, and so said, with a bit too much emphasis:

Coloureds?

The middle-aged man grimaced:

To call a spade a spade: blacks; they all want to get into the country; after all, it's *so* much nicer here, isn't it?

The younger man next to him tutted:

Yeah, but you can't let them all in, can you? I mean we'd be bleeding swamped, wouldn't we?

My thoughts chucked words out with abandon:

What do you suggest we should do about it, then?

The barman chuckled:

You could always build a bloody great fence!

The booming gentleman shook his head:

Not very practical. But there certainly are other solutions.

We looked at him. The younger man frowned:

Like what, Dad?

Ah, of course, father and son. Father hesitated, shrugged, raised a prevaricating hand:

Repatriation, for example.

I polished off my beer, got off the stool.

Had father, son and barman been just a matchstick's worth more unpleasant, I might have smashed my glass on the bar, taken a shard, taken a grip of father and pushed it into his throat.

I gave a chummy farewell nod to all present:

G'night.

Night.

Night.

*

I walked back through the cold, drunker than I realised at the time: I had some trouble fitting the key in the lock and then, once in, I tripped on the doormat, narrowly avoiding a pratfall. I had just righted myself when the hall light was switched on, dazzling me. The shopkeeper was standing a few feet away, in his shopkeeper's jacket:

Had a bit too much, have we?

Nothing accusing in his tone. I smiled:

Just a little, perhaps.

He looked at me inquisitively:

Are you a religious man at all, Mr Cole?

What was he getting at?

Not as a general rule.

He then laid a speech on me:

God is everywhere—he muttered—a presence that thickens the air wherever we go, a tingling force at the universe's very edge;

and that only a few have truly heard his word and drunk his message down just as I—meaning me—had drunk down whatever beverages I'd just had down the pub.

Mohammed, now, he was a good God listener, Mohammed, who saw Gabriel and never looked back, Mohammed who fled to Medina, where Jewish and Arab tribes dwelt side by side, descended as they all were from Ibrahim; and then—he added, after the briefest of pauses—we must not forget Jesus, Jesus baptised in the River of Jordan, Jesus who preached humility and peace; all these prophets—he mumbled—had been spoken to by the ineffable and unknowable One of ineffable and unknowable things, and these prophets had then turned these things into simple words that every person, even a child, could understand, *especially* a child—he said, his whisper rising now to a hiss.

I don't know how long he would have gone on in this vein if at that moment a real flesh-and-blood child hadn't walked out of the darkness at the back of the passageway; she must have been about nine, and had light brown skin; she asked if everything was all right and he, fleetingly irritated, told her to get back to bed, at which she turned solemnly and walked away; he looked back at me and, as if I had just that moment come in—instead of having stood there for Lord knows how long listening to his sibilant rant—said:

Good night, Mr Cole, sleep well.

All that sobered me up. Once in my room, I didn't have to put my head under the cold tap before checking my watch, pulling the wireless spark transmitter from under the bed and tapping: *Tonight*.

I WAS TWELVE

(Sunday 14th, Easter Day)

A bit of an odd morning, it turned out to be, given that Easter was supposed to be an important holiday; in my own (sibling-free) family, for instance, Easter was a red-letter day, involving exchanges of presents—like it was a dress rehearsal for Christmas—and the ceremonious handing over to myself of a largish chocolate egg.

But *chez* Whitebone, Easter was a far less auspicious occasion. Once we kids were seated round the kitchen table, Mrs Whitebone served us our Weetabix and Long Life milk, just like on any other day. I ate subdued, somewhat miffed. Once we had done the washing-up (me and Roger scrubbing, Eileen and Lucy doing the drying-up), Mrs Whitebone said, in that jolly tone of hers which got on my tits so: *Now! Everybody sit back down at the table and close your eyes!* We did so, Lucy with a perceptible sigh. I caught a whiff of Mrs Whitebone's make-up powder as she placed something in front of me.

Eyes open!

After all this palaver I was expecting something really special—spectacular even—so it was a let-down to see that in front of me she had placed a chocolate egg as small as a real one. I examined the wrapping. It was one of those ones that had a white and yellow filling designed to imitate the insides of a normal egg. I'd tried one of these for the first time last year, and had nearly puked.

Simon the paratrooper came in and dumped himself down: *Black coffee would be nice, Mum.* He looked dead tired, despite having got up later than all of us. He was followed a moment later by Dr Whitebone: *Make that two, please, Marjorie.* He noticed us: *Got an egg each, have you?*

Instant all right?

Mrs Whitebone—having given us her vomitous yucky cheapskate eggs—started to get on with a business-as-usual breakfast for the grown-ups, waving a frying pan in the air: *Eggy bread or cheese on toast?* Simon and Dr Whitebone muttered, not quite in unison: *Cheese on toast.* The pan on, she turned to us: *What do you fancy doing today, children? How about an afternoon trip to the Needles?*

The Needles—advertised all over the village on a poster which carried the slogan 'Isn't It Time You Got The Point?'—were some chalk cliffs that poked out of the sea, westward up the coast from Coldwater Bay. There was a small funfair on a nearby promontory, with a chairlift that took you down to the beach, where you could catch a boat out to these Needles. Hey, maybe Easter Day would be fun after all. We gave Mrs Whitebone a unanimous yes.

*

That afternoon, however, it started to rain hard, as if the entire village was being walloped by water.

(A decade later, when I was twenty-something, in a London room whose thick curtains had cast a pall across our hungover morning, I watched my girlfriend of that moment urinate into a chamber pot right in front of me, hitching up her crotch so I could get a better view; the sight brought to mind that relentless Easter rain. Maybe God *is* a woman, I thought, putting two and two together as I watched her pee).

No sooner had the downpour got underway than Mrs Whitebone—whose life, I had already surmised, was not abounding in moments of excitement—immediately stood up, went to the window and exclaimed: *Good heavens*, as if she'd seen a celestial portent. Dr Whitebone turned his head: *What's that, dear?* She gestured to the window with both arms: *Well, there's no point taking the children out in this! Better wait 'til the morrow, methinks.* Eileen said: *Drat!* and Lucy: *What a pity*, and Roger: *I was rather looking forward to it.* I said nothing. I liked the cosiness of the rain, not being at all averse, anyhow, to spending a few more hours indoors with Lucy (with whom, and it thrilled me to recall it, I now shared the newspaper secret).

Dr Whitebone smirked knowingly at Simon: *What do you think?* Simon shrugged: *Yeah, why not?* Mrs Whitebone put on her false-scolding voice: *Oh you're not off to the pub again, please!* upon which Dr Whitebone said: *It's a dreary day,*

Marjorie, and I'm curious to hear what the locals have to say for themselves, if you get my drift. Lucy and I exchanged the fleetingest of glances. *We* got it. His wife harrumphed: *It seems to me you've spent a rather large portion of the two days we've been here so far, in the public house; I don't think it's very good for Simon: he's supposed to keep fit.*

Oh come off it, Mum, if you don't drink in the army, you're dead.

Dr Whitebone boomed: *Just so!* and off they went, with brief waves and briefer goodbyes and a rustle of anoraks being unhooked in the hall and a clunk of door.

I think I'll go and lie down for a bit.

Lucy said, in a voice suffused with responsibility: *That's fine, Mum, I'm sure we'll find something to keep us busy.*

Mrs Whitebone nodded: *See you a bit later, then.* She left the kitchen and tramped upstairs. We had finally been left to our own devices.

Lucy pointed at me: *This young man and I had a gander at an interesting news item yesterday morning.* 'Young man' sounded flattering coming from her, but I was disappointed she and I would no longer have our secret, having shared it successfully for almost a day. She was clearly so fascinated, so flummoxed, by this event that she wanted to air it with the others.

Eileen cottoned on at once: *Are you talking about what happened yesterday at the beach?* She leaned forward over the table, breasts pressing against her forearms. Even Roger, not one for visible displays of enthusiasm, turned his head in Lucy's direction. Lucy nodded with wide eyes: *Oh, yes indeed.*

She gave a concise summary of the article she and I had read, checking the odd detail with me.

When she'd—we'd—finished, there was a hush, made quieter by the rushing of the rain against the window. Then Roger said, in his brontosauric way: *Why do you think your father tried to avoid the subject yesterday?*

Lucy and Eileen looked at him, then at each other. *Who knows?* said Eileen *Maybe he thought it would upset us.*

Lucy scoffed: *Typical! Treating us like children!* and shook her head with vehemence: *I would really, really like to know what this business is all about; poor bloke...*

Which bloke?

The black bloke they found on the beach, Roger!

Having been mulling it over, I said: *Blacks always seem to have a tough time of it, one way or the other; it's like they're under a curse.* Lucy looked at me, surprised: *How d'you mean?*

Well, I mean, look at the negroes in America: if they're not training for the Olympics or playing an instrument, they're cleaning toilets or they're on the dole.

They don't have the dole in America.

So they have to beg, then, Rodge, and that's even worse.

Lucy adopted a schoolmarmish tone: *It's true that Africa's in the most dreadful mess; most of the population have to walk* miles to wells full of dirty water, many only eat a kind of sticky white paste, and plenty of them have kwantiakor, I think that's how you say it, which means their legs swell up big as an elephant's. I raised an emphatic index finger: Their bellies swell up too suddenly remembering a couple of photos glimpsed years before in an article in a Sunday supplement about a place which was also a war, Biafra, that couldn't be found on any map.

Roger shook his head: When I don't finish my food my mother says I should think of the starving Africans; but I can't very well send them my Brussels sprouts, can I?

Eileen piped up: The charities give them buckets of aid anyway.

Lucy raised her own emphatic index: My geography teacher told us the Chinese have a saying which says that you shouldn't give a hungry man a fish so he can live for a day, but a fishing rod, so he can keep himself alive for years; I thought that was a smart thing to say, but when I repeated it to Dad, he didn't buy it.

How'd you mean?

When I came to the bit about the fishing rod, he laughed and said that the chinky-Chinese were an industrious people, but if you gave a fishing rod to an African he'd throw the thing away 'cos it was too much like hard work: easier just to sponge off Oxfam; naturally lackadaisical, that's how he described them.

Lacka-what?

It means lazy, Roger.

I thought of the extremely few black people I had come across. There had been just one at primary school, whose name I never learnt and who kept himself pretty much to himself. At least, I never saw him talking to anybody. There was also a black cleaner at the school, whose skin colour contrasted strongly, I recalled, with his green overalls. And that was that. These thoughts led me to think aloud: *I wonder what it would be like to live next door to a coloured family?*

After a pause, Eileen said: *I suppose it would be like living next door to anyone else.*

Roger shook his head: *I've heard they're a lot noisier than us.*

Dad says they have a different smell to them, because of the spicy food they eat.

That's if they can get anything to eat at all, Lucy.

Dad also says that some people go on about racism but that blacks are just as racist with us as we are with them.

I'm not racist.

I think everyone's a bit racist deep down, they just don't want to admit it.

By 'everyone' Lucy meant, I suppose, white English people (we did not think of non-whites as being English, not back then). There's a thought, I thought: that we're all racist, every last mother's son of us.

LOG OF PROGRESS

(Sunday 14th, Easter Day)

A dream that came to me when I dropped off last night is now creeping back through the hangover.

I was in a hotel that reminded me of one I stayed in once in Accra—the Hansonic—although my dream hotel had no name, no fixed address. I'd been given a small room, its walls a grubby blue. It contained an old cupboard, a couple of old chairs and an old dresser with a mirror, its mercury spoiled by brown stains. The cupboard's door was ajar, revealing an old mop jammed into an old bucket. A map was tacked onto the wall. It showed a chunk of West Africa, an inward-reaching strip of which was highlighted and named **GOLD COAST**, in a font large and bold.

Gazing at it, I found myself assailed by waves of recollections too bygone to have been mine: memories of ancient fears, of paths leading nowhere but to hostile forest. To get rid of the depression which was burrowing into my head, I looked away from the map and round again at the room, imbued though all of it was now with the sadness of those two outdated words: **GOLD COAST.**

I left the room and walked out of the hotel straight onto the wide saucer of a valley bottom. Ahead and to either side were dozens of mountain peaks behind which some sunlight was itching to rise and as I walked on, the valley grew broader and the mountain peaks more numerous; the sunlight finally made it up to the gaps between the peeks then flashed into the sky and across the shallow valley, sending shoots of fire into my eyes until the only thing that mattered was that ever brighter light, as it crept up the mountains, setting the valley ablaze until the whole morning was burning up, until each and every morning that I would ever live was burning; and they would go on burning, those valley dawns, not caring whether any of us were alive or dead. An African dream. My African dream.

I rubbed my eyes, spooned some instant.

*

I needed milk, but my shopkeeper hadn't opened up yet. I was on my way back upstairs when I heard him reciting behind the door of his living room in a jittery voice in which only the word lord was fired with conviction:

O *Lord!*, rebuke me not in thine anger, neither chasten me in thy hot displeasure. Have mercy upon me, O *Lord!*; for I am weak: O *Lord!*, heal me; for my bones are vexed. My soul is also sore vexed: but thou, O *Lord!*, how long?

Answered the careful voice of the little girl:

Joy! joy in bright Ayodhya gladness filled the hearts of all. Joy! joy a lofty music sounded in the royal hall; fourteen years of woe were ended.

Silence. Wanting my milk, I knocked. After a little while, the door opened a notch. My landlord was wearing a black polo neck:

May I be of assistance?

I told him what I wanted. He glanced at his watch.

Just a sec.

He went back in and closed the door. It stayed closed. Biding my time, I wandered over to the hall. There was a pile of old magazines on a table near the street door. The Buddhist Review, The Watchtower, Al Jumuah, Young Believers. All their covers with garish colours and crude drawings of expressions intended to pass for serene, everything overarched by fun-park-ish heavens. My landlord stepped out of his sitting room, now in his shopkeeper's jacket:

Semi-skimmed or whole?

Whole.

I followed him through to the shop's back door; he opened the three padlocks:

Can't be too careful!

The shop smelt of plastic and tin. He unlocked the door that gave onto the street, turned the CLOSED sign round to OPEN, removed a bundle of recently dropped Coldwater Bay Parish Presses from the pavement and slung them onto the counter before producing a bottle of milk:

Anything else?

I nodded at the bundle:

A Parish Press, please.

He cut the string and eased one out:

Here we call it the C-B-P-P; that's twenty pee all told.

*

I found the drowned man in a brief column on the autopsy result—'death by suffocation in water'—which also gave details of the burial: yesterday, 8am, a public nook in a Newport cemetery. It took me a few minutes more to spot a reader's letter on the subject, headed: 'A stray youth'. I wasn't too put out by the slurs on our smartness, but the signature, well, that did get to me. Anyone well-informed enough to use Carl Peters as a pseudonym was enjoying a jet-black private joke.

So who is it that's lurking behind that carefully chosen criminal's moniker? Who's the educated, letter-writing bigot? We don't want any unwelcome surprises. This stretch of coast had been selected with care. This coast is supposed to be clear.

*

I'm writing this in the café where I had breakfast yesterday. Today, just a cup of tea. Before coming here, I took a stroll round the village. Little more than a hamlet though it may be, the houses have the same imperial veneer as those in the larger towns on Wight, built as they were when the Empire—price-

59

fixing, English-teaching, membership-excluding, servant-scolding—was supposed to last for ever. And a day.

On leaving, I spotted an Arab gentleman—the only one I've seen in Coldwater Bay so far—in full regalia. So lost in thought that he almost bumped into me. He stared at me for an instant, unsettled by something. Could it be that he managed to see what other people here cannot: my having passed, my hereditary fluke?

I WAS TWELVE

(Monday 15th)

The day after Easter was blustery, but at least the rain had stopped. At breakfast, Dr Whitebone was in a chirpier mood than the day before. At one point he handed the local paper to Simon: *Chap here's written rather an interesting letter, see what you think.* Simon squinted at the page: *Nail on the head, if you ask me.* Dr Whitebone nodded: *My sentiments exactly.* We might have taken more interest than we did in this exchange if Mrs Whitebone hadn't butted in: *Come on children, it's off to the Needles with us! No nasty rain today!*

We dutifully put on our anoraks. Mrs Whitebone laid a map on the table. The route was simple enough. The one road out of Coldwater Bay—a continuation of the high street—led inland to a T-junction that headed off leftward to the west and rightward to the east. We needed to go west, past Freshwater, all the way to Alum Bay, off which the Needles lay.

She turned to her husband and son: *I suppose there's no point at all in asking you two to come along?* Dr Whitebone, still in an amiable mood, said: *Next time, without fail.*

We set off around ten o'clock, zipping up our anoraks as soon as we stepped outside, for it was most cold. Mrs Whitebone said: *Simon told me he parked the car somewhere near Matcombe Beach.* Lucy snorted: *Near the pub, no doubt.*

Sure enough, we found the Whitebone family car parked smack opposite the entrance of the King and Country. It was a Vanden Plas, a rather rare car even back then, in its brief heyday.

When we were about to get in, I spotted three fully fledged bovver boys—bomber jackets, steel-capped boots—approaching at twelve o'clock. They were some six or seven years older than us and were effing and blinding freely. One of them had an Alsatian on a close leash. Mrs Whitebone stood stiff as a poker by the half-open driver's door, watching them carefully. Lucy tugged at her sleeve: *Mum, please don't say anything.*

But once they were within literal spitting distance, say something she did: *Would you mind not using such foul language? There are children present!* They stopped in their tracks. Then, pointing at Eileen, Roger, Lucy and myself they started to bark further epithets until the one with the Alsatian, who appeared to be the leader (he was certainly trying to outdo the others with the variety and volume of his invective), turned to face Lucy and Lucy alone, who was staring at him: *What are you looking at, you fucking bitch!*

I didn't think twice, I didn't hesitate, the anger rose straight up my throat and emerged as a plummy bellow: W*hy don't you shut up!* He rounded on me: *What did you say?* Still beside myself, I said: *I said bloody well shut up!* My heart was shivering with adrenaline. He walked smack up close to me, his eyes as cold as an otter's, his face blotchy (too much cheap fried food,

I surmised); from a chain round his neck dangled what I recognised as the German Iron Cross, First Class.

Here he was, in the flesh, one sample of all the nasty, violent boys I could never be, not having been born of the same world that bred them; all those boys I feared and loathed because I would never have one iota in common with them, despite their being as British as I was; all the boys whose only function seemed to be to frighten and harass and say things as ugly as those said by this lean yobbo (a hackneyed word, I know, but I can think of no other) who now looked as if he were about to do something I would soon regret. Mrs Whitebone stepped in: *If you do not go on your way right this instant I shall call the police.* The boy looked her way: *Fat cow,* and took the approving titters of the others as an exit cue: *Ah, fuck it.* He and his companions turned, and slouched away. When they'd gone a few yards, he raised a nonchalant two fingers.

Before I could open my mouth, Mrs Whitebone snapped: *Get in the car; I don't want to hear a word more about those dreadful boys.* Roger, Eileen and I squeezed into the back, while Lucy, being the oldest, got the front seat. Mrs Whitebone slammed her door shut and jammed the key into the ignition. The motor failed to start at the first two tries: *Bugger.* Finally, third time lucky, we pulled away. Mrs Whitebone put on the heating, which filled the car with the smell of exhaust fumes, then turned sharply up the high street, zooming past the café and the clothes shop, past the row of terraced houses that paraded their way up the slope. We were calmer now, the boot-boy incident seemingly behind us.

Lucy said: *That's a posh-looking place.* We looked left at a huge stand-alone house that was a wing short of a mansion, enclosed by low brick wall with a metal gate. A brass plaque fixed to one of the gate pillars read STOCKSIDE MANSE.

Just then, drizzle began to spatter the windshield. Eileen groaned: *Not again!* Mrs Whitebone shook her head: *I don't think it's going to pour down like yesterday, though; onward Christian soldiers, through rain and shine!* She gunned the car further up the slope, out of the village precincts.

To the left, beyond a dry-stone wall, we passed a row of telephone poles, stretching away across a field. Just then, God turned his tap full on again. It sounded like furry ping-pong balls were bonking off the roof. Mrs Whitebone tutted: *I certainly hope this eases off* as we entered a gauntlet of overhanging trees. The shush of rain on the surrounding leaves now joined the ping-pong balls on the roof. The road curved quite sharply at this point, so it was impossible to see what lay just a few yards ahead.

When we did see it, it was such a surprise that Mrs Whitebone jerked on the handbrake; the car jolted like it had been kicked up the bum, and we in the back yelled: *Watch out!*

Mrs Whitebone turned off the ignition. We were just feet from the trunks: six long, thick trees, placed across the road, three on the bottom row, two on the second, one along the top.

Mrs Whitebone, frowning like a child, peered through a clear patch of windscreen: *What on earth...?*

The metal sign propped up against the pile—'Road Closed Ahead. Works Traffic Only'—seemed almost more incongruous than the obstacle itself. Mrs Whitebone waggled a finger at us: *Don't you dare leave the car.* She got out and walked over to the trunks. Eileen's voice was a half-inch away from a falsetto: *What's she up to?*

I peered out of the side window. Through the droplets I could make out the trees, their bark dark, and the abundant ferns that were flopping about under the rainfall, and the thorn bushes, clustered willy-nilly. All glistening wet.

An eye? My heart twitched and a prickle sprang up on the back of my neck. There in the green, peeking? I peeked back.

Ferns, trees, bushes, nettles and weeds.

Having given the trucks and the sign a cursory once-over, Mrs Whitebone came back to the car: *I can't hear any roadworks. This is most peculiar; unless they're on strike too.*

Lucy was staring at the obstacle: *What are we going to do now?* Before her mother could say anything, we heard a car. Roger twisted to see: *Morris Minor at one o'clock.* I squinted through the rear window as it trundled up in the downpour: *Late-model Traveller.* It stopped behind us. Its slats were worn, faded. I didn't recognise the driver at first, taken aback as I was by his blackness, but by the time he'd called out *Hello there!* I realised it was the same coloured man I'd seen sweeping the high street in those bright PVCs.

He got out of his Morris and plodded past us: *Morning there*. He examined the obstacle at close quarters for some minutes. Mrs Whitebone used a horsier than usual voice: *I say, do you have any idea what this is all about?* His wet black face filled her window as he pointed at the trees lining the road: *Trees weren't taken down from the edges here; must have been sawn further in. Don't know why the authorities went to all that bother; they could've just put some of their metal barriers up.*

So you think this is official, do you?

He shrugged: *Must be.*

We were just trying to get to the Needles; what could possibly be the matter? I'm going to check with the police.

The man nodded: *Sounds like a good idea to me* and, with a friendly slap on her door, headed back to his vehicle, got in, started the ignition, three-point-turned and drove off.

*

Back in Coldwater Bay, Mrs Whitebone practically dived out of the car: *Come on!* She was in the kitchen in double-quick time. Dr Whitebone and Simon, who had opened a bottle of wine between them, looked up, startled, when we burst in. Mrs Whitebone's voice brooked no objections: *John, we have to call the police.*

Now why exactly should we do that?

66

A question which—together with his accompanying quizzical smile—me, Roger, Eileen and Lucy took as our cue to blurt a baker's dozen of details about what we'd seen, until Simon held up a hand: *Whoa, whoa, are you telling us someone's put up a road block?* Mrs Whitebone got a word in edgeways: *Well, not really; it does say there's some work being done further up, not that I could see any.*

Dr Whitebone's smile vanished in a puff: *I think we'd better hear this from the beginning.* He held up a hand. *Just you for starters, please Marjorie.* She told her husband about the sharp bend in the road, the obstacle, the warning sign, and finally the coloured man who had driven up shortly after. Dr Whitebone leaned forward: *What coloured man?* She looked at him, nonplussed: *I don't know, John, I'm not familiar with every coloured man in England.* I barely noticed Simon's snigger before I put in my ha'penny's worth: *He's a sweeper in the village.* Dr Whitebone passed a slow eye over me before settling it back on his wife: *What did he do, exactly, this sweeper fellow?* Mrs Whitebone tutted impatiently: *He just said hello, took a look at that pile blocking the road, and went off when I told him I'd get in touch with the police, which is what we should be doing right now.* Dr Whitebone's eyes narrowed: *I do believe you're right* he rapped the table *In fact, I'm going to do it myself.*

The local phone book was on a trestle table in the hall. I watched through the door as he flipped open the first page and ran his finger down the local emergency numbers. Cradling the receiver between shoulder and neck, he placed finger in dial hole and made the call.

Hello?

He tapped the cradle, staccato: *Hello, hello?* He turned to us, receiver lolling in hand: *The landlord's bloody well had it disconnected.*

John, you know perfectly well that every landlord in the land does that with short-term rents, please don't go on about...

But he please did go on about it: *He obviously doesn't trust us not to phone Australia or Alaska; mingy so-and-so must be a bloody—* Mrs Whitebone cut in: *John! What are you going to DO?* He poked the phone book: *I've got the address of the police station here; it's just a moment away.*

He was off before anyone could say a word more. Our hush in the aftermath of the slammed door was disturbed after a mo by a long sigh, issuing from his wife.

I'M NOT A

(Monday 15ᵗʰ)

The village police station was at one end of the esplanade, just opposite the Community Centre. Before going there, however, I decided to take a quick look at what it was that had got Marjorie so worked up.

To judge from the neatly sawn trunks, whoever was responsible had used a handheld two-stroke. The surface of the wood had a peculiar sheen to it, not unlike that of monosodium glutamate, which at the time I put down to the rain, still falling with force. The sign didn't look like standard police issue: it didn't even have a stand.

On my way back to the car, a twitch in the vegetation stopped me in my tracks. I glanced both right and left. Although I could see nothing untoward, I stood my ground a moment longer. Nothing.

*

Once through the police station's swing doors, I found the counter deserted except for a Bakelite phone from the year dot and a large walkie-talkie placed upright, its receiver light blinking. On a shoulder-high shelf behind the counter was the local phone book, plus a Yellow Pages, and a fat black binder. The sound of typing had me turning to the only other room on the premises, on my right, its door open to reveal an austere, whitewashed space with two desks facing each other and a filing cabinet placed against the far wall. The typist was seated at one of the desks: a dapper-looking girl in a close-fitting police-issue sweater; her hair, of an attractive burnished hue, was done up in a braided loaf at the back of her head, rather like a forties Fräulein. Just on the right side of thirty, I surmised.

I couldn't help wondering for a moment what it might be like to bend her over that desk of hers, her ungainly trousers yanked down and her lacy knickers pulled to one side to reveal her eager little

"What can I do for you, sir?"

A policeman had suddenly appeared to a chorus of recently flushed toilet somewhere in the building's nether regions. The double chevron on his sleeve told me I was dealing with a sergeant. He had a round head, over which several strands of black hair had been brilliantined into prostration. He was stout enough for his uniform to look a tad too small. I held out my hand.

"John Whitebone. My family and I are lodging at Seaview Heights."

"I know the one. We're not getting many of you grockles this Easter. Worst season in a while. The weather."

He had a Hampshire accent, but with a curious nasal intonation to it.

"My wife wanted to drive over to the Needles this morning, but had to come back. A pile of tree trunks has been placed right across the access road. Roadworks, apparently."

He nodded. "That's right. My constable was just off to Brook, y'see, and called in about the obstruction. Funny, because if there's work needs doing to the road, we're usually the first to be told."

"So it's nothing to do with you?"

Out of the corner of my eye I saw the woman PC was looking at me. The walkie-talkie crackled. "PC Walker to Sergeant Hyman. Are you reading me, Sergeant? Over."

Hyman. The name, I now recalled, had been in the newspaper report. No prizes for guessing the origin of that nasal twang, then. The Chosen One picked up the walkie-talkie. "Andrew, that you? Over."

"I'll be over in a jiff, Sergeant. Over."

"Quick as you can, now. Over and out."

No sooner had Hymie-Hyman released the send button than a squad car draw up outside. A young, be-capped constable climbed out.

He came through the doors sideways, as it were, shoving them open with his shoulders. He was clearly in a state of physical discomfort. His circumcised chief leaned forward on the counter.

"Something the matter, Andrew?"

The constable held up his hands. They were covered in pale red blotches.

"These are burning like hell, Geoff."

I went over. "Might I take a look? I'm a doctor."

His teeth clenched in unexaggerated pain, PC Walker proffered his palms. They had an odd sheen to them. I landed a fingertip gently on one Mount of Venus. The man flinched.

"How on earth did you do this, Constable?"

"Thought I'd have a go at trying to shift one of those tree trunks blocking the road. Gauge its weight, at least. It wouldn't budge, but my hands started itching. Just a little bit at first, but now it feels as if they've been soaked in petrol and set alight. Jesus."

That wood, gleaming in the rain like a Chinese meal.

"Why didn't you put on your Kevlars, Andrew?"

The WPC's voice was smooth and taut. Just like latex, came the thought. Almost posh. Grammar school, most likely.

"Kevlars?"

PC Walker gingerly reached a hand into the jacket under his cape and removed a pair of black gloves.

"I'm not daft. I had another go with these on, but the itching got even worse. Look."

He turned the gloves palms outward. By this time, Hyman had come out from behind his counter for a better look. That pert piece of prime British in the other room watched, eyes a-goggle. The palms and even the upper fingers of these police-issue gloves had been thoroughly blanched by whatever it was they had come in contact with.

"It felt like the stuff, whatever it is, was coming right through the leather."

I took hold of one of the gloves and, taking care to avoid contact with the affected areas, peered at the lining. It, too, was partially blanched.

"That's exactly what it *was* doing, Constable. Now, what kind of chemical could have done that?"

I examined the stains on the inside of the glove. They didn't look like the work of any laboratory corrosive I had come across. I transferred the thing to the counter with pincered fingers and motioned to Walker to show me his hands again. The blotches were reddening up.

"A very unusual form of contact dermatitis. Not poison ivy, not sumac. Not xylene, not lye... Whatever it is that caused this, I'd say that it's possible these rashes could soon form welts or blisters if not attended to."

"So what do you suggest then, Doctor?"

The PC's voice had a vexed lilt to it. I turned to the fine-skinned filly.

"Do you have a first-aid kit here?"

Her smile was more generous than the circumstances required.

"Of course, Doctor."

73

She got up, walked through the door to the counter, slipped behind her Hebrew headman and trotted down to those mysterious nether regions.

"Bloody heck!"

Every muscle of PC Walker's face was now tensed to the full.

"Pain increasing, is it?"

"Not half, it isn't!"

My mind was spinning like a whirligig now as all the oddities to which I had recently been a witness shot into close-up one after the other: the dead blackie on the beach, the roadblock, the carefully placed signs, the toxic substance on the policeman's hands, the blackie on the beach, the roadblock, the toxic

"Sergeant!"

A breathless man in his early thirties had bumbled in through the swing doors. Our bar-mitzvahed officer breathed out audibly, the very picture of someone who was getting more work in a day than he usually did in a month.

"What seems to be the trouble, sir?"

The man pointed.

"The only road out of this place is blocked! And I absolutely *have* to leave!"

"We know all about it, sir," the sergeant pointed at his Bakelite museum piece, "I was just about to see if those roadworks have been properly authorised. Might I ask your name, sir?"

I already had the measure of this intruder, what with his beige flares, his corduroy jacket, his shoulder-length hair, and his phony working-class slur.

"Woolman, Jonathan Woolman. I'm head of humanities at Fearnhill Comprehensive in Letchworth, and if I don't get back by this..."

A Labour-voting Trot, like half the bloody teachers in the country; but I ceased dwelling on him, the WPC having reappeared. She was holding up a white metal box marked with a red cross.

"Here you are, Doctor."

I found her winsomeness quite delicious. I snapped the box open, and set about attending to PC Walker's hands, whose blotches had hopped a couple of spectrum wavelengths to the left and were now violet. I soaked a square of lint in calamine lotion and applied it as gently as I knew how.

"SHIT!"

To a man, we frowned at him.

"I'm in *pain.*"

"I'm being as gentle as I can, Constable."

As I went on applying further squares of doused lint, the teacher went on with his hissy importuning.

"Sergeant, what do you intend to *do*? I'm *stuck* here, for God's sake!"

I glanced over at the counter. The Jew was taking that fat black binder down from the shelf.

"Lorraine, any idea who we need to get in touch with to see if that highway obstruction is legitimate?"

Lorraine. Lorraine. She shrugged, fetchingly uncertain.

"The borough, most like."

"Let's take a look-see. Here we are: 'Borough Services'. 'Abnormal loads'. Not really. 'Accident prevention'?"

It was like watching a film in slow motion. The lint duly applied, I unwrapped a length of bandage.

"I think there are several headings in there that start with the word *roads*, Sergeant."

"Roads it is, Lorraine."

He ran his fingers down the list.

"Here we are. 'Road adoption', it starts. I wonder what that means? How d'you adopt a road?"

He glanced about him with a cheery smile.

"'Road cleaning'. That isn't it... Here! 'Roads and Highways—Obstruction'. This is a Newport number, Medina Borough. It says here: 'The courts allow the highway authority to remove obstructions and recover reasonable costs incurred in doing so from the offender.' If it turns out that no authorised roadworks are involved, some prankster's going to have to pay a pretty penny, wouldn't you say?"

He looked up at Lorraine, whose pearly upper teeth were subjugating her lower lip in a concerned pout

"Shall I call the number for you, Sergeant?"

"No, I can do that all right, Lorraine, thank you very much."

Laboriously, he began to dial the numbers.

"One. Nine. Eight..."

We were all on tenterhooks by the time he clasped the receiver to the side of his head. Then he pulled it away and stared at it as if it'd just stuck its tongue into his ear.

"What's wrong, Sergeant?"

"You try it, Lorraine. Something wrong here."

Lorraine, Lorraine, took hold of the receiver, paused to listen, then jiggled the cradle. Another pause. She jiggled it again. Just as I had done not long ago with the phone at our rented holiday home, believing the landlord had disconnected us.

"The line's dead."

"Are you sure about that, Lorraine?"

"Dead as a dodo."

Lorraine placed the receiver back on its cradle with a sound halfway between a clunk and a click that fairly echoed in that by now most silent room. A silence broken in seconds by our loony lefty.

"What the *hell* is going *on*?"

Another slide had been added to the carousel still whirligigging about in my mind's eye: no phone line, the warning sign, the poison-covered and cleanly sawn roadblocks, the black boy, no phone line, the poison-covered logs

"Now, now, keep your shirt on, Mr Woolman. Let's rack our brains a bit. All we need to do to clear the road is make contact with the Medina Borough offices at Newport. Now, if we can't drive there, and we can't telephone..."

"Are you telling me this bloody village is *cut off?*"

Getting on my nerves as he was, I decided to put this Woolman man in his place.

"This is a police matter. I suggest we let them deal with it as they see fit."

Hyman of Dock Green was still thinking aloud.

"Now, it looks as if we can't very well shift this obstacle by hand, doesn't it, Doctor?"

He looked meaningfully at the constable, who was wringing his bandaged hands in agony.

"If the substance coating the obstacle can go through those police-issue gloves of yours, it can go through practically anything. I would strongly advise against any physical contact whatsoever. But surely you must have a grappling hook of some kind? For getting cars out of ruts and that sort of thing?"

The sergeant, the constable and my pert-faced WPC exchanged the briefest of glances. Hyman scratched the back of his head.

"We have just the one panda car, Doctor, and pandas don't come equipped with hooks, winches or cables. I dare say that's because they don't have the horsepower to haul away anything much bigger than a Reliant Robin. If a vehicle gets bogged down or is involved in an accident, we have to call the Freshwater station and ask for a tow truck. So. I'd say our best bet would be to get the phones back on, pronto."

Oh, come on.

"But don't you have an FM transmitter? Wouldn't that reach one of the towns here, at least?"

"Well, there's one in the panda, of course, but it's no good to anyone until you get at least five miles out of Coldwater. It's only then that it can link up to what's known as the hilltop relay network, otherwise it's not much use, see..."

Dear God.

"Yes, yes, I've got the picture."

Hyman turned to the two PCs.

"I suppose you remember the drill from the last time we had a line down."

Through his winces, the constable managed to say, "You mean Mr Feather, Sergeant?"

"I do indeed, Andrew." Hyman turned to me. "Retired telecommunications engineer, lives on the seafront. Spent half his life up a telephone pole. Saved us loads of trouble not so long ago."

"This has happened before, then?"

"Nineteen-seventy. Force 8 gale. Almost sank a tanker over by Ventnor. It was in the papers."

Not in the ones I take. Then *she* spoke.

"Do you want me to give Mr Feather a lift, Sergeant? I don't think Andrew can drive in those bandages."

The itch in my crotch whispered Give *me* a lift, woman, give *me* one, while she looked at Hyman with a subordinate's attentive respect (putting on an act, most likely: a girl like that, head on her shoulders, couldn't possibly take that slow-witted Israelite seriously). He, meanwhile, had fallen once more to musing.

"Let's take this step by step. Those obstacles are a public health risk. They need manning." He rapped the counter. "All right, here's what we're going to do. Lorraine, I want you to take a walkie-talkie and drive over to Mr Feather's home. You know the address, don't you?"

Lorraine nodded.

"Now, as you are aware, the utility poles start to the left of the access road, just before you reach Worthwood Copse. Drop him off there, check the walkie-talkie's set up properly, and leave him to get on with the job. All right. Then continue on up the access road until you reach the obstacle, and park in front of it. You'll be responsible for turning back all vehicles and pedestrians approaching from the village, until further notice."

"What do I tell them, sir?"

Good question, Lorraine, a very good question.

"Well I... I don't know..."

He tapered off. I ventured: "As someone has already put up a sign declaring the road closed, perhaps that would serve as an interim explanation for any drivers heading that way. We could explain that the roadworks are urgent, that the road is unsafe, a fault line in the tarmac—something along those lines."

Lorraine glanced at me approvingly.

"Sounds believable enough. And Geoff, what if anyone tries to come in to Coldwater?"

"Then of course you tell them to get help pronto. But I'm not betting on there being much incoming traffic, if any. There'll be no deliveries, no post: the strikes have seen to that."

The pedagogue started up again.

"Surely there *must* be people who pass through the village from time to time?"

"That's just the point: Coldwater Bay isn't a place that gets passed through. We're a hamlet of little consequence and we're well off the beaten track. The only people who come here at this time of year are the Easter grockles, which this year means you and the doctor here. No holidaymakers will be turning up now that the Easter week's practically over."

"My *God*."

"Now, now, not to worry, Mr Woolman, we should have all this settled and back to normal in no time."

The Woolman man tutted.

"I bloody well *hope so*."

The constable, edgy with pain, looked at me.

"No matter what we tell the villagers, there isn't any fault line in the tarmac, is there, doctor? I mean, who could possibly be responsible for this? It beats me."

My carousel was whirling ever faster: no phones, a warning sign, a toxic substance, roadblocks, black boy, no phone line, a toxic substance, a sudden twitch of vegetation

"Just thinking off the top of my head, Constable, it could conceivably be some kind of short-term military manoeuvre. My son's in the army, and he told me once they do quite a lot of stage rehearsals for when they'll actually be in the field. They tend to choose remote spots and have been known to give no advance warning. It makes the exercise more realistic, apparently."

The constable re-examined his bandages.

"A bit too bloody realistic if you ask me."

I addressed the sergeant.

"Either way—whether it's a military exercise or something else—it occurs to me that it might not be such a good idea to leave this Feather chap of yours on his tod."

"He'll have his walkie-talkie open on my frequency, Doctor," Hyman nodded at the winking, Hovis-sized device on the counter, "so if anything untoward happens, we'll know just like that." Upon which he raised his hand, placed pudgy thumb against pudgy index finger and got a floppy little snap out of them.

The teacher wasn't reassured. :

"And just exactly *what kind* of untoward something do you think might happen, officer?"

"Oh, here on Wight we have our fair share of undesirable elements, Mr Woolman: people who are capable of all kinds of shenanigans. In my view, all of this business is as likely as not a bit of elaborate buggering about by some local troublemakers."

I found that rather hard to believe.

"I find that rather hard to believe. The roadblock is well constructed, which is not what one expects from mere hoaxers. Then there's the question of whatever it is the tree trunks were smeared with. Not a substance amateurs could obtain easily, in my humble opinion."

"Well, Doctor, there's a bad bunch of lads over by Wroxall way. Professional hooligans, they are. You wouldn't believe what they're capable of."

Hooligans. Not to be ruled out, perhaps.

"Right then! Lorraine, you'd better pick up one of the two-ways from downstairs and be on your way."

"No sooner said than done, Geoff."

"As for me, I too shall get out from under your skirts, so to speak."

I was already at the door when the chevroned Hebrew called after me, "Dr Whiterose?"

"Whitebone."

"Dr Whitebone, beg pardon. Are you particularly busy right now?"

"Well, I'm on holiday and that's always hard work, is it not?"

"Would you mind very much waiting here until WPC Woodstock has radioed in to confirm she's reached the obstruction? You see, should anybody have got to it before she does and tried to shift it, like Andrew here, they may well come in here seeking medical attention."

"And how long, pray, would this confirmation take?"

"Not more than half an hour."

Why not?

"I think I can spare thirty minutes, Sergeant."

"Thank you very much, Doctor. It's the young 'uns I'm especially worried about."

Oh, the children, the children. How very like a Jew. The schoolteacher had started to fidget once more.

"Look, it's *most* important that I get back to my school at Letchford as soon as I can!"

I didn't believe a word of it. He was nothing but a predatory poofter, most likely, itching to get back to some brainwashed teenage busboy. His school, my arse. The sergeant shrugged.

"The best thing you could do for the time being, Mr Woolman, is to return to your lodgings and wait until we get everything back to normal. As I said, it shouldn't take long now."

LOG OF PROGRESS

(Monday 15th)

We have no idea how the inhabitants will react.

The English, from what I've seen, pride themselves on being a good-natured lot; prone though they are to fits of rage as ugly as goitres.

I've seen English soldiers on television—with a dispassionate streak peculiar to them alone—beating up the locals of whatever strange land they happened to have been posted to, urged on by officers with voices taut with thrill, like they were watching a stripper go all the way.

I suspect there's nothing the English might not do, given the circumstances.

In that sense, they are much like us.

I have, after all, seen women forced by their children's murderers to dance on their children's graves; seen mothers forced to bury their children alive with their shot fathers, seen these children scramble up again and again out of the ditch, imploring their mothers not to shovel more dirt on top of them, screaming goodbye to years unlived, until reduced to a single, shifting, stuck-out limb; I have seen hands and whole arms, feet and whole legs, macheted off the old, the infirm, the children—always the children—simply because their villages had got in the way; I've seen *kadogos* of twelve gang-rape under orders; I've seen infants placed together in baskets and lowered into a green and yellow river, caterwauling as they drowned.

Little wonder we decided to go for a while to a place where conditions would simply not permit such things to come to pass. Here where peace is run of the mill, taken as read, for given, for granted.

I'M NOT A

(Monday 15th)

Mr Feather spoke a dialect thick as cud, which I could have sworn got even thicker once the Semitic sergeant had informed him that also present in the station and listening in, was, as he jestingly put it, a 'city slicker'.

Once Mr Feather (and, a moment later, Lorraine) had radioed in—from the utility poles and the roadblock, respectively—I made to leave the station again, that being the agreement between Hymie and me. However, no sooner had I zipped up my windcheater than further crackle from the walkie-talkie stopped me in my tracks.

A Negro corpse, stacked trunks, glistening irritant, shuddering leaves and something more, some piece in the puzzle that was slipping my mind.

"Are you there, Geoff?"

Ka-chhhh, went the metal loaf, *ka-chhhh.*

Hyman pressed the receive button.

"Hello there, Pete. Remember to say 'over' at the end of each call. How're you doing? Over."

"There's heavier rain on the way, sure as my name's Peter Feather. Over."

"Hope you're wrapped up well. How's it going? Over."

"Oh, I've come prepared, wellies and all. Over."

"Have you found the problem, Pete? Over."

"I'm just... Over."

A sound of rustling mac and squeaking boots.

"What have you found, Pete? Over."

"I've never seen anything quite like this. Over."

"What is it *exactly* that you've seen, Pete? Over."

"Someone's gone and removed the wires at a point where they go through the insulators. I tell a lie: at *two* points."

Hyman looked at me, and I looked just as blankly back at him.

"Pete, could you put that into language that's a bit plainer? Over."

"Well, Geoff, you know those T-shaped porcelain objects you get on the crossbeams of all the utility poles? Over."

Hyman looked perplexed. I nodded furiously, Yes, tell him yes, we've all seen those damn things.

"I think I know the ones you mean, Pete. Over."

"Well, those are insulators. They make sure poor weather doesn't damage the signal between poles. Are you with me so far? Over."

"I'm with you, Pete. Over."

"Well, the ones we happen to have here in Coldwater are multipart insulators. Which means they consist of two pieces. Now, what's happened is that the phone lines have snapped— or been cut—*exactly* at the points where they pass through the insulators. The breaks are almost invisible, even to the trained eye. It was a hairline crack in the insulator in question that made me take a closer look. Otherwise I'd never have noticed a thing. Over."

"Pete? Over."

"Yes, Geoff? Over."

"So what is it we've got here? An accident or a bit of larking about? Over."

"I reckon it's been done deliberately, Geoff. And I have my reasons. Over."

"What's that then, Pete? Over."

"It's a neat job. Whoever did it used tools. There's one thing I don't understand. Over."

"What don't you understand, Pete? Over."

"Well, these are joint poles, see. They carry power lines as well as phone lines. Over."

"What are you getting at, Pete? Over."

"Well, the power lines, which are right next to the phone lines, haven't been touched. Over."

"Well, we know that, Pete, because otherwise I couldn't switch on the bloody light. Over."

"I know, but I was thinking, what kind of self-respecting hooligan would damage the phone lines and not take the opportunity to cut the electricity off as well? Over."

But it would all make perfect sense if this were an exercise of the sort my son mentioned: unannounced manoeuvres. They wouldn't do anything as drastic as blacking out an entire village, but leaving it incommunicado for a spell might make sense for a strategy rehearsal. I made a mental note to talk it over with Simon. Yet... Yet a washed-up black boy, unusual toxic substances, and now

"I honestly don't know, Pete. But can you repair the damage? Over."

"It's going to be tricky. I'll have to rethread the faulty insulator and then check the other ones, just to be on the safe side. I'll be needing some copper wire. Over."

"Well, how long would that take you? How many of those insulator things are there? Over."

"Sixteen. Two or three hours, I reckon. That is, if there's nothing wrong with the other fifteen and I don't have to rethread them as well. Over."

"All right, Pete, you'd better call it a day for now. Not much you can do until we fetch some wire. I'll radio Lorraine to pick you up in the panda. Over."

"I'd be enjoying quite a nice view if it weren't for all this rain. Over."

Again, we got a chorus of rustling and panting as Feather clambered down. The rain was intensifying, just as the old fart had predicted. He huffed upon regaining terra firma.

"It's fair pissing down now, Geoff. Over."

"All right, there, Pete? Over."

"I would be if you didn't keep—"

A sudden silence.

At that moment, I simply *knew,* beyond the shadow of a doubt, that we were, at the very least, up against something out of the usual. Hooligans be damned. Hymie slammed his chubby thumb down on the press-to-talk.

"Come in, Pete! Over!"

Not so much as a whisper of static from the other end. Hyman twisted the frequency knob.

"Lorraine, are you reading me? Over."

"All quiet on the western front. Over."

"Well, it's a bloody sight too quiet over by the phone poles. Get that panda to the T-junction, where you left Mr Feather. Quick as you can! I'll meet you there. Over."

"Roger and out."

Hyman was beside himself.

"Could we go in your car, Mr Whitebone? WPC Woodstock has our only official vehicle."

I kept him in suspense for a mo.

"Doctor."

"Doctor, of course, Doctor. Beg pardon."

I pulled the keys from a pocket.

"Shall we go?"

He lurched out from behind the counter, walkie-talkie clutched in one hand while the other placed his cap upon his head.

*

I put on a spurt up the slope of the high street, past the village limits and the stately manse, before braking to a halt. We clambered out, slamming doors, at the exact same moment as Lorraine pulled up sharply in the panda. Film-like timing.

With a feminine trot, she headed for the wall of the field where Feather had been checking the utility poles. They stretched away across the field, into the invisibility of the downpour. The first pole was just a few feet from us. Ice-cold drops fell from low clouds. Hymie surveyed the field.

"Coast seems to be clear."

And with that he hitched himself up and over the wall. I followed suit and found, when righting myself, that Lorraine had done the same and, with Hyman, was already stepping over to the first pole. I caught up. Lorraine and her sergeant set at once to examining the ground, but I could see for myself there was nothing of interest there. No dropped tools, no abandoned walkie-talkie. Just grass shivering in the rain. As they bent over, seeking clues, I peered at the furthest curtains of downpour.

At first, I wasn't sure of what I'd spotted just beyond those veils. I called out to the others.

"Look. There!"

Those two unlike officers of the law stood up straight and squinted at where I was pointing.

Three figures could just be made out—they were no bigger than squirrels at that distance—heading away across the grass. Despite the poor visibility, I clocked the flanking males as nig-nogs. The figure in the middle, by contrast, was shorter, and was wearing a dark blue mackintosh and a sou'wester, shiny with rainfall.

"That's Pete, in the middle!"

Hyman started to stomp ahead across the cake-soft ground, howling Mr Feather's Christian name. Idiot. I turned to Lorraine and felt my voice deepen in a way that surprised even me.

"He shouldn't be doing that. Very foolhardy."

"Foolhardy?"

She giggled, just for an instant.

"We don't know who those people accompanying him are, or what they're capable of."

Hyman came to a halt. He was panting hard and pointing to the grassland beyond.

"I've lost sight of them. They vanished over the dip there, sharp. Must have sprinted or something."

I harrumphed.

"I doubt if your Mr Feather is much of a sprinter, Sergeant."

Lorraine stared at the horizon.

"There's definitely no sign of them now."

Hyman scratched the back of his head.

"I'll be buggered".

My mental whirligig was clicking like a cricket what with a drowned piccaninny with a white armband and a warning sign on a pile of trunks on the access road painted with a toxic substance to dissuade removal and the cutting of the phone lines followed by the immediate abduction by two blackies of the one person qualified to repair them. And then.

The military hypothesis refused to go away altogether. Simon had mentioned to me once that there were quite a few Negroes in the army. Could this be some kind of an aptitude test for them? To see if they were up to scratch?

Only then did I realise what it was that had been slipping my mind all day long. When Marjorie discovered the obstruction on the Freshwater Bay exit, she was joined by the road sweeper, popping out of nowhere—accidentally on purpose, as it were—and this road sweeper just happened to be another black, another Negro, another niggy-wiggy-piggy.

On our way back to the cars, I mentioned, in passing, that the abductors seemed to me to be of the coloured persuasion.

I WAS TWELVE

(Monday 15ᵗʰ)

Around half six we got frozen food for dinner, and I use the word 'frozen' advisedly, given that Mrs Whitebone, distracted as she was, didn't heat it up enough; if Lucy hadn't complained with a tactful *Mum, they're a bit hard in the middle* and her mother hadn't duly popped them back in the pan, we would have had a tough time getting those fish fingers down our throats.

By then it was black as the ace of the spades outside, but the rain was still drumming its fingers against the sash windows. Dr Whitebone hadn't come back from the cop shop, and Simon had gone out somewhere (to the pub, probably, we children had agreed in whispers).

A little later, having done the washing-up, we all sat round the table, wondering what to do with ourselves. Mrs Whitebone's poorly disguised restlessness had got to all of us. In fact, it was she who tired first of the silence, broken only by the above-mentioned sallies of rain against the pane: *Why don't we play cards?*

Lucy tutted: *Cards are boring, Mum.* I was relieved to hear that, not wanting her to discover how terminally hopeless I was at any and all card games.

Lucy.

Mrs Whitebone gave a jagged little sigh and looked at each of us in turn: *What about a round of I-Spy?* This was a suggestion so spastic none of us dared to so much as look her in the eye. She clicked her tongue in what amounted to near-desperation: *Well does anyone have a better suggestion?*

Lucy half raised a hand: *Could we put the radio on?* Mrs Whitebone frowned a touch: *I suppose so, if that's what you really want.*

Lucy turned to us: *Is it OK if I put on Radio Caroline?*

Hearing our categorical murmurs of approval, her mother sighed: *I don't see why not.*

We chimed in *great*, feeling our cockles warm, given that Mrs Whitebone clearly didn't know that Radio Caroline was an illegal station which meant that listening to it was equally illegal, and so a lot more exciting than Radio One. Lucy switched on her transistor radio—a Roberts, good make that—and started fiddling with the dial: *I've been told you can pick it up really well here on Wight.* After a moment of screeching and scratching, a presenter's voice—half plummy, half laid-back—came full on.

The temperature had gone down since nightfall. It struck me, as I waited for the voice to introduce the next song, that for a long time now (a year?) I had been waiting for something—I knew not what—which would perk me up; a gate which would open of its own volition and leave itself enticingly ajar; for me to peek through, then to step through, for good.

We fell silent as the DJ spoke at speed: *In my books they're still the greatest rock and roll band in the world.*

A guitar started strumming, and out of the transistor a high-pitched voice uttered a woman's name and then the song swam along with its built-in farewell to a love affair and I was stealing glances, my heart a-flutter, at Lucy, my heart thumping left and right and up and down, my heart flaring orange; I would have liked to tell her there and then, slap-bang wallop in mid-song, that I was charged from toe to head with longing and love, that I had longing and love poised to spring, cat-like, behind my eyes, that my body whole was in thrall to the longing and love running up and down my muscles and bloodstreams, stretching them to the full before letting them snap back into place, in a continuous, painful game; I would have liked to weep or whisper or bellow all this to her, I would have liked her to know that this was who, what and how I was and was surely who, what and how I was always going to be, right up until the last day of my life, the last hour even.

Who knows, I might have actually opened my mouth and tried to convey some of this to her if Dr Whitebone hadn't then come barging into the kitchen, smelling of wet anorak, his black hair—which he normally kept swept back over his bonce—all at sixes and sevens. His eyes were narrow, focussed; he demanded loudly that the radio be passed to him at once. Mrs Whitebone, who seemed to have been in a kind of reverie, picked up the transistor in both hands, its song dying.

...can't say we never tried.

Her husband snatched the thing out of her hands—*for god's sake, woman*—and having checked his watch he twiddled the dial knob furiously this way and that, until finally: *You are listening to Isle of Wight Radio, and this is the seven o'clock news, with Simon Arkwright.*

Dr Whitebone placed the radio back on the table as carefully as if it were made of blown glass. He swung a pointed finger at us: *Hush, all of you.* Cowed, we listened as the newscaster ran through his headlines.

A victimless road accident in Nettlestone. An interview with the owner of a new fish and chip shop in Ryde. A slump in Easter holiday hotel bookings in Shanklin. Dr Whitebone flattened his ear against the speaker when Freshwater was mentioned, that town being fairly close to us, but it turned out to be an item about the opening of a new branch of the Midland Bank. When the bulletin finished with the local sports news, he switched off Lucy's tranny with a jerk of the knob: *Not a bloody word about what's going on here! Not one. Bloody. Word.*

Mrs Whitebone enquired: *Do you mean about the road being obstructed?*

He looked at her: *It's not just the road, my dear.* He took a breath: *You should know that there's something very serious going on.* He paused again, and took a deeper breath. His wife said: *John, maybe you should try and relax before you...* He turned to her, lips pursed tight: *Shut up, Marjorie!* Lucy stared at him in surprise. He lowered his voice: *It had occurred to me that the army might have been behind the whole thing, but I've just had a little chat with Simon and he has disabused me of that idea.* He slumped into a chair: *It would appear that the army would never have primed a roadblock with a chemical irritant that could injure members of the civilian population.*

Lucy frowned: *A chemical what?*

Her father leaned forward: *There's a local policeman whose hands are covered with the nastiest blisters I've seen in a very long time; he made the mistake of trying to shift one of the logs.* He glanced from bewildered face to bewildered face: *Simon has also assured me that for the same reasons, the army would never interfere with the phone lines; there could be a chance, no matter how remote, that that might put a civilian life in jeopardy: somebody who needed to call an ambulance urgently, for example.* It took his wife a few seconds to ask: *What's wrong with the phone lines?* Dr Whitebone, in a voice strong with the calm of someone about to divulge impressive news, let his words out slowly: *The phone lines that connect Coldwater Bay to the outside world have been severed.* He paused for effect, quite unnecessarily. My stomach was taut as drum skin and my brain—despite Dr Whitebone's unfeigned seriousness—was a-twitch with an inexplicably excitable kind of pleasure.

Mrs Whitebone broke the spell: *I'm sure that can be fixed, John, it's not as if we're in darkest Timbuktoo.* But her husband made his spell hymen-whole again in a jiffy: *The only man in the village sufficiently proficient in matters telephonic has just been kidnapped in broad daylight.*

Mrs Whitebone looked at him, a disbelieving frown furrowing her face: *What do you mean, kidnapped?* Dr Whitebone looked away. *John, I asked you a quest—* His hand shot up: *Shut up, Marjorie*—his second uncharacteristic 'shut up' in almost as many minutes: *I'm trying to think.*

Which he did aloud: *From what I've been able to gather, both the setting up of the roadblock and the cutting of the phone lines were the work of professionals.* Another pause. Eileen grimaced: *Professional whats?*

Dr Whitebone looked like he was about to give her a bollocking, but managed to restrain himself: *If we knew that, Eileen, we'd be more than halfway to solving the whole dilemma.*

My faith in the ability of the grown-ups to cope with things was still intact, and I was longing to be somehow useful in the midst of this brief, unusual emergency: to be handed a small but exhilarating piece of the action.

John, couldn't it be the unions? They've been holding the country to ransom since the beginning of last year, and it wouldn't surprise me one iota if they decided to take matters a step further.

She sounded truly edgy. Silly old thing, did she not know that nothing really seriously serious could happen, not here, not in this little village? Not amid all these sturdy locals, with their firm grips on their pints, their bread-crumbed fish and muddied wellies and their wind-blasted faces, so sure, so certain, so implanted in their home village with their island patois that I had caught on the wing here and there: oh-arrgh, the phones don't ackle, everything's flittershitters, but we'll sort it all out somewhen. And yet, there was Mrs Whitebone all of a dither, lighting up—*for God's sake, John*—and dragging hard at a Peter Stuyvesant.

I never realised she had the habit. Her husband turned to look at her as if she was something the cat had brought in, something that needed to be thrown into the outdoor bin and its smell shut off by a galvanised rubber lid: *Getting your knickers in a twist, dear, is not going to help us one jot.*

He next addressed us younger folks: *Time to sort this mess out, don't you think, children?* Lucy grimaced: *What exactly are you going to do, Dad?* He stood up, put his hand on the kitchen doorknob, his anorak still heavy with soakage: *I'm going back to the King and Country, where Simon and I are trying to persuade the local yokels to get up off their backsides.* With that, he opened the door and, with a tight smile, closed it behind him.

Mrs Whitebone mashed her cigarette end into oblivion: *He's spending much too much time in the pub, if you ask me.*

We children exchanged glances, itching as we were to consort amongst ourselves, to speculate, make guesses, test hypotheses and sketch out a role for ourselves in this curious situation whose reasonable explanation the adults had not yet found. One glance at Mrs Whitebone, however—staring as her stern face was at the remains of her Stuyvesant —was enough for us to realise that in order to feel free to talk freely, we would have to wait until we were out of her earshot.

I'M NOT A

(Monday 15ᵗʰ)

Off I toddled to editor Johnny's first floor offices on the high street, the same three little rooms smelling of damp and dust I had visited in order to deliver my reader's letter, just two days ago, when things were—if one excepted the drowned black boy—quite normal.

I walked through the two tiny anterooms—their walls hidden by shelf after shelf, each piled to near-bending point with box files and back numbers of the local rag—guided by a frantic clicking which came to a sudden halt as I reached the editor's office, the only room with natural light.

"Buggeration!"

It was Johnny, sure enough, a more driven, active Johnny than the easy-going chap of forty-eight hours ago. Only half-visible behind a Remington electric, he was trying to Tipp-Ex out a typo, eyes screwed up in concentration, his mouse-grey hair flopping over his forehead, his hand trembling a touch. To the right of the machine, I spotted a half-empty flask of Scotch.

"Busy are we, Johnny?"

He didn't seem particularly astonished to see me.

"Extremely so, Doctor. What with all this excitement, there'll be bumper sales tomorrow."

He screwed the top back on the Tipp-Ex, unscrewed that of the whisky, took a brief swig, then started to hammer away at the keys again. He had not been at it longer than a minute when he stopped and squinted at what I presumed was another typo.

"Buggeration!"

"Plenty of news, is there?"

He looked up at me with the bleary gaze of the weak-souled.

"*Plenty of news?* Doctor, haven't you heard? The whole village is talking about it. The local road's blocked. The phones are down. And nobody has a clue as to who's responsible."

"Have you heard about Mr Feather?"

His jaw dropped far enough to make him look like a nincompoop.

"Pete? What's happened to *him*?"

"He has been abducted. By two black men, so it would seem. His whereabouts are currently unknown."

"Abducted? Are you sure? Are there any eyewitnesses?"

"Myself, Sergeant Hyman and—whatshername—the woman police officer."

"That would be WPC Woodstock. Lorraine to her friends."

And Lorraine to me, Johnny.

He sank into his chair's padding, swept his hair back with a hasty hand and gestured at the Remington.

"Well, that takes the biscuit, that does. On top of everything else. I'm buggered if I know what to do, Doctor. I mean, I've never had to deal with anything more earth-shattering than poultry competitions and heavy babies. What do you think? Should I go sensational and sound the alarm with a banner headline, or should I underplay the whole thing so as not to alarm people even more, given that we don't really know what's happening exactly? It's a responsibility, it really is."

His hand went back to the flask. A moment later, his eyes primed by Cutty Sark, he wagged a finger at me.

"Know what? I think I'm going to go for a big splash: Pete Feather—him especially—the roadblock, the phone lines, the lot! Present it all as a big mystery, see? It might throw our readers into a panic, it might scare the living daylights out of them, but what the hell! Publish and be damned, I say!"

Then and there, even as I registered the increase in his slur, I experienced a kind of revelation. My previous speculative thoughts—which until then had been all at sixes and sevens—now came together with the precision of a puzzle's last pieces, dawning on me as it did that the burden of dealing with this state of affairs had fallen on me, and me alone. That these out-in-the-sticksers had had a stroke of luck, which was my coincidental presence in their village at this particular time. That providence had provided me, so that I might take matters in hand.

I felt a shot of adrenaline bless my brain with confidence in all that I would do from now on.

I turned to Johnny, who had gone back to poking his typewriter. I held up a restraining hand.

"Just stop there a moment, please. Johnny, we need to think very carefully about how we're going to deal with this situation."

He shook a frowning face.

"Think? I've got to get tomorrow's copy out and I'm behind schedule as it is."

I leaned over the typewriter. He stared at me, awkward as a bum-fluffed adolescent.

"The news you rather precipitately see fit to print will indeed scare the living daylights—as you so succinctly put it—out of the citizens of Coldwater Bay; and when people panic, they have an unpleasant habit of taking the law into their own hands. That, Johnny, is the very last thing we want."

Even I was a tad surprised by the iron-clad conviction of my tone. He took another swig.

"What do you have in mind, Doctor?"

I had quite a few things scuttling about in my mind. First things first, I told myself. First things first. Order.

"Who's the civil authority in Coldwater Bay?"

"Civil authority? Well, I don't honestly think we have one as such."

"Not even a parish councillor?"

"The nearest parish council's in Freshwater. Coldwater's too small even to be registered as a tun."

He stressed the unfamiliar word.

"Tell me what a tun is, Johnny."

"Well, here on Wight, it's a subdivision of the parish council. Freshwater's got five tuns, you see, but we don't have..."

"I get the picture. What about a vicar?"

"Haven't had one of those for years now, Doctor.""What about a JP?"

"Nearest JP's over in Ventnor. We only get petty sessions once a year."

I stood up straight.

"Allow me to correct you, Johnny."

"Come again?"

"The nearest JP is talking to you right this minute."

"I thought you were a doctor."

"Doctors, being considered upstanding members of the community, Johnny, are authorised to take over the functions of a justice of the peace in the absence of an existing incumbent. Under British law."

"Is that right?"

I remained patient.

"Indeed it is. Now, are there any other local worthies that come to your mind?"

"There's Geoff, of course. Sergeant Hyman. He's one person that people round here respect all right. Staunch man."

"When I said 'worthies', I was referring more to social position."

"Well, there's the Arab family up in the Manse. They're not wanting for anything."

"And what kind of standing might they have in Coldwater Bay?"

"We don't see that much of them, matter of fact. Keep themselves to themselves. But they're the most well-to-do people in the village these days, by a long chalk."

"Let's leave them to one side for the time being. Are there any respected *local* notables? They don't have to be millionaires, necessarily."

Johnny took a swig more of whisky.

"Well, I suppose Laura would be the best bet."

"And who, pray, is Laura?"

"Laura Wortle runs the fish and chip shop on the esplanade, a few doors past the sweet and souvenir shop. Everybody knows Laura."

So. A fishwife. The Judaic flatfoot. And myself. Christ.

"All right. Now, how big is the village hall?"

"It's called the Community Centre now."

"Yes, whatever it's called, how many people does it seat?"

"About eighty, maybe ninety. You could probably squeeze over a hundred in there if you allow standing room."

"Oh, I'm going to allow standing room, all right."

Excitement, that was what I felt. Excitement. But not the kind of fast thrill I suspected my daughter Lucy felt when she listened to her pop stars. No, something quite different. Now, not one false step. Get it right.

"Johnny!"

He shuddered, he actually shuddered.

"Doctor?"

"Listen carefully, if you would. I need you to go right now to both Sergeant Hyman and Mrs Wortle, in that order, and tell them that, considering the recent exceptional events affecting Coldwater Bay, in my capacity as justice of the peace, I am inviting them to chair an emergency meeting at the Community Centre, tomorrow afternoon at five-thirty pm, sharp. Once you've done that—and ensured they've got the message loud and clear—I need you to return to this office, double-quick, and put together an eye-catching front page which will inform the village of said meeting. It would be wiser to refer to the current state of affairs in general terms; certainly, Mr Feather's disappearance should not be mentioned. You may claim, if you wish, that your very own Parish Press is convening the event. Some people might find it odd for an outsider such as myself to do so."

He couldn't have wiped the beam off his face if he'd tried ten times as hard.

"I can assure you they wouldn't, Doctor, but I do appreciate the gesture. The Parish Press is well-respected here. Bit of an institution, you might say."

"Couldn't fill the bill better, then. Please try to convey how important it is that as many households as possible are represented at the meeting."

Johnny jotted down details with tipsy enthusiasm.

"I've already got the headline, Doctor!"

"Well?"

"'Hear ye, hear ye, hear ye!' Reminds us we're back to the times of the town criers, you see, when people depended for all their news on one man with a bell in his hand. Well, hundreds of years later, that man is me!"

"That's very good, Johnny. Now, if you will excuse me, I have to make preparations for tomorrow."

No sooner had I reached the door than he called out: "Doctor!"

"Yes?"

"Why are you going to all this trouble on our behalf? After all, you're not even from here!"

"I don't think it really matters where anybody comes from, do you?"

He nodded, the faintest shadow of a doubt on his old apple of a face.

"Fair enough."

I walked down to the ground floor and stepped outside, back out into the rain.

COLDWATER BAY PARISH PRESS

Tuesday, April 16, 1974

HEAR YE, HEAR YE HEAR YE!

PARISH PRESS CALLS EMERGENCY ASSEMBLY * ALL RESIDENTS WELCOME * ATTENDANCE RECOMMENDED

By John Craddock, Editor-in-Chief

In order to inform residents of the measures to be adopted regarding the current anomalous situation in Coldwater Bay, the *Coldwater Bay Parish Press*, at the behest of the local authorities, has booked the Community Centre (68, The Esplanade) for an open parish meeting at 6pm this evening, at which prominent residents and local authorities will address the public.

Interviewed early this morning, Police Sergeant Geoffrey Hyman recommended people should remain calm, despite having their telephones cut off and not being able to leave the village by motor vehicle. He stressed that these were 'purely coincidental contretemps', as he put it with his usual pithiness, which could and would be dealt with as soon as possible. The steps which should be taken to achieve this end, he said emphatically, will be amongst the priority items on this evening's agenda. He added that residents should refrain from trying out any 'ad hoc' solutions. 'Murphy's law', he added waggishly, 'can only be dealt with by rule of law.'

The editor and staff of the *Parish Press* look forward, then, to seeing a splendid turnout at our Community Centre at six o'clock today.

PART TWO: SAFETY FIRST

LOG OF PROGRESS

(Tuesday 16th)

Five to six, and the venue's all but full. A policewoman and constable are on duty at the entrance, nodding welcomes to the incomers. I'm in the back-most row. Before the audience is a low stage with a long table placed on it. Set into the wall to the left of the stage is a closed door. The floor smells of dust and the walls are painted in a blanched blue up to the midriff, where a grubby cream takes over. The chairs are of the plastic, stackable kind. The citizens chat away, expectant, eyes darting. I've never seen so many of our ivory brethren packed together in a confined space. Nor smelt them so much, either: cindery mouths, not always shampooed scalps; sallies of BO from armpits. They do whiff a bit, some of these people.

My landlord is sitting on his tod: no sign of his little girl. The Arab man is a couple of rows in front of him, in a suede jacket zipped up snugly over his belly, gold-plated watch strap gleaming under the fluorescents.

A man to my left has been testing out various theories on his wife: the IRA; Baader-Meinhof; a second Angry Brigade. The wife tells him not to be so bloody melodramatic and to wait for the authorities to tell us just what, exactly, is going on.

The black street sweeper has just come in and found a spare chair near the front. No one pays him much attention, though his PVC uniform makes him stand out. Time moves on, the conversations rise in impatience then fall silent on the nonce when four people emerge from the door to the left of the stage.

A police sergeant, who seats himself at the centre of the table; a man I can't place, middle-aged, red-faced, sits off to the right. The woman in a white apron—who I now know runs the fish and chip shop—sits to the right of the policeman, flashing grins of greeting at the audience.

To *her* right, at the far end of the table, is a straight-backed man whose features are ringing one very loud bell. That sprawl of hair.

The policeman coughs:

May we have your attention, please?

The policewoman and constable at the entrance close the door behind them. I spot the bandaging on the constable's hands. A-*ha!*

The sergeant tries to smile:

Most of you know most of us as are sitting up here, but I shall introduce ourselves all the same; my name is Geoffrey Hyman and I am here in my capacity as a police sergeant with the Hampshire Constabulary.

He nods to his left.

You all know Johnny Craddock here, our very own ace reporter!

The red-faced man grins at this small joke. The sergeant turns to the woman.

And you all know Laura Wortle, of course.

She sits there, green eyes gleaming; a few members of the audience holler:

All right, Laura?

Laura. The policeman waves his arm in the direction of the man who is on the tip of my memory's tongue:

Now, who you won't know is Dr Whitebone; a medical man from London, he is currently on holiday here with his family. As acting justice of the peace, he has volunteered his services to help us to get to the bottom of what is going on in Coldwater Bay and to find some solutions—and there is no doubt they will indeed be found—to the problems we currently face.

The doctor nods. Polite clapping. The policeman consults a sheet of paper:

Coldwater Bay has, for the last twenty-four hours, found itself in a dilemma of an unusual and unexpected kind; firstly, by-road B-3422 has been blocked by a wilfully placed obstruction masquerading as a warning about roadworks, which has effectively cut off all traffic to and from the village; this obstruction—invisible from the A-3055, the nearest main road, also known as Military Road—has been painted or pasted with a toxic substance which penetrates both cloth and rubber and which, and Dr Whitebone has asked me to emphasise this in the strongest terms possible, should not be touched under any circumstances; children, especially, should not be allowed anywhere in the general vicinity of the obstruction.

He pauses. The young policeman by the door is flexing his hands; he looks *really* uncomfortable. Maybe someone overdid it with the unguent. On the sergeant goes:

Our second problem, which came to the attention of the police approximately ninety minutes after the discovery of the obstruction, concerns the tampering of the utility poles which connect us to the Isle of Wight grid; this, in effect, means that all residents will be unable to make or receive telephone calls until the necessary repairs have been effected.

An outburst of chatter. Hands are raised. The policeman raises a mollifying hand:

If you don't mind...

More chatter, more hands shooting up.

If you don't mind...

The hands subside, the chatter quietens. He raises his voice:

If you don't mind, I would like to finish my report first.

Of a sudden, he looks tired:

I'm sorry to have to inform you that our first attempt at repairing the phone lines was unsuccessful. Almost all of you here know Pete Feather; he agreed to inspect the utility poles for us; he was interrupted in the course of his inspection and his current whereabouts are, at present, unknown.

Silence. An elderly lady, shrill:

What do you mean 'unknown'? Do you think he's in danger?

The sergeant coughs again:

Given that when last seen he was in good health, and in the absence of any further information, I believe we can safely assume that he is alive and well. Having said which, we are keeping all our options open at the present time.

Up shoot even more hands than before. The sergeant leans over towards the woman in the white smock and whispers. Serious, she nods and points to one of the questioners:

I imagine you all want to ask much the same thing, so let's just have the one talk for everybody; Greg?

A loaf of a head, close-cropped hair, earrings glinting, a smear of tattoo peeking out of his T-shirt collar.

Just what the *bleeding hell* is going on here? Excuse my French, but I think that's what we all really want to know, isn't it? *What is going on?*

The audience murmurs assent. The sergeant looks down, looks flustered:

Having weighed up all the most probable scenarios, we believe that this could be an elaborate practical joke, carried out either by local hooligans or undesirable elements from the mainland...

Greg bawls:

If so, I'd like to get my hands on those jokers! I'd bleeding...

And again I glimpse that English rage I've glimpsed before: shouts flashing in pubs, yells in side streets, spit hissing out of the blue. The sergeant wags a finger:

If it *is* a practical joke, those responsible will be detained and punished with the full force of the law. We're talking about obstruction of the Queen's highway, tampering with vital amenities, possibly abduction... Yes, Mr Woolman?

A man in a corduroy jacket:

May I ask if the yahoos responsible for this situation have made any attempt at extortion?

The medical man whose face I've been trying to place speaks for the first time:

Whoever is behind this has so far made no contact whatsoever with anyone in the village; that includes the police and the local press.

That voice: the man at the bar. That father of that son. Another hand goes, up, black skin slipping out from yellow PVC. The woman on the stage nods at him:

Winston?

The sweeper coughs:

What else does the panel think it could be if it isn't hooligans?

The mildest of mild Trinidadian accents. Dr Whitebone looks at him, chin raised:

We have considered the possibility that, given the current security situation in the UK today, some kind of military manoeuvre might be involved; I discussed this option recently with my son, who is a Private First Class in Five Para, now currently on leave after a six-month tour of duty in Ulster; he assures me that it is highly unlikely that this could be the case.

He nods at this son, to whom people are turning their heads. There he is: the late teens or twenty-something who was in the bar; shiny, short black hair; he seems flattered by the attention.

The doctor goes on:

The first thing myself and Sergeant Hyman here have agreed upon is that our top priority for the time being is to locate Mr Feather as soon as is humanly possible, while also doing our utmost to guarantee the safety of every man, woman and child in Coldwater Bay.

A sprinkling, just, of hear-hears.

To that end the sergeant here has prepared a formal announcement. Sergeant.

The policeman looks back at his piece of paper:

I would like to make a formal call for volunteers from the resident population to assist the police in the course of their duties. To wit. One: the maintenance of law and order within the municipal boundaries of Coldwater Bay; two: the twenty-four-hour manning of the obstruction on byroad B-3422, with a view to ensuring that no resident approaches, much less attempts to move, said obstructions; three: to ensure, until such time as the current anomalous situation has returned to normal, that nobody leave the immediate vicinity of Coldwater

Bay, given that, as things stand, we simply do not have the means to guarantee their safety. I would also recommend that people ensure their doors and windows are kept locked at night.

He looks up:

These volunteers will also be expected to report any suspicious behaviour or object immediately either to the police, to wit: myself, PC Walker and WPC Woodstock; or to any one of the three civilian members of the emergency committee here present, to wit: Laura Wortle, John Craddock, or Dr Whitebone. To facilitate matters, the Coldwater Bay police station will be manned around the clock, in order to attend anyone wishing either to be informed or to offer relevant information of their own.

A lad in a bomber jacket calls out:

Why don't we just boat over to Freshwater? Half an hour and you're there—problem solved!

The policeman leans forward to address the doctor.

I think our guest might have something to say about that. Doctor?

Dr Whitebone turns unhurried eyes in the youth's direction:

Landlocked Londoner though I am, that possibility had actually occurred to me. However, as we are currently unable to evaluate the risks involved in making such a move, we have deemed it prudent to allow for a wait-and-see period of twenty-four hours starting at midnight tonight. Safety first. If no further incidents have taken place by then, a squad of volunteer seafarers from the village will promptly man the fastest local vessels available. Is that arrangement to your satisfaction?

Relieved laughter. A smile creeps up one side of the youth's face:

Fine by me.

More laughter. I catch an undercurrent of thrill. Wartime memories spiralling in their heads? The doctor mock-seriously says:

I'm glad to hear it.

The red-faced man, Craddock, the one who puts out the local paper, leans forward, tilting his eyes towards the doctor's:

Do you know, I've thought up an immensely simple solution to the whole problem

His voice has a touch of slur. The doctor eyes him:

Yes, Mr Craddock?

Craddock immediately starts waving his arms about:

I mean just how difficult can it be to get rid of a pile of bloody logs! We could burn them, couldn't we? Douse the bloody things in petrol, throw a match at them, and Bob's your bloody uncle!

The doctor looks down at the table for a second before refocusing on Craddock's now even redder face:

First of all, the roadblock is by no means the only problem here. As Sergeant Hyman has just explained, we don't know who is behind this, but I don't think anyone would deny that in the circumstances, we would be wiser to err on the side of caution: we have no idea of how many people are involved, nor what their intentions are, nor indeed where they are positioned. However, we do know that they are in the vicinity, and have already shown their ability to physically intervene when they see fit to do so. This in itself would make any kind of tampering with the roadblock inadvisable. But even were we to assume that we were quite alone, I certainly couldn't recommend setting the obstacle alight: the unidentified but clearly noxious substance with which it is coated might well be inflammable; we can't even be sure that it isn't some kind of explosive.

A beginning-of-symphony silence in the room. He coughs.

Sergeant, please to continue.

The policeman checks his script.

We have prepared a legal document which all volunteers will be obliged to sign.

He holds it up.

The aforementioned volunteers should be males aged between eighteen and forty.

A woman yells:

What about us girls, Laura!

Laura grins:

Nothing I could do about it, love; I'm in a minority up here!

More laughs. The sergeant reads on:

Between twelve and sixteen volunteers will be sufficient to meet the security requirements of the village at this time; upon conclusion of this meeting, volunteers will kindly remain seated until the other attendees have left the building.

I should get back to my transmitter, chop-chop.

I'M NOT A

(Tuesday 16th)

The goats having departed—including Johnny, who left to write about the meeting for his rag and, doubtless, to top himself up—myself, Mrs Wortle, Hyman, PC Walker and Lorraine had a good three score of potential sheep left before us. My son Simon was there, of course. So was the man Mrs Wortle had addressed as Greg, who looked like rather a rough diamond: just the type of fellow we would need, indeed, should the going get the least bit tough. Also present was the loud-mouthed juvenile who had been somewhat amused by my wry handling of his impertinence. It was the younger chaps like him that I was perhaps most interested in: restless lads, a tad oikish, perhaps, but all of them eager to be of use. There was also a handful of stern-faced old men, *Dad's Army* types who had wilfully ignored the rule about keeping the age limit to forty. Finally, there was a little problem, insomuch as the street sweeper—the person Mrs Wortle had addressed as Winston—had also chosen to offer his services.

We managed to badger the codgers into going home. They protested a bit, mentioned their medals, asserted they were a match for any youngster and so on, but we finally persuaded them to leave with a solemn promise that they would be kept on a reserve list and called up immediately should their services be required. We couldn't have said fairer than that, so off they doddered, leaving us with a more or less acceptable selection of volunteers. Sixteen in all. Plus Winston.

I quietly suggested to Mrs Wortle that we send him home too. She looked at me a touch oddly. I leaned into her ear and briefly mentioned something she was still unaware of: that the two men seen with Mr Feather on the rainy field, were, in my opinion, Negro types.

"Which makes this man before us, Mrs Wortle—innocent thought he probably is—a security risk."

"Winston? How d'you make that out?"

The woman just didn't get it. Watching our small audience—now shifting impatiently—out of the corner of my eye, I spelt it out.

"Suppose, for the sake of argument, we suspected IRA terrorists of being behind the recent events here. Surely we wouldn't accept a full-blooded Irishman into the ranks of our volunteers, no matter how innocent he might seem, now, would we?"

"But I'm sure he's completely trustworthy."

"I'm not saying he isn't. But would everybody in Coldwater Bay see it like that? After all, it's vital that every single villager trusts all the volunteers, without exception. To the hilt."

Then Hymo leaned over.

"Everything all right there?"

"Dr Whitebone thinks it could be bit risky to take on Winston. It is true that some folk might not see eye to eye with him being a volunteer."

The Hebrew's jowls dropped a mite.

"I'm not with you, Laura."

She winced, lowered her voice.

"Well, Geoff, he's *coloured*, and, apparently, so were those blokes you lot spotted with Pete. When that gets out, which sooner or later it will, well, you know what people can be like."

Then and there I spotted a hardening in Hymie's eyes, a knee-jerk sympathy with someone else who has been cold-shouldered and spurned, who has had nasty things said to him at school, who has been beaten and kicked and spat on at random just for being... well, just for being.

"I grant you that the doctor believes that the abductors—if abductors they be—were people of colour. But neither Lorraine or I got a good enough gander to verify that observation. Look, let's please just get on with this recruiting business or we'll be here all evening. We can leave Winston till last, if you prefer."

He asked Lorraine to write down the volunteers' particulars. In turn, we asked each one to approach the table and sign a three-point pledge, to the effect that in the course of their duties they were (a) not to divulge any untoward incidents encountered in the course of their duties, to the general public, so as to avoid unnecessary alarm, (b) not to indulge in excessive use of force in those circumstances where restraining action was called for and (c) not to bear or employ weapons of any kind without specific approval from the justice of the peace or the sergeant. When we had sixteen forms filled, I gathered them up and tapped them together against the tabletop, until the pages were flush, and smiled at Winston solicitously:

"Thank you for showing willing, Mr Francis. Should we need an extra hand, we won't hesitate to let you know, but for now our quota has been more than filled."

He was glowering at me.

"Now isn't that odd, that it's the black man doesn't get the responsibility of being a volunteer?"

Mrs Wortle stepped in.

"Winston, Winston, please, it's nothing to do with that. It's like the doctor said, we've already got more than enough people. If we're short of a man, you'll be the first to be notified."

He rose to his feet, and with that po-faced dignity proper to his race started to button up his yellow coat.

"Thirty years I've lived in this country..."

The new recruits were looking at him listlessly, or averting their eyes.

"...and there are times, you know, when I have to check my watch just to make sure I haven't travelled backward in time. But I know that's not the case, of course..."

Now buttoned up, he plodded towards the door.

"…because at least now they serve me in the bloody pub, don't they!"

He slammed the door behind him. The loud-mouthed young chap whistled.

"Touch-*eee*!"

The others did not react to the lad's little joke, watching me and Hyman as they were with let's-get-on-with-it faces. So we got down to cases, as our American cousins say, and established a twenty-four-hour patrol rota, pairing up volunteers and giving each tandem a particular route or posting. When all that was sorted out, Greg put his hand up.

"One question. Shouldn't we be carrying some kind of guarantee?"

Mrs Wortle was shaking her head knowingly.

"I beg your pardon?"

"Well, I don't know that I agree about the bit which says we have to ask the doctor or the sergeant for permission to carry a defensive weapon. What if we get attacked first?"

Hyman spoke with a severity that took me quite by surprise.

"What exactly are you getting at, Greg?"

"Well, you know, I think we all need to carry something for our own protection. You know what I'm talking about."

"There will be no armed vigilantes in Coldwater Bay as long as I'm in charge here."

"Just a suggestion."

"I repeat: there will be no armed vigilantes in Coldwater Bay as long as I'm in charge."

"All right, all right, point made."

I gave the table a little, decisive slam.

"Gentlemen, I thank you for your time. I do believe we can declare the session closed."

People stood up, lit cigarettes, talked in groups, headed for the door. Mrs Wortle slapped Hymie on the back.

"I'm off to fry some fish while there's still some fish to fry."

Hymie nodded without looking up from the table's grain. I tapped his shoulder.

"I think we did rather well there, Sergeant."

I looked at my watch: seven twenty. I stepped down and sought out Simon, who was having a quick word with Greg and the loud-mouthed youth.

"What would you say, Simon, to a quick one before tasting the delights of Mother's cuisine?"

"Spot on, Dad."

The two of us duly bade our farewells and sallied off to the King and Country.

I WAS TWELVE

(Tuesday 16th)

Around about eight in the evening of our fifth day in Coldwater Bay, we children, we kids, we minors were seated at the kitchen table, listlessly playing rummy (for my part, 'playing' would be an approximate word, having failed as I had to grasp even the rudiments of that particular game).

Lucy's Dad and brother had headed off, keen as mustard, to the meeting at the village hall (though not Mrs Whitebone, who had professed a headache and gone for a lie-down). Us kids, left behind though we'd been, were not under the impression that we were missing out on anything, given that the summons to the meeting, as printed in the local rag, had been distinctly unsensational.

We had by now done a fair bit of conjecturing of our own about the roadblock and the cut lines, so much so that Dr Whitebone felt it necessary to sit us down and explain with grown-up straightforwardness, that there were 'two possible explanations': either it was a serious case of holiday-time hooliganism perpetrated by ruffians from another part of the island; or it could be part of a top secret army exercise. At this point he looked meaningfully at Simon who chimed in that that might well be a likely possibility. Simon's endorsement, gospel for me and Roger, clinched it for us.

In short, we were all given to understand that, one way or the other, the grown-ups had the full measure of the situation.

As for the black boy, whose presence on the beach four days ago was still unaccounted for, he was on our mental back burner, so to speak. We knew from sneak reads of the paper that the corpse had been placed in the hands of the authorities in Newport, who were presumably doing whatever had to be done in such cases. End of story.

It was my turn to play. Eileen looked at me impatiently: *Come on.*

I shook my head: *I don't know*, then whipped out a card at random but never got to place it on the designated spot because after a moment's fumble with the knob, Simon and his father burst into the kitchen: *It's in the cupboard; break it out, would you, Simon?*

Dr Whitebone looked at Lucy: *Where's your mother?*
In the master bedroom.

Her dad cocked his chin up, and bellowed: *Marjorie, you awake?* Simon, after rummaging for a while in the cupboard under the kitchen sink, hissed *gotcha* and turned to us clutching a bottle of dark rum. The doctor slammed down two glass tumblers, Wild West style, on the table. Rubyish liquid plopped out of the bottleneck, and one smooth hand and one black-haired hand grasped those glasses and raised them to opening lips: *Cheers.* No sooner were the glasses back on the table than Dr Whitebone poured out some more.

Mrs Whitebone was plonking down the stairs. The moment she opened the kitchen door, she stood stock-still: *What on earth are you two doing?*

Her husband snapped: *This is an emergency, one bloody great emergency, Marjorie! We need to have a bit of a powwow; be so good as to sit down.*

Their son nodded: *He has a point, Mum.* Down she promptly sat.

Dr Whitebone looked at us: *Are you children all right?* We mumbled *sure* and *yuh*. I glanced at Lucy; she was watching her parents and her brother like a hawk.

Mrs Whitebone turned to the two men: *So, are we any the wiser as to what's going on? I think it's the unions, myself, up to their old tricks again.*

Dr Whitebone glared at her: *Of course it's not the unions, Marjorie, don't be so bloody obtuse.*

Mrs Whitebone lowered her head a touch: *Perhaps it is the army, then, and*—only to be interrupted: *And as you know perfectly well, dear, Simon has already ruled out whatever slight credibility the military exercise hypothesis might have had.*

Roger raised his hand: *but you told us...*

That was then, young man, and now is now.

Outside, the darkness lightened for an instant, like someone had just taken a snapshot of the street. Dr Whitebone jerked his head up: *What was that?* We four kids scrambled to the window, Lucy in the lead. In the confusion, my groin bumped suddenly up against her bottom (a surprise prize won by fluke). The window was shut tight to keep out the cold, but we heard the footsteps nonetheless: they were going right past the house, pat-pat-patting, like someone tapping time on a tabletop.

What's happening over there, children?

People, Dad; they seem to be running; it's hard to see with the lights on.

Her father yelled: *Then somebody bloody well switch them off!*

His wife did it. The sky's brightness knob was tweaked up again for a second; the frontages opposite flashed. This time Dr Whitebone came over in person: *Out of the way, please.* He pulled up the bottom sash, stuck his head out of the window and looked up and then down the street: *Oh my God.*

He rattled the window-frame shut: *The boats! We have got to get to the boats!* His eyes straight as a doll's, Dr Whitebone downed his drink in one: *Simon, let's go!* It was only then I realised he was quite drunk.

*

On reflection, it was decided that if it was unsafe for the rest of us to stay at home without any man about the house, so we ended up leaving with Simon and Dr Whitebone, who were striding so fast we had to break into trickles of scurrying in order to keep up.

135

Within minutes, I smelt a not-quite-rightness in the air. Faster than ever Dr Whitebone and his son headed towards what at this distance was still just a blinking flicker down by the beach.

*

A panda car was parked at an angle across the foot of the high street, its doors flung open, its seats empty, its beacon rotating blue. Along the esplanade railings, backs were packed shoulder to shoulder, heads facing dancing yellow light. To our right, the pub garden was chock-a-block with silhouettes backlit by the building's windows; the silhouettes jabbered, swigging drinks and pointing in the direction of the beach.

Dr Whitebone went up to a spot in the railing: *May I insert myself?* People made way: *There you go, Doctor.* The rest of us squeezed in after him.

All the boats on the beach—I tallied five—were on different degrees of fire. The furthest to our left had already been burnt into near uselessness and was still releasing grubby wisps. Directly below us a second boat had already gone black as a rasher of charred bacon. The other three—one ahead of us and to the left, the other two further to our right—had flames seething up their sides then joining hands in the middle before rising in a blaze topped off by spinning smoke.

Our neighbours at the balustrade stood stock-still, fire fluttering on their stares until to a man they joined in a sudden pointing of fingers at the boat ahead of us: *That one's going to blow!*

Its Mercury outboard was smothered in shifting yellow. After a crack loud as a slammed door, a spout of flame whooshed up high past our gawping faces and lit up the sky and the paring of moon for seconds until the fuel burnt out after a jiffy, leaving the boat, blackened further by the blast, to continue to crackle and cackle.

Over at the pub garden, the silhouettes drank and prattled.

A song came back to me that I had often played on the mono in my room at home, the home I had been picked up from by Dr and Mrs Whitebone what seemed like aeons ago, being as I had been the last child to get on board in London for the ride down to Coldwater Bay. The lyrics ran thick and slow—boys, boys, hamburgers and—Mrs Whitebone half-whispered, half-declared: *Perhaps we should go, John,* and on the song went—*if you want it, come and get it*—those vessels so much firewood now, a village dead as a rock behind us, drinking people being unpredictable to the right of us—*there's a bar at the end where I can meet*—from time to time one of whom let drop a laugh of the kind usually described as mirthless—*get it here now*—the sea was its usual withdrawn self, a black shoulder shrugging coolly—*some make you sing some make you*—right then I lost my still-lingering sense of adventure to the discovery that anything whatsoever might happen here, that the grown-ups were not in control any more, that perhaps there was no control at all anywhere, that we were wide open to whoever might be waiting to pounce, to the vandal in the shadows with his brain like a crushed spring, everything that was not us but which could toy with us as it would, be it human, animal, alien, bacteria or a voracious walking plant with the pitcher mouth of a hatched bird.

My eyes were fixed on the beach, but I was aware of the bulk of Dr Whitebone just next to me, and that of Simon to the doctor's left, and that of Mrs Whitebone behind me, and they no longer generated the slightest bit of reassurance, not one iota of security; I wanted more than anything to be out of there, to be wrapped in a blanket and placed in the back of a car that would take me straight back to London; I wanted to, no, I longed, I itched, I was screaming without moving a muscle: just take me back to London, please, get me back there, please remove me from this spot and I will say thank you, thank you, thank you, thank you, I will thank you as many times as you want and more, I will kiss your knees and hug your arms, I will make you smile by jumping for joy like the little boy you still suppose I am and what is more I will remember you as long as I live, I will mention you to everyone in glowing terms for years and years, and years more on top of those, but please, please pluck me away from these railings, out of this dumb-struck crowd, pluck me out of this unplugged, crippled village and send me home.

All right there, Doctor?

Lucy's Dad turned round, startled by the hand on his shoulder: *Oh, hello Greg.* A name I remembered him mentioning not long ago, which I now saw belonged to a man half the size of a hayrick, wearing a beige, knee-length leather jacket. A yard behind Greg, two teenagers in bomber jackets were standing at ease, army-fashion. One of them had an Alsatian dog on a short leash.

I forgot about the beach aflame, fretting urgently as I was now at the sight of this young man with his dog who turned out to be none other than the yobbo who had been so foully obscene to Lucy just a couple of days ago. My stomach hollowing, I averted my eyes but he, he addressed me: *All right?*

I glanced at him, certain as I was that he was extracting the michael as a prelude to another ugly scene, but no, his enquiry was dead serious. My reply came soft as daisies: *Yes, thank you.* He acknowledged this with the slightest of nods, tugged mechanically on the dog's leash, and looked over to Dr Whitebone, who was deep in quiet discussion with Greg. I realised that for this oafish teenager, the doctor was the man of the moment, to be both served and protected together with his entourage, myself included.

Dr Whitebone started to walk in the direction of the police car, accompanied by Greg and Simon. The boy tugged on the leash again and nodded at Lucy's mother: *I've been told to escort you and your family back home, Mrs Whitebone.*

LOG OF PROGRESS

(Tuesday 16th)

Just spent an hour at the promenade, to see how the villagers are taking the boat-burning. Not on the chin, that's for sure. Sobless tears were seeping out of their eyes. The children looked as jittery as they were excited. The OAPs stared bewildered, more lost than usual. A sizeable crowd sought refuge in the pub, to Dutch-courage away their apprehensions.

Half a dozen years ago, to escape the war in my country I slipped over a border into one that was at peace. For days ,I strolled along its yellow roads, looking at its frizzy green expanses, watching schoolchildren making their way along the grass verges, their faces solemn, half-concentrated as they were on the next step of their bare soles on the clumps of grass and bumps of earth, stepping over the dead cans and paper scraps, their white shirts and blue shorts and skirts petal-bright, the girls' and boys' heads of hair cut equally short; I walked for miles, under the bleached clouds that were belting their way across the sky, past the endless parades of roadside kiosks, their owners and their owners' friends sitting out front, morose, short of customers, while dala dalas paused to brake at unmarked stops before releasing themselves from milling queuers, shifting gears upward until gone from sight; I passed houses with iron or thatched roofs, their walls of wattle plugged with cement bricks; I saw the fine buildings where the charity workers lived, on the roads into the capital, below whose shopworn, grey-to-white skyscrapers men with elephant guns guarded the currency exchange shops as cripples pulled themselves along the pavements on wooden boards, one hand proffered for coin, while young people—fit as horses and itching to do something, anything—thronged the streets.

I ended up spending year after year in that place until, despite the niceness of the people and the beauty of the countryside, I found myself asking if that was all there was ever going to be. As if the endless vistas of clouds and vegetable fuzz were nothing but pictures painted over a canvas plastered along the inside wall of a steel circle inside which I was hemmed.

It was then that I started to keep a lookout for people who might be thinking along similar lines to my own.

*

I've been interrupted by my landlord's voice, flat as a pancake, loud as a street preacher's, coming from the living room downstairs. Must have left the door ajar by accident:
And did those feet in ancient time
I recognised the song, of course, who wouldn't
Walk upon England's mountains green?
Caught me off guard when the girl joined in
And was the Holy Lamb of God
On England's pleasant pastures seen?
With the sweetest, most precisely pitched intonation

And did the Countenance Divine

Also with a hint of desperation, as if trying to escape something

Shine forth upon our clouded hills?

Perhaps her adopted father or step-uncle or whatever he was

And was Jerusalem builded here

Letting the part of herself that mattered fly upward with the song

Amongst these dark Satanic Mills?

Hurling the words higher than the shopkeeper

Bring me my Bow of burning gold

Shrill but sure

Bring me my Arrows of desire

He went on droning

Bring me my Spear: O clouds unfold!

A droning that clashed so with her clean trilling

Bring me my Chariot of fire

I started to mutter along

I will not cease from Mental Fight

Following just her voice

Nor shall my Sword sleep in my hand

Taking the words out of my mouth, she was

Till we have built Jerusalem

Voicing the hopes of all waiting to disembark

In England's green and pleasant land

So to speak.

I'M NOT A

(Tuesday 16th)

It was as plain as a pikestaff that we had to agree on a plan of action before things turned into a god-awful shambles.

Not wanting any of the by-now-alarmed and in many cases inebriated villagers barging in on us, Simon, myself, Lorraine, PC Walker, Greg and Hymie locked ourselves into the Community Centre. Lorraine flicked on the fluorescents. The Jew methodically pulled down the blinds.

"Get us something to sit on, would you, Simon, love?"

He walked over to the chairs stacked against the back wall, and hefted six in one go.

Moments later, we were sitting in a circle. The sergeant kicked off.

"Now, the way I see it, of the various options open to us..."

I tried to be polite.

"With the best will in the world, Sergeant, there is only one option open to us now."

Before our limp limb of the law could get a word back in, Greg snapped, "What you got in mind, Doctor?"

I couldn't help glancing at PC Walker, whose brave-boy attempts to disguise his discomfort had given way to a permanent grimace of pain.

"Just a mo. Let's see how you're doing, Constable."

No wonder he cried out as I unwound the bandage. The palms and backs of his hands had gone a nasty shade of yellow, and were dotted with orange blisters, about half of which had begun to issue mixed discharges of pus and blood.

"We have to get PC Walker out of Coldwater Bay to somewhere he can receive adequate medical attention. Where's the nearest place with a first-aid station?"

"Freshwater. Once you're on the main road, it's not more than twenty minutes' drive."

"Right, Sergeant. So we can kill two birds with one stone: whoever's been escorting PC Walker can also contact the authorities, tout de suite. We'll need a suitable vehicle. Any Land Rovers in the village?"

Hyman had a little think.

"There's a couple, old series twos. If it's a four-wheel drive you're after, though, your best bet is the Range Rover the Arab up on Stockside's got. State of the art. Drive over any kind of ground. Fast too: runs on a V8."

"Well then, Sergeant, I think it behoves you to ask our foreign guest for the loan of his vehicle."

Our Yiddish friend demurred, having qualms about unauthorised requisitioning, but in my finest bedside manner I reminded him of the state of his own constable's ravaged hands, which I had left exposed, and then, of course, of the urgency of the situation, which I summarised in the most phlegmatic terms I could muster, aware that all the others were already an itchy mix of panic and exasperation.

When I'd finished, Hymie was the focus of four urgent stares.

"All right, then. I'll ask the Arab gentleman for his car. I daresay you're right, Doctor: this is no time for shilly-shallying."

Hyman stood up and let himself out. Lorraine, having followed him to the door, locked it behind him. A moment later, we heard the panda's motor eek into life. He even put the siren on. Greg looked from one to the other.

"So who's going on this day trip, then?"

Simon raised a hand.

"I am. I'm the only person here with military training. I can handle a vehicle in rough terrain. Whoever it is who's trying to keep us cooped up, they can't be worse than your average Bogsider."

"In Belfast, you were armed."

Simon shrugged.

"Well, so here I'm not. That's no reason for not giving this a try, Dad."

"It makes me a little concerned, that's all."

PC Walker said, "In the station we have a licensed firearm. Under lock and key."

Simon looked at him.

"What is it?"

"A Webley & Scott, I think. It's been a while since I last took a look. Neither myself or WPC Woodstock have the combination. Just the sergeant."

Lorraine said, cool as the proverbial cucumber, "I'll walk up to the Manse and persuade Geoff to give us the number. Back when I'm back."

I raised an entreating finger.

"WPC Woodstock!"

She turned.

"When you pass by the station on your way back, would you be so kind as to bring me the first-aid kit, yet again?"

"Of course, Doctor."

With a small smile, she upped in a flash and left.

*

I suggested to Greg, Walker and Simon that we adjourn to the anteroom, where—I remembered from our little wait there, before addressing the village meeting—there was a map of the island on the wall. It was a tourist board affair with a garish compass obscuring the south-east corner and a slogan in coloured capitals arching across the top—NO ISLAND GIVES YOU THIS MUCH—but a map nonetheless. Walker looked on, grimacing in his usual agony, as the rest of us discussed possible escape routes.

The roadblock had sealed us off from both of the closest ports of call, Freshwater to the west and Brook to the east, to get to either one of which would now require breaking through the dry-stone wall flanking the access road then taking a cross-country route, northward over the fields now sodden with rainfall, that led up to the main road. Greg, as befit a corkhead born and bred, knew the terrain best and we all fell in with his suggestion of heading west to Freshwater, it being, he assured us, marginally closer than Brook. Once safely on the main road, he added, Simon and PC Walker would find the nearest phone in the offices of the Freshwater Bay Golf Club, located on the easternmost outskirts of that village, and alert the authorities.

"Hopefully," he muttered, "it'll be in working order."

Lorraine and her matzo-munching superior appeared in the anteroom, she carrying that white metal box with its red cross. Hyman dug into his jacket and pulled out a leather holster. I relieved Lorraine of the first-aid kit, and opened it up on my lap. Hyman lay the holster down on the table. Simon snapped open the clasp, removed the revolver and checked the chambers.

"Fully loaded."

He re-holstered the gun. Hymie informed us that the Arab had consented to lend us his Range Rover. We agreed that we would rendezvous at the Manse tomorrow, at seven am sharp.

"Shouldn't Simon and PC Walker take a walkie-talkie with them in the car?"

I looked at the Hyme, who scratched his head.

"Problem is, we've only got two pairs of two-ways and we need those to keep in touch with the safety patrols."

I was about to protest, but Simon raised his hand.

"We don't need one. We'll make Freshwater Bay in no time."

My son, I trusted.

"If you say so."

"I say so."

Simon left, wanting to get some 'kip', as he put it. Which left myself, Greg, PC Walker, Hymie and Lorraine. I asked Walker to hold out his hand.

"As ointment only seems to make it worse, I'm simply going to re-bandage you. If all goes well, and I don't doubt it will, you'll be seeing a specialist tomorrow."

Walker winced as I applied fresh gauze. His hand wrapped, I removed a vial from the kit, broke it off at the tip, and drew its contents into a syringe.

"This is a very moderate dose of morphine, Constable. Just enough to take the edge off the pain for a while."

"Morphine?"

I asked Lorraine to help him remove his jacket and roll up his sleeve.

"Don't worry, you'd need a great deal more than this to become addicted."

He looked more comfortable only seconds after I'd withdrawn the needle.

"Sergeant, I wonder if you'd be so good as to help PC Walker home. The medication might make him a little faint to begin with."

Greg stood up.

"I'll give you a hand, Geoff, he looks right woozy."

Which left myself and Lorraine.

*

I drove back to our holiday home (ha ha) trying not to think too hard about everything that had happened in the last twelve or so hours. It was all but dawn when I stuck the key in the lock, and yet there they all were in the kitchen, looking edgier than ever: daughter Lucy, and those kids I was beginning to wish we had never agreed to take along with us. There too, of course, was Marjorie. God, how old she now struck me as being! God, how fifty-plus shows on a woman! The wrinkled cheeks, the wrinkled eyes, the wrinkled bloody everything. She was saying something to me, asking me why I'd taken so long, asking if the powwow—she used that expression—had gone well, asking if I wanted a cup of tea, and I nearly let fly. I nearly hissed and barked at her because of her stultifying lack of intuition, that quality which women are supposed to possess in abundance and of which she had not a jot. I wanted to lean down and stage-whisper into her ear that just an hour ago, in the Community Centre's anteroom, finding ourselves alone, I had made some appreciative comment to Lorraine and she had quickly planted a cold kiss on my lips, a cold young kiss, and then I had hitched down her trousers and yanked down her tights and thrust my hand between her legs and stuck a finger into her young, fresh and already sweating cunt, thrusting it in and out until she started to give little cold young moans and then we had clambered up onto the table—great minds thinking alike—and there she had grabbed hold of my prick with her cold young hand and had massaged it hard, and then knelt on all fours so that I could lift her shirt up over her back and jam that same dick into the waiting flaps and that then I had fucked her hard, harder than I realised I was capable of, my God, I wanted to spell out to Marjorie, I've never fucked a girl so hard in my life, not ever, my balls were flopping up against her still only partially pulled down knickers and I fucked and fucked, excited more and more by her cold, young moans until I had deposited a full load of fine white liquid right into her tight, now sopping cunt, and that then we had slid off the table without a word and put our clothes back into order and gone off to our respective digs without another word, and that's what fucking should be like, Marjorie, that's what a good fuck is, you disposable excuse for a wife (none of the song and dance you used to make when we occasionally made love, as you liked to put it, you prim and proper moaner). That's what I needed and that what's I got and that's what I'm going to get as long as I'm able to, which is I don't know for how long but believe you me I mean to make the most of

it while I can, I mean to fuck and fuck that tight, finely lubri-
cated pussy until I've had enough of it to last me a few years,
long enough so I never have to get it out for you ever again,
you fretful, interfering, frozen-in the-past *bitch*.

I WAS TWELVE

(Wednesday 17ᵗʰ)

We are bloody well coming along, John!

I woke up, dizzy from a crevice-deep sleep, dreams still prancing about in my head. Morning was breaking.

What the bloody hell for, Marjorie? The less people around the better, don't be so damn stupid.

In the bunk above me Roger was snoring still, a childish snuffle of a snore.

I want to see him off, John, and I rather think his sister has a right to do the same.

I was yawning to the full now, mouth stretching like an elastic band. A sharp knock at the door was followed by Mrs Whitebone, rushing in.

She stopped at the foot of the bed and looked down at me with that smile which seemed to be the only one she had left in stock, a weary tugging at the corners of her mouth. *Hello there! Roger still asleep, is he?*

The mesh supporting Roger's mattress creaked and shifted, and from the top bunk came a grumble: *I'm awake now, all right.*

Mrs Whitebone clapped her hands: *Rise and shine!* I blinked: *What time is it?* She peeped at her wrist: *Half past six.*

A few minutes later, mouths smacking of toothpaste traces, Roger and I went into the kitchen and nodded hello to Lucy and Eileen, who looked every bit as sleepy as us. The kitchen smelled of recent burps. There was no breakfast on the table.

What's going on, Mum?

Without answering, Mrs Whitebone went out into the hall and plucked our anoraks off their hooks. Standing by the front door, looking impatient, were her husband (in wellies and a grey windproofer) and Simon, who—Roger and I noticed with a synchronously muttered *wow*—was wearing camouflage fatigues, and a holstered gun on his left hip, its butt facing us thrillingly. Mrs Whitebone snapped: *Put them on.*

*

Mr Whitebone led the way up the high street to where he'd parked the Vanden Plas. Not a soul was in sight. The sky was a shadowy sprawl of grey and off-white—like a huge pigeon dropping, as I would have put it then.

Simon and Dr Whitebone got into the front. Once the females had filled the cramped back seat, Mrs Whitebone said: *Younger on older, is the general rule.*

Which meant, I realised with both embarrassment and pleasure, that I had to sit on Lucy's lap, which I did, as politely as I could: *Not too heavy am I?*

Tart came the reply: *As long as you sit still.* Once Roger had placed himself on Eileen's knees, Simon pulled away from the kerb.

Despite his and Dr Whitebone's imposing adult silence, I could not stop a tantalising ache travelling from below my pelvis up to the back of my throat, given that Lucy's bejeaned groin was nestling just below my bottom, our skins separated by the thinnest of cloths through which the feel of her charged me up so relentlessly, that had someone stuck a light bulb into each ear, I would have popped the filaments. When our car finally came to a halt, I—in the clutches of an urge— had to make an effort to remove my weight from Lucy's electric body and clamber after Roger's flannelled bottom into the morning cold.

The Manse was on the left, a few dozen yards past the end of the high street. Standing next to a brand-new Range Rover and the panda car, grim as pallbearers, were a fattish officer; a thinner (and younger) policeman, his hands swaddled in bandages; the Arab gentleman—now in a swish suede jacket— who'd walked past the pub on our first day; and Greg.

Dr Whitebone walked over, his wellies scrunching the tarmac: *Good morning.* They mumbled *morning* back.

I still didn't have a clue as to what was up. Dr Whitebone looked at the stout policeman: *Your WPC off duty today is she, Sergeant?*

The sergeant's face was so serious it made me want to giggle amid the tension: *WPC Woodstock is on duty at the police station and will remain so until someone is able to relieve her at her shift.*

All right, let's get going.

Simon pulled open the driver's door and stepped into the seat. He wound down the window: *The keys would be useful.*

The foreign man dug into one of his suede pockets, remarking in a rather posh voice that had only a hint of the woggish in it: *I'm so sorry, I wasn't thinking.* Without a word, Simon grabbed the bunch, examined it, then jammed a key into the ignition.

The motor gave a healthy snarl. Roger and I glanced at each other knowingly: what a smashing, state-of-the-art car that was. Dr Whitebone pointed at the passenger door: *OK, Greg and I had better get in the back.* He turned to his wife: *The sergeant will follow in the patrol car; Marjorie, you can bring up the rear in the Vanden.*

All right, John.

The foreign person sounded put off: *Excuse me, but you don't appear to have assigned me a role in all this; I am the owner of the Rover, you know.*

Please feel free to accompany my wife and the children, Mr... I'm sorry but I don't think I know your name?

The foreign johnny snapped: *Khoury.*

Dr Whitebone pulled open the passenger door: *Oof! Those soubriquets from the land of Araby are rather hard for us to pronounce; OK, everybody in!*

He, Greg, and the sergeant clambered into the back seat, leaving the bandaged policeman to be helped into the front by

Simon, who then leaned across him, pulled the door to, then drove away up the road.

What're they doing, Mum?

Simon and the constable are going to drive cross-country over to the main road, and thence to a place where they can contact the proper authorities; and we have come to see them off.

So, Simon the paratrooper—we had the best-trained troops in the world and he was one of them, ergo, he wasn't going to slip up, nor put a foot wrong—was about to do something brave in order to get this village out of the unnamed, uncertain trouble in which it found itself.

Well, what are we waiting for?

We started to climb into the Vanden Plas. Lucy took the front passenger seat. The stout policeman, about to get into his patrol car, turned back to where the Arab man was watching us: *Are you not coming along, Mr Khoury? Plenty of space in the panda.*

The Arab gave him a perfunctory smile: *No.*

*

We parked alongside the Range Rover, just yards from the roadblock. Everybody—except the policeman with the bandaged hands—was busy dismantling part of the dry-stone wall that fenced a field across which a row of telephone poles stretched away in a curve that led up and then over the slope. Mr Whitebone looked up, a stone in his driver-gloved hands:

Why don't you children give us a hand? He pointed at the dislodged field stones scattered about on the asphalt: *You could clear these away and stack them neatly somewhere.*

Like a shot, we put in our ha'penny's worth of elbow grease, picking up the pieces of flat grey rock one at a time; but barely a moment had passed before Roger frowned at the grown-ups: *Where exactly should we put them?*

Simon glanced about for a suitable place: *On the other side of the road; just as long as they're out of the way.* He lit up and nodded at the growing gap in the dry-stone wall: *Come on, let's get this done.*

He and Dr Whitebone and the Greg man and the fattish policeman set to work with a will, barely giving us kids time to carry off the dislodged stones. A muddy odour drifted off the fields. The thin policeman had remained in the Rover, his tie loose, his collar undone; he was taking deep breaths.

After a quarter of an hour or so, the gap was pretty wide. The adults stopped and took a breather. Greg and Simon conferred.

All set?

All set, Dad.

Simon walked round the Range Rover and got into the driver's seat, next to the constable.

Dr Whitebone signalled to us to back away: *Let's give them a bit of space to manoeuvre.* His wife tugged me and Roger backward by our anorak hoods.

You too, Lucy and Eileen, step back!

Simon reversed the Range Rover so that it straddled the road, its nose planted squarely now in front of the gap in the wall. Greg flapped his hand to urge the driver forward: *Plenty of space.*

The Rover's muzzle began to inch through the gap; the sergeant was beckoning too: *You've got a good three inches on this side; keep going, son.*

The rest of us kept still as window dummies until Simon had edged the Range Rover right through the wall and into the field. He braked and switched off the ignition. Dr Whitebone walked through the gap, over to the car. Simon wound down his window.

Remember, keep it steady at forty when going uphill; when you get to the main road, honk three times before letting her rip.

Simon closed the window. He restarted the engine, giving it lots of choke, then let it rev. Purple fumes spiralled from the exhaust.

Simon put his foot down. The Range Rover bumped and swayed, following the line of telephone poles. He went into second and straight through to third, until the car was fairly bolting away over the grassland.

While Dr Whitebone and the police officer waved farewell, while Greg watched from the centre of the road, while Lucy and me and Roger and Eileen stared, swallowing, launching darts of telepathic support at the shuddering car, behind us, Mrs Whitebone squeezed out: *Oh, God.*

Greg was muttering: *Turn right, now.* Just as if he'd been the backseat driver, the Range Rover veered right, then paused at the foot of the slope that led up to the longed-for main road. Simon changed down to first gear to take the slope, and began the climb. The car pitched back and forth as it rose. What luck, I thought, to have such a perfect vehicle for rough terrain, with its high ground clearance and coil spring suspension. Just the ticket.

It drew to a halt just before reaching the crest, then vanished slowly over the brow. Dr Whitebone turned to us: *He'll be on the main road in no time now.*

Greg raised a hand: *Wait for that horn.*

The V8 was out of earshot. I counted up to sixty. How long, I wondered, was 'no time' supposed to last?

Then we heard—oh bliss—three parps.

Off they go.

In my mind's eye I saw the Range Rover whizzing along in top gear towards a town where people moved freely about their business on sea and on land, to where there were unlimited supplies of food and drink, and, above all, to where the authorities could be contacted with ease.

So absorbed was I, I barely heard Dr Whitebone's voice, all plummy and man-to-man: *What would you give them, Greg?*

Greg looked at his watch: *Say fifteen minutes tops to the golf club. If they can't call from there for some reason, they'll be in Freshwater proper before you can say Jack Robinson.*

Mrs Whitebone looked at Greg, a smile trembling on her mouth, her voice notched up into a higher gear of posh: *Are you quite sure about that?*

Greg waved at the crest over which the Range Rover had disappeared: *They're home free, Mrs Whitebone, home free.*

Thank the Lord for that.

The stout police officer coughed: *I'd better be getting back to the station; anyone want a lift?* Greg and Dr Whitebone, who were still looking up at the crest, didn't so much as say good-bye as he headed back to his panda.

*

It was in a jubilant mood that we piled into the Vanden Plas: Dr Whitebone in the driver's seat, Greg next to him, and Mrs Whitebone crammed into the back with us four kids, Lucy on her mother's lap, Roger on mine and Eileen crushed un-comfortably up against the door. We cruised down the hill. When we drew level with the Manse, Dr Whitebone stopped and tooted twice. The Arab gentleman appeared on his porch. The doctor wound the window down: *It looks like that crate of yours will be in Freshwater in no time.* As Lucy's Dad wound his window back up, the Arab was disappearing back into his house.

It was around eight when we got back to the high street. We passed the café and the clothes shop—both closed—and continued down to the esplanade, turned right and parked in front of the sweet shop-cum-novelty shop, which was heart-eningly open, its window display sporting fake fangs and pink rock and picture postcards and marzipan fry-ups. Dr Whitebone got out of the car: *I rather think this calls for a celebration!* Out we scrambled, Eileen first, then me, then Roger, then Lucy.

Prompted by Dr Whitebone, I asked the old lady in her blue apron if she had toffee apples. She handed one to me with the same friendly smile with which she'd handed me an ice cream on our first day here: *There you go.*

We came out, holding our chosen confectionary. Lucy, who had opted for chocolate cigarettes, flicked one out of the pack and inserted it coolly, so coolly, between her lips. Dr Whitebone pointed: *I trust those chocolate ciggies aren't going to be a prelude to the real McCoy.*

His wife stood on the pavement, smoking. As if by mutual accord, we crossed the road at a leisurely pace, leaned on the esplanade railings, and stared beyond the burnt-out boats, at the sea.

We spent a while there, aware of time slipping past.

It's been just over half an hour, Doctor.

We'd better check at the police station; if the authorities have been alerted, they might have gone there first.

161

Off we headed.

Coldwater Bay had been built in the shape of an asymmetrical, upside-down T, the stalk of which was the high street, running as it did down to the sea; where a longish arm of that T stretched off to the east in the form of the esplanade and then petered out at the foot of low cliffs. The other arm of the T, thalidomide stubby, ran off to the west, past the pub, past the Community Centre on the left and the police station on the right, and went on for just a few houses more until the tarmac came to a full stop at some grassland; beyond that there were the seaside cliffs running westward.

We walked along the esplanade, me and Lucy and Eileen and Roger and Dr and Mrs Whitebone and the man Greg, the beach to our left, onward, past the pub that was a folly, onward, in silence, gusts of sea breeze scratching at us as we approached the spot where the Community Centre faced the police station. The panda was parked outside. Mrs Whitebone yelped: *John!*

What the hell is it now?

She pointed. Feet beyond the tarmac, on the grassland, parked skew-whiff—three-quarters on to our line of sight— its two doors wide open like wings about to try to fly, was a Range Rover that bore an uncanny resemblance to the one that Simon and the constable had driven off in.

Simon!

Mrs Whitebone was already half running, half waddling along the road, the rest of us in hot pursuit.

Marjorie, wait, damn it!

But Marjorie didn't wait. By the time we caught up, she had stuck her head inside the vehicle. Dr Whitebone grabbed Lucy and me—who were spearheading the rush forward—by our sleeves: *You children are not to go one step further.*

Lucy and I stopped as if stun-gunned, at the limit of the road, our toes just off the tarmac. Dr Whitebone and Greg went quickly over to the car. Lucy's mum was standing a little apart, her face crestfallen in its scarf frame: *John, it's empty!*

Dr Whitebone and Greg checked the front seats, then jackknifed them forward and clambered into the back, where they poked about for a while, before squeezing themselves back out onto the grass. Mrs Whitebone was smoking again. The men slammed the car doors shut.

Greg looked at the doctor: *Shall I do it?* The doctor nodded. Greg tramped round to the back of the car. First he peered through the back window, then gave the tailgate doors a tough tug. His eyes widened a little as he stared in. Mrs Whitebone was watching him. We all were. Greg shook his head: *Rags and a jack.*

All four hubcaps and mud flaps were splattered in sludge; the tyre treads were dotted with churned-up blades of grass.

Mrs Whitebone threw her fag end away: *Is it the same car?*

Dr Whitebone covered his eyes with one hand: *Of course it's the same bloody car.*

*

The next thing we knew, Lucy's dad was holding open the swing doors to the police station for us. It smelt of carbolic, like the corridors of mine and Roger's prep school at morning-time.

Inside, a flustered, long-haired man in a corduroy jacket was being placated by the sergeant—*Mr Woolman, we're doing everything we possibly can to rectify the situation*—while the policewoman—standing, like her superior, behind the counter—looked on.

Dr Whitebone walked straight up to the corduroy type: *Get out.*

Excuse me, I have a right to—

Dr Whitebone slammed his fist down on the counter: *I said get out!* The man literally jumped, though not all that high.

Greg was beside him in a flash: *Better come with me, sir.* And, having grabbed one corduroy-clad arm firmly enough to make the man wince, Greg escorted him to the swing doors, where we promptly parted ranks to allow them through.

Then Greg was back inside with us; even as the swing doors flapped themselves still, Dr Whitebone, his face taut as a butler's, looked at him: *I rather think we should try a different tack, don't you?* Then he turned to the stout sergeant: *Might I ask you to get one of our security patrols on a two-way?* The sergeant picked up a walkie-talkie off the counter: *Any particular patrol, Doctor?* Dr Whitebone squeezed his chin between thumb and index: *What's that lad of yours called, Greg?*

Kevin, Doctor.

The sergeant twiddled the frequency selector, then pressed the push-to-talk: *Come in, Kevin; repeat, come in, Kevin; over.* The sergeant looked over at Dr Whitebone: *What do you want him for, Doctor?*

Kindly instruct him and his patrol partner to apprehend Winston Francis.

Who on earth was Winston Francis?

The sergeant frowned: *What's Mr Francis got to do with anything?*

He is now undeniably a suspect and as such must be brought in for questioning.

The sergeant kept his thumb off the push-to-talk: *I'm afraid I don't follow you, Doctor.*

When my wife first discovered the obstacle in the road she was joined a few seconds later by Mr Francis, who, apparently, just happened to be in the vicinity; quite a coincidence, wouldn't you say?

Dr Whitebone brought us into his line of reasoning with a lawyer-like sweep of his arm: *Then you may recall that Mr Francis also volunteered to take part in the patrols and was highly displeased when told that the quota had already been met;*

exactly the reaction one would expect from someone who had an ulterior motive for taking part in our security arrangements.

The sergeant's frown showed no signs of lapsing. Lucy's Dad rapped the countertop for emphasis: *Besides which, we all know that the two figures who were glimpsed on the day of Mr Feather's abduction were of the same hue as Mr Francis.*

The sergeant butted in: *As I've had occasion to point out to you before, Doctor, that's only what you thought you saw; it certainly wasn't corroborated by anyone else.*

I know perfectly well what I saw, Sergeant, enough to swear to it in a court of law. Now if we may assume my observations to be correct, we have two, two—he held up a V-sign to the now-a-touch-flushed sergeant—*as yet unidentified people of colour involved in this business, and we also have, right here in the village, another man ditto who has behaved more than suspiciously on two separate occasions. I propose that all of the aforementioned circumstances together provide reasonable grounds for suspecting that Mr Francis may be aiding or abetting the aforementioned outsiders—I have the impression, by the way, that there may well be more than two of them—who would appear to be responsible for the current state of affairs; and what is more,* his voice rose, *I would remind you that the whereabouts of my son as well as one of your officers are now unknown—they are missing, for God's sake—so, if you have no objection, Sergeant, I wish to insist on my prerogative as justice of the peace, and have Mr Francis placed in custody immediately.*

His head was now a-tremble. The policeman said not one word. Dr Whitebone muttered: *Give the order, please, Sergeant.* Then, unexpectedly, he turned to his wife: *Why don't you take the children and go hunting for vittles or something?*

Mrs Whitebone ushered us out, turning to him before the door swung to: *I hope you know what you're doing, John.*

For God's sake, Marjorie, this is about Simon! This is about our son!

LOG OF PROGRESS

(Wednesday 17th)

I went downstairs this morning to buy some bacon and ran into quite a queue. Stony face after stony face ordering larger than usual quantities of staples: pasteurised milk, canned meat, flour, eggs.

For ages—yonks, donkey's years, a month of Sundays—people here have breathed in a sense of their own safety along with ozone and sizzling batter and the smell of bathed children and all the other sweetish, musty or dusty odours that are to them familiar. They've walked their grey-brown streets and gone about their business with no crow of a plague hovering in the air, no drugged men walking out of the bushes with malice aforethought, no people lying so still in the gutter only the occasional twitch of flesh reminds you they have not quite died.

Ahead of me in the queue was a haggard-looking woman this side of sixty, surrounded by four children—two girls, two boys—in their early teens. The taller of the girls, standing just in front of me, was pretty, with silky black hair. The other was red-haired and all but expressionless. One of the boys was awkward, thin-headed, freckled. The other, bashful-looking and green-eyed, was stealing a glance at the tall girl as she said: What do you think's happened to Simon, Mum?
Oh, I'm sure we'll have him back home in no time, Lucy.

The redhead stuck her oar in:

But where d'you think he's got to, Mrs Whitebone?

The woman lowered her voice:

His father's doing his utmost to find out just that, Eileen.

And the freckled boy said:

Is that why he had that black man arrested?

And Mrs Whitebone, aka Mum, made a face:

No need to shout it from the rooftops, Roger.

The shy-looking boy chipped in:

Is the black going to be interrogated?

My husband will probably have to ask the man some questions, if that's what you mean.

Then she nodded hello to my landlord:

Do you have any Hovis left?

Once they had been served and I had got my bacon, I headed straight for my room; I locked the door, set up the transmitter and tapped out my concern as regarded this new development. Only then did I realise the thing wasn't working properly: the batteries were flat.

I hurried back down to the shop, queued again, and asked for two Ds. My landlord shook his head, said his batteries, be they Ds or double As or PP3s, had sold out long ago. And his was the only establishment, he clarified before I had time to ask him to, in all Coldwater Bay that stocked such items.

Which left me with no choice.

I'M NOT A

(Wednesday 17th)

I was in the process of calming myself with a third cognac—impatient as I was for news of Mr Francis—when Kevin showed up. In just two hectic days, this youthful rustic had become a reliable trooper who was carrying out his orders with pride and alacrity.

"We finally located the sweeper, Doctor. He's down in the cells right now."

"Fine work, Kevin. Did he offer any resistance?"

"Played it innocent, more like."

"I'll be right over."

I followed him out of the pub, and over the road to the station. Lorraine—the pulpy walls of her vulva still fresh in my memory—was on duty.

"Good afternoon, Doctor. Sergeant Hyman and Mr Crofton are downstairs with the detainee."

For an instant I wasn't sure who Mr Crofton was. I tended to forget Greg had a surname. She flicked up the entrance flap, and indicated the staircase leading down to the cells.

"They're in Number One."

I passed through the flap and down some steps into a narrow corridor. There were just two cells, their doors, massive iron affairs. The one marked One was wide open.

He was seated on a narrow wooden bench in a pyjama top, crumpled brown trousers and a pair of checked bedroom slippers. It was a pokey little space: fading yellow tiles, no window, and a corner toilet bowl suitable for people no larger than dwarves. Our bagel-loving sergeant had bent down and was talking in a low voice to the inmate. Greg was watching them.

"Good morning, Greg; Sergeant; Mr Francis."

Hyman put me in the picture.

"Winston claims, most emphatically, that he has nothing whatsoever to do with the recent events, Doctor."
The black looked up, his face registering that curious mixture of anger and trepidation with which so many of his kind react when faced with a contretemps. I had made up my mind to remain even-tempered.

"Surely that's just what he *would* say, isn't it, Sergeant? Emphatically or otherwise."

Greg spat on the floor and addressed the detainee.

"You've got to know *something* about this business. Stands to reason."

"I know nothing whatsoever about all the recent bother. What on earth do you all think you're doing? I insist upon being released this instant."

It spoke! I turned to the others.

"Might I have a few minutes alone with this gentleman?"

Greg looked Hymie square on.

"He's the JP, Sergeant. Maybe we should take a hike."

Hymie huffed.

"Well, I suppose it *is* time I checked in again with the patrols."

"Who has the key to this cell, Sergeant?"

"I do. But what I'll do is, I'll leave it upstairs, with WPC Woodstock. She'll lock up after you, should you deem it necessary to hold Mr Francis in custody until the following morning."

He paused on his way out, and turned back to me.

"The maximum period allowed under British law."

As I have already stated, I was determined to keep calm.

*

For two full hours, I questioned Francis about his activities over the last seventy-two. It was like talking to the proverbial brick wall, off which his negatives bounced back with increasingly wearisome insistence.

My sixth sense, however, assured me he was directly involved in all this.

"Would you please let me go now?"

"I'm not convinced, Mr Francis. I'm not convinced."

Uncertainty spread over his face like oil. I bent low, as if talking to a child. Close enough to smell his mustiness. Apparently about to speak, he abruptly shut his mouth. This black, this duffer who had imposed himself—along with so many of his kith and kin—upon my country. My splendid nation.

This intruding spawner of equally black jackanapes who—I had no doubt—would instil fear in the generation of my grandchildren: those little chaps and girls that Simon and Lucy would eventually bring into the world.

Why did these pigmented people not simply go away, why did they not just catch the first boat back to their shambolic republics, why did they not go back to stewing contentedly in the heat and compost of Jamaica or Barbados or Ghana or Kenya or wherever their shanties happened to be? Why, indeed, had they ever come over in the first place?

More to the point, what had Winston Francis and his cronies—whichever and how many blacks they happened to be—done with my son?

I peered closer. He watched me, wary as a cat before an approaching toddler. It was not until I was within an inch of him—his opaque eyes wide, his face tensed—that it dawned on me to just what an extent I still found these people so otherly, so *alien*.

My hand closed in on his cheek, and, as if it were the most natural thing in the world, I pinched that cheek's saggy black skin tight between my thumb and my digitus secundus manus. He grimaced. As I pinched harder still, I discovered that I had enough of a grip to move his bovine head from side to side: first to the left and then to the right, left, right, left, right, like I was making him nod his head in time to bongo-bongo music. His eyes winced.

"You're staying right here, old boy, until I say otherwise."

I let go, with a flourish that, I confess, was rather theatrical. He raised a hand to console the cheek in pain. As I left the cell, he grunted rather than mentioned that he hadn't had anything to eat for nearly twenty-four hours. I turned, still calm.

"You will be fed when you provide me with some information which will help me to locate my son, Constable Walker and Mr Feather."

"Please," he supplicated, "please." And I dare say there may well have been a third 'please', but I didn't catch it as I had already shut the cell door firmly behind me.

Upstairs, I found Lorraine was on her own.

"Hello, Lorraine."

Her face remained appropriately solemn.

"Any luck, John?"

"Not so far. But he's guilty as sin, it'd take a fool not to see it. You're on duty here this afternoon, I take it?"

She grimaced.

"Now that Andrew's gone, I'm doing a double shift, all the way through to midnight. *C'est la vie.*"

"Well, I'll be back presently. I need to have a more serious talk with the arrested man. As a matter of fact, I might need some assistance."

A most scrumptious hardness appeared in her eyes.

"I'd be delighted to help in any way I can, John."

"Splendid. For now, all you have to do is keep him under lock and key."

Once out in the windy drizzle, I headed for the pub.

*

I was back at twilight.

I won't deny—as louts tend to say in their own defence—that I had had a few drinks. Having indicated to the landlord that I wished to be left alone, he cleared a stool for me at the far end of the bar, thus ensuring I was not bombarded with the questions and snippets of useless information that my new standing in the village was beginning to oblige me to endure.

I had learnt from Simon about what British Intelligence had on occasion found it necessary to do in order to obtain information from detained suspects. As well as what the officers of his own regiment, in field situations which required them to improvise, had resorted to when in urgent need of data, always with a view to protecting the lives of their own men.

In my case, one of the lives at risk was that of Simon himself; and as I mused in the pub smoke—if *mused* is the word to describe a blend of outrage, distress and tumbling recollections—I took comfort in the idea that in a situation so anomalous, in which anything might happen at any moment, obliging one to be constantly on one's guard, certain information—such as knowing what has happened to your own son—becomes vital and needs must be procured immediately, and not necessarily by those methods considered de rigueur in peacetime.

It was with this in mind that, some few hours having passed, I requested a full bottle of cognac from the landlord, who kindly refused my offer of payment. I then removed myself to the police station—with this item in hand—for the second time that day.

I took care to ensure that my demeanour was not that of an inebriate as I placed the cognac on the counter, before Lorraine's surprised eyes.

"You took your time."

I looked at my watch.

"It's only just past teatime."

She smiled in a softly salacious manner that made my testicles tingle like sparklers.

"Would you like to talk to the prisoner again, Doctor?"

"I wish to do a little more than just *talk* to him this time."

The hardness flashed back into her peepers.

"What precisely is it that you have in mind, Doctor?"

"Shall we go downstairs? Do bring the key."

I took hold of the cognac and the two of us trooped down into that narrow corridor. I rapped on the door of Number One: tak-a-tak-*tak!*

"Still there, Mr Francis?"

"He won't be able to hear you, Doctor. Thick doors, these."

(A memory of her mackerel-coloured cunt lips, ostentatiously parted following the removal of my gentleman, flashed before my eyes.) She pressed the cumbersome cell key into my palm.

"Would you mind fetching the first-aid kit? I'm always asking you for that damn thing, aren't I?"

She went to the little cupboard at the end of the corridor where it was kept, took it out and held it up to me.

"You're the doctor, Doctor."

I turned the key in the lock and shoved the door open. Winston Francis was resting on the bench—or rather trying to rest, because there wasn't enough room on the thing to accommodate his bulk. When we entered, he sat up as if cattle-prodded. I stood the cognac on the floor. He checked his watch. Cross, he was.

"It's getting on for six! What is all this about?"

Lorraine came in with the first-aid kit, and clunked the cell door shut. I repeated my earlier request.

"Just tell us what you know, why don't you?"

He stood up.

"I do not know one thing! I have told you again and again! Not one thing!"

Lorraine placed the first-aid kit on the floor next to me.

"Please sit down, Mr Francis. Unless formally charged, you will be released first thing in the morning."

Calmed by the firmness of her voice, he sat back down.

"I will be seeing a lawyer after this."

Would he now?

"As is your prerogative. But I'm sure you wouldn't object to asking a few routine questions right now, would you?"

"I'm not saying anything without a lawyer present."

"The current circumstances render that impossible, Mr Francis. I am therefore legally entitled, in my capacity as a JP, to insist that you answer the said routine questions. You wouldn't object to that, would you, Mr Francis?"

A flinch of doubt.

"What is your full name, Mr Francis?"

"Winston Henry Francis."

"May I ask for your date of birth?"

"The twenty-ninth of December, 1933"

"And where would that illustrious event have taken place?"

"Are you trying to be funny?"

"My apologies. Dreadful public school humour. Where were you born, Mr Francis?"

"I was born in Kingsvale, Jamaica."

"What about your next of kin? Would they be here or there?"

"Why do you want to know that?"

"Should we find it necessary to detain you for longer than the legal seventy-two-hour period, we are obliged to inform them of your whereabouts."

"I've got a cousin in Wolverhampton."

"Would you have the address or phone number handy?"

"No, I wouldn't. We don't see much of each other."

"The rest of the family still back in the tropics, are they?"

"My mother lives in Jamaica, if that's what you mean."

"WPC Walker?"

Clever lover that she was, Lorraine entered right into the spirit of things.

"Yes, Doctor?"

"The police could locate Mr Francis's family if necessary, could they not? In Wolverhampton? Or even in Jamaica?"

"Certainly, Doctor. The Jamaican branch would take us a little longer, but we'd find them."

"Good. So we're all shipshape and Bristol fashion, as regards the legal side of things."

He was staring at us. He didn't look reassured. I addressed the girl.

"Talking of kin who might take some finding, my son—my missing son—who, as you know, has recently completed a tour of duty in Northern Ireland with the Fifth Battalion of the Parachute Regiment, once informed me as to the standard procedure regarding the questioning of those suspected terrorists who have refused to talk during the preliminary interrogation."

She kept up a fine façade of formality.

"Indeed, Doctor. And what might that involve?"

"Stripping a prisoner of his clothing, Simon says, has the immediate effect of making him feel vulnerable, and hence, more inclined to cooperate."

I looked her smack bang in the eyes. She held the look. Our wavelengths, to use the jargon of the hippies, were as one.

"Doctor, do you consider that this is the correct course to be taken with regard to the present prisoner?"

She was with me. She was *with me*. I turned to our captive.

"I do indeed, Constable, but only insofar as it proves to be an efficient means with which to convince the subject to supply the intelligence we so badly require."

Mr Francis was now the very picture of Negroid fury, what with his dilated yellow-white eyes and pursed fat lips. I half-expected that at any moment his hair would stand up in strands, golliwog-style.

"I will not submit to this kind of humiliation! I demand to be released. Immediately!"

I enquired of my partner, sotto voce: "*C'est la vie. Tu parles français,* by any chance?"

Her half-smile read, silent and clear: *This is going to be rather fun.*

"*Un petit peu. De l'école.*"

"*Celui-la ne le comprend pas. Il faut que tu le freines avec les menottes. Très vite, s'il te plait.*"

"*Menottes?*"

I glanced discreetly at where her handcuffs were clipped to her hip. She looked away from me to the black man:

"*Allez-oop, m'sieur!*"

As for him, he frowned like an old bear.

"What's that?"

In a surprisingly stentorian voice for one so pert, she let him know what was what.

"Turn around please, sir."

"I demand—"

"*Turn around, sir;* that is an order."

Shake his head though he might, our West Indian gentleman did as he was told. In a display of professional dexterity, she tugged his arms behind his back, then cuffed his wrists before you could say Uncle Tom.

"*Très bien! Faits que il fasse un demi-tour.*"

She gripped his immobilised forearms and swung him round to face me.

"What are you people doing? Where is my son being kept? And the constable; and Mr Feather, for that matter?"

"Please. I just want to go home."

Subdued now, his voice. So we were getting somewhere. I leaned forward and started to unbutton his pyjama top.

"What are you doing?"

I smiled briefly.

"Why, I do believe I'm unbuttoning your pyjama top."

A laugh short as a fart broke out of Lorraine's face. In my estimation, that was when the coon really realised he was in a spot of real trouble. I unfastened the last of the buttons.

"Let's get this thing off, shall we?"

I had originally intended to remove that stripy top as gently as any mother, but at the last minute I thought, no, no kid gloves: this man is in cahoots with a person or persons unknown who have Simon at their mercy.

I stepped behind him, took firm hold of the collar and ripped that pyjama top off his black back. The ends of the sleeves snagged on the handcuffs.

"Constable Woodstock. If you pull on one sleeve and I on the other, we shall surely succeed in removing this garment."

We took hold of a sleeve each.

"On my mark, Constable. One, two, three."

We tugged the pyjama top free, though part of a dismembered cloth cuff remained snared in the handcuffs.

"Ow! That hurt!"

We went back to our original position: facing his face, now wrinkled with ache.

"Constable, *le pantalon!*"

"*Tout de suite, Docteur!*"

She stepped forward—so formal, she seemed, in those ungainly standard-issue trousers—and bent down and unfastened the waist button of his crumpled trousers.

"Please step out of your slippers."

"I will not do that! This has gone far enough!"

"Sir, I asked you to step out of your slippers."

Then our jungle bunny lost it, to use a contemporary expression, and tried to make a break for the door while roaring his nappy head off.

"This is not normal procedure! I demand to see someone higher up!"

Before he had taken more than a couple of steps, however, Lorraine grabbed his cuffed hands from behind and pulled him back down on the bench.

Off balance, he sprawled backward, legs a-splay; she seized the opportunity to yank the slippers from his feet and then straightaway jerked his trews open at the fly, accidentally popping a couple of buttons—which joined the discarded slippers on the concrete floor with a click—before grabbing the leg ends and giving them a good yank. The trousers whooshed off like—like what?—like accelerated snake skin, perhaps, leaving our black buck looking disconcerted in nothing but a pair of white Y-fronts. He started to kick the air, obliging us to take a step back.

"Someone higher up, Mr Francis? That would be me. Constable, perhaps you could put his trousers to good purpose and ensure that his feet have rather less freedom of movement than at present?"

As she lashed his ankles together, I opened the first-aid kit, from which I removed a roll of surgical tape and a pair of scissors.

His ankles were now bound by his britches.

"Thank you, Constable. I wonder if you could just stand behind him and keep a firm grip on his shoulders?"

As she did just that, I unpeeled a long length of tape and snipped it off.

"What is this? What are you going to do?"

I nodded to Lorraine, who steadied his head while I fastened a stretch of tape over his lippos, then wound the rest round the back of his head. I repeated this operation several times, snipping fresh strips off the roll until the niggy-noggy's face was a mesh of tape from just below his squat nose to just above the tip of his chin. I stood back. My handiwork wasn't quite complete.

"Don't let go of him just yet, please, Constable."

I put the scissors down, and, holding the roll in one hand, with the other I wound the tape up across his left ear, over the top of his head, and stretched it over his cranial fuzz and then straight down hard over the right ear, continuing under his chin. I went on doing this until only his eyes, nose, and forehead were visible. Looking a bit like a Negroid mummy, he started to wriggle about in a vigorous manner.

"We need to tether him to something before continuing our questioning, Constable."

We looked around that spartan cell. The bench's iron legs were fastened to the floor. I tugged at one. It seemed firm enough.

"Let's roll him onto the floor."

Lorraine hefted him up by the armpits while I held his legs. We swung him off the bench and down onto the concrete. Quite a team, we were making.

"*Maintenant, il faut ouvrir les manottes temporairement, parce que on le veut attacher au pied du lit.*"

"*Pas de problème, Docteur!*"

We each took hold of an arm while she unfastened the cuffs and then relocked them in such a manner that his hands were now manacled together to the bench leg. We stood up. His eyes glowered from my improvised wimple; incomprehensible mumblings shifted about under the tape. He budged his behind from left to right and back again, in a vain attempt to unfetter himself. Lorraine touched the small of my back. My trouser snake quivered.

"You know, I think he looks quite wonderful."

Her eyes had flared, her lips had flexed. I raised my voice.

"Now, Mr Francis. For the last time: kindly tell us everything you know. Who are your accomplices? Why and where have they taken my son and the other missing persons?"

The blackie's eyes narrowed. He shook his head.

"Still beating about the bush, are we? Oh, dear. Constable, be so good as to remove *le slip de monsieur*."

185

"*Naturellement.*"

He closed his eyes as Lorraine squatted over him, took firm hold of the Y-fronts at the hips and yanked them down to the knees, thus rendering our native bollock-naked.

"Oh, Doctor!" Excitement caught her voice.

"*Qu'est-ce que c'est*, WPC Woodstock?"

She cleared her throat.

"His organ is rather smaller than certain rumours might have led me to expect."

It looked like an expired slug. I picked up the bottle of cognac I'd brought over from the pub, twisted off the top, and passed it to Lorraine, who pouted.

"But I'm on duty."

"It's for purely medicinal purposes, Constable."

She giggled.

"Well, in that case."

She took a big swig.

"You see, Constable, these people—and this has been scientifically proven, time and time again—"

"Which people, Doctor?"

Naughtiness sparked in freshly glazed eyes. I took the bottle, and had a nip myself.

"Negroes, Constable; blacks, coloureds, whatever you wish to call them. Proven, it has been, beyond reasonable doubt—and there are whole batteries of IQ tests to prove it—that their race is intellectually inferior to that of us Caucasians. But what is really so upsetting about them..."

I gave two indicative little kicks against the soles of his feet.

"...is that, far from acknowledging this inherent slowness of thought, they insist on portraying themselves as permanent victims; as diddums who are forever being persecuted, no matter how much one shows willing to be charitable."

Two kicks more to his soles, harder this time.

"Yet one always finds them at the bottom of the heap, doesn't one?"

I addressed myself to him.

"A conversation I had with Mrs Wortle, she of the fish and chip shop, revealed that here in Coldwater Bay, pre-Easter orders on the part of the local establishments ensure the virtual absence of incoming commercial traffic, an absence made complete by the postal and transport strikes. Most accurate, such timing. Surely only someone local could have provided such strategically viable information. But what really aroused my suspicions was the swiftness with which the boats were burned on the beach, just hours after it was asserted in a public meeting, which you attended, that those boats would be our first recourse if the situation did not improve. Definitive proof that reliable information has been reaching our assailants from an inside man; and it is my conviction, Mr Francis, that that reprehensible spy is none other than yourself."

The shakes of his head grew emphatic. He had a bit of a pot belly. I held the bottle to my lips and tippled with determination.

"Constable, in the first-aid kit you will find a pair of surgical gloves. Be so kind as to put them on."

The coon watched wide-eyed as Lorraine did as I said.

"For the purposes of our interrogation today, Constable, I'm afraid we will need to get his little soldier standing to attention."

There was not a flicker of doubt in the glance she gave me. Rather the opposite: I sensed her cunt was dampening already, as much as if I'd just wiggled two fingers into its elastic confines.

"One can only try, Doctor."

She took his floppy member in one hand and began to work the foreskin backward and forward. He shut his eyes tight. The visible part of his face was covered in sweat. His muffled complaints notwithstanding, his percy was becoming more substantial by the minute. Once the erection was brought to completion, Lorraine flicked it. It swayed.

"I think that's as huge as it's ever going to get, Doctor."

"Beggars can't be choosers."

She giggled. "Doctor!"

I looked at the floor.

"Now, where did I put those scissors?"

There they were, next to the roll of surgical tape. I picked them up. I opened and shut them twice. Then I squatted next to the black. He smelt bad.

"Constable, he seems to be losing impetus."

"My apologies, Doctor."

She repossessed his member and began to stroke it so smoothly, I almost envied him.

"Not circumcised, Mr Francis?"

He paused, eyes bewildered, before shaking his head again.

"Of course not. That would be the Hebrews, wouldn't it? However, there is a first time for everything. Constable, allow the erection to diminish just a touch."

Lorraine released the penis from her grasp.

"Mr Francis, are you going to cooperate or are you not?"

Again, that what-are-you-talking-about frown of his eyes, framed so absurdly by the tape.

"The glans has slipped back into the foreskin but his member is still firm. Perfect. Constable, I would like you to hold a pinch of foreskin out from the glans."

Employing finger and thumb, she held the skin away from the penis as instructed, while her other hand kept the shaft steady. She was looking at me with an expression that was positively grateful.

"Like that, Doctor?"

"Precisely. Now please do the same on the opposite side of the glans."

When she was done, his penis looked like a little boy who was having both his ears pulled at the same time.

"Excellent. Now, whatever you do, don't let go. I shall cut through the skin you have so skilfully made available, then snip it off at the base."

She peered at the scissors.

"They look a little rusty, Doctor."

"We shall have to make do, Constable. Some droop is setting in, so speed is of the essence: let's get this over with, chop-chop."

I cut through, then snipped off the pinched segments of epidermis. She then pinched out another two, which I cut and snipped off in turn, and so we went on.

With each clip of the scissors, I felt I was pricking into a million blacks, a million trillion of shiny blacks: ballast to a human race that deserves to float free as a bird, but is forever held back.

I snipped and snipped, until his Negro cock was flaccid and shrivelled, as abject an object as could be imagined. It was bleeding fairly profusely at the base of the head. I looked at old Sambo there. Tears were streaming down his taped cheeks. A cat-like keening could just be made out.

Lorraine was taking another shot of cognac.

"No one could call this ill-treatment, you know, Mr Francis. Circumcision is a standard operation. Are you absolutely sure you don't want to be of assistance to us?"

A pleasant surprise: instead of shaking his head, he nodded, eyes a-pleading. Then he said something, which, of course, could not be heard properly.

"*Passe-moi les ciseaux*, Lorraine."

I rolled the double-R in her name, Frenchy-style. With a complicit smile, she handed me the scissors. I grabbed the black by his sweaty frizz.

"Hold still."

I cut an opening in the tape, around the lips.

"Now, Mr Francis, what is it that you wished to say?"

"I want to help, I really want to help."

A voice with its stomach knocked out.

"Where are my son, Constable Walker and Mr Feather?"

He stared at me.

"I don't know."

"In whose hands are they?"

The thick lips opened, exhaled, closed. He shook his head, once.

"You did say you wanted to help, Mr Francis."

He sighed like a small tyre puncture.

"I do, yes."

"Do you have any accomplices here in the village?"

He shook his head, whispered: "No."

"So you are the only person here we can hold responsible for the situation?"

"I didn't say that."

I held the rusty scissors up to his eyes.

"Tell the truth and I assure you, upon my honour, that you will not regret it."

His eyes rolled from left to right and back again.

"I..."

"Come on, man, out with it!"

A few seconds.

"All right, there must be someone else. There's got to be."

"That's a start. Calls for a bit of a celebration, I'd say. Constable, *le cognac, s'il te plait.*"

I took my fill, and looked at him, pleased.

"So. If we've understood correctly, you are not the only infiltrator?"

He shook his head. Breathed out. Whined: "Please, would you release me?"

"Mr Francis, I am by no means an unreasonable man. I can accept your denial of any knowledge of the precise whereabouts of my son and the other two men. It is plausible that your superiors may have left you in the dark—no pun intended—for reasons of secrecy. But I must insist on being provided with all pertinent information as regards your activity in the village. I can assure you that if you refuse to cooperate any further, well, what can I say? Your troubles will have only just begun."

I fetched the tape, and placed a fresh strip across his mouth. Lorraine held his head steady. While winding a further strip around it, I noticed my left foot was underneath his testicles. I jiggled them with my toe cap. Lorraine released a peal of laughter. I put on an over-deep voice.

"Tell me, Constable Woodstock, where shall we take it from here?"

More peals. Music to my ears.

LOG OF PROGRESS

(Wednesday 17th)

If only I'd had some brandy handy.

Come nightfall, heart cringing, I put on the duffle coat and shoved a pencil torch in the pocket (or the nearest thing to one my singing shopkeeper stocked: a kids' biro which provided a thin orange beam if you twisted its joint). I pulled the hood over my head and let myself out.

Greg's patrols were pounding two beats, round the clock: the high street and the esplanade (other volunteers took turns to stand guard at the obstacle).

I entered the esplanade at a point not far from the sweet and souvenir shop. I heard talking: a two-youth patrol, complete with Alsatian. They—like the other recruits—wore bomber jackets, turned-up jeans and boots. I caught snippets:

Bitter's running out down the King

Skol man myself

Cat's piss

I stepped back and followed the side streets until I was closer to the western end—the stub—of the esplanade. I now had the Community Centre opposite, and the police station was two doors along to my right. I made out two other voices, coming from station: Greg's and the doctor's. Hugging my corner, I risked a peek.

Greg was smack in the middle of the road, signalling—his hands faint flags—that the approaching lads should come to a halt. Behind him was a squat purple car.

The swing doors of the station flapped and thunked. Then, a woman's voice:

There you go.

I heard shuffling feet, a grunt of effort, a hissed

Jesus wept.

More shuffling, then the clunk of a gently shut boot.

The doctor stepped quickly out of the station and slipped into the passenger seat, while Greg got behind the wheel. They closed their respective doors with equal care. A rumble of starting engine.

The car, its lights off, taxied slowly to the far end of the esplanade. It halted. The driver's window came down and Greg leaned out and said back at the lads, one hand brushing away invisible gnats:

Not a step further; your shift's cancelled; go on, shoo, get out of it.

Having watched them retreat, he drove right off the tarmac, onto the rough ground beyond. I moved closer, creeping past the frontages. The car—now fifty metres off the last of the tarmac, a buff shadow now—coughed once and shut up. Treading the soggy earth, I gave the thing a wide berth and crouched in the shadow of a shrub.

The two men got out, leaving the doors open. The doctor's voice carried on the breeze:

Kindly remove it.

Greg opened the boot and hefted out a black sack which at once slithered out of his grip and bumped onto the ground.

Fuck, that's heavy.

The doctor pointed:

Pull it away from the car, would you?

Which Greg duly did, while the doctor removed two spades from the back seat.

Shouldn't we be doing this in a remoter spot?

The doctor coughed:

This is as remote as we dare get. But we're still further out than anyone from the village would dare go.

He gave the bag a sharp little kick:

He might have ended up telling us something really useful, you see. A name. Pity the heart went.

Greg took a breath:

Better get to work.

The doctor handed Greg a spade:

A shallow tomb shall suffice: this soil is loamy and will thus subside of its own accord under the weight.

Greg worked for a good half hour. The doctor took things easier, a spadeful here, a spadeful there.

Quickly now.

They dragged the sack over the ground to the tip of the hole.

In it goes.

It fell in, quiet as a footstep. They shovelled the dug earth back in, then padded it down with the backs of the spades.

Time we were on our way.

They dumped the spades in the boot and got back into the car. They headed for the tarmac, and drove away along the esplanade.

I stayed down on the grass for ten minutes, timed, then crawled over.

I clawed out clumps of earth with cupped hands until enough plastic was exposed for me to take a look-see. I took out my biro, twisted the joint, and aimed weedy orange light at the bag. It was of the common central zip type.

The feet were tied at the ankles. Sweeping away soil with one hand, I ran my light up the naked legs, noting puckered slits in the skin.

With what instrument had they poked his flesh? I nudged the zip open. Swathes of tape had been wrapped tightly round the body at crotch-level, but not so tightly as to stop the genital bundle from having leaked blood fresh enough to still shine a touch.

I carried on up the torso and its cigarette burns, then jerked the zip up as far as it would go. The face was taped up to the hair line, except for a chunk of chin and a raggedy opening for the mouth. The tape itself was speckled with liquid stains. I leaned in. Urine, some bleach.

I popped my pen in my mouth, reached over and eased the body up on its side, just a few inches. Where the duct tape was criss-crossed over the man's buttocks, a hole had been punctured, presumably to gain access to the anus. The rim was circled by dried blood.

A dog barked and a couple of familiar voices whined at each other. I clicked off the pen, and flattened myself out.

The two youths halted right where the road died into the field. A lone streetlamp paled their breath vapour. The dog barked a little more. One of those boys' voices quavered in the darkness:

We'll get you, you cunts!

Leave it out, Kev; your old man wants us scarce.

They headed back, the Alsatian pulling at its creaking leash.

I rose to a crouch and took a last look at the cadaver. England, always out to surprise you. I zipped the body bag shut, replaced the dislodged earth and took my time patting it smooth. No mound betrayed the grave.

Nigh time it was, to move on. The cliff edge was a longish sprint away. I scarpered across the field, bent as low as I could go. Metres from the precipice, I sucked in the air, gathered my thoughts; then whisper-called:

Hodi, hodi.

I could smell the sea's breath and hear the flicker of its waves against basalt, way down below.

Hodi, hodi.

A hatch shot up out of the ground:

Karibu!

He chuckled, Twaibo, as he stuck his head and shoulders out of the ground. His teeth were ghost-white. I bent over, hands pressed against knees:

Kwa mapango; sasa hivi.

He hoisted himself, satchel in hand, out of the foxhole, and kicked the hatch shut. I pointed at where I knew the grave to be and gave Twaibo a potted account. He shook his head:

Mungu wangu...

Then took my arm, laughter gone:

Uje.

Though firmly steered by Twaibo, I stumbled here and there on our way along the cliff edge. Flashes of stained corpse and pierced tape kept coming to mind. From time to time I glanced at the weight of the water, lit a bit by the moon.

Twaibo tugged at my arm and we came to a halt. Perched on the bottom-most lip of the Isle, we faced the sea, dark sparkles to the right of us, dark sparkles to the left, a breeze flapping our hair.

Njoo hapa.

Squint though I did, the steel pegs were driven so deep into the grass I couldn't make them out until he had fastened the upper strands of a rope ladder (tipped out of the satchel in a trice) to them. With a fisherman's flick, he sent the ladder clattering down the cliff, whose face looked sickly in the moon rays.

I had been hoping I would never have to do this.

Twaibo slapped me on the back:

Kila la heri.

I touched his arm:

Nakwenda, tutaonana baadaye.

I lay down my stomach, gripped the side ropes and eased my feet downward until they touched a rung. I started to sweat. My balance once found—and checked and rechecked—I started my descent, gingerly, concerned of a sudden about the snaggable toggles on my duffle coat. What if they caught?

I completely forgot about the corpse in the loam.

One sweaty slip of the hands and down I would've gone, through that clean-smelling island air. (Which would claim me first, the rocks or the sea?) I clung to those thick strings, negotiated those clumsy rungs, kept going only by the certainty that I didn't have a choice in this matter.

I took my time (not wanting to set the ladder swaying from side to side), feeling the luxury of the ocean behind me, fat, complacent, still.

A gust blew me into a pendular swing. I gripped the ropes even harder, and tried to think of worse situations I'd been in, to keep present fear at bay (jet roars, explosions that deafened for minutes on end, crowds releasing shivers of shrieks while running through dust billows).

By the time I finally inched down to where the ladder terminated feet from the sea's spangles, my arms were quivering uncontrollably. My feet planted on the final rung, a steady zephyr tilting me persistently to my right, I had a clear view of the cave opening.

One of the Isle's many water caves. Nice and loud, now: *Hodi, hodi*!

I swung, for what felt like minutes on end—sweat mushrooming on my nape, between my buttocks, under my testicles, fizzing under my arms—until a dark slit of a boat slid out of the hollow. A voice I didn't recognise called out.

Karibu, Jonas. *Shuka chini, taratibu. Teremsha*!

I duly lowered myself a couple of rungs until my feet were dangling free. Someone gripped my ankles.

Achia!

I dropped free and shouted once from fear, but in an instant my hips were clasped and my arms held steady so I could be lowered into the stern of the skiff. Above me the ladder was already clacking back up the cliff face in the moonlight, fast as a lizard. My hosts sat with their backs to me on the crossboard and began to paddle. Within seconds, we were gliding into the darkness of the cave. The paddlers veered the boat round a bend into a second stretch of gloom, at the end of was the merest suggestion of yellow light.

As we headed for it, I also got wind of some chit-chat. To the sound of dipping wood in the placidest of waters, we emerged into a circular enclave. Its ceiling was being danced across by blue-grey leaping cobwebs reflected up from the water by kerosene lanterns hung from the prows of four more skiffs, all moored to the walls. My two-man crew stalled their paddles in the water to stop the boat. The other vessels' occupants—both human and avian—were observing us, solemn and silent.

Two and four and five and four made sixteen people, there in the gaslight. Ubalijoro, ever silent, ever scarred, but so fine a chemist; and Regina, a big girl now—unlike when what happened to her happened—and a whizz at telecommunications; and Bwenje, once-a-soldier-forever-a-soldier. In each and every boat, pigeons cooed in wicker cages whose lattice tops peeked out above the gunwales. A younger man I didn't know couldn't take his eyes off me:

Hakika unaonekana kama mzungu!

I bowed, flourished a hand:

Gentlemen, that is the way God made me.

For a whole week these people had huddled here, taking turns to make the up-cliff sorties and man the foxholes, to stake the village out, huddled in camouflage. I alone had been moving freely about topside. Living the life of Riley.

I raised a hand:

Hamjambo?

A few smiles, some nods, some hands raised, a couple of calls:

Habari na safari?

Laughter. (An open secret, apparently, my chronic vertigo.) I was surprised to see everybody was so fiddle-fit, their clothes clad against trained-up muscles, the women's plaits drawn back tight, utilitarian.

All this to show that we can do it; all this, too, to make a request we suppose cannot be ignored. How important, then, not to slip up. Not yet. I explained that my transmitter had broken down, which was why I had come in person. I took another look around:

Na wazungu?

Regina pointed to a tunnel which led off from the cavern, from which drips could be heard plonking into the water:

Njoo hapa!

A voice made it, echoing, out of the tunnel's depths:

Sawa!

The splash of a single paddle, faint at first, grew louder until finally another skiff hove into the cave's yellow light, under the doddering reflections. Besides the paddler at the prow there was a guard at the helm, his eyes fixed on the three men who were slouching in the centre of the boat, waiting-room expressions on their pink faces: the doctor's son (black hair falling greasily across his forehead); the constable, still in uniform minus the cap; and a grey-haired man in his early sixties who I presumed to be Mr Feather.

As the boat swirled in the centre of the cavern, and as the paddler made to steady it, the white passengers spotted me and sat up straight, alert as whistled dogs, galvanised into baf-flement. After seconds of silence, the old man pointed at me:
You're a white man.

The doctor's son pointed a gunnish finger at me:
I know you.

I chose to address the policeman:
How are your hands, Constable?

He held them up, beaming.
They're fine; they put something on them soon as I got here.

The old man squinted at me:
You come to get us out of here, then?

Ubalijoro, Regina and the rest watched as our two boats faced off in the cavern's centre.
Not just yet, Mr Feather; but it won't be long now. I trust you're all in good health?

The policeman and Feather nodded affably enough, but the doctor's son, serving soldier he, called out, stentorian:
I don't know what your little game is, but when it's over you lot will be in straits so dire you'll wish you'd never set foot on English soil.

My paddlers steered our skiff over to a free length of wall; as they clove-hitched the painter to a hook driven into the basalt, I thumbed to the white men's crew that it was time to return their cargo to the tunnel.

Let me reassure you, as I'm sure you have already been reassured by the people here, that no harm is going to come to you or anyone else in Coldwater Bay.

The paddlers had turned their boat around and were heading back towards the mouth, the old man and the policeman frowning, the soldier boy's odium limited to a twist of lips. Their guard at the stern waved us goodbye with a mock smirk of resignation:

Naenda sasa hivi.

A ripple of laughter. Once the captives were quite out of sight, Regina shrugged at me:

Tatizo ni nini, Jonas?

I asked first about all the others. Reassured that everyone was as well as could be expected—Mzee included—I informed those present of what I'd learnt about the fate of the Jamaican street sweeper, sparing no details. Crestfallen, they shook their heads. I suggested that, given this circumstance, they request Mzee to advance matters before anything else got out of hand. The transmitter being out of order, from daybreak onward, I assured them, I would be in spot, visible from the tarmac's edge, ready to give directions.

Daybreak, said my watch, was a couple of hours away. I was paddled out of there with their blessings, back out into the moonlight and its jittery line on the open sea. I took a deep breath: that damn rope ladder again. One of my boatmen touched my arm:

Subiri kidogo.

He blew a nigrita's call up the wall. Not a minute went by when the ladder came clattering down. The boatmen manoeuvred me under its ropes. I grabbed ahold, hoisted myself up as best I could and tried to get a foot onto the bottom rung, but missed one, two, three, four times.

Siwezi kufanya hivyo.

The boatmen snorted:

Ujinga huo!

One of them balanced the boat while the other dumped his paddle and stood up:

Subiri kwanza!

He hoisted me upward, until I finally managed to gain a foothold on the ladder:

Sawa!

The boatmen were already splashing a path back to the cave:

Ndiyo, ndiyo.

I climbed back up to where Twaibo was waiting for me, in my own good time.

I WAS TWELVE

(Thursday 18th)

Mrs Whitebone slammed our cereal bowls down on the table unnecessarily hard, talking in bursts so concentrated she sounded like a semi-articulate dog: *None of you* (thunk of cereal bowl on oilcloth) *are to so much as step outside the house today. I want the door bolted* (another thunk) *and no one is to answer it under any circumstances* (thunk), *is that quite clear?* This last, a touch tremulous, to Lucy, who nodded: *Sure, Mum,* in a voice inflected with disappointment.

After Mrs Whitebone had plonked the Long Life and a packet of Rice Krispies (Weetabix being now unavailable) next to the bowls on the tabletop, she disappeared for a moment into the hall and returned in a trice wearing a scarf, coat, and woolskin-lined mittens. She surveyed us anxiously: *I'm just going out to get some provisions.* Lucy glanced at her watch (a snazzy Tissot self-winder): *But the shop won't be open for another hour, Mum!*

Mrs Whitebone paused: *There'll probably be a queue; in fact, I suspect you're going to have to sit tight here for quite a bit until I get back.* She pulled a what-a-pity face. *Just as well we brought this along.* She disappeared again and reappeared after a minute with a board game, which she left on the sideboard. *Lucy'll teach you all how to play, won't you, Lucy?* Mrs Whitebone frowned around, checking she hadn't forgotten anything: *Like I said, no opening that door now! And Lucy, don't you go worrying about Simon; I'm sure he's all right.* Lucy shrugged, two tears welling on the brink.

Under no circumstances should you disturb your father—he needs to get some sleep.

Finally the woman left, as confirmed by the welcome sound of the front door slamming behind her.

We were left sitting round the table in the morning's usual ashy light. Roger reached for the cereal: *I'm famished.* He rattled some into his bowl. We filled our own, poured milk and started chomping.

Roger, mouth half full, pointed to the board game: *I don't know that one.* Lucy started to unpack the box.

Careers turned out to be a thinly disguised imitation of Monopoly: instead of houses and streets, the players had to accumulate qualifications and then work their way up through the rungs of various professions until they became successful people whereupon they could drop out of the game, victorious. When Eileen lost by failing to make Detective Superintendent in her chosen Occupation Path of 'Police', Lucy asked us if we wanted to go on. We didn't. Listlessly, she repacked the cards, dice and whatnot into their pigeonholes, pressed the lid back on and returned the box to the sideboard: *Anyone want a cup of tea?* We said yes. She settled the kettle on the hob and scratched a match alight. Roger looked at his watch: *Your pa's having quite a lie-in, isn't he?*

Lucy was dropping teabags into the pot: *Please don't call him pa—I never do.*

She had her back to the sideboard now, fists and face half-clenched: *I don't know about you lot, but I simply cannot stand being cooped up in here.* She leaned forward, eyes shining: *Why don't we—* At which point the kitchen door opened and there stood her father.

I'd seen him before in such formal wear: tweed jacket, woollen waistcoat, white shirt, yellow tie and camel-coloured flannels; what's more he was shaven and brilliantined and smelt strongly, even at that distance, of Old Spice. His eyes didn't gel one bit with the hang of his face.

Are you all right, Dad?

The doctor gave a watery smile, stepped into the kitchen and sat down between me and Roger. He really had put on a great deal of aftershave.

Lucy, be a dear and pour me a cuppa too, would you?

He glanced at our faces, that smile still clinging: *So, how are we all bearing up?* To which we mumbled OKs while Lucy placed a steaming mug, the teabag label dangling out of it, in front of him.

Thank you. Do you know, Lucy, that last night we came very close to finding something out about Simon's whereabouts?

Lucy stiffened: *And?*

Her father raised the brim to his lips, sipped: *It's going to be a bit more complicated than I thought, but we're definitely on the right track.* Her face fell. From upstairs a voice crack-led something incomprehensible and Dr Whitebone stood up: *Silly me, left the two-way upstairs.*

A moment later he was peeking back through the door, walkie-talkie crackling in one hand.

Calling Dr Whitebone, calling Dr Whitebone; your presence is requested on the esplanade, Doctor, smack opposite the fish and chip shop; over.

I'll be right over Greg, over.

He waved goodbye with a shake of his walkie-talkie: *You all stay put now, d'you hear?*

Lucy went to the kitchen window, hands jutted into her front pockets, her bejeaned behind more attractive than ever, at least in the eyes of this beholder.

I move for taking a walk.

Eileen winced: *But Luce, your dad just said—*

Lucy spun round: *Well, he's not here now, is he?* She turned to me: *What do you reckon?*

No way was I not going to be on her side: *I reckon we all could get some fresh air.*

Lucy smiled: *Don't be a stick-in-the-mud, 'Leen.*

We're not supposed to.

Roger, meanwhile, was rereading the Careers instruc-tions: *I don't think we played this according to the proper rules.*

Eileen looked at him then back at us: *On second thoughts, maybe I could do with the exercise.*

Roger still being my friend, I didn't want him left behind: *Come on, Rodge, we can act as bodyguards.* Roger frowned at those game instructions for what seemed aeons before saying yes.

We trotted down the stoop in silence. Off to our right, two middle-aged men were walking quickly past. Eileen watched them: *Where are we going?*

Then one of those village louts came tearing round the high street corner, off like a whippet in the same direction as the two men, bumping Roger—*Mind yer back!*—bomber jacket flapping in the slipstream.

He might have apologised.

Lucy pointed: *I'd say it was obvious which way we have to go.*

I nodded: *Bet you anything you like we'll end up smack opposite the fish and chip shop.*

Eileen signalled us—arms raised—to stay where we were: *But then we'll run into your dad, Lucy!*

Lucy shrugged: *So what?* She headed towards the next corner, with us in tow.

*

On the esplanade, in front of the fish and chip shop, there was what looked like an impromptu gathering of a dozen or so villagers, including Greg, Dr Whitebone, the men and the bovver boy who'd scurried past us, and a big-bottomed woman in a white pinafore. A few other people were converging from left and right into the crowd from which tuts and grumbles were rising like steam from a kettle. We were standing a little way away, but the crowd—shifting, brown-grey—was too occupied with its own business to pay any attention to us. Random raised voices were bowled my way.

This can't go on.

We're being held hostage.

Something has to be done.

Popular demands, faint cobweb-laced words.

We won't stand for this.

We've been patient long enough.

It's more than a body can take.

Lucy's dad was remonstrating with them—hands placating—trying to get them to listen to something he wanted to say.

Roger held up an alert finger: *Listen!* No mistaking that doo-doo-doo-doo of police siren. The panda braked abruptly in front of the crowd, blocking the esplanade. The siren stopped, but the flashing light didn't, and before you could say Jack Robinson the front doors had swung open and the woman PC was popping out of one of them, and the plump sergeant was scrambling out of the other.

I'M NOT A

(Thursday 18th)

"A good morning to you, Sergeant Hyman, WPC Woodstock."

I gave her the subtlest of bows, duly returned, her eyes fixed demurely on the paving.

The crowd had gone silent.

"Morning, Doctor. What's going on here, then?"

What with the gusts of wind and the wash of the sea, it was still necessary to shout. I especially wanted my words to reach Mrs Wortle (a sociometric star if ever there was one). I would need all the support I could get, when it came to rooting out the insiders. Had the unfortunate blackie not confirmed that he had an accomplice when questioned insistently on this point? I jabbed a theatrical finger at the crowd.

"This, is what is known as a spontaneous act of protest, Sergeant. Greg here was chatting with his son and some friends, others joined, and all began to vent their frustration verbally. Greg called me in the belief I should hear what they had to say, and I'm very glad that he did: the good people of Coldwater Bay have, quite simply, had enough. They demand action. I have to confess I couldn't agree with them more."

The uniformed Yid was looking at me circumspectly.

"I don't suppose you got any useful leads from Mr Francis?"

"As it happens, I did. WPC Woodstock was also present when Mr Francis freely admitted to the existence of another accomplice here in the village."

Hymie turned to Lorraine.

"Is that correct?"

"That is correct, sir."

"Did Mr Francis mention any names?"

"No, sir."

"Where is he now?"

Lorraine's shift having lasted through to the small hours, the Jew, I knew, must have come here straight from his home, picking her up in the panda on the way. He most certainly would not have inspected the holding cells.

"Still in custody, sir."

"Properly looked after, I trust?"

"Absolutely, sir. I took him down some breakfast this morning. Circumstances being what they are, it wasn't much, but I did what I could."

For a moment, she even convinced me. What a find, this hot-cold bitch, this fuck-loving filly. Hymie turned to Greg.

"What do *you* make of this?"

Disturbingly deadpan, Greg's face.

"Who's the black's accomplice, that's what I want to know. Whoever he is, I suspect he knows a lot more than Winston, who, with the best will in the world, wasn't—I mean isn't—exactly Albert Einstein, is he? This accomplice could probably tell us a lot more than Winston about what's going on."

He glued a stare on me, almost letting the cat out of the bloody body bag.

Hyman stroked his chin.

"So who could this accomplice be?"

"I can make an educated guess."

Greg laughed, just the once.

"You're not the only one."

Kevin drew in his mucus with the most revolting sound.

"So who's that, then?"

Greg looked at me, looked at him.

"Have a think, son."

Wishing to help, I removed some of the deductive obstacles. "Here's a clue: someone who's clever, from out of town, and not short of a few bob."

"Sounds like you."

Greg scowled.

"Don't get lippy. Use your loaf."

I leaned down until I was eye to eye with this none-too-bright adolescent. Our audience's ears were positively bristling, I could tell.

"I'll give you another clue. When I said 'out of town,' I meant a long way from here; so far away that its inhabitants look quite different."

A gratifying light—mere forty watt bulb though it was—appeared in widened eyes.

"The towelhead up the hill?"

"Is the correct answer, Kevin."

"You sure about this, Doc?"

"I'm positive of it, Greg. We know, from Mr Francis's deposition, that he was in cahoots with someone else. Mr, whatshisname, Curry, is the obvious candidate. The general feeling about him and his family, from what I can gather, is that they are in the village but not of it. Given that the Manse is relatively close to the spot where the roadblock was set up, while being at some distance from the centre, Mr Curry would be pretty easy for outsiders to liaise with. And, talking of outsiders, he is not of our ilk, of course. He is of another faith and another phenotype. Another race, if you will."

An anonymous caller: "Black in my book!"

I surveyed the crowd.

"Ladies and gentlemen, Sergeant Hyman, I rest my case."

And resting it, I saw as if all was painted before me in the sharpest of primary colours, that the English world, and that of Europe too, were like cradles made with no thought for failure, cradles in which cathedrals, castles, great ships, jumbo jets and merrily glinting skyscrapers nestled side by side with their builders, with our wholesome masses: ruddy-cheeked farmhands, matrons in gardens wielding their trowels, families content to make a decent living (with soccer and rugger and cricket and cribbage and the taste of ale by way of relief from their jobs); and all of them knew themselves to be kith and kin and that blood went deeper than water, and that all of them could be called upon if their precious sameness were to be threatened by those whose blood swirled in different patterns, whose brains were tinged with perfidy, with sticky and saggy thoughts, with extraneous aims.

"Now, Sergeant, if we can assume that I'm right—"

Mrs Wortle interrupted me. "—and you're not wrong!"

I chuckled. After all, 'twas the sociometric star. "Pray do tell, Mrs Wortle, what makes you so certain?"

She looked grimly at me, then turned and looked grimly at the others. The common touch, she had.

"I don't like saying it because they've never given me any trouble personally, and they've always kept themselves to themselves, they have, and I think I speak for the whole community when I say that. And what's more they stopped that place from getting all run down, did it up something proud, they did, but..."

She gave me a rueful look.

"It can't be anybody else, can it? When you think about it? That Arab gentleman seems nice enough, but you never can tell with them, can you? Pretty two-faced, some of them."

A nice murmur of approval from the others.

I looked at Hyman.

"QED, Sergeant. I think we should get up to the Manse as soon as poss."

A louder murmur, the odd hear-hear, the odd what- are-we-waiting-for.

"Now hold your horses, Doctor, just what is it you have in mind? We don't want people taking the law into their own hands. We're not in Tombstone, Arizona, you know."

There were never any lynchings in Tombstone. Sikeston, Missouri, that was a famous one. Relatively recent, too.

"I'm sure the last thing anyone wants is for this to turn into a free-for-all. That is simply not the English way. Having said which, time is of the essence, Sergeant. I suggest that you, constable Woodstock and myself lead the way."

"What is it, exactly, that you have in mind, Doctor?"

"We must needs go to the Manse, Sergeant, and detain the Arab as a possible suspect."

My words were picked up by a higgledy-piggledy chorus.

"To the Manse! To the Manse!"

Sober approval, firmly voiced.

"Sergeant, WPC Woodstock, I wonder if you would be so good as to give me a lift?"

I WAS TWELVE

(Thursday 18th)

Lucy, your Dad's going off with the police!

Indeed he was, Eileen. We watched from our spot—where nobody, as it happened, was watching us—as Dr Whitebone got into the panda with the two police officers. They drove off with a short screech. The rest of the crowd started to head in the same direction—up the high street—on foot. A cluster of yobboes gathered round Kevin until Greg said something to them and they made chewing-gum motions with their mouths and slapped each other's shoulders, then fairly sprinted after the crowd, Greg in tow.

Let's follow; we can stick to the side streets, that way Dad won't see us.

Eileen moaned: *Another blooming traipse?*

I surprised myself by snapping at her: *Haven't you got any sense of adventure?*

She looked blank: *If you ask me, all this is just a tremendous pain in the bottom—the whole thing.*

I looked at Eileen's long face and spotted in her a certain type: the people who drift expressionless onto Tube platforms or along grey stone streets, who drive past green hills in carefully cleaned cars, babies on board; danger might slip in and out of the corners of their eyes, but all that mattered to them was to return to the standing still of the run of the mill, to lives free of incident. It wasn't that I despised Eileen's gormless sulk in the face of the strange, it simply irked me that she was not making the best of our unusual situation, probably the most unusual she'd ever find herself in, a red-letter situation.

Come on, Eileen, said Lucy, *we don't want to miss anything.*

*

We huffed and puffed up side streets then out onto the high street, then up to where the Manse sat six-windowed and light grey, just without the limits of the village proper. A crowd had assembled on the lawn, beer cans in more than a few hands. We opted to keep a safe distance, on the far side of the road opposite the house. The wooden gate had been left open.

Present was the long-haired man in the corduroy jacket who had so got Dr Whitebone's goat at the police station yesterday. The white-pinafored woman was there too, chatting to a couple of other women. Dr Whitebone, Greg and several of the local youths were conferring quietly near a rose bed.

The building's front door was of black wood and arch-shaped, and adamantly closed. At the foot of the steps leading up to it, the woman officer and her podgy superior were standing feet apart, hands clutched behind their backs.

Then Dr Whitebone left his confab, nodded at the two police officers, trotted up the stoop, and began to bang the door's stag-head knocker against the wood, not once, not twice, but on and on bam bam bam, on and on bam bam bam, on and on and on until the door opened a crack. He said something to the coy opener. The people on the lawn had started to mutter amongst themselves, but shut up on the nonce when the Arab gentleman stepped into full view.

I'd seen him in the village once when he was in his traditional garb and the second time when he was in civvies. On both occasions he looked impressive: well-heeled, good posture. Now, however, while talking to Lucy's dad, he seemed to have shrunk in size, his face a fretful frown. Greg and the bomber-jacketed youths were watching this doorstep scene attentively.

As for us, we were distracted from it for a moment when the shopkeeper and that little girl we'd seen once behind his counter stepped through the gate into the garden, and stood bang in the middle of the lawn. Lucy whispered: *He must have closed his shop; that means Mum'll be back home and will've seen we're not there and'll start getting all hysterical.*

I'M NOT A

(Thursday 18ᵗʰ)

I told my white lie to the Arab gentleman, without beating about the bush: we had been reliably informed that he was a key informer for the persons unknown who had blocked the road, shut off the phones, kidnapped a police constable, old Mr Feather, and my son. When he asked me, in that oily-woily voice of his, where I'd obtained this information, I said from his fellow accomplice, who had now been placed in custody.

Of course he denied having either an accomplice or anything at all to do with the recent events which—so he rather cunningly claimed—had affected him just as badly as anyone else. My accusation, he said, was not only unfair, but smacked of discrimination. Discrimination! The first recourse of the dark-skinned! I lowered my voice.

"You have a lady wife, do you not?"

That wiped the righteousness off his face.

"And two small children? A boy and a girl, fiveish, sixish?"

"What are you asking me these questions for?"

I looked him straight in his date-coloured eye.

"People here—and quite a few of them are standing in your front garden as we speak—are understandably angry about what's been going on. I would be failing in my duty as justice of the peace were I not to warn you that I cannot answer for their behaviour—there are so very many of them—if they decide to step outside the bounds of the law. Now, the longer we continue dawdling here on your doorstep, the edgier our spectators will become, and I have no wish to put you and your family at risk. To that end, I think it would be better if you and I spoke further in the privacy of your living room."

I glanced back at the chatting, drinking crowd on the lawn. His token smile came out wonky. Nerves.

"I suppose you had better come in then."

I called down the steps to where Hymie and my tight-vulvaed lady copper were standing guard.

"Sergeant!"

The matzo Fatso plodded up the steps, followed by Lorraine. I signalled to Greg, who strode over with his son Kevin and two other patrol boys in tow. The Arab remonstrated.

"I thought you wished to talk in private."

Hyman and Lorraine entered the house first.

"Good morning, Mr Khoury."

Followed by Greg and the three burly boys.

"All right, mate?"

He stared at them as they passed into his hallway.

"Greg!" I said. "Be so kind as to have your boys locate this gentleman's spouse and offspring."

Again I had to reassure the Arab—as Greg and the boys started up the stairs—that they were there to keep a safe eye on his kin: an elementary precaution. Frowning, he ushered me into a large drawing room. On my way in, I spotted a dining room and a kitchen, towards the back.

Once in the lounge—in which the sergeant and Lorraine were already standing politely, waiting to be offered a chair—you could see that this desert-born gentleman had made a conspicuous effort to make everything seem British: the place sported a Bradley coffee table, framed reproductions of Stubbs horses, padded leather armchairs, and stand-alone plate holders garnished with lace doilies. French windows gave onto a trim back garden considerably larger than the one to the front of the house.

The patrol lads came in with the little boy and the little girl. Greg followed a moment later, holding their mother firmly by the arm. Both Mummy and youngsters had their eyes wide open. She moaned something in Arabic at her husband. A pretty twenty-something, she was, her face wrapped up in one of those Muslim headscarves.

"You boys take the children into the kitchen, please, and don't let them out of your sight. Greg, I wonder if you'd mind confining the lady of the house to the dining area? I'm sure she'll feel safer in there."

Greg looked a bit itchy, not his usual bluff self at all. "It'd be a pleasure, Doctor."

"Why are you separating them?"

"Please calm down, Mr Curry. Trust me, we know exactly what we're doing."

The bairns ouched a little bit when lugged off into the back by the three lads. Maintaining that grip on the woman's upper arm, Greg, all red-faced now, muttered, "This way, madam," and steered her swiftly into the dining room, shutting the door behind them. I turned to the wog.

"Time to take a pew, methinks."

I ensconced myself in an armchair. Hyman remained standing. Lorraine closed the living room doors and stood, at ease, in front of them.

The Arab spluttered, "If anything should happen to my wife and children..."

I shook my head.

"Nothing will happen to them, Mr Curry, not when two British police officers and a justice of the peace are on the premises."

Was that a twitch of mistrust I detected in his dusky features?

"Please do be seated."

He perched his behind on the edge of the sofa, his legs pressed together (rather after the fashion of the doily-collared virgins of whom there seemed to be so many around when I was a young man). He was wearing an Aran sweater and smart tweeds: Scotch House stuff which nonetheless failed to add as much as a smidgeon of dignity to his demeanour.

I leaned forward, no-nonsense, man to suspect.

"Mr Curry, we are under some kind of concerted assault by an unknown number of people who are almost certainly of foreign provenance. Their tremendous efficiency so far can only be accounted for by the existence of a source of strategic information within the village itself. From what little intelligence we have been able to gather, it appears likely that these people are of colour. We all know that like helps like, Mr Curry. Birds of a feather, and all that. Mr Francis, who, as you know, is the village road sweeper, being ethnically similar to those few assailants of whom we have eyewitness reports, was the first suspect to be detained and questioned. As mentioned, he eventually admitted his guilt, and confessed that he had an accomplice."

Rueful, my smile.

"Mr Curry, there's no point in denying it."

He closed his eyes, the prig.

"And as I already told *you*, Doctor, I have nothing whatsoever to do with these terrible events."

"You speak with the coolness of a newsreader, sir! Kindly remember my son is amongst those missing."

"I am aware of that, Doctor. Like my fellow villagers, I hope and pray that he and the other missing people will be found safe and sound."

My fellow villagers. I turned to Lorraine.

"WPC Woodstock, perhaps you could ask Greg and the boys how Mr Curry's family are getting along?"

She turned to go. The Arab was up like a rocket.

"If you lay so much..."

"Of course not. But do bear in mind, do *please* bear in mind that the situation is a most desperate one. I am not making any threats, Mr Curry. I am simply stating the obvious."

He plopped back down onto the sofa. Lorraine was hovering by the door, eyes on Curry, playing her part to perfection.

"Let's have whatever information you can give us, Mr Curry. In toto and on the double."

"I don't have any of this 'information' you talk about. None at all."

'Twas a feeble voice that spoke. The inverted commas were especially grating. I had had enough. More than enough.

"WPC Woodstock, we all know that our Greg is a rather excitable man. As I said, perhaps you'd better check that everything is in order."

Lorraine left without a word. It was not far to the kitchen. From there—the door had been left open—we heard the Curry spouse call out what sounded like a complaint.

The Jewboy sergeant, of course, didn't care for this one little bit.

"Doctor, exactly what is going on here?"

Lorraine came back into the room, giving a theatrical puff of relief.

"Can't leave that man on his own for two minutes, Doctor. I think he's taken rather a shine to the woman. If I hadn't told him to keep a grip on himself—"

Hymie positively yelled at her.

"Constable Woodstock! This is not a game! If Mrs Khoury does not feel secure with Mr Crofton, for whatever reason, she must be removed from his presence forthwith!"

Enough.

"Sergeant! I would remind you that I am legally in charge here and will take full responsibility for whatever measures might prove to be necessary. Now, please, calm yourself!"

Hyman looked at me with unaccustomed sternness.

"What sort of measures do you have in mind, Doctor?"

I turned back to my interrogatee.

"Quickly now, Curry, the facts."

"I told you, there's nothing—"

It cut like knife through butter, that heartfelt female complaint, once more and louder and in English this time.

"No!"

And again:

"No!"

Heavens, Greg really did seem to be losing control of himself. Our Arab turned to the door guarded by Lorraine, through which we now heard his wife's remonstrances transmogrify themselves into whines. Or perhaps she had switched to Arabic.

"What is it, Mr Curry?"

He turned to me, palms out in the world-known pleading gesture. How typical of Johnny Muslim: the begging pose.

"I would tell you anything useful if I could, please, just order this to be stopped. Please!

The whines continued. Curry collapsed back on the sofa, head in his hands. He was mumbling. Perhaps he was finally going to tell me the truth.

"Speak up, sir!"

His face was a mess of tear-strewn wrinkles.

"What do you want me to do, invent something that is not true? I'll do anything if you put a stop to this. Money, if you—"

"Do not insult my integrity, sir!"

Still feigning, still play-acting, still lying. I pointed at him.

"What did you think this was when first you got involved? A jape? A prank? You and your friends have engaged in belligerent behaviour, sir, and do you know what we say in this country? All's fair in love and war, sir!"

I might have been trembling by this stage. Why wouldn't he come clean? Even now, when his wife was obviously in a pickle?

"WPC Woodstock! Be so good as to see what Mr Crofton is up to."

"Right away, Doctor."

As she left for the dining room, I stood up and made my way to where the Egyptian's (or whatever he was) hi-fi system stood. He had made an excellent choice: Marantz amplifier and receiver, Linn Sondek turntable and Bose Nine-Oh-One speakers. Lorraine was back in no time.

"Mr Crofton has been duly reprimanded for his excessive behaviour, Doctor. He has assured us it will not happen again."

Amongst the sheik's records were a few popular classics, and a handful of singles for the youngsters: "Noddy at the Seaside", "Peter and the Wolf", and, ah, now what was that one there? "I'd Like to Teach the World to Sing". The year before last's hit. I placed it on the turntable and, holding the stylus above the groove, I addressed the Arab once more.

"Go on, Mr Curry, I know you're dying to tell us something."

Beside himself, he was.

"I want to see my wife, this instant."

"All in good time. Constable Woodstock!"

Lorraine, by that stage, had a fervent look in her eye.

"Doctor?"

"Tell Kevin and the other boys to get on with things, would you?"

"Certainly, Doctor."

No sooner had she left than I lowered the stylus, thus releasing lyrics once chorused—a couple or so years ago— by my daughter Lucy.

I'd like to build the world a home

And furnish it with love

Just as the first bellow came from the kitchen—a real whopper of a howl from the little boy—I turned up the Marantz. A further howl nonetheless managed to slip through:

"PAPA!"

Up a notch. I didn't want the watchers on the lawn to get unduly upset.

Grow apple trees and honey bees and snow-white turtle doves

"PAPA!"

The woggo was on his feet again, understandably flabbergasted.

"Stop this! Stop it now! I will do whatever is required..."

I turned down the volume until it was a ghost of its former self.

I'd like to teach the world to sing

"Tell us what you know, sir!"

Again, the child's howl.

"PAPA!"

His daddy shook a shaking head. I put the tune back to full blast.

In perfect harmony
I'd like to hold it in my arms and keep it company

Then, inexplicably, it wound down.

neeeeeee

There he was all of a sudden, that kosher fool, glowering at me with a pulled plug in his hand. He was ever so red, as if he'd gone through some strenuous exercise, an impression reinforced by his unbuttoned collar and skewed tie. Once again, we heard that by-now almost familiar shriek.

"PAPA!"

Hymie threw the plug down and jabbed a finger against my chest.

"Soon as I put a stop to this, you're under arrest!"

He headed with uncharacteristic swiftness for the door through which the returning Lorraine, I suppose from customary deference, allowed him to pass. By the time I caught up with him, he'd reached the kitchen.

Greg's son and a second lad had hoisted up the boy child, in a state of undress, and sat his bottom on the top of a decidedly warm AGA cooker. He was screaming non-stop, not 'papa' anymore, only nail-on-blackboard shrieks, with barely a pause for breath. The little girl was being held a little way away, next in line as it were—her face buckled in alarm, her clothes not yet removed—by the third patrol boy. I caught Hyman by the elbow.

"Sergeant!"

The face which Hyman turned to me was streaked with tears. The unexpected punch which he drove into my midriff had something of the rabbit to it, though it winded me enough to elicit a cry of pain. The two lads who'd been keeping a hold on the boy let go and rushed to my aid. They had already restrained Hyman when Greg turned up, the curved-tip collars of his jacket askew, his mostly unbuttoned shirt revealing a shark's tooth pendant dangling against the man's admirably hirsute chest.

"What happened?"

Still bent over, I took a deep breath.

"Our guardian of law and order momentarily forgot himself."

Greg looked at Hyman, his arms pinned back by the two lads. The boy child had leaped off the AGA and was howling, prostrate on the floor (his little bottom, I admit, was not a pretty sight); the girl, still in the grip of the third patrol boy, had gone still and blank-eyed.

"You lads, take these two into the dining room with their mother and make sure they stay there."

As soon as the patrol boys had removed the children from the kitchen, Greg glared at Hyman.

"Don't let the fucking side down, Geoff. This is a fucking emergency and you fucking well know it."

The Jew's head shook a tiny 'no'. I took the decision.

"Greg, Sergeant Hyman has both challenged the authority of, and physically assaulted, his superior, in the midst of a most grave crisis. He has left me with no choice."

Iron in my voice.

"Police Sergeant Geoffrey Hyman of the South Wight Constabulary, I am hereby using the powers invested in me as acting justice of the peace to remove you from your post, effective forthwith."

You have to make things *sound* honest-to-God true, every doctor knows that. Hyman didn't blink.

LOG OF PROGRESS

(Thursday 18th)

I was dreaming I had been hauled off to the police station, just like that poor council employee; I had sworn to myself that there would be no more bystander victims, and yet there I was, another one, being taped up, prodded, violated.

The nightmare woke me up after just thirty minutes' sleep. I jumped up, splashed water on my face, hauled on my duffle coat and left.

Daybreak. For an hour, I leaned on the esplanade railing, pretending to look at the sea, which looked pretty gormless that morning. To my right was the still closed pub and beyond that, the end of the tarmac.

Some chat made me look away off to my left, up the esplanade's main stretch. Three or four villagers had stopped to talk outside the fish and chip shop, the doors of which then disgorged Mrs Wortle, who immediately joined them, as did a couple who were strolling past. Greg and his son stepped out of an adjoining street, the former with a walkie-talkie in his hand, and young Kevin, an Alsatian on a leash: they were being on patrol. They, too, joined the cluster. In the houses that gave onto the esplanade, a couple of windows clanked open, several curtains fluttered apart. It wasn't long before more people had come down, until there was quite a crowd. Voices were being raised, enough for me to catch the tone: indignant, enervated.

I crossed the esplanade to a less conspicuous vantage point at the corner of the high street. The crowd grew a little more.

It was joined by the doctor.

A gaggle of kids poked their heads out of one of the adjoining streets. I recognised them from my landlord's shop.

The siren took me by surprise. The car parked with a screech and out stepped the sergeant and the woman police officer and they, too, joined in the conversation. After a few minutes, the police and the doctor got in the car and drove straight past me, up the high street. The villagers, too, started heading in my direction, with Greg and the youths bringing up the rear. It struck me, watching this crowd waddle over, that somehow I'd been rumbled, discovered, caught out. But no, they ignored me, straight past me, following on the wake of the police car, faces purposeful, legs brisk. One called out to me:

What're you waiting for? People reckon it's the Arab!

As for the kids, they were nowhere to be seen.

*

Only when Greg and the young men became the last to disappear up the high street did I spot Twaibo. He was standing at the tarmac's edge, and waving.

I trotted over.

Mzee hajapoteza muda wowote.

Baada ya kumwambia, nini ulituambia sisi, aliamua kuende-
lea. Wote tuko tayari.

I pointed up the high street:

Kitu kilijitokeza, Baadhi yetu walihitaji kwenda mpakakule
kwenye jingo kubwa upande wa kulia.

That fazed him:

Sisi sote?

Nyinyi nyote. Haraka iwezekanavyo. Tunahitajika kuwakama-
ta kundi la watu wakorofi na kuwaweka pale.

I pointed back at the Community Centre—scratched
wooden doors, walls of tired-looking brick; he stepped forward for a better look.

Hapa?

Hapa.

Sawasawa.

He started to sprint back across the grass. I removed my
armband from my pocket and tied it, with some difficulty,
around my duffle coat sleeve.

I WAS TWELVE

(Thursday 18th)

The police officers, then Greg and the bovver boys and finally Lucy's dad, had all entered the Manse. The bystanders in the garden had begun to witter amongst themselves. Those with drinks occasionally chucked their empties on the lawn and, in their own good time, pulled out reinforcements from pockets and handbags.

I am tapping these keys with one hand and with the other I now take a king-sized swig that does my head one big fat favour. Installed in my cough-grey room—it does not matter where in London it is, all London is forever under the same shroud of clouds—in liquid bliss I watch the past pass me by.

Lucy nudged me: *Listen.* The shopkeeper had started to chant, right there in the open air, his voice inflating and fading depending on which way a fickle breeze was blowing: *Give thanks unto the lord, for he is good, his mercy endureth forever, oh give thanks to the god of gods, for his mercy endureth forever, oh give thanks to the lord of lords, for his mercy endureth forever.* Heads were turning his way, but as he was addressing no person in particular, excepting God (he had tilted his head upward), people soon went back to their chatting, paying no heed as he droned on: *To him alone who doeth great wonders, for his mercy endureth forever.*

Eileen shook her head: *Right nutter if you ask me.* Before any of us could reply, another voice sneaked up on the shopkeeper's, a voice crystalline, the breaks between the monotone of the psalm verses. His little girl—I assumed she was adopted—had a pitch-perfect plaint that went beyond sweet, that made *sweet* a corny adjective in this circumstance: *Amazing grace, how sweet the sound that saved a wretch like me!* after which the shopkeeper moaned: *To him that by wisdom made the heavens, for his mercy endureth forever* followed on the nonce by her reprise *I once was lost but now am found, was blind but now I see,* which rose over the house—in which no one knew what was happening—and when it was his turn again: *to him that stretched out the* a fat lady hissed *ssssh!*

The shopkeeper looked quite put out when she pointed to the girl whose voice was now freewheeling in the air: *'Twas grace that taught my heart to fear.* She was being watched now by just about everyone, including that fretful long-haired man in the corduroy suit.

And grace my fears relieved.

When she paused for a breath, a sound of another ilk altogether came from the house. I couldn't put a finger on it, still tuning in as I was to her as she went on: *How precious did that faith appear the hour.* The housebound noise returned, loud enough this time to drown her out. Lucy looked at us agape: *That's the Coca-Cola song! I used to listen to it for hours on end!*

It was coming out clear enough now through the ground floor windows, that line about trees and bees and doves, snow-white ones followed by those words that had thrilled me too, when I was ten: *I'd like to teach the world to sing in perfect harmony,* and which, I now discovered, no longer did. *I'd like to hold it in my arms and keep it company*—Then the song broke right off and in the fresh silence—the little girl having stopped her singing—the trees, pestered by gusts, rustled loud as cellophane.

Mrs Whitebone steamrollered into us from the rear, giving us all a fright, her voice a careering squawk: *I thought I wouldn't find you anywhere!* Before Lucy could reply, we all heard what could only be described as a muffled yelp from inside the house. Excited murmurs from the lawn brigade. Mrs Whitebone stared at the Manse: *Good od in heaven, what was that?* She put one hand on Lucy's shoulder and the other, I uncomfortably noticed, on mine. In a voice kept to a stage whisper she asked no one in particular: *Who's in there?*

Eileen blurted: *The Arabs who live there and your husband and the policeman and the policewoman and that big villager and three of the local oiks.*

Mrs Whitebone looked, slowly, from the black door to the lace-curtained windows and back again: *What on earth is John doing in there?*

It took everybody a while to catch on, as bangs and shouts came from the back of the house, the part that gave onto the fields: shouts that sounded strange and bangs that sounded precipitous, followed by the unmistakable sound of breaking glass. On the lawn, not a soul stirred, not even to raise booze to lips.

The black door shot open and slammed against the outside wall and Dr Whitebone was bundled outward by two black strangers who had popped out of God knew where: a man and a woman, quite young, about Simon's age, perhaps (I couldn't tell, back then, with people of colour). I stared; Jesus, everybody was staring: perhaps because these strangers weren't coffee-coloured like so many of the coloured people I'd glanced at in London, no, they were black as night, as pitch, as jet. They were tall and thin, had short hair and wore jeans and V-necked jerseys over white T-shirts and they had strips of white cloth tied around the biceps of their right arms.

The female black said something to the male one and the two of them started to half-guide, half-pull Lucy's dad down the steps. Dr Whitebone couldn't have looked more taken aback if they'd been trying to poke him up the bum.

Niggers, these *niggers*—the word turned up like a bad penny, spoiling my thoughts, killing all the questions I so wanted to ask—silent *niggers* were manhandling an intelligent, qualified Englishman.

Who began to hang his head as those *niggers* led him down onto the lawn. Both the black man and the black woman had a military bearing about them, and for an instant I found myself trying to spot their guns. There weren't any: no shoulder-slung rifles, no holstered pistols, not one single firearm. Nonetheless, all us white people moved not a muscle.

Oh, John...

His wife slapped a hand over her moan, by which time I had spotted the thin pink clothesline placed around Dr Whitebone's neck: an improvised noose, the line trembling its flimsy way back up the stairs where Greg now appeared framed in the doorway, the pink nylon wound in turn round his thick neck.

A lurker in the doorway shadows gave Greg a shove, forcing him to stumble his way down the steps. He was halfway to the grass when the lurker called out from the dark: *Sawa, twende!*

Looking downright miserable, the three village lads and the local policewoman (her hat placed skew-whiff over her partially undone hair) emerged from the portal and followed Greg and Dr Whitebone down the stairs in single file, linked up one and all neck by neck to the same nylon line.

From a far corner of the lawn, a teetering villager with a bottle in her hand cawed: *There's just fucking two of them.* Her Dutch courage spread to several more, who started to bellow at the black man and woman, who were now busy arranging their captives in a straight line on the lawn, unflappable eyes on the job in hand.

What d'you think you're doing?

Hoy!

You stop that right there!

Someone might even have taken action, if the lurker in the hall hadn't stepped into the light. Lucy gasped. He was tall enough to have to stoop when crossing the Manse's threshold; he wore a baggy sweater with a faded floral pattern, and faded jeans, and shiny, patent-leather loafers and, like his companions, he had a length of white rag knotted round his upper arm. But these were details registered in passing. My eyes were locked on his face on the right side of which two scars ran from mouth to neck the one, and from eye to ear, the other: thick rifts of white, like streaks of dried cow gum. As soon as he started descending the stoop, the bawlers on the lawn shut up.

Perhaps Scar Man's unlovely face had shocked them; or perhaps they'd realised there might have been yet more blacks laying in waiting, ready to be sicked on them if the occasion called for it.

Sawa, twende!

Having made them turn round so they were eyes-front, the three blacks indicated by slight pulls and pushes that the six prisoners were to walk towards the gate. The girl led them, the younger man flanked them to their left, and Scar Man brought up the rear. All filed across the grass, through the gate and out onto the road, where the girl gave them a slow-down wave: *Simama.* The queue halted.

Scar Man, the slightest of smiles shifting his gashes, positioned each captive—laying a huge hand on each one's shoulder—at an equal distance from the ones before and behind. Then he pointed down the road: *Vipi wewe!* The black girl at the head of the queue reached out to Dr Whitebone's neck and gave a little tug on the pink noose, forcing Lucy's dad to bend forward.

Sawa, twende!

The boy at the side frowned at her: *Ukosawa?*

She nodded, smiling easily: *Sijambo.*

This human chain began to head off, down to the where the village lay, its noosed components—I imagine in order to avoid pulling at each other's necks—treading as if flat-footed. Another whine escaped Mrs Whitebone: *John.* She gave a half-hearted wave to her husband's disappearing back. Lucy, black eyes a-glimmer with tears, patted the maternal hand still tight as a vice round her arm: *Mum, Mum.*

Some of the villagers on the lawn had dared, cans in hand, to skulk up to the gate, through which they were now slipping. Keeping their distance, they began to follow the column, in dribs and drabs.

We stared after them, at a loss as to what to do next. Mrs Whitebone, to judge from the tremulous sounds spat from her lips, had abandoned human language for the time being. As was fast becoming a habit with me, I looked to Lucy for guidance but she was gawping at the Manse: *Jeepers.* At the top of the stairs, two more black women—in sweaters over T-shirts, jeans and loafers, their armband knots flapping in the breeze— were helping two twitching, blanket-wrapped children down the steps, followed closely by the Arab man, who was doing a certain amount of twitching himself, while from somewhere back in the hallway came fat, hiccupy sobs.

Mum, what's going on?

Mrs Whitebone's glance back at the Manse lingered. Then her head jerked back round to us and her lips, held silently ajar, got going: *Right now it's your father I'm concerned about.* With which she started to descend the road in the wake of the chain gang and its cautious village followers.

The man in the corduroy jacket was strolling level with Scar Man, looking confidently over at him, nodding from time to time as if to express approval: *You know, I think what you're doing is splendid, absolutely splendid; high time; never thought I'd see the Panthers in the flesh; I mean you guys are just—*

Scar Man's arm snapped up, pointing to where everybody else, ourselves included, was hanging back: *Rudi!*

The long-haired man raised understanding hands: *Sure, man, I'm cool.* Upon which Scar Man positively roared: *Rudi!* The corduroy man jumped back, tripped and fell into a bush.

The young black chappie who was flanking the column called to the woman at the front: *Wanakuja?*

She pointed down the road: *Watakuja.*

The man stole a quick peek away from his wards and pointed: *Wakopale!*

And the girl looked back and nodded: *Wakopale!*

We spotted them too, waiting at the bottom of the high street, two men on one side of the road, four women on the other, leaning against the walls, against the lampposts, arms folded, several large, lidded wicker baskets at their feet. They hailed the descending blacks: *Hamjambo!* and the descending blacks waved back: *Hatujambo!* before halting their captives at the bottom of the street.

Mrs Whitebone muttered: *Where have they all come from, for God's sake?*

The waiting blacks walked languidly over to the others. A conversation started. One of the women who'd been at the foot of the street pointed back and to her left: the direction of the Community Centre. We palefaces had stopped in our tracks, some yards behind Scar Man, who had remained at the rear of the queue.

Having apparently reached some kind of decision, the blacks parted and the procession continued on its way, not towards to the Community Centre, as I'd surmised, but over to the esplanade railing that gave onto the beach, onto the sea. The blacks that had been hanging about at the foot of the high street picked up their wicker baskets and moved off in turn towards the railing.

We edged down the street until we had a clear view of the esplanade. Lucy's dad and his fellow prisoners had been lined up against the railing, faces seaward, the young man standing at their right end, the young woman at the left, while Scar Man watched their backs.

The villagers who'd stayed in the pub all this time were huddled together on the terrace, conversing. The six blacks with the wicker baskets were trotting down the steps that led to the beach. Mrs Whitebone muttered: *What on earth have they got in those things?* We were close enough to the baskets to make out sporadic shufflings, flashes of soft white.

Eileen peered: *Woo, I think they're...*

Without taking his eyes off the captives, Scar Man pointed with one hand at the woozy-looking folk on the pub terrace and with the other thumbed back at us and the other villagers who were now on the esplanade: *Achana nao, achana nao!*

Without understanding a word, we and everybody else stopped in our tracks. Then Eileen fluttered her hand in the direction of the twittering baskets: *Look, they're...*

I'M NOT A

(Thursday 18th)

Jungle-boy and ape-girl led us all the way down the hill, past the café and the clothes shop, right down to the railing.

A whole damn pack of hidden cards had just been laid on the table. I was determined to find out exactly what game was being played and not to lose my nerves, not betray one iota of fear. To keep a stiff upper lip, if you will. There was a time when that now-passé expression actually stood for something.

Naturally, I ruled out any kind of escape attempt while we were all still trussed together like so many Congolese rubber-tappers: our assailants were pretty dab hands when it came to knots, and should any one of us have attempted to make a break for it, the rest of us would have been choked on our own nooses.

The blacks kept waving to us to move faster, yelling something, in wog-talk, that sounded like 'vippy way-way'.

Once we had been led across the esplanade to the sea-view railings, I could see that the outdoor tables of the King and Country—which were off to my right—were packed with onlookers. I felt like a prize heifer at a country fair.

Our guardians urged us to 'panga mas tarry,' something which needed no translation, given that they had started to grasp our shoulders, with their black hands, and turn us so that we faced the sea. I was to the far left of the line, Greg being on my right and the three lads to the right of him. Lorraine was stuck at the end of the lads. Like a bloody chorus line, we were. Flanked by nig-nogs (including that scar-faced brute of a buck who had broken into the Manse, along with our other two guards; he had now positioned himself about a yard behind us).

Of course I could not help but venture that our end might be nigh; that right here, the wind blowing on our faces as cold as cold could be, we'd receive a bullet—or a stab—in the back. Just the kind of precipitate behaviour one could expect from these people. I was acutely conscious of the wind blowing cold as cold could be on my nape. For I couldn't tell how long, we faced the grey sea, the grey sky, breathing deeply.

'Twas a certain relief, I felt, when our keepers gave cheerful shouts in their bongo-bongo patois. It was not until a few minutes had transpired that I realised what was going on: we were no longer alone. Shuffling feet, coughs, and the odd white man's voice, told us that people were being lined up at the railings, off to the left of our little chain gang. I dared to glance.

Beyond the girl guard's gorillaish nose—she had her back to the railings and was grinning like a simpleton—I saw dozens of villagers clutching the iron, their nonplussed faces stretching all the way to the far end of the esplanade, noses sniffing, scarves fluttering here and there. I was unable to make out Lucy, my wife or the other children.

An elbow dig from Greg had me facing the sea once more. He leaned less than an inch towards me.

"The beach."

Across which six blacks were walking towards the shoreline, stepping around the burnt-out skiffs. Each was carrying a closed basket.

A booming voice made me turn my head. A car was cruising slowly along the esplanade. One black drove while another rode shotgun inasmuch as one can with an Austin Allegro, leaning awkwardly out of the passenger side, one hand braced on the open door, the other clutching a cardboard loudhailer through which he roared something along the lines, if memory serves, of 'Taffy ad hari subi reeny pally.'

My first, hurried, hypothesis was that all this was something to do with those urban council estates which had recently become virtual West Indian colonies, where swarms of children hung about doing bugger all through their formative years except form private languages and silly ways of greeting each other, only to emerge into wider society with the resentment of the chronically undereducated weighing heavily on their shoulders. Perhaps a horde of them had targeted this isolated, peaceful village to run amok in. The white armbands which one and all sported, it now occurred to me, were probably a kind of gang insignia. Perhaps all this was an out-of-control offshoot of some kind of 'turf war', as the journalists dubbed them.

I had been trying to keep a tally of the buggers ever since the first three had broken into the Arab's house. My estimate so far was that there were a baker's dozen at large in the village. If so, they were hopelessly outnumbered.

A female darky I hadn't seen before—shivering a touch, hands plunged into the front pockets of her denims—had been stationed in front of Mrs Wortle's fish and chip shop. Against one of the blue iron columns of the only other establishment on the esplanade, the sweet and novelty shop, leaned another young jungle bunny, plump and male, this one; which now made fifteen blacks in all. The rest of the buildings that gave onto the esplanade, local residences all, had gone as still as a stiff: no quivering voiles, no peering biddies.

The car did a three-point turn, then parked at a rakish angle, straddling the tarmac. Again, a nudge from Greg.

"Doctor."

The six coons on the beach had converged at the water's edge and were fiddling with the catches on the baskets; not quite at the same time, they managed to fling the lids open. The silence of both villagers and blacks was so complete I could hear the hinges of the baskets creak and squeak.

For seconds on end, bugger all happened. Then those six blacks made choo-choo noises, puckering their fat lips as if soliciting a kiss. One after the other, as if on cue, wood pigeon after wood pigeon fled the coops. Twelve in all. They shot straight up, circled in a moment's confusion, then got their bearings and headed west as one fowl. Cliffward.

Why, I mused, this looks just like one of those ghastly symbolic shows so beloved of the duffle coat brigade, doves being thrown into the air to show us all what a bloody wonderful thing peace is. Perhaps this wasn't a gang, then, perhaps it was some sort of British offshoot of one of those American 'civil rights' movements.

I tugged my noose an inch or so free from my gullet. Then the fellow with the bullhorn, who was standing by his badly parked car, started bawling: 'En-go-jar! En-go-jar! En-go-jar! Sooby-reeny!'

His calls came to an end, however, without anything untoward happening. On the contrary, we were exactly as before, our noses sniffing ozone, our eyes facing an eventless main. I felt a twinge of optimism. Perhaps, I reflected, they weren't intending to do anything serious to us prisoners at all. Perhaps the noose was just to humiliate us while they put on this shambolic little show of theirs. Perhaps this was nothing but a bit of amateur theatrics. Which would mean that Simon would be all right. And that Lucy, who for all I knew was somewhere close by, was in no danger. My bloody wife, neither. A bunch of clowns, that's what these intruders were! Probably la-de-daaing about like this just to get a headline for their 'cause'. As my thoughts were running along these lines, I noticed the villagers had started to chatter and mutter. Greg gave me his third elbow dig of the day.

"The sea!"

They were no bigger than ants, the lifeboat-sized craft that were moving steadily landward in a wide arc, steering in from the general direction of the cliffs, outboards a-hum.

The first row of vessels coasted up to the beach, practically gunwale to gunwale all the way across the entire bloody bay, and every bloody vessel—as I saw when the first ones ran up onto the sand with a whoosh—was chock-a-block with men of all ages and women of all ages and tykes of all ages, and every bloody one of them was as black as the ace of bloody spades. Greg shook his head.

"Christ! They must've been hiding out in the caves."

"Caves?"

"The sea caves. There's warrens of 'em, all the way from just beyond Coldwater Bay to the Needles."

The first passengers clambered out and hauled their boats up onto the beach. This done, they waved dazedly up at the handful of their confreres on the esplanade; 'hoe-dee', they called, 'hoe-dee'. Then turned to watch the remaining rows of boats approaching the bay, three rows of bobbing black heads, eyes on the qui vive, all idling smoothly in, wave after wave, to land on our land.

Those already on terra firma greeted those who were swarming onto it. They smiled and hugged. There must have been some two hundred of them all told: mothers and fathers piggy-backing piccaninnies, young 'uns walking tall, old 'uns hobbling with the assistance of their more youthful relatives; on they kept coming, prow after prow, whoosh after whoosh, most in jumpers and jeans, though some of the older women wore garish wraps. No armbands. It took a moment to register that a fair number of these newcomers were missing bits of limb. As they milled and mingled on the beach, all the villagers could do was stare, struck dumb as dolls. I looked at Greg, who turned out to be looking at me. His eyes were wide as a marmoset's. His mouth twitched about in search of words until finally he managed to croak, "Gordon fucking Bennett."

I would have put it differently, myself.

LOG OF PROGRESS

(Thursday 18th)

Dusk of the day! The light a soft and innocuous grey, the streets curfew-calm, the native inhabitants tucked away in their cubbyhole homes, their criminals under lock and key in the Community Centre, now pressed into service as a jailhouse.

I took a walk alone along the esplanade, the boats stashed stem to stern below the railing, cosied up to the wall, tucked up in tarpaulin, leaving the beach bare—its shoreline sand lapped by soapsuds-coloured surf—just as if nothing had ever happened.

The evening breeze had never felt so good, so salubrious, so perfumed with future. TVs were flickering here and there in the odd window; and here and there too, the occasional eye looked out from the shadow of a porch: our lookouts, sensibly wrapped up in anoraks duly removed from the high street clothes shop, and distributed accordingly.

I exchanged a nod with the woman leaning guard against the Community Centre's door before turning up the high street. I took in the rising swathe of macadam and the muted shimmer of windows. I tramped up the middle of the road, counting off the doors. I had this village off pat, there now being no nook or cranny of it that I hadn't taken a peek at. I stopped in front of number eighty-four, its door paint chipped and dusty. It was part of a long row of three-storey terraced houses, jostling each other like bread queuers all the way up to the village limits. I peered at the bell console, then pressed the second buzzer, twice and long. A sash window above opened with a clatter:

Who's that?

Nervously loud.

Good evening, Mr Craddock; would you be so kind as to open up?

Up a creaky flight I went, into a cramped anteroom piled floor to near ceiling with back numbers stinking of ink, along a narrow corridor and into his office where he sat before a type-writer whose high back stuck out of a disarray of papers, paper clips, ink pots, discarded ribbons, staplers, hole punchers and a couple of empty half-pint flasks. He had a half-full one half-way to his mouth, its liquid honey-coloured in the light of a gooseneck lamp peering at it from a shelf behind. He sighed with relief as soon as he clapped eyes on my as-good-as-white skin. I held out the text. So inebriated he was, that even his first word,

Yes?,

tottered out lopsided.

Mr Craddock, we'd like you to have this printed in your local journal by tomorrow midday.

We?

You know perfectly well to whom I am referring, Mr Craddock: you too were at the railing today.

He held the document so close to his face he could have blown his nose on it:

Some of this isn't in English.

You're looking at the original; the English part is a translation.

He looked up:

What?

I smiled:

We want the translation—the English—published next to the official text.

He squinted at me, squeezing one eye shut, shifting the full burden of vision to the other:

I've seen you around in the village.

I pointed to the document:

Just make sure that comes out tomorrow, please. We're counting on you, Mr Craddock.

I raised a palm in farewell when he called out, drink hampering his flow:

You can't expect me to print all this gobbledy-gook, surely?

I had a foot in that dismal corridor of his:

Mr Craddock, we insist on it.

I heard the trickle of a swig before he blurted:

Why are you messing about with them in the first place, if you're not, you know, like them?

I called back joyously as I opened the door:

By tomorrow midday, Mr Craddock! Or I'll sick my black friends on you! One or two of them haven't yet lost their taste for human flesh, you know!

I left the door open, traces of desk light flickering on the tarnished brass plaque: COLDWATER BAY PARISH PRESS. I felt my way down the staircase.

Outside, it had taken it upon itself to drizzle. I pulled my hood over my head and headed back to my room.

COLDWATER BAY PARISH PRESS

Friday, April 19th, 1974

COMMUNIQUÉ

PARISH PRESS ORDERED TO PUBLISH EXPLANATORY DOCUMENT * FULL BILINGUAL TEXT PROVIDED * CLOSE PERUSAL STRONGLY RECOMMENDED TO ALL

By John Craddock

As Editor-in-Chief of the *Coldwater Bay Parish Press*, a periodical which has done its best to uphold the highest standards of journalism for the benefit of our small coastal community, I have taken the decision to dedicate the current issue to a bilingual communiqué received by hand yesterday evening. The said text would appear to offer not only an explanation of certain recent dramatic events, but to supply a declaration of intentions, of sorts, on the part of those responsible. It may be read below verbatim.

Kwenu wakazi na raia wa Coldwater Bay, Kisiwa cha Wight Muungano wa falme za Uingereza na Ireland kaskazini.

Sisi, ambao kwa sababu yoyote hawatakuwa wamesainiwa, watakuwa wanaelewa fika kwamba hivi karibuni wakazi wa Coldwater Bay wamekuwa na wakati mgumu sana kwa ujio wetu. Kwa hiyo tungependa kuwahakikishia kwamba hatuna dhamira ya kuumiza hata unywele katika vichwa vyenu. Tume kwisha sema nini, Bila shaka hamjakosa kuweza kujiuliza kwamba sisi ni kina nani na tupo hapa kawa ajili gani, katika Coldwater Bay ambayo tumeikata kwa muda kutoka Wight na vileva popote.

Dear citizens of Coldwater Bay, Isle of Wight, the United Kingdom of Great Britain and Northern Ireland.

We, who will not and in some cases cannot be the undersigned, are well aware that recently, the residents of Coldwater Bay have been having a distressing time on our account. We would therefore like to assure you that we have no intention of harming any of the hairs on your heads. Having said which, you will probably be unable to avoid asking yourselves just who we are and what we intend to do here, in a Coldwater Bay which we have temporarily cut off from the rest of the Wight and indeed, from everywhere else.

Tunashuhudia kwamba hatufikirii kama kuna umuhimu wa kujitambulisha kwa maelezo. Inatosha kusema kwamba tuko kundi la watu mia mbili ,wanaume wanawake na watoto. Ambao hatuna muda rahisi kama hivo. Tuna tokea katika dazeni ya nchi mbili tofauti ambazo majina yake tungeyataja kama tuna fikiria mojawapo ingejenga taswira katika fikira zenu kwamba haikuwa bahari ya nyuso nyeusi.

Baadhi yetu tumejikuta tukipigana vitani, na miongoni mwetu wamekuwa wahanga wa vita hivyo wenyewe kwa wenyewe. Lakini sasa tumezika uhasama wetu. Tunaendelea. Tumekuja hapa.

We confess to feeling no need to identify ourselves in anything approaching detail. Suffice to say we are a group of some two hundred men, women and children, who have not had an easy time of it so far. We come from some two dozen different countries whose names we would mention if we thought any of them would conjure up a single image in your mind that was not a sea of anonymous black faces.

Some of us have found ourselves fighting in wars, others amongst us have been the victims of those selfsame wars. But we have all buried the hatchet now. We have moved on. We have moved here.

261

Mnashangaa tumechaguwa Coldwater Bay kutoka orodha ndefu ya fukwe kwa sababu iko katika ukanda wa mapango ambayo nusu – yamezama, kama mjuavyo. Karibu njia yote kuelekea Needles. Mapango hay yamekubalika kuwa yanafaa kwa kutunza siri na vyombo mbalimbali kwa muda. Tunafikiri hakika mtaelewa kama tulivyo fafanua maelezo ya kina ya mpango huo wa kusafiri toka sehemu zetu za asili mbali na kuja hapa.

Lakini kwetu inatosha.

Kwa urahisi wenu na wetu mtandao wa simu utaunganishwa tena kwa saa mbili (na kwa masaa mawili tu) kuanzia kwenye saa 12:00 leo, Ijumaa Aprili 19th

Should you be wondering, we selected Coldwater Bay from a long list of possible resorts because it abuts on the string of half-submerged caves that run, as you are aware, nearly all the way to the Needles. These caves have proven ideal for the concealment of numerous small vessels over a brief period of time. We feel sure you will understand if we decline to explain the details of the complex operation by means of which we transported ourselves here from our diverse and distant points of origin.

But enough of us.

For your convenience—and ours—a single telephone line will be reconnected for two hours (and two hours only)

mahali pa kupokelea simu patakuwa mbele ya jumba la umma.

Wale wakazi wa muda ambao kwa kawaida watakuwa wakirudi kwenye nyumba zao za kudumu siku chache zijazo na wale wanakijiji wanaotazamia kuonekana kwa majirani wenyeji kwa sababu yeyote ile watatakiwa kuwasiliana na sehemu zao za kazi na yeyote anayewategemea kurudi, na sababu tarajiwa kwa kuchelewa kwao kwa majuma mawili zaidi. (Tunapendekeza mvurugiko wa tumbo aina ya kisingizio tunachokielewa mara nyingi katika nchi hii).

Waathirika wote wangetakiwa wenyewe kuwasilisha malalamiko yao katika eneo

starting at 12.00 today, Friday, April 19th. The receiver will be located in front of the public house.

Those temporary residents who would normally be returning to their permanent homes within the next few days— and those villagers who might be expected to make an appearance in neighbouring localities, for whatever reason— will be required to call their places of work and whoever else might be expecting them back, with plausible reasons for delaying their return a further two weeks. (We suggest a lingering stomach bug, an excuse of a kind which we understand is frequent in this country; you may add, if you wish, that there is a local epidemic.)

lililotengwa na masaa yalio chaguliwa.

Miito hii itakuwa iki-dhibitiwa kwa ukaribu katika muda muafaka. Tunasikitika kwa kuingilia mambo binafsi lakini siyo kwa kiasi kikubwa kama kitisho cha kushindwa kutii amri za kimahakama zi-lizowekwa. Kwa maana hiyo atakaye kamatwa akijaribu kutumia simu kuwajuli-sha au kujulisha ulimwen-gu kuhusu ujio wetu hapa atajuta kwa kitakachom-pataambako tusingependa kuingia huko sasa hivi.

Kwa taarifa nzuri ni kwam-ba yale maduka yanayo hudumia vyakula muhimu na vitu vya kuburudisha vitahifadhiwa kwa njia mbadala.

All those affected should present themselves at the aforementioned location, at the appointed hours.

These calls will be closely monitored in real time. We regret the intrusion of privacy, but not as much as we do the implied threat should you disobey our general injunction to silence. By which we mean that anyone caught trying to use the aforementioned telephone to inform the outside world of our presence here will invoke consequences we would rather not go into just now.

The good news is that those shops dispensing vital foodstuffs, and in some cases entertaining items, will be stocked by alternative means.

Tunapenda kuweka wazi kwamba vizuizi vya barabara havitatolewa, Hamtakuwa, tunaogopa kuwaruhusu kuondoka kijijini hapa aidha kwa gari au kwa miguu kwa muda wa majuma mawili. Kuondoa hatari ya majaribu. Petroli itakuwa ikiagizwa kwa magari yote isipokuwa yale machache ambayo hayana huduma kwetu. Tunasikitika sana kwa usumbufu wowote utakao jitokeza kwa sababu hii.

Kwa upande wa mbali wa kizuizi cha barabara alama za maonyo zaidi na alama za kuonyesha kazi zinafanyika zitawekwa. Tunaelewa ya kwamba migomo katika nchi hii ni ya mara kwa mara. Kama kuna washawishi wageni wowote

We wish to clarify that the roadblock will not be removed. You will not, we are afraid, be permitted to leave the village either by car or on foot, for the aforementioned two-week period. To remove the risk of temptation, petrol will be requisitioned from all vehicles except those few which might be of service to us. We apologise for any inconvenience this may cause.

On the far side of the roadblock, further warning signs and a simulacrum of an abandoned roadworks site—we understand that strikes are prevalent here—should dissuade any incoming visitors, if any, indeed, do appear. If they are not dissuaded, our lookouts will escort them into the village, where they wajitokeze. Kama wajashawishiwa uangalizi wetu utawasindikiza mpaka kijijini ambako mara moja watawekewa taratibu sawa kama zilizopo kwa muda huu kwa wakazi wahapa kwa muda ulio tajwa hapo juu.

Mwisho, tunapenda kuwajulisha kwamba kuondoka kwetu kutakuwa kama ilivyopangwa na itakuwa kama ilivyo amriwa. Vyote historia na uzoefu binafsi vimetufundisha ya kwamba shughuli za nchi ya kigeni (Ya sehemu moja) ni hasara kwa pande zote.

Kwa kipindi hiki cha mpito tunafurahi kuona serikali za mitaa katika mikono ya wale miongoni mwenu mnajisikia furaha kuwapatia.

will immediately be subject to the same restrictions as the current residents, for the time period stipulated above.

Finally, we would like to inform you that our departure will be punctual, and will take place in an orderly manner. Both history and personal experience have taught us that the annexation of a foreign country (or a tiny part of one, in this case) is disadvantageous for both parties.

For the interim, we are happy to see local government in the hands of those amongst you who feel happy about providing it. We will only interfere if we feel our personal safety is threatened, in which case the aggressors will be

Tutaingilia tu iwapo tutahisi usalama wetu uko hatarini. Na kwa watukutu watawajibishwa kutokana na matendo yao ambapo tumesema (kwa hakika tusingependa kufika huko)

Tuna waomba na hii isiwape wasiwasi sana kwamba uamuzi wetu wa kukaa hapa kwa muda uheshimiwe.

Lengo letu kukaa hapa? tumesikia mkijiuliza. Coldwater Bay ni fukwe za likizo. Tupo katika likizo. Tuna hitaji siyo moja tu, hatutapata nyingine tena. Hapana, siyo muda mrefu kama tunavyo ishi.

See you soon, people!

subjected to the consequences to which reference has already been made (the ones we don't really want to go into).

We do ask you—and this cannot be stressed enough—that our decision to sojourn briefly in your village be respected.

The purpose of our stay?, we hear you asking. That should be obvious. Coldwater Bay is a holiday resort. We are on holiday. Not only do we need one, we may never get another. No, not as long as we live.

Tutaonana, watu!

PART THREE: LUCY

LUCY

(Friday 19th)

The funniest thing was, you got used to their black skins in no time. They lounged on the beach in deckchairs if the weather got close to mild, or they sat at the tables outside the pub, and chatted away in their incomprehensible language, their deep-throated chuckles heralding displays of toothpaste-ad teeth.

They had moved into all the available lets in the village, of which there were plenty: it was an exceptionally slack season that year (indeed, we the Whitebone contingent were practically the only holidaymakers). I still wonder sometimes what the blacks would have done if they'd found NO VACANCY signs displayed in the parlour windows of all the village B&Bs.

I was just fourteen, but knew myself without a doubt to already be a girl and no longer a little girl, one of those little girls who had the world laid out before her wide like the sea we saw every day of that fateful fortnight; no, a girl I was now, who woke up every damn day with her skin tautened into a body-wide almost-itch.

Long before *they* came, I was in a state of fervour that might wax and wane, but which never left me, injecting me as it had up to the last vein with expectation; and I expected plenty, oh, loads: lashings of blandishments, and glances fired with desire; and then sex, I expected, not a specific man, just sex. And in the wake of sex would come oodles of self-confidence, and parallel with this pride would come some kind of success: by 1974, I knew, a girl could do anything she set her mind to, and my mind was set on things both bright and big: I was going to rip a tear in the tissue of a life that up until then had been humdrum as hell; I was going to make my female mark.

As I say, I'd been feeling like this for I don't know many weeks before Dad drove us into Coldwater Bay, 'us' being me and Eileen and Roger and Roger's friend—whose name I will not be mentioning for reasons of my own—squeezed up tight in the back of the Vanden Plas.

The Boy Who Shall Be Nameless was the last passenger we picked up on our way out of London, and I noticed as soon as he wheeled his bum into what little upholstery space was left, that he already fancied me something rotten. I was not always able to avoid his furtive glances on the longish journey down to Portsmouth. (If he'd been a bit older, I might have felt flattered.)

Things got more awkward on the ferry over to Wight: although he and Roger spent most of the trip together—they were supposed to be bosom pals, after all—I could hardly turn my head without catching BWSBN's glad eye out of the corner of my thoroughly uninterested one.

Oh God, I thought to myself as we headed south over the Isle, this is one problem I don't need, not for a whole Easter holiday. Though funnily enough, once we were installed in Seaview Heights, I found myself warming to him a mite, this

BWSBN. You didn't have to be a psychiatrist to see that he was a completely different kettle of fish from Roger. Although they were the same age, BWSBN was undoubtedly more mature. Intelligently bashful, to be precise: sharp enough, at least, to realise he was too young to be anything other than reticent in my presence. In his boyish way, he knew the score: a point in his favour.

And when the first strange things started happening in the village, I found I needed someone to confer with, to confide in, to share my hunches with, and BWSBN turned out to be the natural choice, far more so than Eileen, a friend who I'd been happy to see as a kind of younger sister up until then but who, during that period—when each occurrence followed hot on the heels of the previous one—proved herself uncommonly thick.

When I volunteered to go with BWSBN for the bread and then cajoled him into getting the local paper, it was a kind of test, as was letting him in on my occasional pilfering from Mum (that mum of mine who already at that time I pitied, from the bottom of my heart, and that was why I lightened her purse from time to time, to prove that I wasn't plagued by all that pity that welled up in me like sick each time I saw her life buggered up by one lousy marriage which she had stayed in until she had become this automatic wife, this ageing runner-up).

BWSBN passed that first little test of mine with flying colours and when, the following day, I was insulted by a local lout, he astonished me by telling that bully where to get off, in no uncertain terms. Blow me if this BWSBN—who blushed scarlet whenever he got within a stone's throw of me—didn't both stick his neck out and let his feelings fly. After that, I can't say, hand on my heart, that I started to fancy him back. But intrigued, I most certainly was.

Days later, when the blacks landed en masse, he, Mum, me, Roger and Eileen were huddled in the middle of the esplanade, having followed Dad and the other arrested people down the high street. Rather than watch from the railings like everyone else, Mum had wanted us to hang back so we could keep our eyes on Dad. To our left there was a parked car obstructing the road, the driver sitting still as a stone at the wheel and another standing by the open passenger door, staring seaward.

The fact that quite a few of those boat people were mutilated dawned on me in a series of double-takes: that kid there didn't have a hand, that lady there's sleeve was dangling loose... Between them, they packed their boats sardine-style against the beach's back wall, then filed up the steps from the beach onto the esplanade, where their armbanded hosts guided them into the village into whose streets they melted like so much butter.

Only then did the villagers—who had been glued to the railings as if before a firework display—break ranks, the men stifling fake coughs and eyeing the blacks (one of whom had the most horribly disfigured face) who were still on guard. Seeing that these weren't making any moves, the villagers took their spouses or partners or children by the hand—*Come on come on*—and began to walk away from the railings as briskly as they dared. One middle-aged woman was crying on her own, hands pressed to face.

But her fellow villagers didn't do anything, just as people don't when they see someone being mugged in the street or insulted on the Tube, to take two examples I'd witnessed myself. The bystander effect. Whatever.

(Or perhaps, it struck me later, the reason she was ignored was that she wasn't from the village. Had the blacks not warned us in black and white that any stray visitor who chose not to turn back upon seeing the warning signs would be taken into the village by main force and be subject to the new rules—the obligatory phoned excuse, the obligatory stay—now in place there?)

Without a word of warning Mum strode towards the spot at the railings where Dad and the others were still tied together, watched by their three guards. Me and the kids stayed put.

She was a stone's throw away when the girl escort raised a stop sign of a hand: *Usiende mbele zaidi tafadhari.*

I can't understand a word you say; don't you speak English?

275

The girl looked at her, then pointed off to the left, in the direction of the pub, the Community Centre, the police station: *Watahifadhiwa chini ya ulinzi wa kufuri na funguo.*

Mum was beside herself now, her pitch practically soprano: *What what what are you saying, for God's sake?* I glanced at Dad, who had turned his head so it was now in profile, one birdlike eye fixed on us. I gave him a jerk of a wave and what I could muster of a smile. The eye didn't waver.

Next thing we knew, the group of prisoners—Greg, Dad, the village policewoman, three of the village lads, including that lout I mentioned—were obliged by their escorts to face westward. The girl escort raised her voice a tad—*Njia hii hapa!*—and waved them on, casual as a teacher on a school hike. They shuffled along the esplanade and over the road, heedful not to jerk their nylon nooses. The boozers on the pub terrace watched Dad and his little retinue pass by, with a solemnity fit for a cortège.

As did we, until Mum belted out: *John, are you all right?* Dad, like the other prisoners, kept his eyes focussed on the tarmac.

I felt a dash of BWSBN's breath: *I'd say they're being taken to the Community Centre.*

Bingo, BWSBN, bingo. You did sometimes get it right.

Dad and the others were brought to a halt smack outside the Centre. Barbie-sized by distance, the girl escort rapped hard on the door and shouted: *Hodi hodi.* It was opened from the inside and the prisoners were marched in. Two of the escorts—including the man with the horrid face—followed them in, while the girl stayed outside, leaning against the door almost as soon as it was slammed shut.

Mum, trying to keep her hysteria in abeyance, whined: *What in God's name are they going to do with him?*

She was saved from further agonising by countless felicitous cries. Behind us, sash windows were opening and villagers were waving like loons from behind their sills. Those who hadn't yet left the esplanade turned back to look at the sea.

A lone skiff was coming in, rowed at an even pace by two black women. Bobbing in it were Simon, the policeman and that old local, Mr whatshisname. Feather. As soon as the boat hit the beach, the rowers jumped out, hauled it up onto the sand and headed off into the village. The watching locals hastened down to the beach and began to handshake and backslap the returnees. My brother, the policeman and the codger tried to answer the grinned questions. Words were blown in our direction: *fine... treated correctly... chilly down there.*

Simon finally spotted us standing in the middle of the esplanade road, flabbergasted statues. He gave us a wave and a smile. Mum clasped her mouth, as if wanting to shut herself up while the tiniest of tears hung on for dear life to the corners of her eyes. Simon said goodbye to the backslapping locals and trotted up the steps and over to us.

The few blacks who were still around weren't paying any attention to the brouhaha. On the contrary, the three or four blacks that I could see were still looking rather dreamy, pebble-calm eyes surveying the sea.

Simon hugged me, then gave me a smacker of a kiss on the cheek: *All right there, Luce?* I realised for the first time that he'd had what amounted to a kind of secret life ever since he'd joined the army aged eighteen—things he saw, things he heard, things he did and saw done, that I was not ever going to hear about, not from that horse's mouth of his, its teeth bared.

Come on, Mum, no need for the waterworks; I was not mistreated.

Mum's droplets had broken free and were legging it down her cheeks, the eyes at a complete loss as to how to look at her released son.

I'm all right, Mum, right as rain.

He tossed a question to the kids: *Everything all right with you blokes and bints?* They nodded, shy as six-year-olds, BWSBN included. Simon grinned at them, then back at Mum, then back at me, but his eyes weren't seeing us, but the blacks, I could tell: manifold thoughts of the blacks were brewing up those brown eyes of his.

Despite everything, as we headed back to Seaview Heights, the balloon of tension we had all been suspended in was now, bit by bit, thankfully farting itself flat. At least we knew exactly where Dad was being held, and, even more positively, that Simon was OK.

When we got to the door, I turned to Mum, struck by a question so obvious it surprised me I hadn't asked it earlier: *By the way, what was Dad doing, exactly, up there in the Manse?*

Her mouth opened, her eyebrows dove, her eyes shifted: *I don't know, Lucy, I really don't.*

*

Every soul in the village read the fairly reassuring communiqué published the following morning.

We were all at table except Mum, to whom I'd taken a cup of tea in bed. Simon jabbed a finger at the left-hand column: *What's all this gobbledy-gook, some kind of joke?* When I pointed out to him, in jest, that the English half of the communiqué was at least a lot less boring than the usual dreary drivel to be found in the Coldwater Bay Parish Press, he gave me a look that made my crown sweat: *Livelier, sis? Is that all you can think about, with Dad in the clink, Mum worried sick, English people being held hostage in their own village by a bunch of Negroes?*

No, Simon dear, that was not all I could think about, but the way the communiqué had been written had, to a certain extent, taken the sharp edge off my fretting: serious though these people clearly were about whatever it was that they were up to, they were neither roughnecks nor sickos, and appeared, at least, to have come in peace.

Roger put in his ha'penny's worth: *It's a fact that coloured people already spend plenty of time in the sun; so what would they want a holiday for?*

Simon tutted: *They're not on any bloody holiday; when I went out just now, pairs of them were moving from car to car with tubes and jerry cans, siphoning the petrol straight out of the tanks, methodical-like. They're up to something, aren't they?*

Mum appeared at the kitchen door looking like she needed a blood transfusion. Simon jumped up, kissed her on the cheek, and pulled out a seat for her into which she plopped, eyes fixed on her son, ignoring my enquiries as to whether she wanted another cup of tea: *What did they do to you, Simon?*

Nothing, Mum.

She wagged her finger at him: *I want to know what happened.* From her bag, open on the table, she pulled open cigarettes and a lighter and lit up.

Unhurriedly, he told us about the flattening of the Range Rover's pedal to the floor as he and the policeman headed pell-mell for Freshwater; the lone sheep planted in the middle of the road; the necessary braking to a halt; the springing up of two black men and one black woman from the flanking ditches; their forcing of the door locks, the firm removal of Simon and the policeman, the patting down; the driving off of the car by the woman; the trot chop-chop down the hill and all the way over to the cliff's edge, escorted by the two men; the throwing down of the rope ladder, the precarious descent into a waiting skiff, which set off at once into tunnel darkness; the cave in which there were several more manned boats in one of which sat old Mr Feather; the daily meals of fluffy white stodge; the brief visit by a white man in a duffle coat that was too big for him; the eventual return by boat to the village: *They didn't touch a hair on my head, Mum.* He was pulling out all the stops to put Mum at her ease.

She nodded, lips pursed almost into invisibility: *That's all right then, isn't it?*

As I cleared up the breakfast things—the communiqué splayed bilingual on the kitchen table—I ran recent events back and forth: all the kerfuffle at the Manse, then Dad, the other prisoners and the villagers at the esplanade railings, the boats sneaking in from the sea, the black people tramping or limping up the sand, Dad being carted off. Simon's return.

They seemed to have treated Simon pretty much with kid gloves, and the policeman and that local codger ditto. I could only assume they were looking after Dad in similar fashion.

So, I was more intrigued—excited, even—than worried. I wanted to get outdoors as soon as possible, to find out what was up, to get the lie of the changed land.

My darling brother, however, had decided that same morning to keep me under lock and key: *You're not going out there on your own, not with the blacks all over the shop—no way. The door stays locked at all times; as do the windows.*

I snapped my hands onto my hips: *Why, what do you think they're going to do to me, Simon?*

*

Towards midday, when our hermetically sealed kitchen reeked of armpits, smeared Formica and traces of ciggie smoke, Simon looked at his watch and stood up: *Right, I'm going to try and parley-vous with whoever's in charge.*

No sooner had his key clicked the street door shut behind him than Mum too got up, forcing a smile: *I'm feeling rather tired, Lucy, I think I'd be better off back in bed.*

That's OK, Mum, we'll be fine here.

She'd left her bag on the table. BWSBN looked at me expectantly—there always was more gumption to that boy than met the eye (as became only too obvious later on)—as I widened its leather flaps, peeked in and plucked out her door key.

At their own request, Eileen and Roger remained indoors.

*

The first thing we saw, me and BWSBN, as we stepped out into that crisp April morning, was a couple of elderly Negro men having a jaw-wag as they sat on our very wall. A group of coloured children, the oldest couldn't have been six, were playing marbles with pebbles a little way up the pavement.

As we walked, speechless, towards the high street, our attention was caught by a boarding house on our left, in a first-floor window of which a middle-aged lady—the phrase 'big black mamma' did come to mind—in a multicoloured wrap was hanging a waterfall of wet clothes out on the sill. As naturally as if she'd been living here for yonks, she nodded a smile: *Habari za asubuhi?*

When we reached the high street, I laughed out loud: *Wow gosh heavens.*

I was a pupil of Cheltenham at the time, one of the tippest-toppest girls' schools in the country, in whose Lower College human beings were explained to us with a map of the world that showed how they were divided into three races, three: in the north-west sat a clean-cut 'Caucasian'; lurking in the eastern corner was a shifty-looking Chinaman, labelled 'Mongoloid'; even worse was the grumpy monkey crouching in the wastes of the south, labelled 'Negroid'. We gals were taught to carry that map in our heads, not having a jot or tittle of evidence to contradict it, our only contact with 'Negroids' being the music the successful ones sang or the sight of the far more frequent non-successful ones as they packed shelves and scrubbed floors. And swept streets.

But that was as nothing compared to the suspicions about them sucked up since infancy from the colourless air of home, that glum air into which Dad snapped or muttered or roared or pontificated his opinions about people of colour and, although he kept his language battened down, the child that I had been could make out the outlines, shifting and gristly, of the thoughts crawling beneath, hinted at by Dad's timbre and pitch, his delectation in certain ambiguous adjectives, so that suspicions of the dark-skinned were breathed in by me, accumulating until they were packed tight as dust in a Hoover.

Questioned all at once by this sudden surprise, a surprise like that of waking up in childhood winters to find my surroundings fattened up by snow.

For me, that morning still stands out, that morning which snapped the mustiness of home out of me in one go, so that I felt no heavier than my own skin, so that bubbles small as pinpricks rose to tickle the inside of my skull.

Up and down, hither and thither they strolled, the blacks, the young men's backs straight as poles, the elderly ones slouching in their wraps, a few middle-aged ones strolling in open-necked shirts and crumpled chinos (here and there, aided by a crutch). We stepped into this thick trickle of black, BWSBN and I, and the blacks stepped around us, hands in pockets if they had any (pockets or hands), not one of them paying us a blind bit of notice. He splayed his hands to indicate amazement: *This is just—*

I giggled, cutting myself off before the giggle twisted up into a shriek: *I know.*

As we were passing by the café, BWSBN peered through the pane: *Got any change on you, Luce?*

Enjoying breakfast and various beverages were a couple of families, a table of yackety-yakking teenage girls, and a young couple who were holding hands over the top of a corner table. All of an ace-of-spades shade except for the woman who ran the place—blonde, fattish, late thirties—who stood beside the urn, staring into space out of a face flat with shock.

She started upon seeing us at her counter: *You're the first English people I've seen all day.* Mechanically, she poured two cups of tea; hand tremors made the spout quiver: *It's tea or tea, nothing else left.*

When I asked her what I owed her, she leaned forward, close enough for me to sniff gin traces: *I don't know how we came to this.* Then tapped the no-sale key on the till.

From the opened drawer she took a small, oval seashell and placed it before me. I turned it between thumb and forefinger: *Looks pretty.*

Well, this is all you can use for money while this lot are around. They woke me up this morning, told me to open up, which I hadn't planned on doing, and gave me a bunch of these. She leaned closer, her breasts squashing against the varnished counter: *Cowry shells, love; there's not one of them has a penny to his name so they use these—*she pointed to the sample shell—*which I have been told in no uncertain terms are the only legal tender now accepted in Coldwater Bay.* She straightened up and slid the teas over: *This is on the house, loves; next time, make sure you bring your cowries.*

We sat down at one of the few free tables and just looked at each other for few moments. When we got round to sipping our tea, I spotted the girl. The one who yesterday had helped escort Dad and the others from the Manse to the esplanade, and from there to the Community Centre. She was seated next to the window's steamy glass, her plaits pulled back over the crown of her head, and watching the street, eyes alert. A brand-new white anorak sat baggily on her. Her white armband had been retied around the upper sleeve. No one else there was wearing one. I called BWSBN's attention to her. He looked for a moment, before concluding, quietly: *She must be one of the troops.*

What?

He lowered his voice to a whisper so low it practically touched the floor: *All the ones who stand guard, who seem to be organising things, they're always wearing those things, like a uniform.*

And all the others?

Civilians under their protection.

Behind those half-narrowed eyes of his, I knew, lurked all sorts of scraps of arcane military knowledge involving epaulettes and stripes and pips and crowns, Spitfire and Hurricane silhouettes, the different roars made by Stuka dive-bombers and kamikaze Zeros (I had overheard him imitating them), of jolly names for regiments—doughboys and Desert Foxes, Canucks and Anzacs and bootnecks—and those faux foreign phrases he let slip when with his sort-of-pal Roger when they made their dolls lob pineapples at Jerry and fire tracer rounds and cover each other while the enemy dolls spluttered: *Britisher dumbkopfs, Tommy schweinhunds.* In that misty-windowed, black-packed village café, I could see that it was all grist to the mill of this hero to be, the hero he fancied was curled up inside him. He tore his eyes away from the solemn armbanded girl at the window and gave me a confirmatory nod: *Paramilitary backup.*

I suggested we left.

*

There was a shimmer upon the sea, delivered off a reluctant April sun. I saw something going on opposite the pub, and grabbed BWSBN by the arm: *Come on, there's something up.*

A queue of some thirty whites (before I'd never have thought of them as 'whites,' but now they stood out in the everyday blackness like pig's ears in a shepherd's pie) had formed in front of a company phone box: one of those grey pavement objects I'd always passed in the street without noticing but which I had to notice now because its doors had been flung open so that two black girls with wicker satchels slung round their shoulders could sort through the hundreds of coloured cables in there, as confidently as if plaiting hair, applying crimp tools and cable strippers to ply and snip and re-splice. They didn't take long to connect a single line running out of that unkempt tangle to a small blue box no bigger than a pack of fags.

One of them turned to the waiting queue: *Karibia wote wamekwisha!* She removed a set of headphones from her satchel while the other one removed two cables and an orange telephone, from hers.

I nudged BWSBN: *What's with the phone?*

He cupped his hand at my ear: *Lineman's handset; I've seen post office engineers use them to make free calls when they're testing lines.* He really did have his moments.

The girls connected this handset thing and the headphones to the blue box. Then one of them put on the 'phones and listened for a moment, before thumbs-upping the other. The Parish Press communiqué, fresh as lettuce in my mind, had been telling us no lie: at noon on the dot, they had reconnected a phone line.

That big disfigured man appeared, his face as off-putting as ever. He stood behind the company box, arms folded, eyes on the queuers. Amongst them, I recognised the elderly lady from the sweet and souvenir shop and, at the head, that hippieish guy in the corduroy suit. The girl who'd tested the headphones stood up, turned round and waved in the direction of the pub on whose terrace several blacks and one white man were seated: *Jonas!*

The white man—I say white, but he had a bit of the gypsy about him—got up, picked up his chair and negotiated his way with it past the other tables and over to the connection box. He was vaguely familiar. BWSBN got there before I did: *I saw that man once, in the corner shop.*

The man greeted the women—*Habari za kazi?*—and placed his chair next to the box. He sat down and put on the headphones. One of the women dialled a number on the handset and spoke into it: *Kila kitu sawa?* He said: *Loud and clear sawa sawa.* The women burst out laughing. Kids, they seemed to be to me, kids on the last day of term.

He pulled off the headphones, and addressed the queue: *Good morning, everybody, and thank you so much for coming; I understand you each have a phone call to make to someone who may be expecting to see you within the coming fortnight. Please do use our recommended excuse—a persistent stomach bug, there being a local outbreak—for not being able to leave Coldwater Bay. Please say that the doctor has advised you that the outbreak might last as long as two weeks but not longer. If asked who this doctor is, given that some of your interlocutors may know Coldwater Bay lacks one of its own, you will please to inform them that he is a London GP on a holiday visit, one doctor Whitebone—I repeat, Whitebone. The conversations should be kept short but not unrealistically so; I will be monitoring what you say and at the first hint of any straying from the agreed script, I will pull the plug and request that you call back and ensure that your callee does not feel anything is amiss.*

He returned to his seat and re-donned his headphones: *Let's get this over and done with.* One of the black women held out the handset to the hippie type at the head of the queue. The whitish man looked at him, eyes glossy with gravitas: *Please do go ahead.* The hippie, hesitant, took the handset, dialled a number and, face flexed, held it to his ear: *Alex, is that you? Look, I won't be able to make it to Letchford tonight; I'm afraid I'm a bit poorly...*

I would have gone on listening, momentarily tickled pink by the idea of listening to all these grown-ups fib their heads off in the open street. But BWSBN grabbed my arm: *Your bro at seven o'clock.* Damn his sham flyboy talk: *Where?* He nodded over his shoulder. Sure enough, Simon was strolling along the esplanade, eyeing the blacks who were lounging at the railing.

Quick, before he sees us!

Me and BWSBN hotfooted it up the high street and off back home. Or 'home'.

*

Mum was sitting in the kitchen with Eileen and Roger. She didn't give me the dressing-down I'd been expecting for having pinched her keys and gone out without permission. On the contrary, surprise of surprises, the kettle was on and some eggy bread was frying on the stove and she was smiling: *You must be feeling peckish.* She got up and began to dole out the food: *Don't just stand there like a pair of stuffed owls, come and get it.* She turned to the table, full plates in hand.

We were still working our way through the eggy bread when Mum asked us if we wanted to play something to fill in the time until Simon got back. With a wary eye (I knew by now he abhorred cards) BWSBN asked what sort of game she had in mind.

Well, I was wondering if charades would be to everyone's taste.

Charades? Now? With everything that was going on? With these incomprehensible blacks thronging the streets, and us obliged to stay here longer than planned, and, above all, Dad locked away for we knew not what?

Eileen had barely gulped down the last of her lunch: *Charades?*

Mum blew a stream of smoke out of the corner of her mouth: *That's right; why don't you start, Eileen? You know the rules, don't you? You can do a film, a play, or a personage.*

In the main we plumped for flicks, though Roger flummoxed us all by trying to be Churchill, because despite his V sign and air-cigar puffing there was no way we could see Sir Winston in that dour face of his. BWSBN did *The Dambusters, The Bridge Over the River Kwai* and *The Green Berets.* Occasionally someone would encourage Mum to join in, but each time she shook her head until, finally, the fun being on the wane, she got off her bottom: *OK, last one's mine.*

She raised both arms and clasped her hands above her head, then unclasped them and brought them back down to her sides.

Is it a film, a play or a personage?

Mum put on a thoughtful expression: *Personage, in a way, I suppose* and back up went the arms; and again she clasped her hands above her head. Her eyes swept our vacant looks. I was starting to feel a bit embarrassed for her. We ventured a ballet dancer, a circus performer, a mime artist.

No, don't you see?

It being written on our faces that we did not, she put her hands on her hips and with a lilt to stress how easy-peasy it was, said: *God, it is simply God.*

She repeated a speeded-up version of her charade: arms up, hands clasped, arms back down.

God forms an all-compassing whole, so if we could see him, he would be circular in nature.

Not even Roger, the foot-in-bucket boy par excellence, had a word to blurt to that.

*

Brother Simon came back early that evening, carrying a full shopping bag. We were in the kitchen, having a cup of tea. (We had so many cups of tea back then, they practically merged into each other.) He'd tried, he explained, to visit Dad at the Community Centre and had been turned back by the black woman at the door (who had refused to understand his English). For a while, I had been mulling ever more frequently over the scene we'd observed up at the Manse. What on earth might have Dad done there that warranted him being carted off to an improvised clink?

Simon plonked the bag down, his face a sneer: *Guess who's helping make all this shit possible?*

Unfazed by his barracks language, I asked to whom he was referring as regarded the continuance of said 'shit'. He prodded the table top: *That Arab bloke*—another prod—*was spotted driving out this morning, went through the gap that we bloody made and got up onto on the main road, heading out, probably over to Ventnor*—prod number three—*came back with that Rover of his piled up with food and drink, then doled out the goods to baldy in the corner shop and Mrs whatshername with the fish shop and the pub landlord and the woman running the caff and the old bat at the sweet shop*—prod the fourth—*forks out for the lot himself, I've been reliably informed, no skin off his nose, rich as Croesus; and to think he could have taken the opportunity to tell the authorities about what's going on! Christ!*

Our Roger asked the obvious question: *So why do the blacks trust the Arab gentleman so much?* There was what a bona fide author would have called a pregnant pause. Simon muttered something about Dad maybe having been right all along.

I turned to Mum, who was sitting with her arms folded and glaring at her son: *Perhaps your father gave the Arab gentleman good reason to be grateful to these Africans, and they know it.*

Simon blushed, which I hadn't seen him do since I was a little girl and he, an as-yet-unarmed teenager: *What makes you so absolutely sure they're from Africa, Mum?*

Not a jot did the glaring diminish: *It's no good changing the subject, Simon.*

*

(Saturday 20ᵗʰ)

On day two after the Arrival Of The Blacks, Simon came back from a morning walk and announced that we kids could, finally, accompany him outdoors that afternoon if we wished: *Seems safe enough.*

BWSBN got his *yes* in even before I did. Roger and Eileen, on the other hand, shook their heads. They were settling in to what would turn out to be a full-time indoor routine: breakfast, whist, rummy, lunch, Careers, miniature chess, supper and bedtime interrupted from time to time by *The Archers* (which Eileen followed) and *Just a Minute* (which Roger found funny) and occasional countings of Roger's Green Shield stamp collection. Sitting it out, that was all that concerned them now:

waiting for the whole business to blow over, the kitchen their bomb shelter. Mum, on the other hand, only seemed to stop at home to make our meals. After breakfast she went scavenging, as she put it, and that would be the last we'd see of her until around one. After lunch, she would have a wee siesta, as she also put it, and then would be off again until suppertime. She claimed these daily disappearances were shopping expeditions, but I never saw her come back with much to show for them.

*

That afternoon, at Simon's bidding, BWSBN and I popped on our anoraks, and followed him out of the house.

The high street was busier than the day before. I felt not thrilled, as I had been yesterday, but light-headed and at ease. Simon had wanted to walk us up the hill so he could have a word with his ex–fellow captive, the police constable, now posted at the road block: *Amazing how they healed his hands, right as rain just hours after they smeared them with some ointment.*

From the direction of the beach we heard a faint, fast drumming peppered by a faster, tambourine-like rattle. Simon was off like a whippet: *Stay right behind me.*

We hurried past the phone box those girls had been fiddling with—its door now padlocked—tripped down the steps to the beach and joined the crowd (several dozen people, including a handful of fellow whites) that was gathering on the sand.

Half a dozen boats had been placed, keels up, in a semi-circle in the centre of which, their backs almost touching the hulls, stood two drummers in wide-brimmed straw hats, one speed-whacking a set of four barrel-sized wooden drums with two long sticks, the other pawing five wooden bongos as deftly as a find-the-lady man, producing a rhythmic shushing that meshed with the rapid-fire bonks of his co-musician. Together with everyone else, I stared at those dashing hands, those blurred sticks, transfixed by the resulting tattoo.

Everyone else except Simon, who was peering about, clocking the audience, hand-shielding his eyes from that day's surprisingly bright sun: *What's all this in aid of?*

Eti! Eti! Eti!

Half a dozen blacks who must have been crouching out of sight on the far side of the boats now vaulted the keels and began to stamp their feet in the space between the drummers and the crowd, the women dancers in loudly coloured wraps and the men in white shirts and shorts and red fezzes. They fanned out, legs bending and hips shivering to the music. As I watched their feet entwining and separating in moves brief as the briefest of air kisses, I understood a story of sorts was being told, at the centre of which were the men in the fez-zes, whose posturing and stick swishing were having circles danced around them by the ladies.

As those feet beat the sand, as the smiles flashed involuntarily from the dancers' faces, showing they'd got it better than right, as their limbs worked tricks of movement, I felt I was on the verge of making a leap that, once taken, would show me things I hadn't dreamed of until then: the world, which before had seemed such a narrow, regulated space, now puffed up before me, fat with air, then burst, leaving no limits to cling to, no compass points to follow, no rules to abide by.

After who knew how long, the dancers formed a line, turned to show profiles only, then danced off stage right, the men in white giving symbolic swipes to the women in colours, until all had weaved their way out of sight, back behind the upturned boats. The drummers continued for a few seconds before coming to a simultaneous standstill.

The blacks in the audience burst into an applause on whose coat-tails the villagers added a few claps. As the drummers half bowed, a short, grey-haired, bow-legged black man in weather-beaten khaki shorts and flip-flops and a brand-new anorak (from under which a Hawaiian shirt flashed when it got the chance) stepped onto the bottom of the middle-most boat, coughed—he was holding a loudhailer, a cardboard cone, and looked ever so cross—and gave come-on-up waves to someone behind him.

Who, when he climbed into view, turned out to be the off-white man in the duffle coat—the one who'd monitored the phone calls—who stood to the right of the old man, who again looked behind at someone: *You too fat to get up here?* A uniformed leg came into view, as the police sergeant levered himself onto the boat bottom. Once fully on board, the policeman straightened up, feet apart, arms folded. He looked tired.

The old man raised the loudhailer: *We noticed a lot of you local people are spending all your time indoors.* I twigged only then that, unlike his black fellows, he was actually speaking in English.

Jonas, tell them.

The duffle-coated man took hold of the hailer: *Villagers of Coldwater Bay, Mzee is right: you are absolutely free to do as you wish within the confines of the village. No harm can or will come to you. The streets are safe. There will be no shortage of food or drink. What is more, each evening there will be a barbecue on the beach to which everyone is invited. Are there any questions?*

Someone called out: *Where you all from?*

The old man, Mzee, called back: *Haven't you been able to guess?*

The off-white man, Jonas, went on: *As some of you have already discovered, your local currency system has been replaced by one of our own devising.* Walete nje!

This last was called over his shoulder to the members of the troupe, who now jogged out from behind the circle of upturned boats, six from one side and six from the other, wearing their street clothes (jeans and T-shirts and loose sweaters).

They dumped a bunch of net bags packed with shells in front of the crowd, as Jonas continued to shout: *We already have plenty; take them, and hand them out to all the other villagers—free money!*

He handed the loudhailer to the sergeant, who added: *I strongly recommend that you follow Mr Cole's instructions and help distribute the temporary currency which has been placed before us: in an orderly fashion, if you would.*

So this Jonas's surname was Cole. Jonas Cole. Snappy. Without thinking, I ran out past the blacks who were standing in front of me, and picked up a bag of shells. Jogging back, I shook the bag, heard it clatter.

Fun, it struck me, to have this new way of buying things, fun offered to us on a tray by people who—I was starting to believe—wished us no harm and who, for reasons that were good enough for them, would depart in peace at their appointed time, after having released Dad and the others, I now was certain, without incident.

Even as I returned to ranks, other villagers had stepped out and were picking up bags of cowries, with the casual solemnity of customers taking food out of a self-service counter.

The sergeant started up again: *As Mr Cole and Mr Mzee here have assured us, Coldwater Bay is indeed safe as houses, so there is no need for anyone to stick at home. I now wish to make a formal announcement. As you know, last Thursday, Dr John Whitebone, a GP from London; ex-WPC Lorraine Woodstock;*

Greg Crofton and his son Kevin; and two of the latter's friends and accomplices, whose names I will withhold to save unnecessary embarrassment to their families, were apprehended and placed in custody at the Community Centre. Tomorrow, Sunday the 21st of April, at 9am, on the lawn of Stockside Manse, the three minors will make a full confession and apology for their misdemeanours in the presence of their victims, namely Mr Khoury, proprietor of the said premises, his lady wife, and their offspring. Anybody who wishes to attend may do so. Thank you for your attention.

The policeman stepped gingerly down off the boat bottom. As soon as he hit the sand, some of the older villagers went up and buttonholed him. The drummers picked up their gear and hauled it away. Mzee and Jonas Cole strolled over to the steps that led up to the esplanade, Jonas listening, the old man complaining loudly to him in their language. The crowd began to disperse. Simon hadn't moved an inch: *Why isn't Dad going to be at this apology at the Manse tomorrow? What are they bleeding playing at, these people?*

*

When I got back to Seaview Heights, me and Eileen decided to do some housework, seeing as Mum had apparently gone on strike in that department (she was reading a magazine at the table, engrossed, oblivious to all and sundry). Meanwhile, the boys were tidying up their room, having been militarily spurred on by Simon: *I'll be coming to inspect your kit; if I spot so much as one fold out of place, it'll be curtains for you!*

We were finishing up, fiveish, and the boys had just come back down, when Simon slipped his windcheater on: *Off to get a bit more gen.* Roger and Eileen were busy removing the lid from the Careers box, and Mum's eyes didn't budge a millimetre from the article she was reading. Me and BWSBN watched Simon zip up.

Bit bored, are you? I was planning on having a word with the landlord; you two can come along and sit outside on the pub terrace, if you want.

Daylight was barely on the wane, the air was brisk and tinged with unaccustomed, unidentifiable smells.

*

At one of the tables on the terrace, four men were watching their cards, their free hands resting protectively on little heaps of cowries. Occasionally chuckling, occasionally wittering. They weren't drinking much—on the contrary, they seemed to be ticking off the seconds with a certain pleasure, as unconcerned by the passage of time as swans on a lake.

The same woman who'd mopped up some ginger beer spilled by BWSBN on our first day in Coldwater Bay came out bearing a tray laden with cans of beer.

A pong of dregs and ash hit us the moment we crossed the threshold. The barman fastened eager eyes on my brother: *All right there, Simon?* and pointed at us: *They can come in if they want, the old rules no longer apply.*

When we made it through the mainly black clientele to the bar, the man, ignoring us kids, leaned forward, pally-like, to address Simon alone: *What's it to be?* Simon ordered a dark rum for himself and asked what soft drinks were in stock. It turned out that that evening there was nowt but Tizer, which I didn't like (BWSBN neither). Simon nodded at a bowl on the bar: *What's that when it's at home?* The barman tutted: *Some kind of nut they brought over with them; very insistent, they are, that I always keep a bowl handy.* Simon examined one between finger and thumb—a biggish, yellow nut with a criss-cross pattern at one end—before tossing it back into the bowl. He leaned forward over the bar, over which, as I've said, the barman was doing some leaning himself. It was a miracle the tips of their noses didn't meet. The barman peeped left and right: *Geoff's been in.*

I quietly informed a furrow-browed BWSBN that Geoffrey was the police sergeant's Christian name.

The barman topped Simon up: *There's going to be a proper trial later on in the week: your old man, Greg Crofton, and Lorraine as well.*

A little bird informed me something odd happened up the hill; to do with my dad and the towelhead.

Your dad thought the Arab was in on all this, didn't he? And given the way that particular camel-breeding gent is helping this lot out now, well, personally, I think your Dad was right.

Is there a day fixed for the trial?

Geoff said they won't tell him yet; perhaps they're worried we natives might get restless if we know in advance.

Will you?

We might.

The pub began to empty. In a matter of minutes, there was just us and the barman and three villagers, middle-aged men who were sitting in different corners, eyeing each other, like I'd seen homos do once in a park. Simon bobbed a nod at the door: *Tell you what, Luce, I'd like to have a word in private with the landlord here.* The rotter, ridding himself of us like that.

We were just leaving, anyway, bro.

Out I trounced, with BWSBN in tow. Besides, I was curious to see where all the black customers had gone so suddenly.

A gust blew us a clue. Twirls of smoke, flicked hither and thither by sea gust, were rising from the beach. We crossed the road and leaned over the esplanade rail.

The beach was now chock-a-block with blacks seated in circles, at the centre of which were plates full of steaming meat. They hunkered down, clutching knees, or lolled on deckchairs. A little way off was a large metal grill—supported at the corners by large beach stones—on which chunks of beef were being turned over and over by a team of men and women who occasionally ladled out a thin sauce from a bucket that hissed into a spicy-lemony aroma as soon as it hit the flesh. Unaccustomed smells.

The puffy clouds on the horizon were growing grubby, and the shadows of the eating people were lengthening inch by inch, overlapping, criss-crossing. Children were running from circle to circle, their sprinkled giggles barely hearable, their smiles oddly familiar (from all the photos we had seen of the universal black child, grinning in gratitude for our mites on charity tins or in money-grubbing ads surrounded with dotted lines).

These clusters of people, their colourful shirts and pangas half-obscured by lacklustre British anoraks and duffle coats and windcheaters, skin petted by flurries of salted air, covered the sand from esplanade wall to beach edge, snug in the outdoors.

Someone poked my spine; I gave a little yell. Simon had left the pub and snuck up behind us.

Crikey, get a load of that: Butlins for coloureds. Come on, time you two were getting off home.

Trust BWSBN to notice, as we turned away from the beach, that the sweet shop was open. Marzipan things were now visible in the window, and a freshly written sign was hanging from the taps of the Mr Whippy machine: SINGLE CONE ONE COWRY ONLY. BWSBN started to head over: *I wonder how many seashells she wants for a Ninety-Nine Flake?*

I laughed. He glanced at me, pleased. Sweaty, awkward, bumbling, mumbling BWSBN had cracked a joke that I had actually found funny. But not so funny as to make me keep on laughing the way I was—whoops that subsided into gurgles then reappeared as further whoops—and as each whoop went skyward it took with it a gram of tension, an ounce of worry, a pinch of fear. BWSBN didn't take five seconds to start giggling himself, a fit so loud and tremulous that if we hadn't been in this anomalous, edgy, extraordinary and unpredictable situation, I might have worried about the way his jaw gaped and his shoulders shook and his vocal chords hiccupped yuks punctuated by guffaws, and every time we caught each other's eye my whoops and chuckles and his typewriter-fast laughs got another jump-start, and forth came more histrionic merriment. I avoided Simon's irritated stare, bending over, hands on knees, until I had calmed down a bit. BWSBN, too, was at the whew stage, dregs of giggles breaking through deep breaths.

The sweet shop lady spoke so clearly that each word sounded crafted: *My, you two do seem excited.*

She was watching us from her column-flanked entrance. She had fine grey hair done up in a bun, and was wearing a dress covered in blue-and-white flecks: *Well, I suppose it is rather exciting, isn't it, all these people who've come to visit us?*

Exciting? Is that what you think it is? Simon's tone of voice was downright rude. She turned her attention to him, her demeanour unruffled: *I think it's more interesting than alarming, let's put it like that.*

What, you know them or something? Simon glared at her while indicating everything going on behind him—strolling blacks, rising smoke, beach chat in God knew which tongues—with a jerk of his arm.

I can't say I know exactly who they are, but I spent quite a while living amongst people fairly similar to them.

Oh yes?

She was addressing him with the same sweetness as she had us: *My late husband was a district officer in Okigwi, Nigeria, for nigh on twenty years.*

These people from Nigeria then?

The lady shrugged off a chuckle: *No, my dear. To begin with, their language is not one I recognise; and I learnt to recognise all the big Nigerian ones. To go by the look of them, I'd say they come from all over the continent.*

You can spot differences between them?

Oh dear me, yes; Africa is a many-splendored place, you know.

Simon ran an eye over the marzipan items in the window and the tower of cones standing next to the ice cream machine: *You've had stuff delivered recently, haven't you? It's the Arab, right?*

The lady kept smiling: *Perhaps.*

Before Simon could say anything rash, as his freshly clenched jaw told me he was about to do, she stepped to the machine, whipped a cone from the container, and spiralled out a generous ice cream which she handed at once to BWSBN— *There you are, little man*—and while he went redder than velvet she leaned back inside the door, pulled a stick of rock from an open box and handed it to me: *A souvenir from Coldwater Bay, my dear.*

*

(Sunday 21ˢᵗ)

The sun was up bright the morning after. Dazzling enough to make us visor our eyes as soon as the three of us—me and Simon and Mum—stepped outdoors.

*

In the middle of the Manse's front lawn, a rectangular table had been placed, and on the table, a microphone wired to a hi-fi amp, which was connected in turn to a speaker perched in the crook of a branch of the nearest elm. The table had been borrowed from the pub terrace, as had the benches laid out before it. These were already packed with villagers, amongst whom I spotted the long-haired man in corduroy, the fishwife, the sweet shop lady, the shopkeeper with that little girl, and an elderly man whom it took me a minute to clock as Mr Feather (released on the beach, three days ago, together with Simon and the constable). Not a soul was drinking or chattering this time round. Armbanded guards had been posted at the gate, at the door of the Manse itself, and next to the elm. Another was sitting on the sill of one of the first-floor windows, legs swinging.

Behind the table stood the sergeant and that once-captive constable, elbow to elbow, the latter with a black notebook open in one hand and a biro in the other.

As soon as we stepped past the gate guard into the garden, the shopkeeper stood up and waved: *Mrs Whitebone! I have kept some space for your party!* That's nice of him, I thought, as Mum led us past people's knees to where the little girl was saving three places with her hands and bottom. The shopkeeper pulled her onto his lap and voilà, me and Simon and Mum could sit down.

BWSBN had had to stay behind with Eileen and Roger, Simon having insisted that our group be limited to family only.

People sat waiting, eyes fixed mainly on the two policemen, whose authority made the present, perhaps, seem not so strange, nor so unsettling, nor hanging so in the balance.

Minutes passed. Some started to shift in their seats, and others to whisper in their neighbours' ears, and yet others to venture a pointed finger, kept close to the chest, in the direction of the gate, towards which the three louts were being escorted, no pink loops round their necks this time, by a guard at their head and another to their rear. They looked distinctly de-loutified—what with their hung heads and grimy clothes—as they were ushered through the garden gate and over to the table, facing the police officers, backs to us. Their escorts stood at a few feet to the right and left, respectively, of their sorry line-up.

The Manse's black door swung open and out came the Arab gentleman, his wife and two children. He was wearing his desert get-up and she was clothed from the crown of her head to the tips of her toes, with a cloth gate over her mouth; the children were in white shirts and navy V-necks, with grey trousers for the boy and a black skirt for the girl. As they stepped onto the grass, the sergeant indicated that they stand next to him and the constable. When duly lined up, the parents looked at the louts. Their children looked anywhere but.

The sergeant and the constable conferred. The louts' escorts checked their watches and the gate.

It was soon opened with such force that it bounced back from the inside wall with a sharp clack. Head down, Mzee, the elderly bowlegged man we'd listened to on the beach yesterday—still in his tatty khaki shorts and pristine anorak worn over the ever-so-loud shirt—made a beeline for the table where the sergeant and the constable made a space so he could stand between them.

Mzee took a quick look at the downcast louts, and snatched up the mike: *Can everybody hear me?* The amp must have been full on: they could have heard him down on the beach. *I'm late, I'm late, I know. Typical. Right, let us get today's* gachacha *over with.* Gachacha, *for those of you in the dark, is a system of reconciliation employed in the wake of acts of notable wrongdoing; the accused admit their misdeeds if misdeeds they have indeed committed; the victims must then decide if they wish to forgive the perpetrators; and the judge, that is to say, myself, passes sentence after due consultation with a peer, to wit, in this case, Sergeant Hyman.*

The long-haired man stood up, fist raised: *Umkhonto we sizwe!*

The old man glared at him: *No bloody interruptions!* Corduroy Jacket's neighbours shushed him back into his seat.

In fits and starts and a blundering drawl, those three teenage lads pulled us haltingly through the events of the afternoon of the eighteenth, occasionally quibbling amongst themselves over which of them, exactly, had stripped the little boy, or had placed him on the hob—for God's sake—or had held the little girl fast so she too might take her turn. The constable took notes.

When the last of the lads' whines had died away, the old man took back the mike and turned to the Arab family: *Mr and Mrs Khoury, does this account fit the facts?* The Arab man nodded. His children and the woman stood stock-still. The old man looked at the lads: *Say whatever it is you wish to say.* He handed the mike to the one on the right, who began to mutter something. The old man slammed the table: *Look at those you have offended!*

The boy stared as instructed at the Arab man, and began to reel out regrets which, to judge from the robotic delivery, had been learnt by rote: *I am very sorry for any distress caused to Mr Khoury and his family and offer my unconditional apologies...* Only when he passed the mike to the second boy did I notice that the last in line—the little prick who'd insulted me, the son of that villager, Greg, with whom Dad had been spending so much time—was trembling a touch; perhaps fighting back tears of repentance, I thought; but only when he took the mike (the second lad had repeated the regrets of the first, word by poorly memorised word) did I guess from the twitching corner of his mouth that he was fighting hard to keep down a smirk, suppressing it just in time for him to give what turned out to be by far the most convincingly enunciated apology, eyes fixed firm on the injured party, the words made to sound as if they had been dredged from the depths of his ratty little soul.

The old man removed the mike from his hand and passed it without more ado to the Arab man, who held it too close to his lips: *We as a fa—* A feedback shriek; he tried again: *Our family has agreed to forgive the three boys before us; we...* Wobbly lips, a swiped tear, an uncertain hand digging into the folds of his robe for a crumpled crib: *...we understand that they were too young to fully comprehend the evil of their ways, having been coerced into their actions by adults the maliciousness of whose intentions did not diminish their natural authority in these boys' eyes. Sir, it is difficult for us to do, but we forgive them.*

The constable went on scribbling like billy-o in his black notebook. The sergeant looked at the lads, whose heads were back in the hung position. The old man beckoned to the Arab to hand him back the mike: *Thank you, Mr Khoury. Subject to the approval of the native authorities, I sentence you three young men to sweep the streets and empty the litter bins of Coldwater Bay, from seven am to five pm, seven days a week, with a half hour break for sandwiches at midday; you will not be allowed to consume alcohol or any other intoxicating substance, at any time; you will not come within two hundred yards of the Khoury residence and will, on seeing Mr Khoury or any member of his family, give them a wide berth of not less than twenty yards, at all times; and this you will do until we have once more left Coldwater Bay to its own devices.*

Upon which he turned, abruptly, to the sergeant: *Is that all right by you?* The sergeant leaned into the microphone that that little old man—his frown impatient—was proffering: *I think they can count their lucky stars, myself.*

The old man hawked, then spat on the grass: *This sentence will be put into effect as soon as these proceedings have been*

terminated; I would furthermore remind defendants and plain-
tiffs that in four days' time, on Friday the twenty-fifth of April,
they will be expected to testify as material witnesses in the trial
of Gregory Crofton, Lorraine Woodstock and John Whitebone.
Simon squeezed my forearm. Mum gazed on, a bitten underlie
her only outward sign of concern. The sergeant leaned into the
mike again: *The trial will take place at the Community Centre,*
at six pm.

*

(Monday 22ⁿᵈ)

The following morning, Simon stuck his head round the kitch-
en door while the rest of us were still breakfasting. *Won't be*
back till late; toodle-oo!

Mum lowered her cereal spoon: *But Simon, you haven't*
had any brekky.

He was already heading for the hall: *Got my cowry shells,*
haven't I? Get something on the way.

I asked BWSBN, as per usual, if he wanted to go out and,
as per usual, he gave me an eager yes.

We wound up, as per usual, on the esplanade. A few
Africans were coming up from the beach, shaking sand out of
towels or slapping it off flip-flops, while others were strolling

along the promenade. Over by the fish shop, some had formed a queue.

We leaned on the railings and took in the finely chopped sea, the black-skinned bathers and sunbathers. A few yards along from us stood that long-haired man who had so embarrassingly raised his fist at the face-to-face showdown the day before. Same corduroy jacket, same deeply grimy beige flairs. He was staring into space, his lips so pale they merged seamlessly into the rest of his face. He had a bumfluff whisper of a beard—though he must have been nearly thirty—but what really caught my eye was his pronounced stoop. BWSBN was starting to walk a bit like that, I noticed: with that faux-humble slouch, playing that I'm-classless game which was then and still is all the rage amongst the scions of the better-off; within a handful of years I would find myself at parties chock-full of Mr Woolman types, and of (older) BWSBN types with their woolly class-ambiguous voices, drugs slipping down their throats like candy, their scruffiness cultivated, their wide-collared shirts left rakishly undone, their general jibber-jabber loosened by quality drink, and their breath laced by drags on Gauloises Bleues or Sobranie Cocktails; oh, all those living rooms I would eventually stand in, sniffing how plush the carpet, clean sulphate tempering the effects of the Pimm's and the Black Velvets as I tried to seal myself off from it all, assailed as I was by men with that trademark hunch of shoulders, all of them coming onto me like I was going out of fashion.

When I turned away from bumfluff-face, the sunbathers had retired to the edges of the beach, leaving the central swathe clear. A couple of black kids—nine or ten years old—were screwing poles into the sand, two at one end of the cleared area, two at the other. The watchers on the beach applauded as two teams hobbled onto the pitch: four players and one goalie in each, most of the players leaning on at least one crutch, and two of them on two, with the exception of the goalies, whose legs were intact, but whose arms were stumps. A baseball-capped referee, who was in one piece, stepped between the teams and blew his whistle.

The players hopped and kicked and saved with a speed astonishing in people so physically abbreviated. BWSBN was riveted: *Jesus, they're fast, for cripples.* The crowd rooted for one side or the other as the crutches clashed, the ball was tapped about, goals were scored and the players bound and sprang, their new windcheaters flapping, flashing snippets of white T-shirts underneath, their un-maimed legs wrapped in blue jean, their stumps showing below frayed cut-offs, all of it surveyed by creamy clouds and by a growing number of native villagers who had converged at the railing.

Football always attracts a crowd.

As I watched, a premonition grew and grew upon me that all these maimed Africans who were playing so hard, and all the Africans who were cheering them on or queuing for fish and chips behind me or taking it easy somewhere else in the village, and that even all the white-armbanded Africans—who, as I knew now in my bones, had planned everything, had set up the roadblock, located hiding places, brought the cowry shells, downed the lines—had already lost or were losing or would lose whatever it was they thought they might win: the cold English sky proclaimed it, the England that loomed beyond the confines of Coldwater Bay proclaimed it, the bland English faces of the watching villagers proclaimed it.

Inevitable though it was, there was something about this thought of them losing that made me sad, as if a golden opportunity was being allowed to be thrown away and that if it were, impossibly, taken, then all things might turn out different from the way I already knew they were laid out: that there was no other route, no other train standing on the tracks.

Everything stood out so, cut neater and neater into the air, and I knew I had to open my eyes as wide as they could go, to take in the mutilated players as they played and played and played, their shapes shouting, until they were the only beings visible, until all the village vanished into air behind them as they tapped that bloody ball.

The harder I forced myself to dam up the tears, the harder they came.

Luce, what's the matter?

Even though BWSBN had managed to sidle up, he didn't dare touch me. I wouldn't have minded at all, right then. In my lonely and weepy state. My touch paper had been lit, but there he was standing back, poring over the safety instructions as I watched the clacking, leaping, kicking, puffing people down below.

*

That afternoon, me and Simon and BWSBN decided to see if we could get a fish supper (Mum having again returned from her supposed afternoon trip to the corner shop without anything edible). The locals were taking to the cowry shell currency like a duck to water; given that the things were in such plentiful supply, it was like they'd all struck it rich. Even BWSBN and myself never seemed to be out of them. (Roger and poor Eileen, of course—having turned their backs on the whole thing—didn't have a shell to rub between them.)

The fish lady was behind the zinc, attending her now mainly black clientele, young men in the main, who waited their turn in silence or muttered the odd exchange, their tallness and slimness and upright backs in sharp contrast to the diminutive form of the few male villagers in the queue. It seemed quite natural, though: the dark, dark skins of the customers under the chippie woman's fluorescents; the attempts by two of the locals to make small talk with the blacks who would then turn from their contemplation of the goods under the fishwife's glass display to nod and smile and gesture, trying to help these locals out in their attempts to make themselves clear.

317

Simon kept mum.

*

Passing by the sweet and novelty shop—the old lady was in her door frame, crooking her finger to entice a gaggle of black kids in: *I now have strawberry sherbet! And realistic plastic spiders!*—we witnessed our first spat.

A villager standing in the middle of the esplanade, who had had several drops too much, had launched into a tirade at the first blacks to hand—a couple of couples—slurred words blurted at top volume, of which I made out only the odd unprintable word. Neither the couples being maligned, nor an armbanded man who was watching the scene from the corner of the high street, did a thing. Within minutes, three villagers appeared at a trot from the direction of the pub, calmed down their countryman and hauled him away.

A now familiar waft of burning wood was drifting its way up from the beach. I ran to the railing. That old man in the raggedy shorts had told us no lie: the barbecues were on every evening, Monday included. A few people were watching a flat-stacked pile of driftwood take. The grill had been placed over the incipient licks of flame. A skinny young man whipped out cutlets from a bucket and dropped them across the bars, while another closed in to sprinkle them with sauce, this time from a pop bottle. The condiment fizzled. More people were moseying over. Amongst the two or three white ones I spotted the elderly Mr thingy, Feather.

*

(Tuesday 23rd)

On Tuesday morning, BWSBN and I turned up equally early in the kitchen. Simon and Mum had already flown the coop.

We shrugged on our anoraks without a word. On the off chance, I asked Eileen if she wanted to tag along. She shook her head with a frown. Roger didn't so much as look up from his Krispies.

BWSBN pulled the front door to.

Esplanade?

By way of an affirmative reply he did that eyebrow-fluttering routine he imagined was so charming: *Shall we go this way for a change?*

Which took us down a side street.

The Africans were well wrapped up that windy day, but just as much out in force as they had been on previous occasions. Some passers-by asked after our morning: *Habari za asubuhi?* We smiled and gave half-baked waves, still unsure as to what was the thing to do.

We emerged onto the esplanade right next to the old lady's sweet and novelty shop, for which BWSBN made a predictable beeline: *Fancy some fudge, Luce? I spotted some in her window yesterday.* He pulled a handful of cowries from his pocket and rattled them.

I wasn't looking.

On the pavement, a little way away from the old lady's shopfront, a lone trestle table had been set up behind which a tall black boy was having trouble keeping a handful of canvas sheets from flying away. Beyond him, also on the esplanade, two or three black people were laying down blankets, bags of as yet-unidentified wares plumped beside them. BWSBN was dawdling by the window full of fudge. I walked over to the black boy, who was thin but not at all skinny, with deliciously long fingers. He wore a blue sweater over a white T-shirt. Jeans. No armband. The sheets turned out to be paintings. The stones he'd selected to hold them down were too light for the stronger-than-usual wind, and the canvases were fluttering about too much for me to focus on their subjects. I pointed over at the beach: *Shall I get you some heavier stones?*

Then and then alone did he acknowledge my presence: *Nini?* I had his face full on. He couldn't have been much older than me. Maybe fifteen, sixteen tops. He sounded peeved. A sharp gust had him slamming a hand down on a wayward corner of canvas.

Back in a jiffy.

I trotted over to the far set of steps and went down onto the sand. BWSBN, instead of entering the shop to get his blessed

320

fudge, was now watching me intently from the entrance. I got my stones, popped back and unloaded them onto the black boy's table. He laughed: *Asante sana!* I blushed, and started putting the stones on top of his unruly wares. He joined in: *Asante.* I twigged 'asante' could only mean one thing and replied, accordingly: *You're very welcome.*

BWSBN was standing beside me now, still as a toad. Me and the boy worked on for a few seconds until the paintings were all pinned down:

What's this then, Lucy?

I looked at BWSBN askance: *What's what?*

He nodded, unenthusiastic: *These rather simplistic naïf genre paintings.*

God, I hadn't realised till then how smug he could be. The boy watched us both, attentive. Embarrassed, I started to browse through the pictures. Bright colours, schematic forms, bug-eyed people in unlikely postures: naïf, if you will; they were not, however, images of some faraway hottentot land, as I'd expected, but recent ones of Coldwater Bay. There in one painting was the esplanade, sure enough; and there in another was a shopfront in the high street; and there in yet another was the beach with black people on it, some with smiles and others without. And dotted here and there, in this picture and that, were us white folk, of all ages, anoraks bright, hair straight as flax. A tip of black finger touched the back of my hand: *Jina lako nani?*

I didn't get it until he pointed at himself: *Mimi ni Tendai.* He jabbed his chest again: *Tendai.*

I too pointed at myself, Jane to his Tarzan: *Lucy.* Tendai smiled at a flustered BWSBN: *Na we?* Who straight away snapped like a piqued lapdog: *What's he saying?* This was a different BWSBN to the diffident fellow I'd known so far.

I don't speak their language any better than you do, but he quite obviously wants to know your name.

BWSBN gave it, ungraciously. Tendai nodded: *Tendai.* To which BWSBN, to my astonishment, replied: *Yes, I realised that, I'm not an idiot.*

But an idiot was what he was increasingly becoming in my eyes, which I turned back to the pictures, skipping from one to the other until I stopped before a vertical portrait of a man dressed in yellow; though the subject's face was averted, as if ashamed, it was clearly the road sweeper, the black road sweeper we had all seen on our first—or was it second?—day in the village. My nerves started to prick and start. I must have gawped at that depiction of a black man wielding a broom for quite a while because Tendai, thinking I wanted the price, held up four fingers: *Nne.*

In my inexplicable state of alarm (and still in the thrall, I have to confess, of Mum's lifelong remonstrances never to buy anything from street hawkers) I shook my head too firmly and too quickly: *No, no.* Then Tendai, offended, perhaps, by what must have sounded like a dismissive tone, bowed his eyes, took the painting and stacked it carefully with the others. BWSBN butted in: *Well, d'you want some fudge or not?* Bugger his fudge.

I tapped Tendai's trestle table: *Goodbye, Tendai.* He said nothing and wasn't looking up, so I tore myself away, with barely a nod to BWSBN: *I don't know about you, but I'm going home.*

BWSBN tagged along.

*

Over lunch, I recalled my unease over the painting of the road sweeper. It gnawed and gnawed at me, and just after dessert it bit to the quick when it occurred to me I hadn't seen hide nor hair of that road sweeper for days. I got up from the table. Thankfully, Mum and Simon were still out. I'd got to the hall when BWSBN caught up with me, face a-tremble, eyes childishly cross: *Where are you going?*

I opened the door: *Where I bloody well please.* I closed it on him and ran down the steps.

*

At irregular intervals and on irregularly chosen spaces, more and more salespeople had placed blankets or trestle tables all along the length of the tarmac, and were touting canned food, coloured wraps and bangles, little heaps of fruit, stocks of home-recorded cassettes, and second-hand cutlery. Sellers and customers were haggling; cowry shells were exchanging hands here and there. Tendai had a couple of customers.

I dawdled in front of a nearby heap of sandals, pretending not to hear their seller's patter. No sooner had Tendai's clients moved on than I hastened over. He stared at me warily. I smiled—*Hello!*—laying friendliness on with a trowel to make up for what I'd thought he'd thought of as my earlier rudeness: *I'd like the painting I saw earlier, please.* I pointed to the canvases. He hesitated. I mimed someone sweeping a street. He placed the painting of the sweeper before my eyes. The acrylic paint made for a shiny surface, and the figures—there were a couple of passers-by in the background, as well as the sweeper—were marked by strong black lines filled in with bright colours upon which equally bright spots created a mottled effect.

Tendai pointed at it: *Unapenda hii?* He had to repeat this a couple of times before I gathered he wanted my opinion, as if he were the painter.

I pointed: *You did this?*

He gestured at the whole table: *Hii yote rangi nili-ipaka mimi.*

Then I pointed at him: *You?*

He pointed at himself: *Bila shaka.*

Wow.

I concentrated on the picture I'd come for: *Do you know where he is, this man?* He frowned. Again I tried: *You don't know? Where is he? Here? There?* I gestured again, pointing at the village then thumbing at the beach. He shook his head: *Hapana, hapana.*

So where is he then?

Alikufa.

Alikufa?

Ndiyo, ndiyo, alikufa.

Seeing as I wasn't getting any the wiser, he pointed to the painting: *Unataka kununua hii?* He raised four fingers, back to business.

OK, sure.

I counted out four cowries. He took the money, rolled the canvas up and handed it over. I waved goodbye. He flickered his fingers: *Tutaonana.* I tried to repeat the word, got it wrong; he corrected me, I repeated it. He nodded: *Sawa kibisa.*

I weaved my way through the trestles and wares.

*

To go back to the kitchen at Seaview Heights was to step straight into the doldrums, the dumps, the pits. Roger and Eileen lurked there like lumpy spectres. But it wasn't until BWSBN appeared in the wake of a toilet flush that I realised that for BWSBN I had felt something just a little bit beyond friendship, but now, as he greeted me, hesitantly, awkward—*Everything OK?*—I instantly contrasted him with, older, surer, realer Tendai, with whom I vaguely suspected I might vault the barrier of childhood, beyond which biologically primed young people put out feelers to test each other for excitement and love in order to eventually, well, eventually.

I unrolled the painting. BWSBN asked where I'd got it, as if he didn't know. I stared down at him from the rock of age: *None of your biswas, young man.*

Simon came in, early for him. He was pensive, even a touch diffident. He hadn't been drinking, that much I could tell. He sat down at the table and spotted my purchase. He looked at it for a while, speaking as he did so, a tiredness on the edges of his voice, a quiver in the odd word: *Listen, sis, I've been hearing some rumours about Dad; things the local yokels think they've picked up from the blacks, even though they can't understand a ruddy word they say... So if you hear anything iffy about Dad, you should disregard it; let it slide, OK?*

I nodded, unsure as to what he was on about: *OK.*

I dare say everything'll get cleared up at this trial thing on Thursday. He looked around: *Mum not back yet?*

She's been out as much as you, recently; more, even. Hope she's OK.

BWSBN scraped back his chair and left the room without a word.

*

On Wednesday morning I was off early, the hell with breakfast. I walked, anorak open, breasts thrilled by rain flicked by a friendly sky, down the high street, daydreaming of freshly restored mansions, immense estates, vast tracts of landscape, yachts, limousines, Lear jets, Electra Glides... There on a corner was creep Kevin and one of the other little bastards who'd been condemned to sweep the streets, wielding their early-morning brooms with their sourpuss faces and their slow-witted bitterness. And their blood poisoned by sin. I walked on unheeding. A few blacks were already out and about.

The market on the esplanade now included a handful of stalls set up by some of the villagers, who were selling what looked like bits and pieces of tat they'd found lying around at home, in order, presumably, to increase their cowry buying power even further.

Tendai was just setting up his trestle table. I waited until he'd weighted his wares down before going up and browsing his proposals for that day: *May I look?*

I know that girl-meets-boy stories are all the same—all racing pulses and blood-heightened cheeks and lust laced with affection—and I know that it happens sooner or later to just about everyone, but that makes it no less exciting, terrifying even. I was dawdling like a fool before Tendai's stall, but he put me at ease in a jiffy, showing me picture after picture like I was his star client, his talent-spotting dealer come to help him make it big. He taught me his words for *good*, for *OK*, for *bad*, for *yes*, for *no*. *Nzuri. Sawasawa. Baya. Ndiyo. Hapana.* I got them down pat and asked for more. I stood politely to one side when real customers came along, mainly Africans, but there were a couple of curious locals too: *Look at those colours!*

Sales were slow, there being just three throughout the morning I spent there with Tendai; just two teenagers, we were, passing the time as best we could, more aware of each other's presence than that of anyone or anything else. Time flew, I knew, because in no time it was it was already the lunch hour and Tendai was making it clear, with words and signals, that lunch he had to have with his family, a I-wish-this-wasn't-so-but-there's-nothing-I-can-do-about-it expression on his face. Just then, as regret at parting was raising its unwanted head, I felt an equally unwanted tug on my anorak and there was a bright-red BWSBN, doing his damnedest to ignore Tendai and saying in a voice that nerves were making too shrill: *Come with me, Lucy.*

It was pitched all wrong; couldn't, indeed, have been wronger.

What's up with you?

He gulped: *I've found out what your Mum's been getting up to all day.*

Put like that, it smacked of some kind of adulterous affair. *What? Tell me. What, for God's sake?*

He shook his head: *You've got to see for yourself.* Another irritating tug.

I was about to apologise to Tendai for the interruption, but he'd already rolled up his paintings and pocketed his takings and was set to go and dine with his own: *Tutaonana, Lucy.*

I pronounced it back right: *Tutaonana.*

*

BWSBN was all fired up.

Come on, while your Mum's still there!

I had to break into a trot to keep up.

You sounded concerned about your Mum yesterday so I decided to look for her; finally, I spotted her, coming from this place. We had reached the corner shop.

So what? Mum's always going there.

We closed in on the door with the stealth of pantomime criminals. The sign was turned to CLOSED. He pointed at an adjacent door. I went along, knowing BWSBN well enough to suppose he wouldn't be going through all this kerfuffle unless he really thought it was warranted. He put his ear to the door: *They're still there.* He prodded it a tiny bit open: *He keeps it unlocked, in case any more wish to attend.*

I took a deep breath—*Attend what, exactly?*—but he was already stealing into the hallway, motioning with curling finger for me to follow.

The hall whiffed of stale milk. There was a pile of thumbed magazines on a side table; I recognised a Jehovah's Witnesses mag, 'cos we'd once had several issues pushed through our own letterbox, back in faraway London. BWSBN stopped next to a door in the corridor and crouched, eavesdropping. Walking over, I made out the chanting of several men and women.

I looked and beheld a pale horse and his name that sat on him was Death and Hell followed with him...

The subsequent silence was filled by whiny guitar music, after which the voices chanted on.

...and power was given unto them over the fourth part of the Earth, to kill with sword, and with hunger, and with death and with the beasts of the Earth.

Before I could stop him, BWSBN had opened the door a crack. He beckoned me to peep.

There, in what was clearly his living room, sat the shop-keeper himself, on a beige armchair, fat Bible in hand. Perched on an arm of the armchair was the little girl, eyes closed, hands gripping the neck of an odd-looking guitar, its sound box the size and shape of a space hopper; and with her big bottom plumped down on the other arm was—for Christ's sake—Mum, another fat Bible open in one hand, the other resting familiarly on the shopkeeper's shoulder as she now recited, haltingly, off the page: *How long, oh Lord, holy and true, dost thou not judge and avenge our blood on them that dwell on the Earth?* To which the semi-circle of some half-dozen villagers, all middle-aged to old, kneeling on the carpet, fat Bibles open in all their hands, responded—*And the sun became black as sackcloth of hair and the moon became as blood*—and then everyone fell silent once more and the girl returned to her instrument, making those distant-sounding twangs, while the shopkeeper looked up solemnly at Mum through his NHS specs and Mum smiled radiantly down at him.

The girl ceased her strumming and the others opened their eyes. The shopkeeper closed his Bible and looked from one person to the other, whispering with the slightest of lisps: *As we all know, what has happened here in our village in the last few days is not a coincidence, not by any means; though the mundane eyes of the many have yet to see it, the changes in our circumstances are fraught with meaning, a meaning which comes, which can only come, from He on whom all depend, who begets not, nor is begotten.*

Here the others chimed in *Praise be to Him*, except for Mum, who stared at the shopkeeper with unblinking eyes as he warmed to his theme: *Like the summer holidays to which we have so often played host in our capacity as the dwellers of a modest seaside village, life seems endless at its beginning and pitifully short when we realise the final week has—all of a sudden, it would seem—drawn nigh; and yet we live our lives as if it would be high summer for evermore; we gossip and carouse, we fill our homes with glossy goods, we flash our four-wheeled baubles along the roads (which have now been so righteously, so very righteously, placed out of our reach). Some choose to take their pleasures where they can, whereas others plan and plot their futures; but only a few, a blessed few, never cease to bear in mind that no matter which path they take, Azrael, the cautious angel, will be awaiting them at the end. We are fragile, so fragile, so much more fragile than the creatures of the sea or the fowls that fly through the sky or the beasts that creep upon the Earth; None of these are so flimsy as we, we that are blessed with the power of thought and the capacity for invention; we who sin willingly and fear no chastisement; we who devastate from the safety of our hearths and pause not to consider the consequences of what we do or omit to prevent; we are the least essential and yet the haughtiest creatures in the entire cosmos. Do we not repent of such hubris? Do we not long for our duly merited comeuppance?*

At once and as one they replied: *We do!*

He went on, faster than before, almost breathless: *It is no coincidence that those who have chosen to visit us are, we believe, from a place gravely affected by the acts great and small of our compatriots past and present and, indeed, those of our own unworthy selves; by measures our ancestors took upon themselves to take against their ancestors centuries ago, yea, measures which involved coercion, which involved planting, which involved mining, which involved schooling, and theft, and the bilking of millions upon millions of souls; it is no coincidence, I say, that some of these people have landed upon the elfin shore of Coldwater Bay.*

BWSBN tapped me on the shoulder, mouthing: 'elfin'? I made the finger and thumb gesture to indicate very small. The shopkeeper raised his voice a tad: *What is the purpose of their visit?* To which the others repeated as one man: *Restitution.* He nodded: *And what is our reward?* Upon which they chorused: *Atonement!*

Only those trapped in the beguiling optimism of our times can imagine that the folk who have come upon Coldwater Bay after such travails shall depart them without further ado; brothers and sisters, when the prescribed time has passed, the price for our and our fellow countrymen's trespassing on their distant land shall be paid in full; and it is us, us—his otherwise negligible lisp here became more pronounced: 'uth'—*who shall settle this debt; we shall be the beasts of no name who shall atone for the crimes of our countrymen. Brothers and sisters, have no more doubts and have no more fears, for our visitors, these humble sons of Ham, are none other but willing agents of the Most High, of Ishvar, of Ek Onkar, of Yahweh, of Ar-Rahman, sent to release us into a heaven of such sheer pureness we shall, upon entering it, be freed of all blood, freed of all history; until that joyful day comes, we shall and will savour the sweet lull of the remaining days afforded us, the calm before the cleansing swords of requital descend upon us all. Let us pray.*

The others pressed their hands together again. The shopkeeper put his Bible down on the floor and fished a thinner, tatty-looking book from behind the armchair cushion, while

Mum echoed in a chirpy yet sanctimonious voice I'd never ever heard her use: *Let us pray!*

In unison, they droned after him: *I seek refuge in the Lord of the dawn, from the evil of what he has created, and from the evil of the utterly dark night when it comes.*

The little girl gave a decorative flourish on her guitar thingy, and bowed her head. He clapped the tatty book to, turned to my mother, muttered something I didn't catch, then patted her on the back, to which she responded with a grin. I might have gawped on if BWSBN hadn't, through frantic pointing, signalled that the session was up and that soon, presumably, the attendees would be leaving. We hotfooted it out of the corridor, out of the hall. Hit the street.

On which I was whacked by a dizzy spell that made the houses spin, their colours not kosher, their forms queer. Having seen my mother like that, not herself, not like any of her selves I had ever known, perched on the right side of the shopkeeper like a pudgy pet. I understood there and then that from now on I was on my own; I felt as if my hands might have drifted off the end of my arms, that my neck was bending like plasticine.

The situation in which we all found ourselves in Coldwater Bay at that time, now struck me as being tailor-made for just-orphaned me, given that the only person of all the people I knew at that moment in Coldwater Bay who I really felt like seeing was Tendai. The rest, my father included—about whom

I did not want to think, open-ended question that he had become—had had their time, for the time being.

The old man who'd given the speech on the beach strode past us in his anorak and shorts, eyes down and brow knitted. On the other side of the street a woman in a white armband was strolling a little way behind, checking her ward was safe and sound.

*

I went to bed that Wednesday night feeling like a heroine. The evening, to be sure, had not been good, what with Mum pottering about with a saintly graciousness, the provenance of which I now knew only too well. To make matters worse, BWSBN had taken to glaring at me frequently, as if expecting me to apologise to him for something. As for Simon, he had made some loud statements to the effect that Dad was an innocent man and the accusations he would have to face at tomorrow's trial were a load of 'bollocks'.

I went to bed early, not wanting to make even the smallest of small talk with po-faced Eileen who, whenever we coincided in the bedroom, would invariably assure me, *We'll be laughing about this in a few weeks*, before tucking herself in on the top bunk.

I lay on mine, staring at the half moon, my thoughts full of Tendai, but with flashes of Dad interfering on the edges, the latter's face expressionless save for a bit of glitter in his eye.

My sleep was as deep as sleep can get when flashes of white light started nudging at my eyelids until I woke up, saw the window turned into a panel of shine, and shoved up the sash. The flares came as if chained one to the other, each exploding the moment the previous one faded. I would have stayed there ,spectating mesmerised, if Simon hadn't clomped like billy-o past my door and down the stairs: *Where are the fucking car keys?*

I hooked on slippers, pulled on my dressing gown and pussyfooted down the stairs into the hall. The front door slammed like I'd never heard it slam before. Outside, the engine of the Vanden Plas squawked and sobbed, once, twice, a third time. I pulled the front door open as Simon got out of the car and kicked the nearest tyre—*Bastards took the fucking petrol!*—before legging it towards the high street, on the triple. I hurried down the stoop, not minding the cold.

What on earth's going on?

He was panting down my neck, that bad penny, BWSBN. I didn't deign to reply, walking as I already was in Simon's direction; BWSBN, who was in a silly colour of pyjama, vanished from my peripheral vision, but when I thought I'd shaken him off he popped up next to me—this time with an anorak on—as I was turning into the high street.

Yet another flare—which turned out to be the last— poured light into the sky. Simon had come to a standstill about

336

a hundred yards ahead of me. To my right and left, a few villagers were shifting about in the darkness of the portals.

Half a dozen Africans ran past me, men and women, flashlights in hand, beams playing over the centre of the road ahead and Simon's static back.

Pisha njiani tafadhari!

A shadowy villager, catching the drift of their waving, shouted at him to get off the road. He took a few steps back.

The Arab's Range Rover was growling down the asphalt at an easy pace. The Africans lowered their flashlights. The car drew to a halt, its front passenger door was flung open and a man alighted, his build giving him away even before I spotted the face-length scars. The driver, shadowed, cut the ignition. The scarred man opened one of the back doors. Three figures clambered twitchily out: the pub landlord; the Right-On corduroy man; and a wispy-haired, red-faced villager I'd seen around somewhere but couldn't place. All had black woollen caps jammed on their heads. The flashlight beams rose to catch their faces which they jerked their forearms up to shield, but not before I could see they'd smeared shoe polish over their cheeks and foreheads. BWSBN whispered: *Jesus, they tried to make a break for it.*

The fat sergeant, unhatted, his jacket unbuttoned, drew up beside us, breathing mist. The disfigured man nodded at the catch for the night. The sergeant shook his head: *Really, gentlemen; it's four o'clock in the blooming morning.* He looked

337

at the landlord: *Is that whisky I smell even at this considerable distance?*

The landlord coughed: *I don't deny, I might have got a bit high on my supply.*

The sergeant turned to wispy-hair: *Johnny, I wouldn't have expected this from a wordsmith like you.*

The wispy-haired man shrugged: *Thought it might make a good story.*

So: what was the big idea?

We tried to skirt the roadblock.

The sergeant shook his head: *They're black, not daft.* He turned to the now-shivering corduroy man: *Mr Woolman, I didn't think you had it in you.*

The faintest of voices came from behind a curtain of trembling locks: *Letchford...wanted to get to Letchford.*

The sergeant looked at the scarred man: *Can they go home?* He thumbed at the buildings to right and left: *Home?*

The scarred man raised his arms, palms splayed: *Bila shaka.*

The sergeant shook his head at the failed fugitives: *Better get some kip, the lot of you, and please don't try anything like this again.* And please, pleaded my mind, let's get out of this cold, away from this scene, with the watching villagers thinking who-knew-what and the Africans standing still as statues and beams of light pouring straight from the Rover's headlights and from the torches, please, let's wrap it up now, please Simon don't.

But he did, he gave the three a bellyful: *They've got my Dad, they've got my Dad; tomorrow who knows what they're going to do to him. Why couldn't you have done this properly? Why didn't you let me know?* The landlord, wispy-hair and the weedy corduroy man stood there like slide projections.

The Africans were retiring at this point, exchanging banter peppered with the odd laugh. Simon glared at the sergeant: *Why are you helping them out? How could* you *be on their side?*

The sergeant shrugged: *I'm doing what I've always done: trying to keep the peace. It's getting early; good morning.*

The shadowy villagers were also dispersing. BWSBN bothered my ear: *It's true, you know, what the sergeant hinted at: very poor tactics, that, trying to get round the roadblock.*

The scarred man climbed into the passenger seat; the driver gunned the motor and began to reverse back up the road. Simon turned to us as he walked past: *You two; to bed.*

BWSBN ventured: *Lucy.*

Oh Jesus. Through gritted teeth, I hissed: *What is it now?*

The scarred man, didn't you see just now? He was wearing a gun—I'd say a Beretta—it was stuck down the back of his belt.

No, I had not seen that.

*

(*Thursday 25th*)

339

The following day, I went down to the 'market', now a daily event. I wandered about between the stalls and goods-laden sheets, caught snippets of villagers talking pidgin English to get what they wanted.

There was an urgency in the air—ozone-laced! The villagers who noticed me stared. The daughter of.

No sooner had I moseyed up to Tendai and said *habari*, than I understood the first real kiss of my life would take place in the very near future.

He asked a friend to tend his paintings and we went strolling (a respectable distance between us) along the esplanade, past the Community Centre—there where Dad was—on past the police station and then right off the end of the tarmac onto the wild grass beyond. We sat down on the far side of the nearest rise in the ground and talked, and smiled. And kissed, of course.

After a little while, we walked back to the esplanade hand in hand, and, as he wanted to get back to work, we said goodbye for now, catch you later, see ya, *tutaonana*.

S.W.A.L.K.

I sauntered back, taking in the stalls and the buyers and the sellers and the fish shop and the sweet shop and the drab seafront doors and the esplanade railing and the cold sand beyond, glimpsed through the iron. The walking, talking, greeting, limping people on the tarmac stood out bright and clear, limpid under the cloud-filtered light, outlines sharp as the characters in Tintin books.

*

I walked into the kitchen.

Hi there, sis.

Where have Roger and Eileen gone?

They're upstairs with the radio; wanted to listen to The Archers *down here, but I said not on my nelly.*

On the table was an open pack of sliced bread, next to a jar of lemon curd. Mum's presence barely registered, so still she was sitting, staring at nothing in particular. I smeared some curd on a slice. Simon leaned towards her: *Mum, I'd like to have a word alone with Lucy.*

She looked at him, eyes suddenly cow-wide: *Simon, surely there is nothing you would wish to tell her that you could not tell me?*

I bit into the bread; the lemon curd tasted like sherbet: yuck. Simon was making an effort: *Mum, please; just a few minutes. You could check up on Eileen and Roger; I don't know if that programme's suitable for them, Ambridge has been getting quite depraved in recent years, so I'm told.*

You're a trial sometimes, Simon, you really are.

She departed the room. Simon leaned towards me. I put down my bite to eat.

I saw Dad this morning.

For a moment, it struck me that Simon might have spotted me with Tendai as we were passing the Community Centre either on the way to our kiss or on the way back, but there was no censure lurking in his stare.

Dad? You saw Dad? How is he?

Physically speaking, he's all right. He gets enough food. When I called round, they put him at one end of a table and me at the other, and we talked for about half an hour. He dug a pack of ciggies out of his anorak, took one, and lit up. Blown smoke whirled and curled.

And?

He didn't mention the trial at all, not a word; just went on about, you know, black people the way, you know, he's sometimes done.

Physical memories of Tendai started to prod me pleasantly: *And what did he have to say about 'black people'?*

The usual.

Eyes on mine. A rock, Dad had always been. A craggy rock, perched alone on a peak I'd never been allowed to scale. Immune to the elements, he was for me, Dad.

No arguments, sis. You're not going to the trial.

My watch said thirty minutes before it started.

Why not?

I need you to stay here and keep an eye on Mum.

She's not going?

A finger windscreen-wiped back and forth: *She's not herself; I don't want her put under any more pressure.*

Is this to do with those iffy rumours about Dad that you mentioned on Tuesday?

He stubbed out the fag end.

Is it?

You're not going, sis, and that's that.

I wanted to go. Curiosity, more than love: *He's my Dad!*

I said you're not going to go. Is that clear?

I jumped up to answer the door before Simon could.

Outside stood BWSBN, eyes beady as a pigeon's, clothes rumpled, and smelly.

Where've you been?

It was a self-deprecatory smile that he gave me: *Out and about.*

*

Six o'clock. I asked Mum how long the trial would last. She said that it depended, sometimes these things dragged on so. We killed time as best we could, me and Mum and Roger and Eileen and BWSBN.

For supper, Mum made us something simple—what exactly, I have never since been able to remember—which I picked at while the other kids ate and she stood by the stove nibbling at a piece of bread. We did the washing-up, the boys drying. Eight pm. Eileen asked if we could have the radio on and Mum said she supposed so, but no pop music, please. We listened to the tail end of a news broadcast, last sweepings of a world which now seemed so very, very remote: the death of some politician, a royal event, the football scores, occasional showers. Coming up, a documentary about an oil crisis. Mum muttered that she didn't want to hear about a bunch of sheiks holding the world to ransom, and twisted the Roberts off.

Nine rolled around. Eileen and Roger went back to playing at cards. Mum smoked a cigarette as she stared out of the window at the dark street. BWSBN made me nervous by asking if I was concerned about Dad, and I told him that of course I was concerned, and then he nodded, grave as a doctor, and said not to worry, that everything was going to be all right. Which piqued me even more.

The doorbell rang at ten past nine. Eileen, Roger and BWSBN looked up. Mum and I hurried to the hallway. A dark bulk could be made out on the far side of the emeried glass. Mum blurted out Dad's Christian name. A voice we didn't recognise asked if this was Dr Whitebone's residence, and she opened the door even as she answered that it was. There stood the constable, and round the constable's shoulder was my brother's arm on the end of which its owner half-hung, half-leaned as the constable informed us that Simon was a bit the worse for wear. Simon moaned that he could take it from there. Mum thanked the policeman, and my brother walked in, so crouched over I thought he was going to fall flat on his booze-squeezed face, but he made it through to the kitchen, where he blinked like a woken cat under the brightness of the bulb. He slumped onto a chair and looked round at the kids. He was smiling. Mum told them to go upstairs. Eileen and Roger were up like a shot. BWSBN took his time, placing flattened hands on the Formica and levering himself up. Simon told him to please get a move on and off he went. Simon asked Mum to sit down, and turned to me: *You too, sis, take a pew.*

*

Simon described the court: the accused were placed in chairs at either side of a table at which the sergeant acted as prosecutor and the constable, for the defence; a jury of twelve villagers was sitting in a cleared area to the right of the packed hall. Armbanded blacks were posted behind the defendants, at the door and here and there around the room.

The sergeant held up photographs of the street sweeper's body, which he had taken before decomposition set in; these were followed by the eyewitness account of the whitish man, Jonas Cole, who had seen the body being buried and had exhumed it forthwith. And then came the confession of the policewoman, who related what she and my father had done to that poor man (Simon smiled without a trace of mirth: *I shall spare you the details).* The Arab gentleman then took the stand to explain how my father had comported himself and what he had ordered to be done in the Manse, on Thursday the eighteenth last. The wife and the children had then testified, after some coaxing from the sergeant, as to what actually had been done (to them) before a stop was put to it.

Once finished, Simon lit a cigarette. I knew he had left certain things out, above and beyond those he'd said he'd left out. Mum, who'd been chain-smoking her way through a few death sticks herself, asked Simon if he knew what was going to happen to Dad. Simon said he had already been handed over to the civil authorities, meaning the sergeant and the constable, who would keep him and the other accused in the police station's holding cells until the blacks left on their self-appointed day. A week tomorrow.

Mum's voice was brittle as poppadom: *I find it rather hard to believe your father has been found guilty of murder, Simon. Was this not what is known as a kangaroo court? It was hardly British justice, was it?*

Simon kept on staring at nothing: *I saw the evidence, heard the witnesses; there were the photographs.*

Mum stood up. Her head was trembling: *Whatever you do, don't tell the other children. As for John, I shall pray for him.* To do which, she found it necessary to leave the kitchen and, a moment later, the house.

As for me, Tendai's face had formed a smokescreen between me and my shock, my nausea, my plughole-spiralling thoughts. I wanted to get away from it all, from this stuffy kitchen, this mother past her mental sell-by date, that father who had done Christ only knew what. The words sprung to mind crudely and rudely: I've got to fuck Tendai, the sooner the better. I've got to fuck him if it's the last thing I ever do.

*

(Friday 26th)

They buried Winston Francis at seven o'clock the following morning. The weather held. Neither me nor Simon nor Mum went: according to my brother, we might not have been all that welcome. BWSBN, on the other hand, surprised us by saying he did want to go. He left around six. Unnecessarily early.

I slipped out late in the morning—well after the ceremony—and headed straight for the open-air market. There were no villagers around and only a few of the black vendors. Tendai, however, was in his usual spot, selling zilch.

*

When I was walking home from his room, the sky bright but not sunny, the air mild but not warm, odd moments popped up into my head—silent flashes of us going into the bed and breakfast, the white man who ran it or at least who opened the door peering at me with poofy complicity: *Going to try something different, are we, love?* On the first floor, I glimpsed a black brood playing in a room from whose ajar door a firm-eyed mother watched us pass. The poof half-heartedly calling up a catchphrase as I walked into Tendai's room: *Shut that door!*

When walking back past the corner shop (imagining Mum in that living room with the shopkeeper and his girl mascot and the other God freaks), my woman's instinct—me being a woman now, no doubt about that—assured me I was being watched. Simon? BWSBN? Maybe even Mum? After all, I'd spent quite some time at Tendai's place.

I stopped to take stock. There was no one to the right of me, no one to the back of me, no one peeking from the windows to the left of me. There was, however, a disembodied clip-clop of heeled leather on paving stone which turned out to be, as he hove into sight, a white man I'd never seen before, walking up the other side of the street, hands in pockets, overcoat collar turned up, head bowed, a checked cloth cap pulled down low. He didn't so much as glance at me. There were considerable mud stains on his trouser ends.

A quarter of an hour later, I rang the bell at Seaview Heights, recent memories of Tendai still dilly-dallying in my head. The bloody Archers were audible from Eileen's open sash window. Simon answered the door, as unrecognisable from the angry brother he'd been before Dad's trial as he was from the shattered, plastered brother who'd come back from it. He glanced to left and right: *Come on in, sis.* He closed the door tout de suite: *Go on through.*

The kitchen door was half open. A checked cloth cap was resting on the table. I hesitated, but Simon hustled me on in. The man in the overcoat was already standing up, hand outstretched: *You must be Lucy.*

I must have been, but was unable to say so in as many words.

It was exactly then that I knew it was all over.

Simon pressed gently down on my shoulders: *Don't be rude, and sit down.*

He then took the one next to me: *Lucy, this is Maurice.* Maurice had a gaunt face—not unlike that of my father—that middle-age was starting to curdle. His coat was black and of a smart cut and didn't peg at all with the cloth cap that sat before him. Around his neck was a silk cravat.

You have one very brave admirer.

My first thought: had they rumbled Tendai?

Who knows what might have happened, if it hadn't been for—

And blow me down if he didn't mention BWSBN by name.

—who, seeing you were so concerned about your Dad, decided to get help; he took advantage of the funeral ceremony this morning to reconnoitre the village for possible escape routes, and finally managed to sneak out into the wider world, using a route that I, too, found invaluable when entering the village incognito a while later; quite a little hero he has been, and I do not speak in jest.

And all because BWSBN wanted to get back into my good graces.

I don't want to sound rude, but might I ask who you are, exactly?

Luce! That is no way to—

Maurice held up a calming hand: *It's my fault for not introducing myself properly; I'm an employee of Her Majesty's Government, come to get the lie of the land. Quite a little situation you have down here.*

Tendai, I was thinking of Tendai.

I see. So, do you know what the authorities now intend to do?

Maurice frowned, his skin like bending leather: *That all hinges on if we can determine whether the intruders have or do not have access to weaponry. From what I have been able to gather, it would appear, extraordinarily enough, that they do not, with the exception, I have been told, of one handgun in the possession of a gentlemen with a rather unpleasant face wound.*

My, BWSBN had spilled every single bean.

There are certain aspects of the situation about which we are not entirely clear; the armbands worn by some of the intruders, for example.

Paramilitaries, BWSBN had said.

Do you know what they stand for?

It was my eagerness, I suppose, that made him smile.

Well, we think it might be something to do with a custom of a Rhodesian tribe, the Ndebele, who traditionally wore white ox tails on their upper left arms when they went on the warpath for white settlers. In 1896, they killed quite a lot of them in most disagreeable ways. A wee pursing of the lips: *One has tried to do one's homework, you know, despite the rush.*

Simon lit a cigarette, blew the smoke out straight, snapped the lighter down on the table: *So these blacks have come all the way from Rhodesia?*

From what I've been able to observe—face markings and so on—they seem to come from pretty much all over the continent.

The words rang in my head: *nzuri, sawasawa, baya, ndiyo, hapana*—not forgetting *tutaonana!*

Do you know what language they speak?

From the snippets I've heard, it's almost certainly Kiswahili, a Bantu tongue spoken in several East African countries. He leaned forward, eyeing me: *I hear you've got quite pally with the interlopers.*

Just how long had this man been snooping around? Had he spotted me and Tendai together?

Allow me to ask you a question I have already put to your brother. In your considered opinion, if measures were to be taken to oblige them to leave, are these people likely to offer any serious resistance?

Me? He was asking little me? I glanced Simon's way, and Simon gave me a nod.

I really, really, don't think they wish to hurt anyone, if that's what you mean.

I see. And what do you think might be the purpose of their visit to the United Kingdom?

As it happened, I had always sort of somehow believed the official statement they'd had printed in the local paper, to the effect that they were here on pleasure, but it would have sounded laughable to say this to such a serious, mysterious and, I suspected, important man.

I don't think anybody really knows; do they, Simon?

Maurice went on, regardless: *I have managed to have a word with the sergeant in charge here, who, I gather, is holding your father, and two other British subjects, including a woman police officer, in the local station.*

We nodded.

This sergeant has also informed me that he wishes to help broker a somewhat unorthodox deal with our newcomers; indeed, the whole situation is rather urgent: high time I got cracking.

Maurice dug into a pocket in the inner recesses of his coat and withdrew a black box about the size of a bumper one of chocolates together with a dinky microphone attached to a flexible cord. Simon appraised the device: *That's a new one on me.*

Maurice plugged the mike into the back of the box: *Last year's gadget from our American cousins; short range, but far better than a walkie-talkie. UHF frequency, rather handy. Not on sale here yet; only a matter of time, I suppose.*

My thoughts were swinging on trapezes, reaching out to each other, missing each other by inches. Simon sounded as if he were talking from behind glass: *Short range? Can I take it that help is close at hand, then?*

Maurice started twiddling a knob on the black box with one hand, while holding up the mike in the other: *You certainly can. Now, if you would be so polite as to excuse us, young lady, what I have to say on this apparatus is strictly for authorised ears only. Your brother, being a member of Her Majesty's Armed Forces, may stay.*

One foot out of the door, I paused, being in something of a dither: *What exactly is going to happen?*

He stopped twiddling: *Be assured that we're taking a softly-softly approach; the last thing we want to do is cause a ruckus, young lady.*

*

I slipped out of the house, closing the door so that not a click did it make, then ran like the clappers, like the clappers, side street, high street, esplanade, where the market was busier than in the morning, and where, as every early evening, barbecue smoke was rising from the beach. I ran straight to Tendai, who was selling a painting of a giraffe and four tropical birds to the sweet shop lady. She was counting out her cowries when I shouted his name between gasps for air. They both turned. I had to reach out my hands to Tendai's chest to bring myself to a halt, him recoiling slightly, like a train buffer.

My words tumbled out, spilled across the tarmac: *They know, they know! There's a man here from the government! They're going to do something, Tendai!* Then I remembered he couldn't understand. The few words of his language that I knew wouldn't have been much use.

He flashed a smile, then removed it as fast as if by sleight of hand: *This spy of yours, where is he?*

I stared at him like a waxwork: *You speak English.*

Yes, of course. Is he in your house, this man from the government?

Flabbergasted, I managed a nod. He handed the picture to the sweet shop lady, who was eying me wryly.

Take it, it's yours.

No sooner had he grabbed my hand than thunder filled the air and every soul within sight raised his or her head to the as-yet empty sky; the roar expanded, fingernail-on-blackboard shrieks spinning off it for seconds until two green-and-grey hulls shot over the roofs close enough for all of us to see the pilots' metal-wrapped heads.

The jets circled round, uncannily slow, then shot out to sea, their roar fading then re-rising like turned-up feedback as they looped back towards us, muzzles up like snooty dogs, exposing their undersides before making one final, deafening circle around the village centre and going back where they came from, their screams fading to a moan, their thunder, to bouncing echo.

Tendai and I hurried along the esplanade. Armbanded Africans had appeared at regular intervals of every few yards, and were calling out unhurried instructions to their fellow blacks. These began to head off, up from the beach, onto the esplanade then up the side streets. Some walked alone, others in couples or groups; mothers and fathers carried babies or held toddlers' hands, the cripples crutch-hobbled, the vendors abandoned their stalls, cowries and all. The old lady stayed put, watching it all. Tendai was making a beeline for the pub.

A cluster of villagers were peering out of its door, beyond which their jittery expressions made it clear they did not wish to step. Old man Mzee was sitting quite alone at one of the terrace tables, in his tatty shorts, loud shirt and flip-flips, his new anorak looking a bit shopworn now: *Habari gana?*

Tendai pointed at me: *Tell him what you just told me.*

When I'd done that, Mzee shook his head: *And there was me thinking we'd get at least a fortnight's worth out of the* wazungu. He stood up: *You two'd better come with me; the streets won't be safe for long.* He waved at the crowd on the threshold: *Cowry shells are legal tender until you are informed otherwise; have the next one on me.*

I had to trot to keep up with Mzee and Tendai as they strode across the esplanade and up the high street. All around, windows were being pulled to, black neighbour was calling to black neighbour, the eyes of armbanded men and women were taking breaks from watchfulness to check watches. They didn't look concerned. They didn't look pleased, either. Mzee stopped at number 84. The door was ajar.

We climbed a musty staircase into premises that smelt of whisky and untouched dust. Nobody around. Mzee stamped his foot, then screamed: *Mr Craddock!*

A muffled call: *I'm in the basement, the basement!*

When we got there, we found mister wispy-hair, who I recognised from when he'd been caught trying to escape the day before yesterday. Spanner in hand, he was trying to fix something on a greasy machine the size of a billiard table. Watching him, frowning, arms folded, was Jonas Cole—it really was a cool name—his duffle coat open, sweat on his brow: *We don't have much time.*

I guessed as much from the jets; soon as I heard them, I came here.

Mzee stamped his little foot again: *Are they ready, Mr Craddock?*

Wispy-hair looked up, his cheeks smeared with ink: *Just have to bodge it and fix it a bit, and then they'll run off like water. This is a Heidelberg Platen, you know; damn good machine, but a bit temperamental, and its chase only takes two pages at a time.*

Couldn't you have sorted out these technical problems earlier? We gave you four days. Don't you people have any concept of time, for God's sake?

Mr Craddock fiddled with his spanner: *I didn't think you'd need everything in such a hurry. All right, here goes; fingers crossed.* He pressed a red button at the side of the machine, which shuddered, then—slowly but surely—rolled copy after copy of the latest edition of the Coldwater Bay Parish Press off the runners, and dropped them, flat and even, onto a tray.

Mzee grabbed the first stackload and passed it to Jonas Cole, who, without more ado, left the basement and trotted upstairs.

Mzee had picked up the second fresh stack. Tendai reached out: *Nipe mimi.*

Mzee paused: *Hakika?*

By way of an answer, Tendai snatched the stack and followed in Jonas's footsteps. By now the machine had deposited another load, which Mzee picked up in turn and proffered to the wispy-haired Mr Craddock: *Come on, Johnny, do your bit; get these to the villagers.*

Craddock shilly-shallied: *I'm not sure if—*

Mzee dumped the stack in his hands: *We haven't risked so many skins just to swan about on an English beach; take it and go!* Craddock shouldered the stack and walked, wheezing, to the stairway. Another pile was ready and waiting.

Hey, I could—

Mzee held up a palm: *You, little girl, find your way home, post-haste, chop-chop, fast as you can!* He bent down to pick up the stack: *Scram.*

At a loss for a reply, I climbed the stairs and let myself out of number eighty-four.

The minutest of drizzles was falling outside.

The high street was deserted. I started walking down to the esplanade. A few doors along, a black man sprinted across the road, carrying what looked like a.

I slowed up, sticking close to the side of the street, and slammed a hand over my heart when a woman suddenly stepped out of the tea shop. She had a scarf tied tight round her forehead and was holding—her too—a gun, pointing skyward, one hand on the pistol grip, the other clasping the barrel jacket. She took me in with untroubled eyes and thumbed in the direction of the esplanade. I hurried on down, past an armbanded man who had taken up position in a doorway opposite, his rifle aimed prospectively up the street, its curved magazine familiar from remembered flashes of black-and-white TV wars.

I made it to the bottom of the high street. Fretful white faces were still gawping from the door of the pub. The police constable was still standing guard at the Community Centre. I stepped onto the esplanade.

Half a dozen men and women, armbanded and bescarved, their guns shouldered, were standing along the railing, backs to the sea. Two more were guarding the steps that led down to the beach, watching the dozens upon dozens of their fellow Africans of all ages that were hauling out the boats—several to a gunwale—or righting them, or scrubbing their insides.

The old man called Mzee walked right past me, over to the pub's overcrowded door, a batch of broadsheets draped over one arm. He plucked one off.

Please take one, they're free.

Some of the clientele reached out and accepted the proffered issues, which they passed back into what—as I could make out through the gaps between their shoulders—was a packed interior.

Help yourselves! Plenty more where these came from!

Tendai was a couple of dozen yards off to my left, handing one of his own stack of broadsheets to the sweet shop lady. They were talking. Wispy Mr Craddock was nowhere to be seen. Maybe he was handing out his stack somewhere in the side streets; either that or he'd chucked it in the nearest bin and made for the nearest bolthole.

At the western end of the esplanade, Jonas Cole and the plump sergeant were coming out of the police station. Silent and determined of step, they positioned themselves at the bottom of the high street, bang in the middle, Jonas with his broadsheets, the sergeant at ease, both looking up the sentinelled road.

The detonation, taking place as it did on the far side of the rise, sounded at that distance like a gigantic sheet of paper being crumpled furiously up. The pub-door villagers went silent. Mzee, who'd been walking out across the pub's empty terrace, stopped in his tracks. Tendai and the old lady were looking up, as if expecting spent shells. On the beach, all had turned heads in the direction of the noise. I peeked up the high street. From behind the Manse, a thin spiral of black smoke was rising through the spit.

The sergeant's voice carried in the silence: *They're through your roadblock.* Jonas checked his watch: *Taking their time.* He tucked his broadsheets away into his duffle coat.

I felt as if I was being made to see a film I knew I wouldn't like.

Tsst!

From his spot by the sweet shop, Tendai was waving at me to seek shelter, and I would have made myself scarce there and then if the sight of an armoured car edging its way down the centre of the high street—it had a tiny hooded port for eyes, and loose chains clattering against the radiator grille—hadn't kept me rooted to my spot.

All civilians are advised to remain indoors.

Its side windows were battened down. A machine gun was sticking up out of the turret, its barrel swaying loose as the vehicle bumbled forward.

Jonas turned to the sergeant: *Saracens hold ten.* A Saracen, then. A great ugly hulking thing, it turned out to be, as it got closer. It's not the same to see those machines in the newspaper—the only place I'd ever seen them—because the fact is that in England they keep that kind of vehicle out of sight, waiting in the wings, out of politeness, perhaps, not wanting to expose their knobbly bits and ugly grates and sticky-out tubes to the public except in bunting-softened parades. Seeing such a machine in the flesh—in the metal—it made me think of a dangerous dog. Not a jot of the thrills did I feel, that Roger and bloody BWSBN might have, if they had been standing too at this corner, rain on their ruddy faces. On the contrary, I was sweating underneath my hair and had a clump of sick in my throat.

Halfway down, it halted. From a small red tannoy attached to the left headlight, the voice boomed forth once more, sounding like a toffee-nosed Dalek: *I repeat, all civilians are advised to remain indoors.*

The pub door slammed shut. Mzee was still on the terrace. The armbanded Africans in the doorways and on the roofs had trained their rifles at the car.

Anyone in possession of firearms must— One moment, please.

Snap, crackle and pop from the tannoy. The vehicle jolted into motion again, easing its way farther down the street until it was within spitting distance of the sergeant and Jonas Cole.

There it stopped, engine grumbling. It must have been hard to see anything much through that hooded slit.

Who's in charge here?

The sergeant raised his hand.

Please identify yourself.

The sergeant cupped hands to mouth: *Sergeant Geoffrey Hyman, Hampshire Constabulary. May I ask to whom am I speaking?*

The acting platoon commander of Sections A, B and C of the Queen's Regiment of the Territorial Army, based at Jersey Camp, Newtown.

The Saracen's tannoy hiccupped before getting back into its stride: *Listen carefully; I repeat, listen carefully: anyone here in possession of firearms must surrender them at once to the man facing this vehicle, and then await further instructions.*

Through the following silence and the slowly thickening rain, Mzee flip-flopped over from the terrace.

In the middle of the road, the three men conferred.

Then Hyman called out to the armoured car once more: *We need to confirm that have you been correctly informed of the terms of surrender.*

At once, the Saracen snapped: *Any form of parley is out of the question until those in possession of firearms surrender them, as previously instructed.*

The gun turret rotated into life, its machine gun barrel taking beads.

The sergeant, Jonas Cole and Mzee had another confab. The sergeant cupped his hands again: *Platoon Commander, there has been no loss of life here; these people simply wish to ready their boats and set sail. The gentlemen with me are the only ones who, as per the said agreement, have requested an audience with a higher authority.*

Mzee whispered something in the sergeant's ear.

They inform me that they believe they are historically entitled to a palaver.

The Saracen kept silence. The rain was starting to snake down my back, to flatten my hair. Heavier now, it having been nudged into an angle by the breeze, falling over the high street, the three figures, the green-and-grey armoured car, the pub's deserted terrace and the packed beach, where the blacks were now pulling on waterproofs, anoraks, coats.

A tap on the shoulder. I started. The sweet shop lady was right behind me, her head in a pac-a-mac hood. I looked over her shoulder to where Tendai had been. No sign.

He's gone to the beach, dear; like the rest of them.

I nodded in the direction of Mzee and Jonas Cole: *Not those two.*

Not those two, no.

The Saracen piped up again: *All those in possession of firearms must surrender them at once to Sergeant Hyman of the Hampshire Constabulary. If they refuse to do so, appropriate*

*action will be taken forthwith. I repeat, appropriate action will
be taken forthwith.*

The sweet shop lady sighed: *I hope they're not going to do
anything silly.*

*There will be no further warnings; I repeat, there will be no
further warnings.*

Dear, oh dear.

The turret of the Saracen was going round and round and
round, in a slowed twirl, all our eyes, I was sure, as fast as mine
on its even speed. When it stopped with a clank and the per-
forated barrel began to rise, the vomit clump in my throat rose
as if cued.

The ocean of worldliness is so deep sang the ever so familiar
voice—that pious caterwaul I'd eavesdropped on the day before yesterday in the shopkeeper's living room—before being
relieved, not a moment too soon, by a chorused: *and unfath-
omable.* Then Mum piped up once more: *I couldn't reach the
other shore.* Came the chorus again: *and I was drowning.*

Isn't that your mother over there? Goodness me.

Then the little girl at the front of the little procession as
it turned into the high street, at a midnight mass pace—sang:
Then I received Guru's grace, and in a moment I was saved.

The shopkeeper—walking just behind the little girl, side
by side with Mum—turned from time to time to conduct the
others with floppy jerks of his hand, and together they chanted:

Why should I beg for anything from anyone? You, my Lord, give everything with your unseen hand.

Mzee and Jonas Cole and the sergeant gawped, rooted to the spot as the shopkeeper led his troupe until they were lined up in front of the Saracen, creating a buffer between it and the three men.

Oh Lord God of my salvation, I have cried night and day before thee.

Before the vehicle, they plonked their bottoms down, never letting up for a second: *Let my prayer come before thee, incline thy ear unto my cry.*

The turret swivelled round in their direction, the machine gun drooping.

For my soul is full of trouble, and my life draweth nigh unto the grave.

I caught glimpses of diluted hair, of mousy coifs. I couldn't see my mother because the sergeant was blocking my view, but I could imagine her determined stare, her lips open wider than the words required.

I am counted with them that go down into the pit. I am as a man that hath no strength.

Free amongst the dead, like the slain that lie in the grave...

The loudspeaker boomed: *Sergeant Hyman, can you hear me correctly? I wish to be informed of the exact nature of the situation here.*

The singing might have staggered to a halt if one of the villagers hadn't droned, off his own bat, *We shall not be moved*, which chestnut of a chorus was taken up by the others, forming a furry undercurrent of sound.

Platoon Commander, it is my considered judgement that these British citizens are currently involved in a peaceful protest; as acting police officer in charge, it is my duty to remind you they are entitled to do so under British law.

These people are obstructing us in the course of our duty, Sergeant; please have them removed.

I don't have the necessary personnel to enforce that order, Platoon Commander.

Then Mzee whispered in the sergeant's ear.

Platoon Commander, that aside, may I remind you that an agreement has been established with an official of the British government to the effect that the temporary contingent of foreign visitors be allowed to leave peacefully; and that two of their representatives are to be conceded an interview with a higher authority; I have been assured that their armed personnel will stand down at once as soon as this agreement has been confirmed.

No comment. The sweet shop lady tutted: *Get on with it, you idiots.*

The tannoy clicked on: *I have not been informed of how many of these visitors there are, Sergeant, nor of their intended destination.* The sergeant lowered the hailer, and lent an en-quiring ear to Mzee.

They number just under two hundred, counting the chil-dren; they have a vessel moored at an as-yet-unspecified loca-tion in the English Channel which can be reached by the smaller boats in which they are now ready to embark.

The reply was so long in coming, I started to time it.

Before we proceed, I need to ascertain the rank and con-dition of the higher authority to whom they wish to address themselves.

Mzee, Jonas Cole and the sergeant went into another flurried powwow. Then the sergeant hesitantly cupped his hands once more: *They wish to personally present a printed copy of a formal request to the prime minister of Great Britain and Her Majesty the Queen.*

The crooners cut themselves off in mid–*We-shall-not-be.*

Please confirm.

Jonas Cole whipped out the bundle of broadsheets from under his duffle coat and held them up.

On the beach, the boats, each holding a couple dozen peo-ple, had been lined up facing the sea. None of these would-be passengers were taking any notice of the exchange between the two official Englishmen. The first row waited on the water's edge; the second row's prows were slotted between the sterns of the first. A sea of corrugated crowns, I saw, a field in black blossom, the lips of some moving in conversation, the rest waiting still as rocks.

The rain was as yet keeping itself fairly moderate, the liquid only partially visible in the air until it showed up at last glistening on the skin and plastic of all those people who were waiting to go.

I took a last glance at the crowd, knowing I would never see Tendai.

In the end, I knew zilch about him, nothing about what his home was like, nothing about what it felt like to view the built-up bleak and cream-painted world of the Isle of Wight with his particular eyes. Not a clue had I as to what it felt like to have his mother tongue flashing around the brain, nor what flashes of memory might come knocking at random at his mind; I had not a smidgen of knowledge, swaddled in ignorance as I was, so tight I couldn't even twitch my way an inch into the world he'd lived in, grown up in, emerged from.

Over the boats, the clouds opened and shut their tiny mouths.

My dear, I think something might be about to happen.

Mzee stepped forward, within inches of the silent line of believers, within spitting distance of the hooded port of the armoured car, and yelled: *We have received a pledge from a representative of the British government, guaranteeing safe passage to the people now waiting on the beach, and also guaranteeing that myself and one other person would be allowed to speak to a higher authority. We have no intention of relinquishing our weapons until we see some evidence—unambiguous!—that you mean to honour your promises.*

You could have cut the silence with cheese wire. Mzee remained where he was. The armoured car dawdled; not a twitch, there was, from its turret.

How strange, that stand-off in the rain.

A minute went by.

The vehicle started talking again: *This APC is at the disposal of the two spokesmen who seek an audience with a higher authority.*

Mzee returned to his previous spot, next to the sergeant and Jonas Cole.

I must now insist upon the immediate surrender of firearms.

Mzee and Cole looked at the sergeant; the sergeant nodded. Mzee cupped his hands and raised his chin so as to reach those in the doorways and on the rooftops: *Toweni magazini!*

As one person, the armbanded men and women detached those curved magazines from their guns and tossed them onto the tarmac.

Wekeni silaha zenu kando!

The bulletless guns were held up for a moment, horizontal at shoulder height, then placed slowly at their users' feet.

Inua mikono juu ya vichwa na muelekee ufukweni!

With raised hands, the armbanded people stepped out of their alcoves and shinned down drainpipes, and made their way down the high street, down past the Saracen, past my mother and her fellow seated worshippers, across the esplanade's tarmac to the steps leading down to the beach, down onto the sand, where they distributed themselves swiftly amongst the boats until one was standing at each prow, one at each stern.

Sergeant, please approach the vehicle.

The sergeant took a few steps forward. His way was blocked by the seated God people. He leaned down and spoke into the shopkeeper's ear. The shopkeeper signalled that all should rise, and his followers rose to their feet, rubbing backs and loosening up legs. I spotted Mum, her eyes uncertain, her mouth disconcerted. The shopkeeper, holding the brown girl's hand, led his people, at a dignified speed, off into the nearest side street.

A door clanged open at the back of the Saracen. A pasty-faced officer who looked about twenty—his carrot-coloured hair cut short as lawn—extricated himself from the vehicle and, straightening his beret, walked over to where the sergeant waited by the snout.

They talked a while. Then the sergeant accompanied the officer—he had a single pip on his epaulette, which I knew from Simon meant second lieutenant—down to where Jonas Cole and Mzee were standing.

Mzee called out to those waiting on the beach: *Ni muda wa kuondoka! Ni muda wa kuondoka! Ni muda wa kuondoka!*

He signalled to Jonas Cole, the sergeant and the lieutenant, who then walked briskly through the drizzle to the Saracen.

I watched as the old man and the almost white man—the batch of *Coldwater Bay Parish Press*es still in his hand—clambered into the back of the vehicle, followed by the lieutenant. I heard the tinny clank of the door flap shutting to. I saw the sergeant stand back to allow the Saracen room to reverse, turn, and pick up speed up the road until it disappeared over the ridge, inland.

No sooner was it out of sight than the sweet shop lady took hold of my arm: *You should see this.* She guided me down to the esplanade, where assorted villagers were drifting over to the railing.

The armbanded Africans were already pushing the first row of boats into the surf, leaping across the gunwales as soon as they were afloat, as the outboards were slammed upright down the backs of the bows and string-pulled into roars and groans, while the second row of boats was hauled forward across the sand in hot pursuit, entering the water even as the first row of craft was turning into a string of shrinking dinghies, full of toy passengers, their heads dark dots, the outboards faint as bees.

All right, Luce?

Simon. To his left, also against the railing, Roger and Eileen had appeared, emerged from hibernation; they waved: *Hello, Lucy.* A yard or so further along the railing, Maurice, cloth cap raised now, and his overcoat buttoned all the way up to his peeking cravat, was observing the distant boats. Before I could say anything to my brother, a fraught purr filled the sky and a helicopter cast us into shadow for seconds, rotor blades fluttering our damp hair.

The sweet shop lady glared at them. I visored my eyes for a clearer view: *What's that doing here?*

Maurice lowered his head until it was level with mine: *It's from Air-Sea Rescue; safe passage guaranteed.*

The helicopter headed out over and beyond the pitching boats, beyond the dozens upon dozens of wee heads, before slowing to an attentive hover. Roger and Eileen watched it all with the half-closed, half-bemused eyes of the children they still were.

Where are they all going, Si?

Simon didn't take his eyes off the boats bobbing seaward, the helicopter keeping abreast: *Maurice has informed me they have a converted trawler somewhere off Sark.*

Eileen squinted at him through the wet: *Is that a Channel Island?*

The jets' claps of thunder broke over the back of my neck, making me duck a touch as the two green-and-grey fuselages shot over the boats, veering due east, leaving behind echoed roar, vapour trails barely visible against soggy, sprawling clouds. Maurice, eyes still on the boats, anticipated the question I was about to ask: *In unforeseen emergencies—and few can have been as unforeseen as this one—Lucy, one has to be prepared for any eventuality.*

The railing was now jam-packed with villagers. None of their erstwhile awe was manifest now that the boats were departing; on the contrary, the odd snicker could now be heard, the odd outright laugh; odd voices spat odd taunts—*Good riddance to bad rubbish*—that bit by bit dared to get louder: *Don't bother coming back!* The people closeted inside the pub had moved out onto the terrace, drinks in hands; one boomed out: *Bye-bye, fuzzie-wuzzies!*

Thanks to the efforts of Mzee, Tendai, Jonas Cole and perhaps even mister wispy-hair, nearly everybody had a copy of the broadsheet somewhere about their person, and now these pieces of paper came out, one by one and here and there, and were crumpled into uneven balls that were tossed in dribs and drabs from the railing to the keel-scoured sand.

My dear...

As the bobbing boats became horizon pepper, the jeers and catcalls multiplied as did the balls of thrown newsprint that fell well short of short in the chill.

My dear, I think you should have this...

The sweet shop lady was tapping my chest with something.

These are going to be scarce pretty soon, believe you me.

I took it. A piece of paper, folded up thick and small as a pack of pocket tissues.

COLDWATER BAY
PARISH PRESS

Friday, April 26th, 1974

LATE EDITION

PARISH PRESS PUBLISHES FAREWELL MESSAGE * THE VISITORS INSIST ON PUBLICATION BEFORE DEPARTURE * FULL TEXT GIVEN IN KISWAHILI AND ENGLISH

By John Craddock, Editor-in-Chief

The following valedictory statement was handed to me on Saturday, April 20th, by a man who identified himself only as Mzee. At his insistence, it has been distributed today, by hand, throughout Coldwater Bay.

Next week, Monday's issue of the Parish Press will contain a special report on the exceptional events of the last fourteen days.

Kwenu raia wote wa Uingereza, juu na chini na katika mikono yote ambapo ujumbe huu utapokelewa au kuangukia.

Tumekuja katika kisiwa hiki cha likizo kusini zaidi kijiji kilichotengwa chenye madhari nzuri kiitwacho Coldwater Bay. Kwa hitaji kubwa la likizo.

Ilikuwa nzuri. Asanteni sana kuwa nasi.

Sasa ni kwamba tunarudi tulikotoka tunatoa ombi hilo.

Bila wasiwasi hatutahitaji msaada zaidi. Na tunaele-kea katika masikitiko yasi-yokoma kuhusu biashara ya utumwa. Na kitu kimoja tunaelewa fika kwamba wa-henga wetu walishiriki pia.

To all citizens of the United Kingdom, both high and low, into whose hands this message may fall or be delivered.

As we said, we came to your southernmost holiday resort, a delightfully secluded village called Coldwater Bay, for a much-needed holiday.

It was nice. Thank you for having us.

Now that we are on our way back to where we came from, we wish to make a request.

Have no fear: we are not going to ask for any form of aid. Neither are we going to launch into an endless historical lament about the slave trade; for one thing, we know full well our ancestors were involved

Hata ninyi mligeuka kutoka biashara ya nyumba ndogo ndogo na kuwa biashara za kuvuka mabara.

Vile vile tunalalamikia chaguzi zilizo hujumiwa na uchumi wa mazao ya biashara ambapo tunajukumu la kujadiliana kuelekea uhuru wa kisiasa.

Nini zaidi, hatuna lengo la kulaumu nini kilichotokea kiasi cha miaka mia moja na hamsini iliyopita wakati wafanyabiashara wenu ambao wahenga wetu walishugulikiausawa kwa karne nyingi, walianza kuvunja milango ya maduka na kuiba masanduku ya kutunzia fedha.

Aidha tuliwaacha wafanye vile au tulijaribu kuzuia

in it, too. Even if yours were the ones who turned it from a cottage industry into a transcontinental enterprise.

Neither shall we grouse about the rigged elections and cash crop economies with which your governments of the time obliged us to negotiate the road to political independence.

What is more, we have no intention of condemning what happened some hundred and fifty years ago, when your traders, with whom our ancestors had dealt on an equal footing for centuries, started breaking down our shop doors and stealing the tills, to coin a metaphor. We either let them do it, or we tried to block the entrance.

lango la kuingilia lakini waliingia, sio vizuri kulilia mikataba iliyokiukwa. Pia tunatambua ya kwamba miongoni mwenu wengine wanajisikia wakosaji, wakosefu kama zambi kuwa katika taifa ambalo limekuwa kama tuseme chakavu-mbele yetu. Mapigo yao ya moyo yametufanya sisi kushawishika kujali maombi tuliyofanya kwenu.

Siyo kitu kidogo.

Miaka sabini na ushee iliyopita, hakukua na sehemu hata moja ya bara hili ambayo haikumilikiwa na Uingereza au nchi jirani za ulaya. Hata mlipigana kwa ajili ya ardhi yetu miongoni mwenu. Ambapo wachache wenu mngekataa maana ni nje ya uwezo wenu kufanya.

Either way, they got in. No good crying over reneged contracts.

We also know that amongst your very selves there are many who feel guilty—guilty as sin—for belonging to a nation which has behaved in such a—shall we say shabby—way towards us. Their breast beating neither concerns us nor has influenced us as regards the request we now wish to make of you.

Which is no small thing.

Seventy-odd years ago, there was not one part of our continent that had not been earmarked for possession by Great Britain or its European neighbours. You even fought over our lands amongst yourselves. Which, few could deny,

Serikari zetu- falme ndogo, Umoja wa vijiji, Tawala, miji na vituo vya biashara, aidha vilitolewa au kuwa serikari binafsi.

Mengi ya majina yao ki-ukweli haina maana ny-ingine kwenu ila kwa vyo-vyote ni Mossi, Basuto, Maravi, Bunyoro, Kasanje, Ndongo, Mande, Duala... Unafanya kutoa zawadi am-bapo panapostahili kubaki panajulikana kama mataifa yaliyo bakia: Wamasai kwa sababu ni vivutio; Wazulu kwa sababu wal-impiga Michael Caine ka-tika filamu na kushindwa, Waashanti kwa sababu san-aa zao zinaonekana kush-angaza katika majumba ya makumbusho.

was rather a presumptuous thing to do.

Our polities—small monarchies, village nexuses, empires, city states, riverine trading centres—were either eliminated or voided of autonomy. Most of their names, we presume, no longer mean anything to you, but here are some of them, anyway: Mossi, Basuto, Maravi, Bunyoro, Kasanje, Ndongo, Mande, Duala... You do, to give credit where credit is due, remain familiar with a handful of our pre-existing nations: the Masai because they have become picturesque; the Zulus because they fought Michael Caine in a film, and lost; the Ashanti because their artefacts look surprisingly interesting in museums.

Ingawa, katika mwendelezo wa haya katika sehemu zenu tulilazimika kuchukua lugha mbali mbali za ulaya ambazo bado tunaendelea kutumia nyingine za kwetu.

Ingawa sisi (na watoto wetu) tulilazimika kufanya zaidi kuliko muda wetu kwa kugema mipira, kuchumapamba, na kubangua kakaoili kufanya ya gurudumu la uchumi wenu likizunguka. Labda mlitufanya sisi kufanya kazi muda wote kwa sababu mliamini kwamba kubaki kwetu hapa hatuna muda wa maana? Tuliishi hapa kwa nguvu kwa kulinda vilivyo vyetu, mfumo wa masoko bara zima.

Katikati ya karne ya ishirini hakuna roho miongoni

Although, in the course of this prolonged imposition on your part, we were compelled to acquire several European languages, note that we still continued to use most of our own.

Although we (and our children) were obliged to do more than our bit of rubber tapping, cotton picking, and cocoa-tree chopping to keep the wheels of your commerce turning—perhaps you made us work around the clock because of your persistent belief that we have no sense of time?—we survived physically by preserving our own, continent-wide system of local markets.

mwetu haijabadilishwa kwenye uraia wa mojawapo au ya mataifa mbalimbali ambapo nyinyi na majirani zenu mlianzisha kitu kipya kwa ajili yetu (na kwa faida yenu). Mataifa ambayo mipaka ilichorwa kupita katikati ya maziwa. Mataifa ambayo yalikuwa madogo kuliko kingo za mito iliyopanuliwa, Tawala zilitwa katika fikira haraka za wake wa maofisa. Na tawala ambazo zilikuwa katikati ya tawala zingine mipaka yake ilitolewa nje.

Hatukuruhusiwa kusema chochote kuendesha hizi tawala, hata tukiruhusiwa tusingekuwa na muongozo na jinsi gani ya kufatilia yote haya kwa bara zima. Kwa kila shule mia mbili za msingi kuna moja tu ya

By the mid-twentieth century, not a soul amongst us had not been converted into a citizen of one or the other of the various states which you and your neighbours had invented for us (and for your own benefit). States whose frontiers were drawn across the middle of lakes; states that were little more than extended riverbanks; states named at the whim of officers' wives; states that simply filled in the spaces between other states that had only just been traced out.

We were allowed no say in the running of these states, and even if we had been, we would not have had a clue as to how to go about it, given that, throughout the continent, for every two hundred sekondari wengi wetu hatukuweza kusoma kwa wakati ule.

Vita vya kutupiga sisi vile vile havikusaidia pia je jirani zako wajerumani wanawakumbuka Waherero? Nanyi pia mnawakumbusha Wagikuyu, Waembu na Wameru? Hatukupaswa kamwe.

Baada ya kutangazwa uhuru vitu viliharibika.

Ni jinsi gani tunaweza kuelezea?

Hebu fikiria tafadhali tumekuwa katika Nyanja ya suluhisho zaidi.na kwamba tumeiunganisha Uingereza ya kusini na Ufaransa ya kaskazini, Uskochi na Sweden; Cornwall na Ureno…

primary schools, there was just one secondary one. Many of us, of course, didn't make it to primary school in the first place.

The wars against us, of course, didn't help either. Do your German neighbours remember the Herero? Do you yourselves remember the Gikuyu, the Embu and the Meru? We suppose not.

After the aforementioned independence, things got worse.

How can we explain how?

Imagine, please, that we had accosted you first, and had behaved in a similarly arbitrary fashion. That we had merged southern England, say, with northern France; Scotland with Sweden; Cornwall with Portugal...

Fikiri halafu tumeendesha hizi siasa ngumu kwa miongo na halafu kwa sababu zetu mbali mbali.Kuwapa uhuru kwa pigo la kalamu na kwamba hatukusita kuwasaidia mmoja baada ya mwingine kutegemea na msaada aliouonyesha kwetu.

Fikiri siasa zetu za mfumo wa kupanuka. Sasa uhuru ambao tuliupeleka katika migogro mara kwa mara kati ya mipaka ya Tawala zao, Migogoro hiyo tulinogesha kwa kuwapatia silaha na misaada.

Fikiri iwapo wakazi wa asilinyinyi mchague kutoshiriki katika swala hili kwa kugeuzamipaka yote na kufananisha na uhalisia mzuri katika ardhi tuliingilia ili

Imagine that we then ran these awkward polities for decades, and then, for various reasons of our own, granted them independence at the stroke of a pen; and that we didn't hesitate to switch our support from one to the other, depending on the allegiance they showed to us.

Imagine that these our clumsily fashioned polities, now 'independent', were then pitched by us—for reasons of our own—into conflicts, often between rival factions within their own state borders; conflicts we stoked with copious supplies of arms and aid.

kuhakikisha mipaka halisi kubaki kama ilivyo chorwa.

Fikiri ya kuwa hii iliendelea kwa miaka mingi baada ya uhuru mpaka kusema mwaka huu.

Tunaweka kwenu kuomba hii itabaki ni jambo lisilo shikika kikamilifu. Africa.

Kwa hiyo tungependa kufanya pendekezo ili kujaribu kurudia uwiano.

Kwamba tungepewa haki ya kupanga upya mipaka ya tawala zisizoshikamana. Bila ya hila katika kutoa misaada na bila siri katika usambazaji silaha, ili kuhakikisha kwamba hakuna vurugu na migogoro itakayowezekana katika kipindi cha makubaliano mikakati hii itachukua muda mrefu

Imagine that whenever the native inhabitants— yourselves—tried to opt out of this situation, by altering their frontiers so that they corresponded a little better to the reality on the ground, we stepped in and ensured that the original borders were kept exactly as we had drawn them.

Imagine that this went on for years after 'independence'. Until, say, this year.

We put to you that this has been and remains a thoroughly untenable situation.

Africa.

We would therefore like to make a proposal in an attempt to redress the balance.

(Baada ya yote itachukua nusu karne kujenga mfumo uliopo hata kwa bunduki za Maxim kwa upande wake.)

Tunatakiwa kutambua kwamba hata tukiamua kuunganisha tawala/mataifa kuwa shirikisho kubwa au kuunda tawala ndogo au majiji au kuchagua ni mfumo upi wa kisiasa utakaokuwa mzuri kwetu hakuna jaribio litakalofanywa kwa upande wenu kutuzuia sisi kufanya hivyo.

Tungependa pia kueleweka kwamba kama sera zetu zitaonekana kufanya kazi na mipaka ya tawala kwa pamoja na tutakuwa na mamlaka mazuri na siyo wachache kuamua kufanya kilicho sawa,suluhisho labda litaonekana mahali bado

That we should be given the right to rearrange the frontiers of our untenable states, with no disingenuously distributed aid and no clandestinely distributed arms, so as to ensure that no violent conflict will be possible during the processes of negotiation. These processes may take quite a long time. (After all, it took you half a century to create the current set-up, even with the Maxim guns on your side).

We wish it to be understood that whether we decide to merge our states into larger federations or create smaller states or city-states—or, indeed, to choose whichever forms of polity we decide are best for us—no attempt will be made on your part to prevent us doing just that.

basi litawekwa katika meza ya duara ambapo mataifa duniani yatajadili.

Ili yote haya yawezekane, itakuwa muhimu kwenu kuwabana wote ambao ni wakuu wa tawala kwa sasa. walio wekwa katika vyeo vya sasa nanyinyi au wame-shawishiwa nanyi kufanya hivyo.ambaye anaweza ku-toona macho kwa macho katika uwezeshaji wetu.

Zaidi tunawaomba kutumia mabaki ya diplomasia za Uingereza ili kuchochea ku-unda na kushawishi mataifa ya ulaya yasiharibu mab-adiliko haya.

Ni nini kinaleta maswali haya: sisi ni kina nani, ku-uliza yote haya kwenu?

We would also like it to be understood that if certain of our polities wish to dispense with state borders altogether—and we have it on good authority that not a few will decide to do exactly that—solutions may be found so that a place may still be laid for them at the table around which the nations of the world confer.

In order for all of this to become possible, it may be necessary for you to restrain those of our current heads of state—placed in their current positions by yourselves or encouraged by you to do so—who might not see eye to eye with our initiative.

Sisi sote ni wageni wenu, kwa njia moja au nyingine tumekuwa tukishiriki katika vita baridi iliyopiganwa mioyoni mwetu, tulipigana au kupigana kupinga,kabla yakutambua kwamba hakuna upande hata mmoja uliofaidika na hilo.Miongoni mwetu walilazimika kupigana,wengine walipigana kwa sababu walifikiria ni vyema na wengi wao wameishia katika moto.

Bila shaka tumekuja elewa ushindi daima ulikuwa umehifadhiwa machoni petu na kwamba raia wengine walikufa na kuhangaika kuliko wanajeshi kwa upande mwingine.

Hii ni mojawapo wa sababu kwa nini tulihitaji likizo.

We further request that you use what remains of the United Kingdom's diplomatic influence to convene your European neighbours and convince them too, not to obstruct these changes.

Which brings us to your inevitable question: who are we to ask all this of you?

All of us, your guests, in one way or another, have been involved in the cold wars being fought in our heat: we have fought— or been fought against— before realising that there was not a single side it was worth our while to be on. Some of us have been obliged to fight. Some of us have fought because we thought we wished to. Most have been caught up in the crossfire.

(Kuwa, tunatumaini bila kusema maeneo mengi ya bara letu kwa sasa yana amani na furaha pamoja na tumaini la mafanikio ya baadae, tunasonga mbele halafu bila dhamana tume-pewa matokeo ya kwamba maeneo haya hivi karibu-ni au badaye hayatapata kutembelewa na wapanda farasi wanne).

Kumalizia, tungependa ku-toa sauti ya neno la onyo.

Muda huu tumekuja katika amani,tunaonelea vyema kuonyesha sisi ni nani na jinsi gani ni rahisi kwetu kuja na kusema "hello".

Indeed, we came to understand that victory was forever being kept from our sight; and that more civilians were dying and suffering than were the soldiers on either side.

That is one of the reasons why we all needed a holiday so badly.

(There are, we hope it goes without saying, many areas of our continent which are currently at peace, and where cheerfulness— together with the hope of some future prosperity— keeps breaking through. However, there is no guarantee, given the circumstances, that these areas will not, sooner or later, be due a visit from the Four Horsemen).

Halafu tunafikiri ni muhimu kusisitiza kwamba kama maombi yetu tuliyoeleza hapa yatapuuzwa na kutojaliwa yatasababisha turudi hapa kwa idadi kubwa zaidi.	To finish, we would like to sound a word of warning.
	This time we arrived in peace. We wished to show you who we are, as well as how easy it is for us to come and say hello.
Tutafanya hivyo lini na jinsi gani tuwezavyo na tutabaki hapa mpaka makubaliano yafikiwe.	However, we feel it necessary to emphasise that if our requests stated here are ignored so persistently as to give us cause to assume that they will never be given due consideration, we shall return, in far larger numbers.
Kama mtataka kujuwa kwa nini tumejitayarisha kufanya hivi njooni katika sehemu mojawapo ambazo tumetoka na tunasema mnakaribishwa sana.	
	We will do so as and when and how we wish. We will remain until an agreement has been reached.
Hakika mngeona kwamba mambo ya kitaifa kwa sasa na jinsi yanavyotokea, chaguo letu halitazidi mojakatika idadi.	If you wish to know why we are prepared to do this, you have only to come and live in one of the

Moja tunalopendekeza ni. **Tafadhali fanya liwezekalo kutii huu ujumbe kabla hatujafikiri kuwa hakuna njia nyingine ila kujiandaa kuja tena.** **Tafadhari.** **Wakati mwingine tutawaacha raia wetu nyuma.** *Goodbye.*	many places we have come from for, say, a fortnight. You would be most welcome. You would then surely see that—given the current state of affairs and the way things are shaping up—our options are limited to a number not exceeding one. The one we propose. So please, do deign to respond to this message, before we feel we have no alternative but to prepare our next visit. Please. The next time, we shall leave our civilians behind. *Kwa heri.*

PART FOUR: I WAS TWENTY-ONE

Christ, how good it tastes, like mother's milk, old mother's milk. Down, down, down like honey, like White's Cream Soda, like the excitement from when I was eight and nine and ten and eleven, when it was so bloody exciting to be so small and to know without knowing why that you had a life as big as a battleship stretching ahead of you, impressive in the water.

Just a jiffy I require, to tilt the bottle's neck once more, one eye on the honey-coloured liquid as it splashes softly into the tumbler. I scoop cubes from my ever-ready black-and-white ice bucket. I let my poison sit for a bit. As the grown-ups always told me whenever they bought me a can of pop: *Don't drink it all at once.*

My perennial wish to please those I loved, or fancied or fancied I loved, served me by forcing me to make an effort to scrape through my A levels. After which, those wonderful masters at Big School, their fingers laced with pullable strings, got me into a university.

By the time it was time for me to knuckle down for my finals, my entrails were pickled from the liver to the ileum, my brain was stable in brine, and my eyes shone like a Chinese meal.

I attended three specialised clinics in all, two private, at my parents' bidding—my poor parents, they could hardly have guessed wherefore I drank, my not having told a soul—and one public, which I checked into off my own soused bat. In the latter, the psychotherapy being done in groups, I met a lot of people, heard a lot of people spill their woes on the worn carpet our feet all shared. On the day I departed I swore to all those newly made half-friends that this time I was going to stay on the wagon, and that I was going to ride that wagon off into the sunset. Wishing to please: there I went again.

Like I just said, I never mentioned Coldwater Bay, not ever. Not stone-cold sober to the psychotherapists and their nurse sidekicks; and not to anyone else, even when under the influence.

*

During the last days in Coldwater Bay it became increasingly obvious to me that all that was required to find a way out of that village was some serious reconnaissance. Reccying was the key to flight. Didn't anyone except us teeny-boppers read the trash mags?

So I reccied the village with persistence and gumption. (By that stage Lucy, who had fallen lock, stock and barrel for one of the black fellas, probably didn't even notice I was spending most of my time out of the house.)

The armbanded Africans kept a watch on the only road out, on the shops and the pub, and wherever else village people tended to congregate; as well as on the western end of the esplanade, there where it merged into grassland. As for the eastern end, they didn't need to keep an eye on that: it ran into a sheer rock face.

What was more, to judge from their resigned faces, a majority of villagers were more surprised than frightened by the situation. They certainly didn't appear to feel the Africans meant them any harm. Sit it out, seems to have been their philosophy.

So when I started to wander round the back streets of Coldwater Bay, it wasn't as if I was bumping into fellow daredevil escapees on every corner.

Besides, I cut a slight, inconspicuous figure back then, as well as looking too innocent to be up to no good.

On Friday, the twenty-sixth of April, knowing the road sweeper's funeral would be a crowd-puller, I left Seaview Heights early and ambled up the backstreets until I reached the backmost of them all, beyond which there was nothing but a broad upward slope, some of it grassy, some of it bare rock. I knew that slope had to be pretty steep for some couple hundred yards, then would become more gradual: just like the exit road a way off to my left.

There was a condemned house, fourth from the right, with a weather-faded KEEP OUT sign nailed to its door. The place looked as gloomy as a husband left on his tod. A side alley to the right of the house led from the front yard through to the back. I walked on to the end of the street, turned round, retraced my steps. There was no one in sight. Without hesitation—after all, all this I was doing for Lucy—I swung first one leg and then the other over the low wall, crossed the front yard and strode through the alley, my heart boom-boom-booming.

The backyard turned out to be about the size of a tennis court. It had untended flower beds on three sides, a-prickle with skew-whiff plants.

The fence at the back was a thin, dark wood affair, similar to one which a great-uncle of mine had had in his back garden in Pinner (and all his neighbours, in theirs). It was a head higher than I was, but—I guessed from my childhood trips to suburbia—would tip forward creaking worse than trodden stairs as soon as I started climbing.

Lucy, I re-reminded myself, I was doing this for Lucy, and gripped the fence's top end. Sure enough, as I hauled myself up it leaned forward some thirty degrees with an eek and a sough; I flung one leg over, was astride the thing for a ball-poking moment, then swung the other leg over and dropped myself down onto the far side, flexing my knees as I'd been taught when high-jumping at school; I fell over nonetheless. I lay where I was for a moment, testicles smarting, ears straining for stray voices, or shouts, or cries of alarm.

I began to scramble up the slope in front of me, pressing down my hands for better traction wherever they felt grass; after about twenty minutes I ran out of stamina. There must have been a hundred yards or so to go before the steepness stopped.

I recalled an old ploy from when I'd been made to run exercise laps of the playing field: *You're a British bulldog.* That's the image I used to lash myself on with: *Remember you're a British bulldog,* I whispered to myself as I inched forward, face squashed and puckered as the slope grew less steep by degrees until it was all but level.

I raised myself into a crouch and scuttled forward, as low as I could go. The grassy rock gave way gradually to grass pure and unadulterated, which meant that the main road—Military Road—was now just a couple hundred yards ahead.

I ran like I'd never run before. Flat as a pancake the muddy soil was, and it might have slowed me up if my feet hadn't been feather-light now and self-confidence hadn't been blossoming in my mind: All this I am doing for you, Lucy. I will be the angel that will get your Daddy out of confinement and put the clock back to where it so comfortably sat a fortnight ago, and who might even roll into the village on the turret of a tank waving at the flower-chucking girls packing the streets, so that you may see you are not the only pebble on the beach, Luce.

Military Road was flanked by wild grass. My throat was sore with wheezing. No traffic. Not so much as an aural trace of a single bloody car.

Simon, I remembered well, had been driving off west to Freshwater when he'd been intercepted. So I decided to go in the other direction, east to Brook ,and even then to avoid the road.

I sprinted across the asphalt and kept going north over the next fields. I stopped only when I could no longer see Military Road behind me, or the sea beyond that. I felt safer, doubting that the Africans could have posted lookouts this far inland.

I turned eastward, in the general direction of Brook. I kept an orientational eye on the hedgerow to my left, but then the hedgerow ran out, and, bereft of bearings I came up against a copse, skirted it and strode across four more fields, oblivious to the growing cold. At the edge of the last field, the underfoot mush of grass and soil turned into tarmac: Badger Lane. I made one last check for swooshes of vegetation or whites of observing eyes which I now did not expect to find at all. Not in a place called Badger Lane.

Which led me past a mesh of branches, trunks, tussocks and ferns that clicked and tutted as I passed.

The final stretch of the lane was flanked on each side by a single row of trees so closely planted they seemed to be competing for views of me, their tops bumping into each other as I started to trot, then outright ran, all the way to where Brook's first houses were waiting for me to calm down, to smile, to go phew, to look around for the house which would be my best bet.

Now: a top-up of my eternal drinky-poo. Tasty.

I plumped for a building that looked well-off, walked up the garden path and rang the bell. As I waited—in front of a white panelled door with two mock carriage lights on either side—I noticed the tears in my anorak, the earth stains on my cords, the dirty damp that had turned my Hush Puppies black and a squash of cowpat peeping out from under one of the soles. I looked at my Timex: tennish.

The door was opened by a little girl of about eight: *Whatever it is you're selling, we're not interested.* She giggled before slamming the door.

Coldwater Bay! Lucy! Without thinking, I pressed the bell once, twice, three times. The electric dong-dings echoed indoors, over and over and over until a middle-aged man trussed up in a silk dressing down jerked the door open: *What's going on here?*

His voice bore a passing resemblance to that of Dr Whitebone.

Something ever so serious has happened! I have to call the police!

His features softened even as the fluffiness of my accent dawned on his ears: *What exactly is the matter, little man?*

After that, it was plain sailing.

*

The owner had me wait in the living room—silky curtains, thick pile carpet, a bookshelf packed with first editions of thrillers, a boffo stereo with speakers tall as topiaries—while he took his time on the phone in the hall, talking, so he claimed, to the police, his voice muffled, indecipherable. His wife popped her head round the door and said she'd make me some tea. Her husband still hadn't got off the phone by the time she placed tea things on the coffee table.

All right?

Thanks very much.

It wasn't until I was halfway through my second cuppa that I heard a car on the drive. The living room door opened again and there stood the owner; he pointed down the corridor to the front door.

Go on through.

I stepped out onto the gravel, and there waiting was a beige Jaguar, an XJ6 no less, its exhaust pipe puffing. A man in a camel-hair coat sat at the wheel. Another man, in a coat ditto, was holding open the rear passenger door and saying my name with a question mark on the end.

Yes, that's me.

It didn't occur to me to ask them to identify themselves, so impressed I was. I assumed they were CID.

In you get, then.

I bumped my head as I clambered aboard. Bam went my door and bam went my door-holder's as he got in at the front. He waved through the open window at the couple framed in their doorway.

The couple waved back as the car pulled away, their faces bemused and satisfied both.

*

I was driven faster than legal along almost deserted lanes: when the driver did come across a car, he zoomed up to its bumper and hooted until it pulled over.

No sooner had we left Brook than the man who'd asked me my name turned round and asked me to repeat what I'd already told Mr Worseley. His voice sounded like it was working-class and didn't want to be. He jotted things down as I spoke.

*

We passed a handful of places: Chessell, Ningwood, Shalfleet, Newtown, then turned left up a side road to a tall mesh gate set in a tall mesh fence topped with barbed wire.

The sign next to the gate read: NEWTOWN RANGE AND JERSEY CAMP. MILITARY TRAINING AREA. A sentry opened up. A soldier!

Excuse me, but aren't you with the police?
We work with the police, let's put it like that.

401

We drove in, turned right and continued parallel to the fence, past a single-storey building that might have belonged to a good golf club, then along the flank of a wood and over a river then along a squashy track, until we reached a farm. A couple of men carrying pails glanced at the Jaguar as it drew up in front of the main house, pebble-dash façade more or less covered by writhing honeysuckle. The driver turned off the ignition.

Let's be having you.

They took me into the farmhouse, sat me down in a spacious kitchen, and left. A second later, the door opened again and another man came in, above-average tall, wearing a black coat.

How do you do? My name is Maurice.

His manner, his tone, his burr told me that he was OC. Maurice took off his coat—underneath he was wearing a black jacket and a white shirt unbuttoned at the top to make room for a puffy silk cravat—hung it on a wall peg and sat down at the table, opposite me.

Just like the man in the car, he asked me to tell him everything. I went into what was becoming a regular spiel; from time to time, he asked for more details: words I had heard the blacks use, the way they dressed, how many of them seemed to be wearing armbands; the villager's reactions, those of the local police, the reasons for Dr Whitebone's arrest (about which, at that time, I knew next to nothing). How I managedto get out. He didn't take notes. When his questions seemed to have come to an end, I stressed my concern for Lucy. He looked me in the eye: *You've done rather well.* I felt chuffed.

However, even as my heart glowed with pride, ensconced as I was like a bona fide intelligence operative before Maurice's prying eyes, the odd doubt was worming its way into the back of my mind. What was this Mr Maurice going to do with this scoop I'd placed in his hands?

No one in the village is going to come to any harm, are they? Now that you know, I mean?

Harm? The villagers?

Them and the blacks, too.

He smiled fast: *I thought a well-educated young chap like you would know that that is not the way we do things in this country.*

Hunky-dory, I wanted everything to be in the end: *I don't want to seem rude, but can I have your word on that?*

Maurice chuckled: *My word? Rather an old-fashioned concept. May I ask which school you attend?*

I told him.

No!

Yes.

His face shed its former wary coolness and took on the mien of an eager, if inexplicably wrinkled, schoolboy's.
Do they still chuck pancakes over the bar on Maundy Tuesday?

Oh, yes! I've done it twice.

403

And is Little Peter still kept hanging in the HM's cupboard?

Yes, it is, unfortunately. How come you know all this?

How do you think, little man?

The penny dropped with a racket.

Were you a pupil there?

Extra appreciatively, he was looking at me now.

I most certainly was.

Wow.

Long before your time, of course. But I do have very fond memories of the place.

I like it there too.

I'm sure you do.

He leaned forward and patted my hand:

It's occurred to me, you know, that you deserve a bit of a reward for the excellent service you have rendered to your country. You seem to be concerned about the Africans, as well as the villagers; perhaps you might care to see our visitors being escorted safely away from the coast. Have you ever flown in a helicopter?

Not yet, I haven't.

Would you like to take a spin in one?

Would I just!

He grinned, then looked at his watch, then seemed to consult a patch of wall, then nodded.

Do you know, I do believe that's quite feasible. We'll see what we can do.

Bottoms up. All the way down to the icy dregs. And one more, why not? No point in crying over spilt.

*

The remaining events of the day felt like they were being bowled towards me, knocking me for six. A ride, an interview, officials, another interview, my life's one and only helicopter flight, another ride, the final interview. If all that had happened before seemed to have been taking its due time, the end of the last day made a rush at me, hurtling down the approach, time and again, towards my particular pit.

*

My Timex said one pm when the door opened again, and I was surprised to see not Maurice but the nameless camel-coated chaps who had chauffeured me out of Brook. The driver was holding a tray which he placed before me and then removed the tea cloth, to reveal a steaming mug of soup and a plateful of watercress sandwiches. I remembered to say thank you. He stepped back and leaned against the wall. The other man, the one who'd asked me questions in the car, sat down at the head of the table. Both kept their coats on despite the warmth in the kitchen, which for some time now had been steaming my wet shoes dry.

The one at the table pointed at the tray: *You must be hungry.* To show willing, I picked up the mug, blew on it, and took a sip of soup: *Where's Mr Maurice?* The man took out a pack of cigarettes. Dunhill. The fag for shop assistants who wanted to be classy, we'd joked at school, Roger and I. He lit one, exhaled: *Mr Maurice is a very busy man right now; thanks to you.* I took sip number two. It tasted nice.

I ate, cheered by the thought that should all now go swimmingly, I would surely get into Lucy's good graces. Or even her teenaged heart. Or, and why not?, her knickers. After all, at twelve (going on thirteen), knickers were on my mind.

The table man stood up: *Time I was getting back to the mainland.* The man at the door plucked it open: *Right you are.* The table man turned to me and said *Be good,* for which no answer occurred to me as he turned up his camel-coloured collar and slipped out. The door man closed the door after him, and went back to watching me chew.

*

My mug and plate were empty and my watch said gone five when a thudding of rotor blades—recognisable from the cinema, recognisable from the Nine O'Clock News—grew louder and louder until the windows rattled. When the silent man cracked the door to take a peek outside, his face flinched from the air blast, and the longer bits of his short haircut fluttered as best they could: *Time you were on your way.*

He accompanied me out, my clothes fluttering in the squall from the Sea King that had landed in a field on the western side of the farm. It had 'Royal Air Force' painted on the side and the word RESCUE under the cabin and on the tail. He bent down to my ear: *Maurice thought you'd like the ride.*

The Sea King's cabin window slid back, and a helmeted pilot gave a cheery wave. My escort laid a hand on my shoulder: *Let's say hello, shall we?*

We ran into the flurry, the grass bristling, the sky grey way above us. It had started to spit a little.

The blades having stopped now, I could hear the pilot shouting as he pointed at me with a podgy glove: *What's all this about?* My escort shouted back: *Case officer's idea...joy ride for the kid...he insisted...put us in a spot...*

The kid.

...so let's do this properly...straight back to Odiham...no hanging about.

He tapped his watch emphatically. The side hatch swung open, and into the belly of the beast I clambered, helped by the pilot, who sat me down on a metal side bench near a window, strapped me in, and then walked back to his cabin, where the other one was waiting

The interior was big enough to carry my entire class at school. I stared in awe. The pilots adjusted helmets, thumbed-up to the man outside, then turned to look at me trussed up solitary against the fuselage wall for my own safety, their faces wary: *All right?* upon which I thumbed-up in turn, glancing thrilled at the packed rows of switches and dials on the control panel—the only thing I could identify was the round radar screen in the centre—at the bunches of cables packed into the roof, at the pilots' cantilevered seats which looked like they'd been designed for a special type of cripple. The rotors started to twirl back into life, loud and clear and faster and faster.

We rose into the air, pitching and yawing, the fields turning, fast as dizzy spells, into patches, and the lanes into lines, slightly blurred by drizzle. I gulped with joy—derived in part from a certain sense of self-importance—as the machine ascended, its metal shuddering, its rotors, both main and tail, whacking the air.

Once we were well and truly in the sky, the pilot on the right turned round and pushed his mike away from his mouth: *Having fun?*

Yes, thank you!

We're heading south-south-west; should be within visual range of the destination in about ten minutes.

Visual range of the destination! We flew over a small town. Shalfleet? Chessell? Ningwood? Dinky cars, dinky houses, dinky people here and there in their back gardens. An old biddy waved. I waved back, nose pressed to the flecked window. We thud-thudded our way over fields, copses, hedgerows, roads, and over two big woods, their spongy florets Airfix-glued to the ground.

The chopper swung to the right, jerking my face away from the window. The other pilot raised a hand: *Sorry about that.* We swung about once more, this time to the left. I flopped about in my straps. The pilot who'd apologised, shouted: *You should recognise this bit.*

I recognised it like I'd been living there for years and years: the Manse, the high street, all of Coldwater Bay swooping into view, near enough to toss pebbles at.

I whispered: *Coldwater Bay, here I come; beleaguered people, here I come; Lucy! I promised myself I'd do it and here I am, flying in, just for you.*

The pilots' mikes crackled and sputtered: *Roger, two hundred feet...* We went lower, towards the row of people at the pier.

And there she was, I actually spotted her, there she was—Lucy, Lucy!—her face staring out to sea at the little boats which were moving forward in two irregular lines, like strings of beads slapped across the water.

Then we were fast leaving Lucy and the surf-nibbled coast behind; the people at the railing became a row of fluff, the staid houses, a tiny stone array.

The helicopter swung downward, wobbling. One of the pilots yelled through the rotor din: *Every now and again we go in close to see of anyone needs any assistance; standard procedure.* No reply coming to mind, I nodded, and went on looking through the window. The boats below us were close enough for me to see the lace wakes spun by their outboards, and their occupants staring unworriedly at us out of anoraks and shawls and coats and windcheaters. I heard the pilot shout into his mike: *Girl Guide to Rangers, repeat, Girl Guide to Rangers, Brownies heading due south-west, coordinates to follow.*

The other pilot gave me a wave: *Ever been to the Channel Islands?* I shook my head. He thumbed down. A large green blodge and two little ones. Pitched at a slight angle, nose seaward, we flew over one of the smaller blodges, the one that was nearest to the French coast (which lay there, green and smug and Gallic). Below us, between the blodge and *la belle France*, a trawler was anchored, on which the boats, looking pluckier and pluckier in that torn-up sheet of sea, were converging. We dove in for a closer look.

The side of the trawler which gave onto the approaching boats was lined with black men and women, all of them faffing about with cables and ropes.

Brownies about to board. Coordinates forty-nine, twenty-five, twenty-five north; three, twenty-one, ninety-seven west; repeat, forty-nine, twenty-five...

The first of the boats were drawing alongside the trawler, down the side of which now hung an array of rope ladders.

Brownies have commenced boarding. Coordinates forty-nine, twenty-five, twenty-five north...

Tiny people were climbing those tiny ladders. When they reached the gunwale, they were hoisted on deck by the tiny crewmen. Each newly emptied boat was lashed and hauled up onto the mothership, leaving the nearest full boat to move into its place, whereupon the boarding process would start again. We were circling overhead, round and round.

Girl Guide to Ranger; all Brownies have boarded. Have you read the coordinates, over? The pilot on the right turned and smiled: *Back to Blighty any moment now, son.*

They checked their watches. I pressed my face to my window.

The trawler, its deck milling, had upped anchor and was heading away from the blodge of land, in the general direction of Brittany.

The pilot on the.

Just a mo, Joe. One more for the road and sod the ice.

The pilot on the right pointed at the radar screen: *They're early, they're really early. Put your bloody foot down.*

The pilot on the left glanced at me: *Hold tight, son!* The Sea King accelerated up and forward, yawing on its axis, then swung round, its tail to France, its nose to the United Kingdom. I heard a distant jet roar.

Girl Guide to Ranger, returning to base; repeat, Girl Guide returning to base.

The pilot on the right jabbed the radar again, and the two of them started to peer at the sky. The pilot on the left pointed at nine o'clock. Exactly the direction my window was facing.

Let's sodding well get a move on!

A brace of Hawker Siddeley Harriers soared towards us out of the clouds, then above and beyond us in what felt like the nick of time. They were heading in the general direction of the trawler.

The pilot on the right tapped his fellow on the arm, with what seemed some urgency.

Hold tight, son!

The Sea King picked up some speed, but not enough for me not to hear the jets' bellow, muffled at first, then rising to a scream, which waned to something like silence for several seconds.

When the explosion came, the helicopter lurched as if shoved by a lout.

The pilots corrected the unwanted yaw, allowing me—one cheek flattened like a stingray against my window—to see the top end of a billow of smoke, black as oil, that was boiling up and up and up, escaping skyward.

I tried to peer down, but the helicopter was tilted to one side—giving me but a square of grey sky—before shooting off.

Away from it all.

The truth took me a trance-like moment to realise. Then I doubled over, stomach fit to shit, my cheeks full of rising blood. Perhaps I'd got it wrong? What about the children (loathed them though I did, children, at the time)?

Clutching my safety belt with both hands I leaned out into the fuselage and shouted: *What's happened?* They didn't—or pretended not to—hear me. So I raised my voice until it was a screech: *I said, what happened just now?*

The pilot on the right jabbed his finger in the general direction of Britain: *Back in no time, son.*

To think I'd longed for so long to see fire blasting out of barrels, to see the enemy scream while exploding into fragments, to see grenades wipe out machine-gun nests and flamethrowers fry the enemy. To see my comics come to life.

My Sea King bore me in my upset state over a tip of France, across the Channel's slosh, over the Isle of Wight, which I barely glanced at, over Portsmouth and down to an inland base, whose hangars grew from Monopoly houses into building blocks into long buildings, beside one of which we landed on a tarmac pad.

I sat slumped forward in my safety belt, while one of the pilots unclasped my buckle and lifted me bodily and—hoisting me up against his chest with one arm like I was so much baby—took me out into the open air.

The man who'd sat at the table with me was there, leaning against the Jaguar with crossed arms, a pose he broke chop-chop as soon as we landed. He asked the pilots something I didn't catch, then grabbed my arm and yanked me over me to the car, opened the back door, said something I didn't catch either, placed a hand over my head and pushed my head down so low, he nearly squashed my face into the seat leather. He fastened my seat belt, clunk, click, glanced at his watch, slammed my door and slid into the driver's seat. As he turned the ignition key, he looked back at my tear-stained face with an expression I recognised only too well as the one grown-ups use, and I daresay still use, to express disgust with children for being childlike.

*

We were on a motorway for about an hour. Camel-coat didn't say a word. Scenery rushed past, too fast for me to digest the sneering worm of ghastliness that was lolling around inside me. The man looked steadily ahead, overtaking vehicle after vehicle, as po-faced as if chauffeuring a coffin. We drove into a built-up area and finally drew up in front of a walled house painted white. I managed to ask where we were. My driver glanced at his watch again and said Richmond.

He got out, walked round the car, and tugged my door open: *Come along!*

He rang the bell. A thin man, with a haircut that looked wartime, opened the door: *You're late.*

Maurice, in his ignorance, thought the kid deserved a treat; sent him up in the helicopter, which hung around a bit too long.

The thin man looked at my troubled face: *Hello, little man; that doesn't seem to have been a very good idea, now does it?*

*

The thin man pulled me along a corridor which smelt of mothballs: *Sir Michael's in the most filthy bate; he can't abide unpunctuality.*

At the end was a wooden door, painted black. He knocked, then opened the door a crack: *He's here, Sir Michael.*

He opened the door wide.

The room was painted brown to chest height and clotted cream from chest to ceiling, and was as bare as Mother Hubbard's cupboard. Sitting on a plastic chair in the middle of the floor was a portly gentleman in a three-piece pinstripe and speckled tie. He was bald from forehead to rear pate, with thin layers of silver hair flat against his temples. He pointed at an identical chair placed at a yard's distance—the only other item of furniture there—upon which I duly sat, feeling exactly like the hapless infant I knew he took me for. The man who had escorted me in coughed: *You should know this young man was taken up in the helicopter; Maurice's wheeze.*

Was it now? Perhaps Maurice should have been put fully in the picture, clearance or no clearance.

Will you be requiring...?

Not for the time being, thank you, Jeremy. Be an angel and close the door on your way out, would you?

*

Sir Michael turned to me, his funereally serious eyes the colour of cockles: *Welcome to Latchmere House. This is what our allies on the far side of the pond see fit to call a 'special facility'; I always think that makes it sound rather like a lavatory.*

He looked me over with a certain distaste.

What did you see from the helicopter?

Careful, I knew I had to be, even as my face flooded with blood and my nape went moist.

Hardly anything.

He leaned forward, a little.

Could you be a little more precise?

I did hear a bit of a bang in the background.

And what did you think it was, that bang?

I've always been a lousy.

I don't know.

He leaned back.

I doubt that your extreme youth would allow you to appreciate the gravity of the events to which you have unintentionally been made privy; however, it is incumbent upon you to pass through the same security procedure as every other witness. To that end, I must needs inform you that you will be obliged to take an oath not to reveal one single detail—allow me to repeat myself: not one single detail—of what took place in Coldwater Bay, on the Isle of Wight, between April the fifteenth and April the twenty-sixth of this year nineteen seventy-four; including what you say you didn't see from the helicopter today. Am I making myself clear?

I had nothing in my mind's eye but black billows, nothing in my ears but explosion, no gut feeling but alarm.

Should one iota of the aforementioned information find its way into the public domain, the source—even if the source happens to be a minor—will accordingly be traced, debunked and then dealt with, rather severely.

I managed a nod.

As you value all that is dear to you, and that all that is dear to your mother and father—who will be debriefed in due course—you will keep your silence until the time, should such a time ever arise, when the authorities decide it is no longer requisite. Your oath, then, will be for good, in both senses of the word.

His brine-preserved eyes watched me. I found myself holding my breath.

Jeremy!

The hinges squeaked and Jeremy popped his head round the door: *Sir?*

Kindly take this young gentleman to the office. Make sure he understands everything he signs.

I felt Jeremy's spidery hand on my shoulder.

*

In Latchmere House's filing-cabinet-lined office, the pen I'd been lent scraped its way along the dotted lines of sheet after sheet of shushing paper.

It is imperative you understand that failure to honour these pledges would be considered, by any judge in the land, as an act of treason, the penalty for which, I believe, every schoolboy knows.

The documents Jeremy handed me to sign did not make any explicit reference to what had really taken place but referred instead to a war game of a unique, exceptional, but indispensable nature, carried out with the assistance of an (unspecified) Commonwealth country. I presume this was the story fed to all the villagers, whether they chose to believe it or not. They too, I also presume, were subjected to the same intimidation as myself: those with jobs and children, perhaps more so.

I never discovered what kind of 'debriefing' my parents were eventually given, but from the day I was returned home, no mention was made by them of my holiday on Wight, or of the Whitebones, for that matter (with whom they appeared to have completely lost touch).

A month later, I was thirteen.

*

At fourteen, I became a secret drinker, something that's easier done than said, being a simple question of siphoning off discreet amounts of spirits from the family drinks cupboard and supplementing them with the cheapest beverages that an understanding offie will sell you if you can pass for eighteen.

Before, my mind had flapped, trapped in the birdlime of unwelcome thoughts, so I doused it so thoroughly it could barely raise a twitch. Once I'd got the hang of the measures, I never got blotto. On the contrary, alcohol provided the peace of mind which allowed me to function normally at both work and play.

I kept my mouth shut about Coldwater Bay through adolescence and beyond.

As I moved from prep school to Big School and on to university, as if life was as simple as a series of gear changes, occasionally I would run into Roger. The first time, Roger tried to bring Coldwater Bay up in his bumbling fashion. I changed the subject. Or pretended I hadn't heard. Or left the room. I really don't, really can't remember. There are many things now which I have rubbed from recall, alcohol's eraser leaving nothing but shavings in its necessary wake.

I can't even remember the last time I saw old Rodge.

*

Twenty years ago, television was regarded as an ideal source of employment for overeducated people like myself who did not wish to become either merchant wankers or cyril servants. After joining those of my peers who had put themselves into the pertinent queue, I landed a job as an assistant PA for the current affairs department of an independent television station based in London. The job did, indeed, turn out to be ideal for me, given that I did not stand out at all amid the stressed-out and mostly young dipsomaniacs by whom I found myself surrounded. I was twenty.

We toiled at a breakneck pace I found comforting. After work, we jammed ourselves into a nearby pub, one and all, and when closing time came creeping round, it was always a short distance to the nearest Indian, and from that Indian it was a question of a couple or three taxis to trundle us through the London night to this or that club at which, after a brief attempt at maintaining the kind of serious conversation proper to youthful professionals, we would end up either snogging one of our bunch in the many shadows of those clubs or dancing like puppets plopped about by sloshed marionetteers.

In the morning we would awake, alone or accompanied, as the case might be, in our flatlets; but as our work normally didn't start until mid-morning or so, we would have plenty of time to take the Alka-Seltzer, the aspirin, the black coffee or the healing hair of the dog before pulling on clothes and hopping onto the Tube.

At the weekends, we usually went to each other's parties, at which, inevitably, at least two or three people wouldn't calibrate their alcohol intake correctly and would end up screaming obscenities in the middle of a crowded lounge, or vomiting in the master bedroom, or passing out behind the lavatory's locked door.

The liquor continued to take the edge off the insects that were still squirming in that part of my mind to which I had denied myself access.

Thus did I and my colleagues enter the early eighties, watching events great and small unfurl, then get neatly rolled up again.

I wore cowboy boots that no cowboy could have afforded, wore clothes adorned with pocketless zips and had haircuts in brass-plaque-announced establishments where they served you iced Coke as they snipped away at your scalp.

*

As Lady Luck or her live-in boyfriend Sod's Law would have it, my twenty-fourth birthday happened to fall on a Friday, and that particular Friday several parties happened to be on at the same time, most of them happening to be in the same area (just north of Oxford Street). The birthday boy had been invited to all of them.

I treated myself to a little preliminary lubrication in the Argyll, next to Oxford Circus station, then headed for rendezvous number one, a short stroll away in Great Portland Street. Zilch was going on there, and when a young woman came in with whom I had been unable to get it up not too many soused nights ago started pointing at me while whispering into a girlfriend's ear, I left.

The next place on my list—a flat in Langham Street—was packed to the gills. I eased my way through the deafening babble, and nodded hi to those I recognised until I'd made it to the drinks table. I surveyed the offer, and plumped for an enticingly cold can of Carlsberg Special Brew.

Isn't that a tramps' drink?

She was standing at the far end of the table, pouring herself a glass of plonk, her eyes kohl-ringed and her hair in a perfectly cut, through-a-hedge-backward style. She was wearing a soft black leather jacket over a baggy T-shirt, half of which was black and the other half bright white.

Hello, Lucy.

Her stare wobbled a touch before recognition set in: *Hey, long time, no see.*

You look different.

She laughed, and looked me over: *You look different, too. You even dress OK; thought I'd never see the day.*

As she was turning abruptly away, on the point of merging into backs and shoulders and grins, I shoved my way closer: *Lucy.*

If I was twenty-four, then she was twenty-six. Not much of a difference, not any more. She was on something for sure, her pupils being wide and her mouth rehearsing its moves before it spoke.

What is it?

Seize the day, I told myself, seize the day, so I seized my can of beer, and without a moment's hesitation wrapped my lips round that teardrop opening and drank, pointing one finger at her, by way of saying, don't go just yet.

The beer hit the spot, smack between the frontal lobes, where most good it would do.

Why, Lucy, your tone reminds me of certain gentlemen I met from the Ministry of Defence, all those years ago.

What?

Her smile, frozen though it was, kept me going: *There's something I've been wanting to tell you, for years; but perhaps not here.*

She laughed and turned to take in the room crowded out with smoke and jabber and muffled rock: *This party's naff; besides, you're the only soul here I know.*

*

We ambled south, in the general direction of Dean Street. We ended up at the French House, and for the time being made small talk: university, work, love life. Her last flame, it so happened, had flickered out a couple of months ago. I ran my eyes over the De Gaulle proclamation on the wall while the random simpers and giggles of nearby customers buzzed about my lobes, and for a moment I thought: why not just keep it like this? Keep the talk this small and the flirtation this restrained and maybe steal a kiss on the street outside and then make my excuses, and go? Keep life simple and the alcohol sweet and this girl, opposite me, for just a little longer. And my mouth, shut.

So, how're your parents doing, Lucy?

That did for the small talk, as I could tell by the fastening of her eyes on mine.

If we're going to get onto that subject, I'd rather we went somewhere quieter.

I took her a stone's throw farther south to a place I knew off Leicester Square which had a poorly frequented upstairs bar. She ordered a rum and Coke and me a barley wine, and we headed without more ado for the remotest of the many empty tables. She shucked off her jacket and slung it over the back of her chair. Her breasts, which until then I had paid hardly any attention to—not since when I was twelve—were now pleasantly present.

You remember my mum?

Of course.

Mrs Whitebone had ended up following the shopkeeper and his little brown girl and a couple of converted villagers north to where a lot of other like-minded people had converged on a commune in Suffolk, the closest address for friends and relatives being a PO box in Bury St Edmunds.

She told me and Simon that she wanted to do something that gave her life meaning. That was the last we saw of her; nineteen seventy-five, beginning of.

She made an inroad into her drink. I got another barley wine, sat back down: *And your dad?*

He'd already gone off to Jo'burg with his lady police friend; having made a full statement regarding certain events he'd been involved in, to the relevant authorities.

He's in South Africa?

She eyed me over the last of her rum and Coke: *So it goes.* She held up her glass: *I'd like another one of these, please.*

I went to the bar, secured her a refill.

When you say 'events', you mean what happened in you-know-where.

Yes.

You were told not to talk about all that?

You weren't?

She poked me in the midriff, not at all playfully: *Is all this to do with the thing you said you wanted to tell me? Listen, why don't we go somewhere really quiet, if we want to deal with all this? As quiet as we could possibly wish?*

We clinked glasses and downed our drinks in one. She unslung her jacket and we walked out of the upstairs bar. She tapped my arm: *Please, stop looking so shifty.*

*

Once we were ensconced in the cab I got an erection as unexpected as a hunger pang. The rub of shoulders, the close smell of her perfume, of her shampoo, just having her breasts within

425

accidentally-bumping-into distance was combining with my twelve-year-old memories of Lucy which had left their erotic mark on me through the years: the enticing scenery I had sensed behind her swishing hair, her pale face.

We sailed over the bridge.

South of the river, eh?

Her eyes, placid in reflected streetlight: *Oh yes, I've been really slumming it.*

The cab drew up outside a two-storey Georgian house just off Clapham Common. She paid, and fumbled for keys: *Dad would have preferred to have lived in Knightsbridge, the old snob.* She opened the door. The inside smelt dusty.

You live in your parents' place?

She flicked on lights. Dull mahogany furnishings, a chintz-upholstered three-piece around a coffee table, modern-artish daubs on the walls.

Simon's got his army, Mum's practically incommunicado, Dad's a million miles away, and I'm working in a gift shop that pays peanuts; what would you do?

I sat down on a chintz armchair. She brought vodka over from the drinks table, then glasses and tomato juice and Worcestershire sauce and black pepper from the kitchen. She sat on the sofa, pouring and sprinkling.

I'm told I do a pretty mean Bloody Mary. She patted the space next to her: *You can sit here if you wish.* I wished. All but hip to hip, we clinked.

That hits the spot.

I'm guessing you get the spot hit pretty often. I took another swig of laced tomato juice. She patted my knee: *So, do tell.*

Taking my time, downing her booze, I let her become the first person I'd ever told about my helicopter ride, from start to finish: the lead-up to it, what I saw, what I had to conclude. I assumed she didn't know: it had all happened far too far away for any of the watchers at the railings of Coldwater to have had an inkling.

She put her Bloody Mary down: *I see.*

It took me a moment to realise that tears were streaming down my face and transparent gubbins from my nose. So much for seducing this particular childhood sweetheart. When I looked up, a box of Kleenex had been placed in front of me. I grabbed three tissues at once and wiped my eyes, then blew my nose and was about to stuff all that soiled paper into my pocket when a hand appeared: *Give it to me.*

When she got back from the kitchen I was on the sob again.

Why has this upset you so?

The calm in her voice threw me somewhat.

Lucy, all that happened because of me; or thanks to me.

Don't kid yourself that you were so important; they would've done the same thing with or without you. They might've taken a bit longer, but they'd have done it anyway; you mustn't blame yourself.

How pat. The tears had retreated from my face only to gather like rain clouds in my throat.

That's not true; the Africans might have got away.

Her hand touched the top of my head, all motherly: *They really weren't supposed to be in our country, you know.*

I pushed her hand off my crown: *I'm sorry?*

Her hand resettled on my knee: *I've thought about them a lot, of course; and, well, I suspect they were a lot more dangerous than we ever realised.*

I heard myself saying: *This sounds pretty weird coming from someone who went as far as to take a shine to one of those Africans; what was his name?*

She giggled once through a pout: *Shine? No pun intended, I hope. Tendai. At the time I was a bit stricken, but I really had no idea who he really was or what he was really like. I never got to know him. Puppy love.*

Again I heard our flyboys roaring, felt the Sea King shudder, recalled billows black as tar. I wished she would stop patting my fucking knee.

Listen, you silly, everything you've just told me, I've known about it for ages; Simon isn't a crack trooper—now a ranking officer, actually—for nothing. He found out through the high-echelon grapevine about what the RAF had done and told me all about it when I was a bit older; in fact, he told me a couple of things you probably don't know about yourself.

My penis, which not long ago was being whipped into stiffness by two craving testicles, was shrinking like an old lady in a gale: *Like what?*

Like what happened to Mr Khoury.

Mr Khoury?

The Arab gentleman who lived in the Manse, remember? Not long after the army arrived, some people broke into the Manse and gave Mr Khoury a bit of a biffing.

Christ.

Jesus.

'Mohammed' would be more appropriate. Khoury died from a head injury; I don't know what became of his wife and children. And as for that oaf Greg—remember Greg?

I remembered Greg.

Greg, I admit, should have got his just deserts—he'd attempted to violate the Arab man's wife—but he got off scot-free.

And don't you think all those Africans should have been let off 'scot-free'?

It seemed natural to shout.

Calm down. I'm not condoning the way they were dealt with, although Simon did explain the military justifications for it: if those blacks had got back to Africa, who knows what they might have got up to.

Like what?

More of a roar than a shout. Her hands were fluttering.

Take it easy, please. Who knows, maybe they were paving the way for further assaults; perhaps that's what all the immigration we've had in the last decade is really all about: infiltration to pave the way for an even larger invasion. Maybe the incursion we saw was just testing the water.

Testing the water?

I'd gone shrill.

That's why I still think sometimes I should put two fingers up at the Official Secrets Act and tell everybody what happened to us in nineteen seventy-four because, well, like I said, it could happen again. What is it? Why are you staring at me like that?

Thinking, I'd been, for years and years, that instead of arsing about in England as I'd been doing, instead of cramming and memorising through the booze, instead of sitting in libraries and sniffing must and bookworm, instead of making myself dapper and after-shaved to be interviewed by a panel of smooth-voiced people for my current fairly well-paid job, I should have gone, I should have got the first fucking plane out to any place in Africa you care to name, to Abidjan, to Lagos, to Freetown, to Dakar, to Ouagadougou, to Dar es Salaam, and I should have started finding who might have known about Mzee and Jonas Cole and their display of skill and chutzpah, their armbanded supporters, their civilians basking on the beach. Sooner or later I would have found someone who knew what I was talking about, someone who knew the score, someone who'd been involved on the edges, maybe, a sibling or a spouse, maybe, a friend or passing acquaintance, maybe, and I would have told him or her exactly what had happened, I would have mimed the boom, I would have painted the billows, I would have laid it on the line, told it like it was, I would have spared no detail of the few details I saw with my naked eye.

What would he or she have done then, that listener of mine? Just spread the word, surely, just let it burn like fire over stubble, just let it fire the ears of those whose future on that continent was already making it difficult for them to breathe.

What is it?

Nothing, Lucy, nothing at all.

She was watching me, lips taking a sip: *What you don't know about is Dad.*

You told me: he's enjoying apartheid.

There's something else.

What?

A lowering of the eyes: *He got so upset about Simon having gone missing, he went over the top while he was questioning one of the suspects.*

What does that mean, 'over the top'?

The person being questioned didn't make it.

Was that that street sweeper?

Yeah.

I'd been told he died of a heart attack.

No.

Oh.

Dad was given a proper trial. He explained his side of things; the judges agreed it was involuntary homicide in exceptional and extenuating circumstances. It's difficult to forgive him for what he did, but...

But.

But these people, blacks, Negroes, whatever they prefer to be called, I've come to the conclusion over the years that they really—and I mean this in the best possible way—they really are not like us; they're different from us, just as we are from them.

Meaning?

Meaning the bottom line is, like I said, they had no business being here.

So the street sweeper got his just deserts?

The words fell like droppings from those once yearned-for lips: *I didn't say that. I meant that if they had minded their own business and let us mind ours, none of what transpired would have taken place; that man would have come to no harm, and neither would any of the others.*

I stood up and headed for the front door, Lucy click-clacking over the parquet behind me. I fumbled with the latch—a state-of-the-art piece of locksmithery—and she reached an arm over my shoulder to show me how it worked. I pulled the door open.

Hey, are you sure you really don't want to stay? Not even a little longer?

She had rested a hand on my shoulder.

Goodbye, Lucy.

Afore ye go, then, if go you must, please take this; I'm sure you'll appreciate it more than I have.

She pressed an envelope into my hand. What the fuck was that, I wondered?

Her voice followed me down the stoop: *Seeing as how you're obviously one of the ingenuous millions.*

The door clunk-clicked behind me. I walked across the front patio and through the gate and up Victoria Rise towards the Wandsworth Road. Only when I got to the corner, there were the Clapham Baptist Church hung, and still hangs, its weary sign, did I flick the envelope open and fish out a slip of yellowed newsprint.

*

I was living in a bedsit in Earl's Court with a coin-operated gas heater and an electric hob, good for heating canned ravioli on. The low rent was what gave my salary a chance to stretch its arms out to the quality alcohol, the better clubs, the late-night taxis.

That night, Friday though it was, I went straight home: I popped one pound fifty in the meter, lit the heater, and sat on the bed.

I read no books and had none. Drinking had made them unnecessary. Alone with the heater's blue-yellow flames, I unfolded the only thing I had to read, and read it through.

*

When I'd finished, I folded it up again, and put it back in its envelope. I stretched out on my bed and stared at the ceiling, upon which there was a damp stain. The damp stain, after about an hour, turned out to be in the shape of Africa. It was unpeeling the paper and moistening a bit of fresco.

Then the pictures came: smiling faces of children on cans which had coin slots in their tops and charitable slogans on their sides; fly-harassed children from Sunday supplement snaps.

Why—needy though they were—did they look to me like humans are supposed to look, and why did I, conversely, look like a bad copy of the way a human was supposed to look, and when I say 'I', I mean every last mother's son of us pale, pink, ruddy-skinned folk? Why did we all look so creepy in comparison to those pictures, which were now going forth and multiplying all over on the ceiling: faces of actors and street sellers and women with hoes and men with machetes were spinning across the ceiling and down the walls until they were crowding the room, standing before the heater's flames, standing outside on the landing, cramming the staircase and spilling out onto the pavement: white teeth, yellow whites of eyes—faces whose bodies were in wraps, in short pants, in military uniforms, in nurse's uniforms, in T-shirts and torn jeans; they were all around the house now, bumping against the jerry-built walls as they milled about in adjoining rooms. At last, then, they had come.

For I had long imagined that, sooner or later, their anger would do its job, that they would eventually fill their ammo belts and grease their Kalashnikovs and prepare their vessels, welding and soldering until every trawler was battle-ready, until every dinghy had enough oomph to whoosh across the seas, at which point they would come flocking to the coasts, ready to steam out, motor out, sail out and paddle out, if necessary, the AK-47s strapped now to their backs and the coils of bullets sleeping in the bows; millions would mill along the jetties of Banjul, Bissau, Conakry, Monrovia, Accra, Porto-Novo, Malabo, Laâyoune and Luanda, and raise anchor and head north; they would have had a last calm cigarette on Cape Verde before continuing up past the Arabs and the Berbers, up past Portugal into the expanses of the Celtic Sea, hundreds of square miles of water patchworked with tankers, yachts, dinghies, tugboats, barges, hydrofoils, catamarans, feluccas, ferries, ketches, barges, all the way up past Brittany, slipping into the English Channel, rows of dozens of vessels, their occupants' grips tightening on grenades, anti-tank shells, ground-to-air missiles, knives as they approached the southern coast of England, there where people swan about so carefree, so comfy, so self-assured, so self-satisfied; where life is indeed an island, a game disguised as common sense played out within the confines of a coastline bristling with complacency, while those vessels packed with men and women headed direct as dogs for Falmouth, Plymouth, Torbay, Exmouth, Sidmouth, Seaton, Weymouth, Swanage, Bournemouth, Southampton, Portsmouth, Bognor Regis, Worthing, Brighton, Eastbourne, Hastings, Folkstone, Dover, Deal, Ramsgate and Margate too, as the catches were clicked back on their assault rifles, their carbines, their Uzis, their shotguns and semiautomatics, as the edges of their blades were tested by careful thumbs, as they leaped out of the boats and splashed into the oily thigh-high water, strode up to the harbour fronts and stormed the obliviousness that nestled so cosily there, they would gut the terraced cottages and scorch the thatched roofs and loot the snug pubs, taking a breather in Bath, wiring Oxford and Cambridge both with TNT, breaking into the courthouses and shooting the wigs off the judges' heads with a precision the armed members of the British police could only dream of: Africans, Africans everywhere, packing the supermarkets, assault rifles clanking against trolleys heaped with foodstuffs, Weetabix included, Africans everywhere, taking delicate bites of soft cheeses in the delicatessens, perusing the libraries of stately homes, reading the news on the BBC in Igbo and Amharic and on ITN in Xhosa and Susu; Africans, Africans seizing the radio stations, the power stations, the pig farms and slaughterhouses, the banks and the post offices, the arsenals and missile silos, American bases and GCHQ, the green valleys where sheep were grazing and the green fields where cows were lounging, Africans skinny-dipping in Southport and storming the very gates of London, firing skybound rounds from jeeps driven round Piccadilly Circus, musing in the cinemas of the West End, Africans breaking into numbers ten and eleven Downing Street and making the Prime Ministress and the Fat Chancellor hop alarmed, highland-flinging to avoid the bullets which they assumed would be rapid-fired on the ground on which they stood; Africans, Africans, juggling with the stocks and bowling with the shares, filling newspaper columns to the brim, hosting the TV shows, drilling the troops, calling the shots; England overrun at long last, England at a loss, bewildered, gobstruck, nonplussed and flummoxed while posters fluttered in the cold wind of a resort island—on whose remote esplanade Africans were already pouring themselves Mister Whippies—proclaiming in letters bold as brass: 'Isn't It Time You Got the Point?'

At last, they'd made it over.

A movement at the window had me pulling aside the lace curtain, and there they were outside, staring at the area, the bairns trying to stick their heads through the railings, their mothers standing with no smiles as the stain caved in and the walls split inward and all Africa was crushing me like an imploded sky, all Africa was squeezing its four walls closer and closer, leaving me with no room to budge as the ceiling slammed down like a potato masher, while my brain shot off random sparks and shot up random flames, because all Africa knew what was up, all Africa had been put in the suffocating corner where I was gasping for breath, then and there.

All Africa had finally asked me to get the ball rolling by redressing the wrongs I had committed eleven years ago, all Africa had told me to act wherever and however I could act, on my po-faced, indifferent, icing-cool, marble-eyed fellow natives, and towards the end of that sleepless night, I fancied I was going to do it, I was going to contact all the right contactees and get things going. Indeed, I myself could not go on any longer unless I did something to make amends as best I could for all of us curd-cheeked people who had bamboozled whole generations, who had poured previously-unheard-of faiths down the gullets of their sprogs.

By the time dawn gave its first pale cough of the day, appeared beyond the net curtains, the walls had returned to their places, and the ceiling patch was back to being a mere smear.

I went to the basin and splashed water on my face, fingered water through my hair. Action, action. I left my room, padded down the corridor and stepped out onto the stoop. It was sevenish. The buildings were being bathed in watery milk.

*

I got off the Tube at Covent Garden, and walked to the only place I knew where Africans congregated; I'd passed it dozens of times.

But the Africa Centre turned out to be closed until twelve. I wandered to kill time, wondering how exactly I was going to express my intentions to the people in there.

By eleven o'clock, I was getting footsore and the Lamb & Flag was close by; I needed a place to sit and think.

I ordered a healthy Guinness and tucked myself behind a corner table. How was I going to handle this? Might they not get suspicious of a young white man barging in with nothing to offer but his eagerness? What was it exactly, anyway, that I wished to do?

I had thought, of course, about telling them what happened in Coldwater Bay, but decided against it for the same reason I had decided against telling anybody else all those years: apart from the fact that I might be taken for a nut of the conspiracy kind—not having any proof to back my story up except a piece of newspaper that anybody could have had printed up—I never forgot Sir Michael, nor Jeremy's warnings as I signed the papers he slipped before me; I had no doubt whatsoever that any indiscretion on my part would have consequences that I didn't even want to think about, for me, or possibly for my parents.

I switched to bitter because more than a couple of Guinnesses would have given me the squits.

I got back to the African Centre at about two. The blind was up, and goods were visible in the shop window: sculptures, sandals, mats. I walked in. A middle-aged African man was sitting behind the counter, reading a paperback. Inside were more items for sale: paintings, books, bracelets, wraps, more sculptures, more sandals, more mats. I browsed, a touch dizzy after several pints on an empty stomach. But I hadn't come to buy anything. I'd come to help. I glanced at the man, still engrossed in his book. I looked back at the goods, and absent-mindedly picked up a hamster-sized bust.

Can I help you?

I started: he was right behind me. I breathed dregs at his face: *Just looking.* At once, I put the head down and headed for the door. At the threshold, I waved: *Bye.*

Goodbye, now.

*

I continued to work by day, and to head off to the pubs and clubs by night. In some of them I would spot black people, of African or West Indian origin, and for an uncomfortable second or so, I could not help seeing them as foreign children in permanent need of help and succour and love and charity. Just looking. I would then brush by them, my body a mix of glitches and loosened screws, my mind trapped in the jelly of the days in Coldwater Bay.

Not a day passes when I do not hear the jets, feel the shudder, glimpse the black smoke.

Whenever I would run across Lucy, which did happen a few times, I made a point of avoiding her, which was easy enough to do given that I was also avoiding everybody else.

Sometimes, when alone at home, the tears would come. They still do. Thinking about those people.

Just looking.

Barcelona, 2007-2011

ACKNOWLEDGEMENTS

ACKNOWLEDGEMENTS

First of all, many, many thanks to Margareth Yagaza, Viki and Rama for showing me Africa from an African point of view (or a Tanzanian one, to be more exact). Many thanks, too, to the Swahili-language writer Erick Shigongo for sharing his thoughts about Africa and European attitudes to it.

A special thank-you goes to Elias Charles for his fine translations into Kiswahili of the texts I sent him, and which appear in this book either as written communiqués or spoken phrases.

And thanks, too, to Steve Burdett, a good friend who made sure that the printing machine used by the owner of the *Coldwater Bay Parish Press* was a believable one.

SOME SOURCES

The racist crimes of the German explorer Carl Peters—whose name Dr Whitebone uses to sign his letter to the local paper—are documented in Thomas Pakenham's *The Scramble for Africa* (1991). The same book documents the wearing of white armbands—made from ox tails, in this case—by the Ndebele people, to indicate they were on the warpath.

The abrasive home-made chemical that is smeared on the road block is similar to one that appears in an episode of Wole Soyinka's autobiography *You Must Set Forth at Dawn* (2006). Farmers in Western Nigeria applied the substance to the seats of police cars during post-independence protests at a rigged election; it would burn through the policemen's uniforms, causing them to flee the cars and writhe in pain. The exact nature of the recipe, Soyinka assures us, remains 'elusive'.

The descriptions of violence in African wars to which Jonas Cole alludes at various moments come from a variety of historical, autobiographical and fictional sources, including Lucien Badjoko's *Jo Vaig Ser un Nen Soldat* (Catalan edition, 2006); Ishmael Beah's *A Long Way Gone* (2007); Uzodinma Iweala's *Beasts of No Nation* (2005); and Martin Meredith's *The State of Africa* (2005).

The idea, expressed in the visitors' final communiqué, that Africa's borders and political structures need to be rethought and altered through democratic processes, if necessary, comes from the Guinean author Manthia Diawara's essay *In Search of Africa*. The same book also stresses the importance of open-air markets for the African economy: hence the setting-up of one in Coldwater Bay.

The idea that Kiswahili—the common language used by all the African visitors to Coldwater Bay—should become the lingua franca of black Africans, is defended in Kenyan author Ngugi wa Thiong'o's collection of essays *Moving the Centre* (1993).

The *'gachacha'* sequence—in which the village youths are 'tried'—is based on the reconciliation process which took place after the Rwandan genocide, described in detail in Dina Temple-Raston's *Justice on the Grass*.

The references in the visitors' farewell message to the range and diversity of pre-colonial African polities is drawn largely from J. D. Fage's *A History of Africa* (fourth edition: 2002).

Sir Michael (Hanley) was the head of the Security Service between 1971 and 1978. Latchmere House, in London, was used as an interrogation centre by the Security Service (in the novel, that function has been extended into the seventies, given that there were rumours that this was indeed the case). It later became an open prison, which was closed down in 2011, not long after *Snug* was completed.

AK DIGITAL is the online platform of the Antonia Kerrigan Literary Agency. The purpose of this platform is to promote and sell professional-quality copies of books which the agency deems worthy of mainstream publication. As regards Matthew Tree's remarkable novel, *Snug*, Antonia has the following to say: '*This book's a must, and not to be missed. It will grip you from beginning to end.*'

22833940R00265

Printed in Great Britain
by Amazon